THE
WITCHING
TREE

THE WITCHING TREE

• A Natalie Lockhart Novel •

Alice Blanchard

MINOTAUR BOOKS
NEW YORK

First published in the United States by Minotaur Books, an imprint of St. Martin's Publishing Group

THE WITCHING TREE. Copyright © 2021 by Alice Blanchard. All rights reserved. Printed in the United States of America. For information, address St. Martin's Publishing Group, 120 Broadway, New York, NY 10271.

www.minotaurbooks.com

Library of Congress Cataloging-in-Publication Data

Names: Blanchard, Alice, author.
Title: The witching tree : a Natalie Lockhart novel / Alice Blanchard.
Description: First Edition. | New York : Minotaur Books, 2021. | Series: Natalie
    Lockhart ; 3
Identifiers: LCCN 2021027391 | ISBN 9781250783042 (hardcover) |
    ISBN 9781250783059 (ebook)
Subjects: GSAFD: Mystery fiction.
Classification: LCC PS3552.L36512 W58 2021 | DDC 813/.54—dc23
LC record available at https://lccn.loc.gov/2021027391

Our books may be purchased in bulk for promotional, educational, or business use. Please contact your local bookseller or the Macmillan Corporate and Premium Sales Department at 1-800-221-7945, extension 5442, or by email at MacmillanSpecialMarkets@macmillan.com.

First Edition: 2021

10 9 8 7 6 5 4 3 2 1

To Doug.
The dream goes on forever.

Don't stare too long at the Witching Tree,
Defile it not, or cursed you will be.

THE
WITCHING
TREE

PROLOGUE

Veronica Manes, the town's best-known practicing witch, woke up staring at the blank white sky, snowflakes dusting her cheeks. She was shivering cold, lying on the ground in the dead of winter. She looked around and realized she was way out in the middle of nowhere, surrounded by woods and snow.

Veronica struggled to sit up, thinking that she must be dreaming. She took a deep breath, pain flaring inside her head. She blinked a few times and wobbled to her feet. Steel chains clinked. She looked down and realized with a spike of dread that she was shackled to the railroad tracks on the edge of town.

What the hell is going on? How did I get here?

Her throbbing skull made it difficult to think. She was handcuffed to two lengths of steel chain that looped around the railroad tracks—one handcuff per wrist. She twisted and yanked on the cuffs and padlocked chains, desperate to free herself. She knelt down in the snow and clawed at the rusty braces between the rails and rotting wooden ties, to no avail.

Veronica panicked, her heart doing double-flips as she realized the futility of her efforts. She stood up and looked around for a way out of this insanity. Any minute now, somebody was going to pop out of the woods and tell her it was all a joke. A horrible, disgusting prank. *Trick or treat.*

"Help! Somebody help me!" Her screams slap-echoed through the woods and bounced off the drifts.

The place was remote. There weren't many houses built near the tracks north of town. A friend of hers lived along the commuter line and was constantly complaining about the noise—the blare of the horn, the clatter of the boxcars, *clang, clang, clang.*

Veronica scanned the tree line and saw a waft of smoke drifting from a nearby chimney. "Hello, can you hear me? I need help. Somebody help me!" She yanked hard, trying to pull herself free, but each time she jerked on the handcuffs, the rattling steel chains held firm. Her heart rate soared. She knew she was trapped.

Now something even more disturbing caught her eye as she looked down at herself—what kind of weird outfit was she wearing? The world spun for a moment. Veronica couldn't believe it. She was dressed for Halloween as a caricature of a witch—a long black costume and a tall wide-brimmed hat straight out of *The Wizard of Oz.* Lying on the ground next to the tracks was a broomstick.

What was going on? Was this some sort of sadistic joke? Her brain was in a fog. Something terrible was happening. She tried to escape by twisting her hands out of the cuffs, but they were tightly ratcheted around her wrists. The metal was ice-cold against her skin.

Now a distant train horn pierced the silence—a familiar warning cushioned by the gently falling snow. She spotted a single headlight through a veil of fog. Life was so beautiful. Everything glowed. *"Please stop!"* She frantically waved her arms, but the chains would only allow a limited range of motion. *"I can't get away! I'm chained to the tracks! Stop!"*

The engineer didn't see her. The train plowed forward, spitting gravel in its wake. Rumbling and shaking the ground underneath the tracks.

Deep in her gut, Veronica understood that no one was coming to rescue her.

You run and run and try catching up with your life, but then one day time runs out, and this is all you have. One last beautiful morning.

She felt the seismic vibrations underfoot from the deep-bellied rumbling of the oncoming train. The horn blasted its warning. Ornate snowflakes swirled through the air.

At last Veronica understood. *All is lost. Let go. Accept.*

She performed a simple pagan ritual as the train approached—last rites—then turned her head away from the oncoming locomotive and closed her eyes.

1

Mornings were dark in March, cold and foreboding. Chilly floors, hurrying downstairs for coffee, shivering and gazing out the French doors at the purple-black sky. For Natalie, living with Hunter Rose inside his enormous nineteenth-century mansion was like curling up with a leather-bound Charles Dickens novel—deliciously comforting. She loved getting up early, before Hunter was awake, and sneaking downstairs to sit at the end of the absurdly long mahogany dining table, built for a family of twelve, where she had a magnificent view of the manicured backyard and the wild woods of upstate New York.

Last night there had been another snowstorm, but it was dissipating now. She watched the gently falling snow. The backyard was pristine—like an untouched canvas. She could paint the day in any direction she pleased. The plows were making their rounds, and the utility trucks would soon be repairing any fallen lines. Order was slowly being restored.

Natalie relished the quiet of early morning, before Hunter was up with his scratching and yawning and exaggerated gestures of emerging from the cocoon. He was gorgeous to look at. Gorgeous to touch and explore, but this morning she didn't want that. She needed a separate space where she could think, because she had an important decision to make.

In the cradle of winter, March's lullaby, Natalie Lockhart was considering quitting the police force. She'd had enough of the dark side. Four months ago, she was almost killed by a twisted individual who liked to drug and embalm young musicians, and six months before that, she'd solved one of the biggest serial killer cases in the American Northeast. Now, the more time she spent inside the Rose mansion, playacting the lady of the manor, the more she kind of liked it.

And what was not to like? Dinner parties with fascinating people, weekend jaunts to Manhattan to buy art, and basically having enough money and time to do whatever she pleased. An opportunity to explore her creative side. When she was little, Natalie used to love to draw and paint. Hunter had offered her a large room on the third floor to use as a studio space. No more scraping by to pay the bills, no more broken dishwasher, no more waking up in the middle of the night because she'd forgotten something vital to the case she was working on.

Living with thirty-three-year-old Hunter Rose, the founder of Rose Security Software, had given Natalie a chance to hide out from the press. His personal security team was highly skilled at performing background checks on persistent reporters and serial-killer fanboys, screening visitors, and examining the mail. They used closed-circuit TV to monitor the house and grounds. There were alarms and panic buttons. The only thing missing, Hunter joked, was a designated safe room. And he was thinking about that.

Natalie was grateful for the protection. She hadn't asked for the notoriety. It was a fluke, an unlucky turn of events—her being in charge of two sensational murder cases within the span of a year. It would've given any other detective wet dreams, and yet it had happened while Natalie was trying to come to terms with the tragic death of her sister, Grace, and the shocking revelation about what Grace had done. And so it became Natalie's worst nightmare.

As a teenager, Grace Lockhart and her close group of witch-curious friends had killed Natalie's older sister, Willow, by ritualistically stabbing her twenty-seven times and pinning it on Willow's boyfriend, Justin Fowler. Justin had gone to prison for twenty years before the enormity of the truth had been revealed.

The horror and sorrow Natalie had experienced during this past year had calcified into disillusionment. It was like waking up from a bad dream, only to discover that you were still living inside the same bad dream. A hall of fucking mirrors.

Recently, tensions had eased for Natalie when the national media finally left Burning Lake for greener pastures, feasting on brand-spanking-new tragedies in other areas of the world. At last she could breathe again. She could sit there and process her feelings and not feel resentful or defensive each time she stepped out her door.

Hunter, for his part, wanted Natalie to quit her job and pursue other interests—to draw or paint or take up photography, to run a marathon or scale a mountain. He wanted her to evolve, to become more of herself. A bigger, better, improved Natalie. And so, these early-morning retreats to the downstairs dining room with its ornate woodwork and incredible view of the backyard that was more like a manicured park out of *Downton Abbey* were vital to her well-being. Because now she had to decide whether or not to quit the force. And as of this moment, everything was up in the air.

With a determined sigh, Natalie opened her laptop on the dining table and started to type: "Dear Chief Snyder, Please accept my letter of resignation from the position of CIU detective, effective two weeks from today. It's been an honor to work for you, both as a police officer and as a detective for the Burning Lake Police Department. I will greatly miss all my colleagues. My only regret is that I was not able to better protect the citizens of Burning Lake. During the next two weeks, I will help in any way I can to make the transition as smooth as possible. Please let me know if there's anything specific you'd like me to do. It has been a pleasure working for you. Sincerely, Natalie Lockhart."

Her fingers lifted off the keyboard. She felt light-headed for a moment. Was she actually going to hand in her resignation today? Due to budgetary constraints, the town council had passed a motion that, starting in April, the police department would freeze all hiring. It would be in effect from April until the end of September. Natalie had another week or so to decide what to do, because she wanted to give the department enough time to train her replacement. She would have to make her final decision this week.

Footsteps overhead.

She sighed. He was up. She closed her laptop, brushed a casual hand through her hair, and smiled.

Hunter came shuffling down the stairs, talking on his phone and issuing orders to his second-in-command, an older man who was clearly intimidated by the founder and CEO of the biggest software company on the East Coast. Hunter pocketed his phone and stood in the doorway, smiling broadly at her. "Damn, you look pretty."

She smiled. "You're such a charming liar."

"I tell no lies."

"How'd you sleep?"

"Like the dead. You could've driven a stake through my heart." Handsome and disheveled, he crossed the room with catlike grace—feline as a mountain lion—and lifted her out of her chair and folded her into his muscled warmth, breathing his sour-smelling morning breath in her face. "I've got a brilliant idea," he whispered in her ear. "Let's take the day off. Okay? Please? We'll watch old movies and fuck like bunnies and have French toast for lunch. Can't I tempt you?"

She gave him a wry look. "One of us has to earn a living."

"Actually, that's not true. You and I could both quit tomorrow and we'd be fine until we're a hundred." He arched an eyebrow at her. "We *are* going to live to be a hundred years old, aren't we? That was the deal, wasn't it?"

She laughed. Despite her best attempts to have her own space in the morning, she abandoned all her worries and melted into him. Hunter was like a drug, and she wanted to do nothing for the rest of the day but live within the span of his hug.

"We could order that take-out pasta you like for dinner," he said, picking up her coffee mug and taking a few sips. "Mmm. You make the yummiest coffee." His bathrobe was open, and he was shirtless, wearing pajama bottoms and a pair of suede bedroom slippers that had seen better days. "You know, the pasta with the shrimp and fresh basil and aged parmesan . . . where's the delivery menu?"

"In the kitchen drawer with the others."

"Is that a yes?" he asked, drawing her close, the surface of his skin twitching like a racehorse. There was an earthy, peppery scent to his sweat.

She thought about what was waiting for her at the police station—an in-box full of paperwork, more notes to review, digital files to be archived, an accumulation of busywork. This winter had been slow going down at the BLPD. Most criminals didn't like the cold. "I guess I could take a mental health day," she hedged, warming up to the idea—no, scratch that, sliding into it like a hot bath.

"You *deserve* a mental health day. You of all fucking people. God, I love you." He kissed her face all over, making playful smacking sounds.

She squirmed and laughed, trying to escape his sloppy kisses. "Okay, but only if you make the French toast."

"Bah. Who needs French toast when I've got this?" He nibbled on her earlobe, then progressed down her neck toward her collarbone.

She became acutely aware of the blood pumping through her veins, the weakness in her knees, the magnetism of his body and their core physical attraction. Sex with Hunter was frankly earthmoving. Her body was drenched in love chemicals and her mind floated in an atmosphere of euphoria. Total brain fog.

Her cell phone buzzed, interrupting them. It rattled on the dining table.

"Don't answer that," he pleaded, drawing back and staring at her admonishingly.

The sound was so jarring this early in the morning that she swung out an arm while reaching for it and accidentally smacked her hand on the table. "Ouch!"

"Your physical grace never ceases to amaze me," he said with a wry grin. He took her hand and kissed it.

"Fuck you, I know what a klutz I am."

"How very charming of you to bump into things and then swear at me whenever I politely point it out. Double scoops of goodness there."

She tried not to laugh as she picked up her phone. "Hello?"

"Natalie, it's me," Luke said in a solemn voice. "Something's happened. I need you over here right now."

2

Although Burning Lake tended to cling to its holiday season for as long as it could after New Year's Eve, the post-holiday blues had descended upon the town. A month packed with social events had given way to the empty calendar of January and February. This winter had been especially harsh and unrelenting, beginning with an ice storm in November. Even though it was March, there was still a long way to go.

It was seven thirty on a Tuesday morning, March 8. A small army of plows had been sent out after the storm had tapered off around six A.M., and most of the roads on the north side of town had been cleared. The sheer edges of the embankments revealed where the plows had dug into the lawns, exposing clumps of brown earth beneath the white drifts. Shivery cold inside her Honda Accord, Natalie turned the heat on full blast, then found the weather channel. The storm was rapidly heading northeast, according to the weatherman, but outside a light snow was still falling. Her tires hummed on the slippery asphalt as she drove toward the outskirts of town.

Everyone in Burning Lake knew who fifty-eight-year-old Veronica Manes was—a respected Wiccan priestess, head of one of the oldest covens in town. She lived in the historic Bell House at 8 Plymouth Street, and many years ago, she'd written several books under a pen name, Corvina Manse—a clever anagram of her own name. She was known to host quarterly moonlight rituals on her property. She was the best person to talk to if you wanted to understand modern-day witchcraft. She had shoulder-length gray hair and wore informal, mismatched clothes—turtlenecks, cardigans, stretch pants, New Balance sneakers. Her face was kind, with more than a hint of melancholy about it. She was a perfectly ordinary person who just so happened to be a witch.

Now she was dead. Hit by a train.

The last time Natalie had seen Veronica was about four months ago, during the investigation of the Violinist case. Veronica had briefly encountered the victim, Morgan Chambers, and provided the police with helpful information. Since then, Natalie had bumped into Veronica a few times around town—twice at the grocery store and once at the bank, where they'd exchanged pleasantries before going their separate ways.

Over the phone, Luke had skimped on the details and Natalie didn't know the whole story. She didn't know if this was an accident or a suicide, but it was certainly terrible news. Also, quite mysteriously, he'd hinted at foul play, which puzzled her. Was she pushed onto the tracks? Veronica struck Natalie as someone so intelligent, practical, generous, and tolerant, she couldn't have made very many enemies in her life. Certainly, she was beloved by the Wiccan community. But as her father, Joey, used to say, *Accuracy is more important than speed. Don't get ahead of yourself, Natalie. Facts first. Speculation last.*

The northern edge of town consisted mostly of woods—conservancy lands, state lands, privately owned property, and railroad easements. The tracks ran east to west, with a handful of passenger trains running routes several times a day. Most of the vehicular-train collision accidents that occurred along this route happened on Snowshoe Street or Bellflower Hollow, two places where the back roads crossed the tracks without any drop-arm gates or warning signs to deter drivers from thinking they could outrun a locomotive.

The last collision had occurred at the Snowshoe Street crossing two years ago when a woman's Toyota Highlander got stuck on the tracks and was struck by a westbound passenger train. Fortunately, although the SUV was totaled, she came out of it totally unscathed. There had been other victims over the years who weren't as lucky—car accidents at the crossings, or people on foot, who for whatever reason decided to walk along the tracks, believing that the train would give them plenty of warning. Over the past three decades, there had been a dozen collisions, but only five fatalities. An unfortunate few were suicides.

Natalie pulled over to the side of Copperhead Road, an isolated stretch of asphalt surrounded by dense woods on both sides. Other members of the police and fire departments were already there. Loose stones crunched under her tires as she parked behind a police cruiser, got out, and took a fire road toward the railroad tracks.

"Shit." She'd forgotten her winter gloves at home. Natalie shivered and breathed on her fingers to keep them warm, then burrowed them into her coat pockets.

The gravel road stopped at the edge of a clearing. Since this dead-end street didn't cross the tracks and continue northward, there were no warning signs posted here, no drop-arm gates or flashing lights, no bells or crossbuck symbols to warn drivers or pedestrians away from the tracks. The road simply ended in a ditch full of silvery winter weeds.

The railroad companies owned the land on which their tracks were laid, as well as a significant easement of a couple hundred feet on either side. She heard the crunch of footsteps approaching. Forty-five-year-old Detective Peter Murphy came out of the clearing toward her, talking on his phone. He acknowledged her with a stiff nod. They used to get along quite well, but last year his feelings seemed to have soured toward her, and now theirs was a contentious relationship. It all started when Murphy accidentally lost a crucial file from the Missing Nine case, almost a year ago, and Natalie let him know how much his carelessness pissed her off. Murph's resentment and her bitterness had festered quietly ever since.

"Natalie," he said coolly, his thick eyebrows knitting together as he pocketed his phone.

"Hello, Murph. What happened?"

"Luke didn't tell you?"

She shook her head. "He said to get here pronto. No details."

"Well, then, you're in for quite a treat. Go have a look for yourself, if you've got the stomach for it."

"I think I can handle it."

He held her eye, then brushed past her saying, "Of course you can. See you later."

Okay. Chalk that up to another awkward exchange.

Natalie trudged into the clearing where the train tracks cut through the woods and the utility lines ran parallel to the tracks. Here the snowpack was deep. The snow layers had built up since November, and the newer powdery snow lay on top, whereas the older snow was denser with a crunchy crust.

Natalie shivered as the wind rustled through the leafless trees, blowing loose scuffs of snow across the landscape. A cardinal darted over the treetops like a slash of crimson—so quick, and then it was gone. There was a faint smell of sulfur in the air from the train braking.

She followed the footprints of other law officers toward the tracks, then took a moment to survey the scene of the accident—an expanse of snow scattered with bundled-up figures talking in hushed voices. Natalie recognized several of her colleagues from the detective's unit among the state police and rank-and-file officers—Detectives Lenny Labruzzo, Augie Vickers, and Brandon Buckner.

They were looking down at what appeared to be lumps of clothing scattered around the tracks, along with brilliant scarlet splashes in the snow. Her stomach felt watery. She stared at the scene until she nearly went snow-blind. Then she looked away and blinked, the afterimage lingering on her retinas.

Blood in the snow. Scarlet on a white background.

She heard a familiar voice behind her.

"Natalie," Lieutenant Luke Pittman said.

3

Thirty-nine-year-old Luke Pittman had the kind of handsome, weathered face that suited his chipped, rugged personality. He and Natalie had known each other since they were kids. Luke's father had abandoned him, and his mother had to work two jobs to keep them afloat. It wasn't long before Joey invited the fatherless boy over for dinner, and soon Luke was hanging out with the Lockhart girls in their backyard. He'd been there during the most crucial events in Natalie's life. She used to have a dreamy-eyed crush on Luke, but their timing was always off. Over the years, they'd developed a strong, close friendship that her relationship with Hunter was threatening to weaken.

"Luke. What happened?" she asked.

He studied her closely for a moment, then shoved his hands into the pockets of his parka. He had dark circles under his eyes. He looked exhausted. "The train engineer called it in at six thirty-five A.M.," he said. "Veronica Manes was struck by a westbound train going seventy miles an hour. No witnesses saw her approaching the tracks. There are no signs of her car in the vicinity. The engineer spotted her as the train was approaching. He hit the brakes and blew his horn, but it was too late. We haven't found any

ID on her or in the snow. No keys, cell phone, or wallet. Not yet. We're still looking. Several of the officers, plus Brandon and myself, were able to identify her facially. We're positive it's her, but the coroner will confirm with a dental match. We've contacted next of kin. I'm taking the lead on this case. I want you, Lenny, Augie, Murph, and Brandon on my team."

"Was it a suicide or an accident?" she asked.

He shook his head. "I haven't made my assessment yet. Right now it looks like a suspicious death."

"Suspicious?" Again she was confused—a suspicious death meant possible foul play. "I don't understand."

"Natalie," he said solemnly, "there's more you need to know."

She drew her coat collar closer. Although she was deeply involved with Hunter, she had to acknowledge that she still had feelings for Luke. Their friendship was a long-running river, and she couldn't ignore the personal connection between them. For most of her life she'd been secretly in love with the guy, and their crisscrossing paths were braided together so tightly, she couldn't give up on him that easily. She wanted to be friends. Close friends. But Luke had drawn a line. His smile had not changed, but his eyes had. His eyes tended to glaze over whenever she spoke, as if she could no longer be trusted. They were damning eyes.

"The site of impact is twenty yards this way," he said, pointing eastward. "The train is parked half a mile that way." He pointed west. "It took that long for it to come to a full stop. When the train struck the victim, she was shackled to the tracks."

"Shackled?" All the air went out of her. She didn't know what to say.

He nodded. She noticed the green scarf that Rainie Sandhill had knitted him fluttering in the wind. "The department is going to great lengths to play this down. The last thing the chief wants is another drop-everything case. This is his worst nightmare."

She glanced east down the tracks where Augie and Lenny were having a heated conversation, their dueling breath clouds clashing like lightsabers. Assistant Chief Timothy Gossett was with them, looking useless—Natalie despised the pressed uniform, the neatly trimmed hair, the artificial suntan in the dead of winter, the aviator sunglasses for the snow glare.

"Two steel chains were wrapped underneath the rails," Luke explained, "and attached to two pairs of handcuffs. She was handcuffed and chained to the tracks. Upon impact, her wrists were instantly severed, her hands dropped into the snow, the chains went slack, and she was flung fifteen yards north of the grade. Meanwhile, the train kept going." He stomped his bootheels on the packed snow, then rubbed his hands together and glanced at her cautiously. "Blood, bone fragments, and brain matter left a trail about eighty feet long up the tracks," he said. "Officers with cadaver dogs are walking the grade now, picking up pieces of . . . the victim out of the snow. We may not find it all until the spring thaw."

Concentric circles of fear began to open up inside her. The enormity of the implication was earth-shattering. She could feel an acidic rancor at the back of her throat. She wanted to have grown a tougher skin by now, but her past experiences had deadened her to the world instead. Sometimes she felt so much pain, she was overloaded by it. "So you're saying she was murdered," she said, letting it sink in.

He nodded. "I doubt very much she could've chained herself to the tracks. Anything's possible, but physically, in this weather . . . I had an officer drop by her house. Her car's still in the garage. Did she walk here all by herself during last night's storm? Did she carry those steel chains and handcuffs in a backpack? There's no backpack or tote bag nearby. No keys to the handcuffs or padlocks she would've tossed in the snow. At least the metal detector hasn't picked anything up yet. Besides . . ." His lips tightened over his teeth. "There's more."

Natalie braced herself.

"She was dressed up in an old-fashioned Halloween costume. A witch costume. Long black dress with a black cape or cloak. We also found a tall black witch's hat in the snow, and a broom."

"Are you serious?"

"Also, there was a small silver cross draped around her neck."

"A cross?" she repeated, shocked.

"It's unknown whether or not she was under the influence of drugs or alcohol."

"Why does this keep happening?" Natalie interjected.

His eyes grew compassionate, but his voice sounded brittle in the winter air. "Nothing's happening to us, Natalie. This is a brand-new case."

"That's not what I meant."

"I know exactly what you meant."

She felt as if she were standing inside a very deep hole. "The press will go haywire—another crazy case in Burning Lake. Fuck."

"That's why I'm assigning you a secondary role," he said with obvious concern. "You won't be front and center this time, Natalie. I don't want you handling things in a prominent position. Instead, you'll be canvassing and doing other background work. I need your experience, but I won't put you through the wringer again."

She understood that he was protecting her, being a considerate friend. And the truth was, Natalie didn't want another drop-everything-and-go-for-it case. Last year, she'd caught two sensational homicide cases, and that was enough. Any other detective would've given his right arm for either one of them.

But this was Veronica Manes, a woman who was beloved by everyone in the community. And right at this instant, Natalie wanted more than anything to find out what had happened to this wonderful human being.

"Augie and Lenny are in charge of processing the scene," Luke went on. "Keegan's searching the grounds with a metal detector, looking for the handcuff and padlock keys or anything else that might've slipped under the snow. I sent Murphy back to the station to work on a warrant to search Veronica's house and property. In the meantime, there's a road close to the point of impact, Mountain Laurel Road, on the northern side of the tracks, up that way." He pointed eastward. "I need you to take that road by foot, Natalie, and canvass the homeowners in the area, get their statements— did they see or hear anything unusual last night? Any traffic? If Veronica didn't do this to herself, then somebody had to have transported her over here. They must've dressed her up like that and chained her to the tracks, and they had to come down one of those roads that abuts against the grade. It's the closest way in."

"What about the engineer and the railroad company? Who's handling that?"

"Brandon will deal with the train folks—he's talking to the engineer and other witnesses right now. They've got CCTV cameras inside the engines, sort of like a black box for trains. He'll obtain the video and liaise with the relevant company personnel. Then we'll all meet up for a debrief this afternoon around two o'clock."

"Okay," she said, her eyes stinging with emotion, "but first, I want to check out the crime scene."

"Natalie." He touched her arm with his gloved hand. "Are you sure?"

No, actually, she wasn't sure at all. Gruesome crime scenes could change you in ways you might never recover from—they wormed their way into your psyche and had the power to hurt you at the oddest moments. But she said, "I want to know what we're dealing with here."

He nodded slowly, and she could tell by the way he looked at her that this was one of those cases that could scar you all the way to your core.

4

Natalie headed east along the tracks, trudging past solemn-faced officers and detectives bent over a lengthy trail of bloodstains and scattered pieces of organ matter. Everyone was in shock—there wasn't a single jaded expression. The atmosphere was kinetic with fear and distress, even from these seasoned pros.

She came to the spot where the chains had shackled Veronica to the rails. She tried not to stare too hard at the vivid torn-away pieces of flesh lying on the virgin snow or the bright brushstrokes of blood, like some mad painter had done it.

Looking east down the long, straight tracks, Natalie noted that on a clear day, the engineer would probably have had a good line of sight. There were no curves to interfere with his view. There were no trees with overhanging branches to obscure his sight line. No steep grades or signage to get in the way. It was possible that, with better weather, he would've hit the brakes early enough to spare Veronica's life. But last night and early this morning, it was snowing heavily and visibility was poor.

Which brought Natalie to her next question—did the perpetrator deliberately use the snowstorm to hide behind? Because if everything was covered in a fresh coat of snow, there would be no tire tracks or footprints to worry about. Perhaps this crime had been premeditated right down to the weather report? A truly chilling thought.

From the condition of the railroad track bed, Natalie could see that the train had plowed through the snow, hydroplaning, and spitting gravel up from the ballast. The spot where Veronica Manes had taken her last breath wasn't anywhere near a crossing gate, so there were no drop arms nearby, no alarms or flashing lights to warn that a train was approaching.

However, in a twist of tragic irony, Veronica would've been able to see the train's headlight through a veil of snow. She would've heard the horn. A horrifying thought.

Natalie took a step back and focused on the tracks. She noticed fissures in the snow from where the train had plowed through, casting heaps of powder on either side. Two separate lengths of padlocked chain were still wrapped around the underside of the rails, in between the ballast and the wooden railroad ties. There was a set of handcuffs attached to the end of each chain. There was blood on the handcuffs.

Upon impact, Veronica's hands had been severed at the wrists and, freed from her body, had landed on either side of the tracks. The two hands were surrounded by orange evidence cards. Frail-looking and ash gray, they lay on top of the snow with their fingers curled, like two helpless creatures, crimson blood soaking into the drifts.

Fear buzzed through Natalie as she knelt to examine one of the hands balanced on top of a snowdrift. The radial and ulnar arteries had been severed, with thick black blood clotting over the slice. The cuts looked clean, but she was no expert. The fingers were slightly bent at the knuckles, as if tugged upward by the strings of a puppeteer. Some of her fingernails were broken or cracked, with dirt or gravel embedded under the nails, as if she'd tried to scratch and claw her way out of her predicament.

Natalie leaned in closer to study how the chains had been secured to the tracks. The rails were held together at the joints with steel plates. Rusty nuts and bolts held the metal plates in place, and iron spikes kept the plates attached to the wooden railroad ties. The gravel ballast located under the rails and between the ties provided enough space to wrap the chains around the plates, securing them to the tracks without derailing the train.

Not far from the tracks, surrounded by more orange evidence cards, was a black witch's hat, half-buried in the snow. It looked like part of an old Halloween costume. Natalie didn't see a broom. Perhaps that had landed farther away.

She could hear a thrumming sound, and it took her a moment to realize that it was her own heartbeat, the blood rushing through her ears faster and harder than usual.

This scene was full of death, but winter was alive with songbirds flying overhead and a cold breeze blowing through the treetops and people moving around in the periphery of her vision—stalwart officers grid-searching the area, finding gruesome bits of detritus along the tracks. Nothing made any sense.

She stood up and studied the chaotic still life before her—an overturned women's boot, a tall black witch's hat, two perfectly intact dismembered human hands, and various bloody fleshy parts strewn around. The cold made her teeth hurt.

Natalie felt herself going into shock—but she refused to allow herself the luxury. Everything slowed way down, or perhaps it was the result of moving through the dense layers of snow, how the drifts around the tracks had impeded everyone's progress.

She took another careful step back. The body had been flung by the force of the impact about fifteen feet away, where it landed on the north side of the grade. With great reluctance, she turned and headed down the embankment.

Surrounded by orange cones, the victim was lying prone in the snow, her arms and legs akimbo but still attached to her torso. It was obvious her bones had been broken in many places. Her severed wrists were coagulated with blood, and the flesh of her forearms was ringed with bluish-purple bruises—evidence that she'd tried to escape and had struggled with the handcuffs.

Everywhere in the snow around the body were strings of goopy crimson innards. Veronica's torso was a mass of twisted black fabric and exposed flesh, where large lacerations had pooled with coagulated blood. There were ugly abrasions and lacerations on various parts of her body. The victim's boots had been knocked off her feet. Again, orange evidence cards marked the places in the snow where the boots had landed—one here, one there, at least twenty feet apart. Most disturbing of all, the back of Veronica's skull had been partially bashed in and one of her eyes bulged slightly in its socket as if with surprise. But her face was relatively intact and recognizable.

Careful not to disturb the scene, Natalie knelt down in the snow, feeling cold and empty. Windswept of emotion. This was Veronica Manes, a woman everyone in town admired—her sad blue eyes stared beyond Natalie at an unknown evil, as if her death had driven her mad.

Natalie found herself awkwardly kneeling on the ground in front of the body and quickly got up, stumbling to her feet. She saw everything with sudden clarity through a wide lens. Veronica had tried desperately to get away. The bruises around her wrists and forearms proved that. The broken fingernails proved that. As for the grotesque costume, the victim was a devout Wiccan who believed in peace and white magic—Veronica was a thoroughly modern-day witch, and if you wanted to insult a modern witch, then this outfit would've been a perfect vessel for her humiliation.

Natalie blinked and saw coronas of light, afterimages from the brilliance of the sunlit snow. For the briefest instant, she grew faint, and the sky seemed to darken, or else the world was growing dimmer all around her.

She stared down at something so foreign to her, it almost didn't register. The kind of image you didn't want inside your head. A torn-apart doll. A sickening stench of decay. Flecks of blood spatter everywhere you looked. Snowflakes sparkling down around them. Natalie knew that the sight of this poor ripped-apart body would burn itself into her brain. She resented the fact. Death was unfair. Death was never convenient or welcome. But this was something far beyond that.

She took a deep breath, and the light returned, and everything went back to normal again. If you could call this normal.

5

The sky was as gray and overcast as a sickroom with all the shades drawn. Natalie walked in silence along the grade, between the tracks and the woods, then finally turned north and headed up a set of railroad tie steps, spongy with rot, set into an embankment. Mountain Laurel Road began at the edge of the forest and continued on a curved path through the conservation lands.

At first glance, Natalie didn't find any footprints or tire tracks on the snowy dead-end road—just a heavy dusting of fresh powder over older, more compacted perennial snow. When she came to a bend in the road, she could see where the plows had been through earlier that morning. There was no hope of finding any footsteps or tire tracks here—it had all been plowed under. She texted herself to follow up with the snowplow services—perhaps one of the drivers had seen something?

She took photographs of the snow-covered portion of the street, the street signs, and the plowed asphalt, her boots squeaking over compacted snow. Soon the road began to curve again through the woods. It was so silent and peaceful here. She could smell the hickory woodsmoke in the air. A light snow was falling, and everything felt sacred. These woods. This road. The chilly, muffled air.

Veronica Manes had no business being out in the middle of nowhere during a snowstorm on one of the coldest nights of the year. What was she doing here? How could this have happened? As far as Natalie knew, Veronica was a stable and contented person, highly respected by the whole town. If she'd parked her car on Mountain Laurel Road and then walked down to the tracks, they would've found her vehicle this morning. She would've been carrying a flashlight with her, too, since there were no streetlights out this way. No illumination at night. Luke hadn't mentioned finding any flashlights at the scene.

Burning Lake, New York, was one of the most popular tourist destinations for Halloween, rivaling Salem, Massachusetts—perhaps even surpassing it by now—with its monthlong schedule of festivities and events, including haunted guided tours, museum exhibits, Halloween-themed balls, and culminating in the Monster Mash Music Festival on October 31. For centuries, Burning Lake had buried its most shameful secret. In 1712, three innocent women were executed as witches—Abigail Stuart, Sarah Hutchins, and Victoriana Forsyth. Decade after decade, the town fathers struggled to keep this sordid history hidden from view. The city's rebirth began in the 1970s, when a book about the witch trials was published to critical acclaim, drawing hundreds of tourists to Burning Lake on Halloween's Eve. Today, the town's commercial district was full of occult gift shops and New Age boutiques, selling everything from spell kits to magic crystals. Every October, the trees blazed a spectacular orange color, and thousands of tourists came from all over to see the world on fire.

There were only two official historic covens listed in the Burning Lake phone book—the Pendleton coven formed in the late 1800s and the Carrington coven founded in 1926. Each of these covens had thirteen members, who were replaced only when they either moved away, voluntarily left the coven, or died. Veronica was the head of the Pendleton coven, and a woman named Jessie Ashton was in charge of the Carrington coven. As far as Natalie knew, the two historic covens occasionally organized bake sales and held fundraising events together. They were keenly aware of their public image and the town's heritage, and their websites emphasized that they believed in white magic only.

Both historic covens were closed to new memberships, and Veronica and Jessie were constantly turning people away. Even though there were plenty of other "unofficial" covens for people to join here in Burning Lake, the waiting lists for these two historic covens were long. Perhaps some disgruntled person seeking to join Pendleton had taken Veronica's rejection personally?

Natalie was about fifty yards from the tracks when a gray-shingled rooftop with a turret came into view. The house was very old, painted apple green with white trim. The mailbox at the end of the driveway read DREYER.

That was odd, Natalie thought. She wondered if Aimee Dreyer, the department secretary, lived here. She opened the gate of a waist-high wooden fence framing the property. The porch with its old-fashioned rocking chairs reminded her of a bygone era, when people used to make ice cream by hand and fan their faces with their straw hats in the summer.

Natalie knocked, then waited.

The apple-green door swung open, and forty-two-year-old Aimee Dreyer greeted her in yoga pants and a Wonder Woman T-shirt. She had a pretty freckled face and frizzy blond hair pulled into a hasty ponytail. The morning fog hadn't cleared yet from her eyes. "Detective Lockhart?" she said with surprise. "What are you doing here?"

"Sorry, I didn't realize you lived here, Aimee. There's been an accident on the tracks."

"Oh my gosh. Come in!" Aimee swung the door all the way open.

Natalie wiped her boots on the welcome mat and stepped inside.

The front foyer angled awkwardly into a high-ceilinged living room, where the furniture was economical and functional, and where comfort seemed more important than style. Big upholstered chairs. A wide sofa with lots of throw pillows and a blanket. Side tables stacked with books and old coffee mugs. The place was invitingly spacious and smelled of wild roses.

"What happened? Who got hurt?"

"Veronica Manes was killed on the tracks."

Aimee's face flushed crimson. At work, you couldn't see her freckles beneath her makeup, and any split ends were flat-ironed into place. Down at the station, Aimee presented herself as a polished professional, but Natalie sensed that maybe this was the real her—a fun person to hang with. "Veronica Manes? You mean that witch who's so nice to everybody?" Aimee asked. "What happened?"

"We aren't sure yet." Natalie and Aimee had always had a cordial working relationship, friendly but distant, and now Natalie felt embarrassed that she didn't know more about Aimee, but she wasn't good at small talk. "I need to ask, due to the proximity of your house to the tracks . . . did you see or hear anything unusual last night? Any traffic on the road early this morning? Headlights or voices? Anything at all?"

"No." She shook her head slowly. "I don't remember hearing anything. What was she doing down there this time of year?" Her eyes were shiny with heartfelt emotion. "God, what awful news. Would you like some coffee?"

"No, thanks."

"Mind if I get a cup? We can sit in the kitchen. It's nicer in there."

Natalie followed Aimee into her small sunflower-yellow kitchen, with its old-fashioned plumbing fixtures and cozy touches—a Cookie Monster jar, lobster-shaped oven mitts, an assortment of cheery refrigerator magnets. On the kitchen table was a centerpiece of daisies, and Natalie wondered where you could get daisies in the dead of winter. She guessed a flower shop, but Natalie had never been inside one before. She wasn't the type of woman to buy herself daisies in the middle of winter, and for that she sort of envied Aimee.

"Sure you don't want anything?" Aimee asked, pouring herself a cup of coffee.

"Positive, thanks."

"The sound of the train horn is so annoying, not to mention the rumble as it rolls past the house. So I always wear a sleep mask and earplugs at night," Aimee explained. "And even that's not enough. I bought a sound machine to block out the noise. Now I sleep like a log." She took a seat at the kitchen table and stirred her coffee, gazing out the window at the gently falling snow. "The noise from the trains, it gets louder in the fall and winter, because the leaves are off the trees. But then in the summer, you have to open your windows to get a cross breeze, so it's almost as bad. The train noise, I mean." She shook her head. "I guess it's pretty much always an issue. Anyway, when the train passes, it's like living next to a freeway. My earplugs and sound machine block out the noise, and then I can sleep."

"So you didn't hear a thing."

"No. Sorry."

"Who's your nearest neighbor?"

"Oh, we're a select group of stoics. Not too many folks live out this way, as you can imagine." She smiled and settled against her yellow-painted wooden chair. "The homeowner on the other side of the road, about twenty yards down, is Jerry Duckworth . . . he's an old crank. Retired. The next house down is Tabitha Vaughn. Oh my gosh, she'll be devastated. She's a member of Veronica's coven. We run in different circles, but we commiserate about the trains once in a while. She's really nice."

Natalie nodded. "Anyone else?"

"Across the street from Tabitha, farther down, are the Palmeros. They're summer people, so they aren't here now. Then you take a left onto Hummingbird Lane and go all the way to the end, and that's the cottage those two crazy kids were renting, but they're gone now."

"Kids?"

"In their twenties. They up and left about a month ago. I'm not sure why. You should ask Reverend Grimsby. He was renting it to them."

6

The next house down on the other side of the road belonged to a re-
tiree named Jerry Duckworth. The house was Italianate with hood-
like windows and a tower on top. "Ugly Victorian," it was called. The white
paint had long since gone gray, and a rusty tin birdhouse hung from a
nearby tree.

Natalie rang the doorbell.

"Who is it?" came a scratchy, agitated voice from inside the house.

"Detective Lockhart." She held up her shield to the peephole. "Can I have
a word with you, sir?"

After a moment, the front door creaked open.

"What do you want?" A frail-looking, white-haired, hunched-over man
stood squinting up at her. There was a carelessness about his appearance—
loose bathrobe, wrinkled pajamas, stained slippers—and deep bags under
his eyes.

"I need to ask you a few questions. May I come in?"

"Questions about what?" he said irritably.

"There was an accident on the tracks this morning."

"When?"

"Earlier today. Perhaps last night. We aren't sure yet. May I come in?"

"I guess so," Jerry Duckworth grumbled, stepping aside.

A musty smell greeted her. He led her into a living room full of bulky pine furniture. The tall narrow doors and windows made her feel claustrophobic. There were fleur-de-lis on the wallpaper and too many extension cords plugged into the outlets. She was worried that the circuits would overload, and the place might go up in smoke.

"What do you want?" he asked without offering her a seat.

"I need to know if you heard or saw anything unusual last night . . ."

"Unusual?"

". . . or early this morning?"

"Who are you again?" he said with a squint.

"Detective Lockhart from the Burning Lake police. There was an accident on the railroad tracks. A woman was killed early this morning. Her name is Veronica Manes."

"Oh, yes." He nodded slowly. "She's a friend of my neighbor's. Tabitha Vaughn. They're both *witches*," he said in a loud conspiratorial whisper. "They belong to the same *coven* . . ." He suddenly turned and pointed at one of the windows. "About a month ago, I asked Tabitha to talk to those two young people who were living up there in the cottage on Hummingbird Lane. They were practicing witchcraft. Some errant souls, and what is the Wiccan community doing to stamp this sort of behavior out? Nothing. They sit back and let it happen in their name. No wonder they have reputation problems. Those two kids were a perfect example. What if there were individual Christians who went out and did outrageous things in the name of their religion, and we said nothing? Think of the brouhaha that would follow. What's good for the goose is good for the gander. If we didn't disavow those few troubled—very troubled, aberrant—followers then what would they say about us?"

"What did they do? Those two kids?"

He stared at her for a dazed moment, as if he'd abruptly lost track of his thoughts. "What's that?"

"Those kids. What were their names?"

"I don't know. Anyway, what good would it do me to complain now? They're gone. They vamoosed. Good riddance to bad rubbish, is what I say." He scowled and drew his thin plaid robe tighter around his waist. "But speaking of unusual sounds . . . a major road crosses the tracks about four hundred yards from here, and the train will blast its warning horn from half a mile away. Continuously. I've petitioned the town council to declare this neighborhood a quiet zone, but they haven't done a blessed thing." He rubbed his unshaven chin. "Anyway, I can't afford soundproofing or anything like that. To tell you the truth, I've been trying to move from this neighborhood for years, but nobody wants to buy a house near the tracks. But I'm a God-fearing man, so . . ." He looked at her and shrugged, as if he'd lost another thread. His head was inclined in Natalie's direction, but it wasn't entirely obvious that he was cognizant of her presence. "So there you have it."

"Did you hear anything else besides the train horn last night?" she asked.

"Ten times a day you can hear that darn horn blowing. Sounds louder at night for some reason. I'm an early to bed, early to rise type of guy. But the trains will rock the whole house." He pointed at the ceiling. "Do you see those cracks in the plaster? They say trains make the earth move, and it's true. Not just from the shaking and rattling. It's the blasted horn. So loud. First time I heard it, it rattled my teeth."

"Do you have any relatives, sir?"

"What? No. Not very many of us Duckworths left. Why?" He slumped into his armchair.

"Are you feeling okay?"

He blinked at her with his papery eyelids. "I think so. Why?"

"Do you have any friends or relatives close by? Someone who can look in on you?"

He nodded slightly, then pointed at a ceramic bowl with a business card inside it.

Natalie scooped up the card. It had the name and number of a local social worker she knew. "May I sit down for a minute?" she asked.

"Suit yourself."

Natalie took a seat. She would call the social worker this afternoon and make sure she checked in on him today. "Mr. Duckworth, I need to know if anything unusual occurred in the neighborhood last night or this morning? Did you see any headlights or hear voices, or a car backing up? Anything at all?"

"What do you mean by unusual?" he asked with a glassy look. "The train makes a deep annoying rumble as it passes by. I've got foundational damage from the trains constantly going by the house. That's unusual, isn't it?" He stared at her with a mixture of indignation and anger. "A rumbling sound you can't ignore?"

The wind swelled outside, and a shiver ran through her.

7

Farther down Mountain Laurel Road, Tabitha Vaughn lived in an azure-blue house sheltered on all sides by woods. Thin wafts of grayish smoke emitted from the chimney. There was a Jeep Renegade parked in the driveway. Natalie crossed the snowy front yard, and an owl hooted from the treetops. A mouse or a bird had scampered across the lowest porch step, leaving their tiny paw prints.

A middle-aged woman wearing a floral-patterned housedress and a peppermint-striped apron opened the door. Natalie had seen Tabitha Vaughn around town, and the two were at best acquaintances. Tabitha had a chubby face with an upturned nose and a barely there chin. Her thick gray hair was long enough to sit on. She flapped her hands and bit back the tears. "Oh God, Aimee Dreyer just called. Veronica's *dead*? Seriously? Are you sure it's her? Because I just spoke to her yesterday."

"You saw her in person?" Natalie asked.

"No. We spoke on the phone. We were scheduling our next meetup. Listen, Detective, I just baked some cookies. The oven timer dinged, and I have to get them out of the oven. Do you mind?"

"We'd better not let them burn."

"Please, come in." She showed Natalie down a long, narrow hallway with small amateurish oil paintings on the walls—landscapes mostly, beaches and sunsets. "I'm baking cinnamon cookies for the food bank. It makes me feel better to help people who are struggling more than I am. What's that saying? You don't become poor by giving."

The large country kitchen was filled with a delicious cinnamon-sugar smell. The countertops were scattered with measuring cups, bowls, spilt batter, and toast crumbs.

Tabitha put on a pair of pink oven mitts, took the cookies out of the oven, and plopped them down on a cooling rack. "I can't believe it. I'm still in shock." There were smears of mascara under her glazed eyes. "Veronica was a great influence on us all. Please. Have a seat."

Natalie pulled up a stool to the kitchen island. Snow tapped lightly against the windowpanes. Plants and herbs grew on the sills. "I only met her once," Natalie said. "But she impressed me as someone who was genuinely kind and grounded."

"Yes, she was. She'd give you the shirt off her back. But she could be brutally honest, too, sometimes. Sorry, I got dizzy for a second. I feel wobbly. I should sit down." She sat at the kitchen island next to Natalie and rubbed her temples with shaky fingers. "I forgot to ask, do you want a cookie?"

"No, thanks."

"Let me guess. You're on a diet."

"Post-holidays."

"Right. Part of my New Year's resolution is to eat as many cookies as I want. It's the opposite of the things people say they're going to do—lose weight, exercise more, work harder, achieve new goals. Not me. I decided a long time ago, winter isn't the time to step on the scale. Now's the time to be jolly. I'll get serious in April."

Natalie smiled. "I hope you don't mind, but I need to ask you some questions. Did you notice any unusual traffic on Mountain Laurel Road last night? People driving around. Headlights. Voices. Anything."

"I dozed off in front of the TV last night, but something woke me up . . . a flash of light or something. I assumed it was coming from the TV."

"Did you get up and look around?"

"No. I usually have a glass of wine in the evenings to calm my nerves. Then I watch my stories on cable. Helps me sleep." She smiled sadly at Natalie.

"I fell asleep in the living room with the lights on. Sometimes it makes me feel less alone. Less scared."

"You get scared at night?"

"Oh yeah, ever since I was little. Maybe that's why I became a witch. To fend off the darkness with white magic. I had a TV in my room as a kid, and I used to stay up watching reruns with the sound off so I wouldn't wake my parents. My favorite show was *Bewitched*. Natch."

Natalie smiled. "I couldn't help but notice your name . . ."

"Tabitha. Right. My real name's Rosalie Vaughn. I hated Rosalie. So I changed it in my twenties. Tabitha suits me. Growing up, I was the weirdo who everybody ignored, until they needed my help in countering the curse another kid put on them."

"So you got into witchcraft early?"

She nodded. "I was brought up a strict Christian, but it wasn't enough. I wanted more magic, more mystery, fewer rules . . ."

"And you saw a flash of light last night?"

"I do remember seeing headlights, or lights . . . but it was all fuzzy. It was late, I remember that. Could've been a freight train. The horn blast, the rumbling. You get used to it. You stop hearing it after a while. But then, when your friends come over, they'll comment on the noise, and it always surprises me. The homeowner who lived here before me planted a row of hedges along the property line to act as a sound barrier, but the air currents just carry the sound over the hedges."

"Have you noticed any unusual activity in the neighborhood recently?"

"I don't think so. Unless you're talking about the cottage on Hummingbird Lane. Now there's a strange pair. Holly and her husband—Edward, I think his name is. Reverend Grimsby rents out his little cottage, and we've never had any trouble with the tenants until recently. But it's empty now. He had to evict them."

"Why?"

"Partying, drugs, bonfires. They left about a month ago, so it's been blissfully peaceful ever since. What a relief. The reverend hasn't blessed the house yet, but there's always a cleanup in the spring with a team of volunteers from the church."

"Has anyone threatened Veronica that you know of?"

She shook her head.

"What about any rivalries inside the coven?"

"We believe in karma—that any action you take will come back at you three times over. That's the Threefold Law. Also known as the Wiccan Rede—which basically tells us to do whatever we want, just as long as we don't bring harm to others. Of course, we're only human. There is such a thing as coven rivalry, which can escalate into a 'witch war.' But that's not the case here. Everyone in Pendleton gets along really well with everyone in Carrington. Spiritual enlightenment is our ultimate goal. You may get negative energy from solitary witches or splinter sects who do immoral things, but that's not the norm."

"Thanks." Natalie handed Tabitha her card. "If you think of anything else, give me a call. And if you don't mind, I need a list of all the members of both covens."

"Sure. I'll get that to you right away. I can't imagine how they're going to take the news. This is truly devastating." Tabitha put the card down on the kitchen island, then looked up. "She didn't kill herself, did she?"

Natalie shook her head, trying to prevent speculation—an impossible task in a small town like Burning Lake. "We don't have all the details yet," she said.

"Veronica lived her life with great poise and dignity. Everyone loved her. She was working on a new book, you know. Doing research in the town library. She seemed so excited about it. And happy. Looking forward to the future. She's the epitome of what a modern witch should be. She had it all."

8

Each residential lot was like an island carved out of an ocean of woods, isolated from the others by untrammeled wilderness and a desire for privacy. Across the street from Tabitha, twenty yards north, was the Palmeros' summer home.

The squat two-story house flanked by two weeping willows was closed up tight for the winter. There were no cars in the driveway, and the snowy front yard was undisturbed. It was obvious nobody had been there for months.

Natalie followed the road north another dozen yards or so until she came to Hummingbird Lane. She took a left onto the single-lane road, which ran through the woods past a semi-frozen stream and rocky out-croppings with a small waterfall. The snowplow had been through here earlier, but there was about half an inch of accumulated snow on the plowed road. The cottage at the midpoint of the lane had burned down a decade ago and was never rebuilt. Where the cottage used to be was now an overgrown lot.

Reverend Grimsby's dove-gray cottage was at the very end of the lane.

It had seen better days. The picket fence was peeling. A few stunted apple trees grew in the yard. The plow had pushed a heap of snow right into the driveway, where no vehicles were parked. However, there was a trail of indentations in the snow leading up to the front door, indicating that somebody had been here recently. How recently, she couldn't say, since the footprints were partially filled in with snow.

Natalie took a few pictures of the front yard with its visible tracks, then proceeded with caution, making a wide arc around the potential evidence in order to preserve it. There were at least a dozen rolled-up newspapers on the front porch. She tried the door, but it was locked. The window shades were drawn three-quarters of the way down. She cupped her hands over the glass and peered through the bottom portion of the window.

It was dark inside. She could barely make out an old-fashioned wood-stove in the living room, a sofa with newspapers on it, and a card table with four folding chairs.

She stepped back from the window. The birds were fighting over territory high in the treetops. A dog was barking loudly in the distance. It was coming from behind the cottage.

Natalie went around back and trudged through the deep drifts, avoiding the fallen branches from January's and February's storms. Strung between two sturdy birches was a hammock packed with snow and leaves. There was a pile of bricks on the picnic table. Natalie fished an amber beer bottle out of the snow, then heard the dog barking again. It was coming from the woods behind the cottage.

She followed the sound toward a stand of hemlocks, where a large black dog was romping in the snow. It spotted her and barked excitedly. It didn't bare its teeth. Instead, it leapt in exuberant circles, then playfully darted off, practically daring her to chase it.

Natalie slogged through the woods toward a rocky ridge beyond which the dog had disappeared. It had left good-sized prints in the snow, and she easily made a distinction between these and the human footprints she'd seen on the front lawn. As she headed down the slope, she caught her coat on a thorny bush and nearly tumbled into a thicket of wild roses. She stopped herself by grabbing a thorn-studded branch. "Ow," she said, sucking the blood off her finger. Perhaps she shouldn't have come this way, but the dog was barking more insistently now, running farther downhill and to the left.

The woods felt full of watchful eyes. Natalie didn't know why she was following this dog—partly out of curiosity, partly out of instinct—but she figured she was committed now, so she kept going, clambering over a stone wall, dodging fallen branches and half-buried tree stumps. She tramped through knee-deep snow until her feet grew numb.

She was about to give up and turn back when something stirred out of a snowdrift—a wild cottontail rabbit bounding away from her. A flock of crows wheeled through the overcast sky, making her shudder. She looked around and realized she was behind the dove-gray cottage again—and that the dog had taken her on a wild-goose chase through the woods and back toward the property.

Now the dog trotted over to a patch of leaves beneath a sprawling oak tree. It began to whimper, then dug at the snow. It sniffed and barked.

"Hey, good boy. What've you got there? What did you find?"

The dog looked up, alert. It wagged its tail, excited about something. It looked around in all directions, then barked again. Then it began to dig.

"What've you got there?"

Old leaves and twigs and pawfuls of snow went flying in all directions. Soon the dog was gripping a desiccated squirrel carcass between its teeth.

"Yeah, you don't want that in your mouth, buddy. Put that down."

The dog growled. Hunkering for a fight.

"Okay. Your funeral." Natalie backed off. Then she looked up.

Something was hanging from the branches of the tree. Thirteen things, to be exact. Thirteen glass mason jars with screw-top lids, wrapped in twine.

She reached for one, tilting it sideways. The lid was sealed with red wax. The jar was full of a yellowish liquid that had partially frozen solid, and there was something floating around inside the piss-colored murk. Straight pins bent into L-shapes, and what looked like a clump of human hair, along with small rusty nails and something that had once been alive but was now dead and unrecognizable. Perhaps a dead mouse—she detected a tail and a tiny set of claws.

Natalie had forgotten her gloves at home. Her fingers were frozen. She rubbed her hands together, and then, standing on tiptoe, gingerly untied the mason jar from the tree branch. As soon as it was released, the jar slipped out of her hands and crashed to the ground, shattering on a rock at her feet, glass shards and frozen chunks of urine scattering across the snow.

9

Luke stood in the road beside his parked midnight-blue Ford Ranger, talking to Chief Snyder on his mobile phone. His head was inclined slightly as he glanced at the overcast sky. It had stopped snowing, and the wind moved in broad, aggressive gusts through the treetops with an ominous wailing sound, like a warning for the whole town.

Luke pocketed his phone and came over. "Chief says we've got priority—the run of the lab, extra manpower, whatever we need. He says just solve the case."

She smiled vaguely. "Just solve the fucking case, huh?"

He handed her a latte. "I thought you'd want this."

"Mind reader." She took a couple of sips, then secured the lid. She was still shivering from cold and shock. Still having a hard time processing it. Sometimes you got by with a dark sense of humor, but in this case it seemed inappropriate for them to be joking about anything. She had just gotten off the phone with Reverend Thomas Grimsby, who'd given her permission to search the cottage and grounds. "Where's Augie?" she asked.

"En route. He's bringing a cadaver dog to search the ravine where you found those animal bones."

"Not to mention the bottles of urine."

"Thirteen of them, huh?"

"Very creepy."

"Did you get the key from Grimsby?"

She showed Luke the house key. "It was hanging from a hook underneath the picnic table in the backyard."

"Not the world's greatest security," Luke said.

"No, although I doubt a thief would want to steal anything. I peeked through the windows. The place is a dump."

"Let's go."

Natalie took another sip of coffee, then looked around for a place to stash it.

"I'll take that," Luke offered.

Their hands touched by accident, and their skin emitted a staticky spark.

"Sorry." He took her cup and put their coffees on the hood of his Ranger.

Natalie balled her hands into fists and tried to focus, but her mind was filled with him—his opinion of her, his approval. Luke's hair was slightly wavy and amber-colored, and he had the world's most intense eyes. They were crystal blue and thick-lashed, and his mouth turned down on one side whenever he became overly secretive and pensive, just like now.

"After you," he said, handing her a pair of latex gloves, and Natalie led the way.

Time had battered and warped the cabin. The porch was off-kilter. The front door creaked open. It was cold and dark inside. No electricity.

"Wow, smells funky in here," Luke said.

It was true—but not dead-body funky.

They stood for a moment in the blue-tinged darkness before turning on their flashlights. The house smelled of old things—ever-encroaching mold, soggy coffee grounds, wet wool, burnt toast, urine, and incense. The living room needed fumigating. The hardwood floors were crunchy with kitty litter, and you could barely see through the dirty windows. There were dried cat feces in one corner. Water stains mushroomed on the ceiling.

"Windows are locked," Luke said, testing them. "No evidence of a break-in."

None of the furniture had been overturned, and there were no signs of a struggle.

The cottage itself predated the 1950s, with vinyl tile flooring and knotty pine walls, everything buried under layers of dust and neglect. The carpet's padding was rotten beneath the old weave. Natalie stepped on a wedge of glass and it made a distinct crunch.

The place felt evil. Bad.

"What else did Grimsby say?" Luke asked her.

"The last tenants were here for about six months. A young couple named Holly and Edward Host, down on their luck. Grimsby wanted to help them out by offering them a reduced rent, but they took advantage of his generosity. They were having rowdy parties, bothering the neighbors. Grimsby threatened to evict them for failing to pay the rent. They left about a month ago still owing four months' back rent. Now the cottage is empty."

Luke had a weathered squint. "And they haven't been back since?"

"Not according to Grimsby. He's been renting the place out to various needy tenants over the years, but these folks were trouble."

"We should run a background check."

"I'm way ahead of you."

"As usual." One corner of his mouth twitched with a repressed smile. "And no one else rented the place after they moved out?"

"No. It's been empty." She swept her light around the dank living room. A deer's head with antlers hung crookedly on the wall above the fireplace. Soiled laundry and old magazines were scattered over the floor or on the furniture, which consisted of overstuffed armchairs, thrift-store bookcases, and a sagging sofa. There was an art deco lamp and a chipped ceramic clown on one of the secondhand side tables.

Natalie caught her reflection in one of the dirty windows—she had long mahogany-brown hair, blue eyes, a slender nose, and full lips. She had lost weight recently. Hunter called her "beautiful," but whenever she looked in the mirror, she couldn't see it. All she saw, reflected in her face, was all the phases she'd gone through, all the awkward stages and mistakes and missteps, all the blemishes and flaws, the ugly sides of her personality. It was all there like an aura. She couldn't see herself clearly, the way someone brand-new might imagine her.

A large spiderweb drifted across Natalie's face, and she batted it away. "Shit!" She girded herself as Luke walked over to her.

He looked at her with careful eyes. "You okay?"

"It's creepy in here."

"You getting those vibes, too?" he said, shining his light on a crude charcoal sketch that was taped to the wall. "Did you see this?"

She squinted at the drawing. "Huh."

"Do you know what that symbol is?"

She nodded. "It's the international sign for squatters—a circle with a line coming in on one side, meaning they're entering the property and will be staying for a while. Then an arrow going out the other, meaning they're leaving or they've left."

"Squatters?" he repeated curiously. "I thought they were renters?"

"They're supposed to be." Natalie shone her light on a wrought iron wine rack that held half a dozen empty bottles. She picked one up. "Hmm. It's vodka, not wine."

Luke frowned. "What kind of squatters can afford Ketel One?"

"Good question." She put the bottle back.

They went into the small kitchen. On the counter next to the stained sink was a rotten, dehydrated pumpkin that looked like the wrinkled face of a corpse staring at them. The broken handle of a Campbell's tomato soup coffee mug had been duct-taped together. More duct tape was wrapped around the toaster.

In the bedroom, the empty dresser drawers were yanked out, suggesting that the tenants had abandoned the place in a hurry. There were dozens of half-melted candles on one of the nightstands and also on the warped hardwood floor. The cheap laminate headboard of the queen-sized bed was draped with dusty twinkle lights.

On the rickety bureau was a makeshift altar of some sort, composed of thirteen sugar candy skulls and a handmade, infant-sized wooden casket.

"Jesus, is that what I think it is?" Luke muttered.

Steeling herself, Natalie opened the lid and squinted into the dim interior. Tucked inside the velvet-lined casket was a Victorian-era doll with a cracked porcelain face. The doll's head was twisted one hundred eighty degrees around so that it faced its own spine, and there were pins stuck into it. Scattered inside the coffin were a couple of braids of human hair, one blond, one brunette, and what looked like bird remains, including the feathers.

"These people . . . the Hosts? They have a few screws loose," Luke said.

"If that's their real name." Natalie shone her light across the floral wallpaper, then down at the floor. Under the bed was a Nike shoebox containing a collection of drug paraphernalia—a rusty folding pocketknife, a couple of razor blades, several wrinkled squares of tinfoil, a book of matches, and a small spoon.

"Meth heads," Luke said with disgust.

"Nobody says meth anymore."

"They don't?"

She shook her head distractedly.

"What do they call it, then?"

"Tweakers. What's this?" She reached for a folded piece of paper tucked underneath all the other items. She opened it up. "It's a flyer from St. Paul's Church, with a list of all the food drives this winter. There's one at the church today."

"You go check it out," Luke told her. "I'll get things started here."

10

St. Paul's Church was an octagonal brick building in the neo-Georgian style, topped with a copper domed roof and a copper-clad cupola. Located on the west side of downtown, it was large enough to accommodate three hundred worshippers and was known for hosting AA and Narcotics Anonymous meetings in its basement.

Today's mobile food drive was set up in the church parking lot. A long line of idling vehicles had already formed, and Natalie had to park six blocks away and then walk to the church.

Flea markets and bake sales took place in the large parking lot during the warmer months, but today's food bank had attracted a surprisingly large number of families in dire need. Church volunteers were busy unloading pallets of food onto wooden tables—beans, rice, peanut butter, powdered milk.

"Detective Lockhart, hello," Reverend Thomas Grimsby said, coming over to her and shaking hands with a gentle pumping motion. A slender man in his mid-sixties, Grimsby had warm gray eyes that strained to convey compassion even when he was exhausted and overworked. The last time they'd spoken was at Daisy Buckner's funeral a little under a year ago, before Natalie had uncovered the shocking truth about her sister.

Back in high school, Grace Lockhart and her best friend, Daisy Forester, had formed a coven with Bunny Jackson and Lindsey Wozniak. The four girls were so jealous of Natalie's oldest sister, Willow, that one day they lured her to a secluded farm and stabbed her as part of an occult ritual. Then they framed Willow's boyfriend, Justin Fowler, for the murder. He was convicted and sentenced to life at a maximum security prison. The four women managed to keep this terrible secret between them for twenty years. But last year, when Daisy Forester Buckner became pregnant with her first child, she decided to clear her conscience and confess to the two-decades-old crime. When Grace tried to talk Daisy out of it, the fight had ended tragically, with Daisy's death. Natalie was the lead detective on the case.

Once Natalie realized that her beloved sister Grace had not only killed Daisy, but also their sister Willow, and then lied about it for twenty years rather than face the consequences, Grace committed suicide by jumping off a notoriously dangerous cliff and drowning in the lake.

As a result of Natalie's skillful sleuthing, Justin Fowler's sentence was commuted by the governor, and now the ex-prisoner was living at home with his mother in Burning Lake, too traumatized by his ordeal to come out of the basement, rumor had it.

In the meantime, Grace's daughter and Natalie's teenaged niece, Ellie Guzman, had gone to live with her lawyer dad in Manhattan. Now Natalie was all alone. She had no family—mother gone, father gone, Grace and Willow gone, Ellie gone. Her life had been shattered. Who was responsible? Natalie felt tremendous guilt and pain and sorrow.

"Are you all right?" Grimsby asked her now.

Natalie blinked. "Fine, thanks, Reverend."

"The news has rattled everyone."

She tensed and kept nodding.

He pursed his lips and glanced around. "We didn't cancel the food drive, though. Not with so many desperate mouths to feed. People aren't doing very well nowadays."

"It's good you didn't cancel it," she agreed.

"Single mothers. Unemployed fathers. The county food bank was look-ing for a place to host the event, and I told them—that's what we're here for. Let me show you something."

He escorted Natalie over to the wooden tables, where volunteers in green polo shirts with stick-on name tags were handing out boxes of groceries to a long line of cars. "Each vehicle gets two boxes of groceries—meat, produce, canned goods, a loaf of bread, dessert, and a gallon of milk, all provided by the county. We add a few goodies to each bag—protein bars, bananas, trail mix. I want to make sure the kids are getting their nutrition."

A car rolled up, the driver's side window rolled down, and a disheveled-looking woman with three small children in back accepted a box of gro-ceries. "We appreciate everything you're doing," she said with a flustered look.

"No problem," the reverend told her. "A bag of food and a friendly face, that's our motto. No one in Burning Lake should ever go to bed hungry."

A volunteer handed the woman another box, and the car drove off.

"It's a blessing. It warms my heart." Grimsby shook his head. "You look cold, Detective Lockhart. Shall we step inside?"

She nodded and pulled her coat collar closer.

Grimsby's office on the second floor of the church was full of creaking furniture and outdated technology. It was so chilly in here, she wondered if the heat wasn't working. Her impression of Grimsby was that he wanted to help, and if he couldn't help you directly, then he would get others to help. That was his job.

"Veronica preached tolerance. I truly admired her. We were starting to really enjoy each other's company. Her speech was magnificent. Did you happen to hear it?"

Natalie shook her head. "I missed it, unfortunately."

"I invited her to come speak to our congregation on Christmas Eve. Ve-ronica drew parallels between Wicca and Christianity, how pagan religion was actually there before Christianity. She was preaching mutual under-standing and respect. Wiccans and Christians have always gotten along very well in Burning Lake, ever since the 1920s at least, let us say. The twenties were big for spirituality and séances. The occult became quite fashionable. For the past hundred years or so, we haven't had any problems, not really. Not like this." He rubbed his temples and shook his troubled head. "I have no idea who could've done this to her, but it wasn't at the hand of any Christian I know. Certainly not." He glanced up. "So what can I do for you, Detective?"

"Tell me about Edward and Holly Host," she said.

"Right. The Hosts. I consider it my obligation to help people who are down on their luck. I'm a hands-on kind of guy—not just sermons. If you want to bask in God's grace, then you must act in charitable ways. Not just talk about it. Action speaks louder than words."

"So you rent out your cottage to people who are down on their luck?"

He nodded. "People who've attended the AA or NA meetings here at the church, who've expressed an interest in improving their lives. I charge three hundred a month, utilities paid."

"That's a bargain."

He shrugged. "I can afford it. I'm one of the lucky ones."

"And how did you meet the Hosts?"

"Narcotics Anonymous. She—Holly Stewart is her maiden name—she grew up here and felt comfortable enough to open up to me. She had a somewhat troubled childhood, became addicted to marijuana and cocaine in high school, and dropped out midway. A familiar story, unfortunately. She ran away with her boyfriend, Edward Host, moved to Utica, got married by a justice of the peace, and then they got heavily in debt. About six or seven months ago, she decided to come back to Burning Lake and start over. She asked me to help her out. At first, she came alone. But later, Edward joined her."

"What do you know about Edward Host?"

"Not much. He's a mechanic, currently unemployed, but his real passion is music. He and Holly are in their mid-twenties. He came across as quiet and sullen. Holly's the one I made the arrangements with."

"So she has family here?"

"Just a mother, Jodi Stewart, who passed away four years ago. She used to work at Murray's Halloween Costumes out on Route 151."

"Did you do a background check before renting out your cottage to them?"

Grimsby smiled and shook his head. "I never do background checks on my tenants. These are all troubled people. A background check will only confirm what I already know. It won't change my mind. That's why I'm here. To help out the less fortunate."

"So Holly approached you initially, and then what?"

"I offered them the cottage. It was vacant at the time. We shook on it. I have a few simple rules. One, respect your neighbors. Two, no disruptive noise after eleven P.M. or before nine A.M. Keep the place clean and tidy. Do yard work as necessary. Let me know promptly if there's a problem—leaky roof, plumbing issue, and the like."

"Did they follow the rules?"

"At first." Grimsby sighed. He raised his chin. "When I met Holly initially, she struck me as the kind of person who was truly capable of turning her life around. Very friendly and outgoing. She'd say hi to anyone. But after they moved in, I rarely heard from them anymore. They stopped coming to the NA meetings. Stopped paying the rent. They had plenty of excuses. Months went by, and still no rent. So I dropped by one day in mid-December and noticed they'd been drinking. Maybe doing drugs as well. I don't know. He became verbally abusive and kicked me out. She apologized later on, but it was too late. I won't tolerate that kind of behavior.

"In the meantime, the neighbors were complaining about the noise, and around the same time I found out they were dabbling in the dark arts. They hadn't paid their rent for months by that point. I asked Holly to come see me at the church. She brought her sob story along—the unemployment checks had run out, they were both out of work, it was hard, they'd hit another rough patch . . . and oddly enough, she confessed they were into the occult. They thought that by messing around with witchcraft, they might be able to fix their lives. That somehow everything would come together for them. That they wouldn't have to work so hard for it. I tried reasoning with her, but she honestly believed that these rituals were going to make all the difference. These folks weren't looking to change."

"So what happened?"

"I reluctantly told her I was going to have to start eviction proceedings, and that unless they started paying the rent, they'd have to make way for somebody else. Someone who was motivated to do the hard work it takes to improve your chances of succeeding in this life. That was a few months ago. The next day, she called and said they were leaving. She promised to mail me the back rent. Of course, I never heard from them again."

"And they never came back to the cottage?"

"Not as far as I know."

"And you have no idea where they went?"

"They took off in the dead of night. Didn't leave any forwarding information."

"When are you planning to rent it out again?"

"Well, it's been a darn long winter, hasn't it?" He smiled warmly at her. "Traditionally, in the spring, a few volunteers from the church and I will go out and clean everything up—the cottage, the grounds, the public lands around it. Clear the brush, pick up the trash. But this time, I intend to bless the house before I can even think of renting it out again. Get rid of the occult trappings, and the furniture, too. Clear it all out. Then bless the whole house. Only then would I be able to conscientiously rent it out to someone else."

"Does anyone from the NA meetings know where the Hosts might've gone? Did they head back to Utica?"

"I've asked around. Nobody knows."

"Do you have their old Utica address?"

"I can dig it up for you."

Natalie glanced at her watch. She had more questions for him, but she'd run out of time. "Thanks, Reverend. You've been very helpful. Here's my card. Could you text me that information?"

"Sure thing. I'll get to it this afternoon, right after the food drive is over."

She stood up.

"Let me walk you out."

"Thanks, I know the way."

She couldn't be late for her next appointment.

Not again.

11

This past December, the holidays had been especially joyous, with people going out of their way to celebrate—carolers strolling along Sarah Hutchins Drive, music piping out of storefronts, the smell of gingerbread and cinnamon filling the air, pumpkin lattes at Starbucks, and the ringing, charitable bells of the Salvation Army.

After New Year's Eve, there were post-holiday echoes of sadness just around the edges. Fatigue from all the frenzied activity—social events and Christmas parties, the drinks and sugary foods. By mid-January, people began to pack away their treasured ornaments in tissue paper and take down the Christmas tree. The menorahs and yule logs and candles were put away for another year. Back to work. Back to the daily grind.

As the February snow fell, roads closed and schools were canceled. It was cold and dark and easy to give in to winter fatigue. Downtown storefronts were still framed by twinkle lights, but the unusually long winter had ground all the fun and glittering excitement out of the season, mashing it into a soggy gray ball of icy slush. By this point, a blanketing exhaustion had taken hold of Burning Lake. Most people wanted to hibernate and order take-out pizza for dinner.

In March, feelings of hopefulness were beginning to dawn. Although it was hard to imagine during this frigid endless winter that spring would soon be here. Only another month or so, two at the most, and the snow would stop falling, the accumulated drifts would melt away, new grass would grow, trees would sprout new leaves, and the birds would be back.

However, the gruesome death of Veronica Manes had ground any stray glimmers of hope to an ugly halt. The mood around town was grim. Fear was growing. Rumors spread faster than the police could stop them. As she drove past the station house, Natalie noticed a group of reporters shouting questions at Chief Snyder and Lieutenant Detective Luke Pittman on the front steps of the building. She recognized a particularly aggressive reporter from Boston. Last year, he had somehow gotten hold of her private number and called Natalie all hours of the day and night, asking about the Crow Killer case, and then about the Violinist, until she was forced to change her number. Now she carefully guarded who got her unlisted number.

Natalie drove around the block and pulled in undetected behind the police station, where she parked in her reserved spot. She turned off the ignition and sat for a moment, her thoughts churning and tangling inside her brain. She could feel her heart hammering and a roaring in her ears— that was how much she feared the media and their questions. But it wasn't all she feared. Something of tremendous power and force had seized the town. This wasn't a simple homicide. It was an act of pure evil.

She used to think that Burning Lake was a safe place to have grown up in. Every winter, Natalie and her sisters had the best time making snow angels in the front yard, waving their arms and legs through the powdery snow. Years later, Grace always kept her Christmas tree up for as long as possible—weeks after it started dropping needles. She liked to look at the lights and imagine herself drifting into that world of pine-needled branches and exotic ornaments she'd collected over the years. She loved the blue spruce smell. It went far beyond any religious feelings for her. She told Natalie once that she'd imagined Christmas to be a place where you could set aside all your cares and worries, and she liked to prolong that feeling for as long as possible. She kept her tree up until February.

Now Natalie took a deep breath, got out of her car, and went inside the three-story building, where the mood was subdued. Half of the staff was out in the field. Veronica Manes was an icon in this town, and the officers and detectives were united in their determination to solve the mystery of her untimely death.

The station house was a little run-down, a little careworn. The hardwood floors were scuffed from decades of abuse and the radiators rattled and hissed. Nobody had taken down the festive Christmas lights yet. They were strung across the hunter-green wall above the reception area, where Dennis the dispatcher sat flipping through his stuffed Rolodex wheel.

Natalie stopped at the front desk to pick up her messages.

"Tough day," Dennis said, setting aside his paperwork and smiling up at her.

"One of the toughest."

"Phones are ringing off the hook. People asking for you, Natalie. Don't worry, though, it's all being diverted to Luke. But it's crazy, isn't it? Nobody wants to say this out loud, but we all know the town's reputation is going to suffer. Another sensational case in Burning Lake. Another bizarre homicide. We'll either become a tourist hot spot or the world's biggest joke. Anyway, I'm telling any journalists who call that you're unavailable or out in the field, per Luke's orders."

"Thanks, Dennis. Talk to you later."

"Don't let the bastards grind you down."

She waved in agreement, then headed down the hallway and stopped briefly in the break room for a cup of coffee. She ignored the plate of sugar cookies, grabbed her mail, and headed for the elevators. She took a steel car up to the third-floor detective's unit, where the air was stuffy hot. Most of the messages were from reporters and bloggers she knew, people who'd been in touch before asking about today's case. She tossed them on her desk, then peeled off her coat with a stale crackle.

"Hello, Natalie," Lenny said from his corner desk. In his late fifties, Detective Lenny Labruzzo had a receding hairline and a pruny face, with distinct lines of worry between his eyebrows. He'd recently become a grandfather and was a few years away from retirement, and nobody knew what they were going to do without him. Dusty air blew down out of a vent in the ceiling. There were Post-it notes stuck all over his computer. On the wall behind him was a sign that read DO WHAT YOU LOVE AND LOVE WHAT YOU DO. He gave her a weary shrug. "Looks like it's just you and me this afternoon."

"Yeah, well, I had to come back for my appointment. I thought about canceling, but Dr. Mazza's such a hard-ass."

Lenny smiled. "Have a seat. You look beat."

She sat down at her desk and noticed right away that her stapler and pencil jar had been rearranged, and the stack of papers in her in-box was neater than when she'd left it there last night.

"See anything different?" he inquired.

She lifted a corner of the blue blotter. The shiny wood-laminate surface wasn't familiar to her—a glossy walnut finish. "This isn't my desk." She put her hands on either side of the desktop and shook it. The desk didn't wobble. "What the hell—?"

"We wanted to surprise you this morning, but God had other plans."

She looked underneath the desk at the left leg. On her first day as a detective, the guys had given her the worst desk in the unit, the one with the wobbly legs—standard for all rookies. She kept a matchbook tucked under the shortest leg to keep it from driving her insane, but once in a while it slipped out of place and the whole thing wobbled.

She sat up, a surprised smile curling her lips. "You got me a new desk?"

Lenny nodded. "Brand spanking new. Check it out, Natalie."

"What's the occasion?"

"It's sort of a promotion," he said with a chuckle. "How can we possibly call you a rookie anymore, when you've solved two of the biggest cases we've ever had?"

"Oh, Lenny, that's so nice of you."

"Don't thank me. It was Luke's idea."

"Really?" She tensed but kept smiling. Besides instituting a hiring freeze, the town council had also decided to cut back on all services, and now was not the time to be buying anyone a new desk. At the same time, it was so nice of them. It meant she had gained their trust. She was really part of the team now. She would miss them terribly if she left the force. "It's great," she said. "Thanks."

"You're welcome. Anyway. Happy belated birthday. We requisitioned the desk back in December, but it took a while for them to ship the damn thing, what with all the paperwork and approvals, yadda yadda. We had to twist a bunch of arms. But here it is, two months later. Ta-da!"

Natalie's birthday was January 24. Hunter had planned an incredible evening involving a helicopter and the New York City skyline, along with an elegant dinner and a dozen red roses.

Luke had followed their tradition of remembering each other's birthday by picking out what was supposed to be the world's stupidest birthday card. Every year, they competed for the title. But this one was so lame, she couldn't even laugh at it. On the front was a picture of an old lady, her white hair in a bun, blowing out a hundred birthday candles, and inside it said, "Another year, another ache, another piece of birthday cake." She would have to wait until next November to get her revenge.

Now she checked her watch and said, "I'd better get going."

"Team meeting's at two o'clock," Lenny reminded her.

"Thanks again for the desk," she said and left.

12

The building was only a block away—a five-story, granite government building full of city workers. The psychiatrist's office was on the top floor. The waiting room was the usual boring environment that contained the carpeted hush of a dentist's office.

"The doctor will see you now," the sweet-faced receptionist told her.

The office was empty. Natalie took a seat in a chair facing the doctor's imposing desk and studied the diplomas on the walls. One said Harvard Medical School. That was always reassuring.

Dr. Marybeth Mazza came breezing in and took a seat behind her desk. She was one of those crisp professionals who totally had their act together—so together that Natalie felt like a frazzled, disheveled mess by comparison.

Dr. Mazza had short, perfectly cut dyed blond hair and calculating eyes. She was smart, intuitive, and inquisitive—in short, all the things you wanted in a therapist. Sometimes she got excited; other times she seemed bored. Every session, they strolled through a labyrinth of Natalie's most painful memories, and Natalie wasn't sure if it was working or not. Her grief had faded, but her losses pressed dully on her heart.

"How are you feeling?" the doctor asked in a neutral tone. Her handsome face was set to "expressionless."

Natalie squirmed beneath that carefully arranged, assessing gaze. "Not great. I woke up to the news that Veronica Manes was hit by a train."

Dr. Mazza nodded. "How do you feel about it?"

"Angry. Confused. I mean, this town is the gift that keeps on giving, isn't it?"

"So you blame the town?"

"Not literally."

Dr. Mazza tilted her head slightly. "Figuratively then?"

"Well, who's to say? After all, three innocent people were killed in 1712, and right before she died, Abigail Stuart cursed the town of Burning Lake and everyone in it. Maybe we're still paying for it? Metaphorically speaking." Natalie sighed with frustration at the doctor's steady gaze. "Relax, I'm joking."

"Are you?" Dr. Mazza was the kind of shrink who actively listened, always ready to interject some pithy observation that would lead you down another, more revealing path.

"It's not just me. Hashtag BurningLakeIsCursed is trending on Twitter."

"And you think that perhaps everything that has happened to you in the past few years . . . the terrible ordeal you went through with your sister Grace, and the two gruesome homicide cases you ended up solving, are somehow due to Abby's hex?"

"Not really. I said I was joking." She was feeling defensive, and she wanted to be nicer. But these sessions with Dr. Mazza brought out Natalie's rebellious nature, a throwback to her surly teenage years, when she was only trying to be honest.

"Do you remember all the words to Abby's hex?" the doctor asked.

Natalie shrugged. "Doesn't everyone? I used to recite it while skipping rope."

"Would you mind reciting it for me now?"

She looked down at her hands. She didn't feel like reciting anything, but the words came tumbling out of her mouth. "May he who rules the underworld, Remit himself to Burning Lake, And bring great harm to those who take . . . the lives of three innocent girls, And rain curses on this place of strife, And hex those who would take another life, And hex your children who come after you, And hex all those who come after them, too.

"May you forever suffer and never unlearn, The sins you birthed like twisting worms, And may this monster whom you fear the most, And the witches' deaths of which you boast, Be avenged over great distances of time. He will send his webbed flock as a sign, And they will feast upon this unsacred ground, And burn this wretched town and all its inhabitants down."

They fell silent for a moment. Abby's curse seemed to ring inside the room.

"I can understand why you might think the town is hexed," Dr. Mazza said. "The recent spate of murders has affected the community on a deeply personal level. And from a certain perspective, it appears that you, Natalie, are at the center of it all. Has it hit you what kind of impact this new case will have on you?"

"It's already having an impact."

"Such as?"

"Well, for one thing, everyone's gone into protective mode."

"Protective of whom?"

"Me," she said. "Dennis is filtering my messages. Luke is shielding me from the press. He's taken the lead in the case, and I've been assigned background work. Everyone's walking on eggshells to make sure I don't crack."

"You think they doubt your ability to handle another case like this?"

"I don't know what they think. But they're treating me like I'm breakable."

"Are you?"

Natalie shook her head. She wondered if her stomach was growling too loudly, since she hadn't eaten all day. "No, I'm fine."

"Okay. And yet you seem resentful of the fact that Luke is concerned about the high-profile murder cases you've been handling quite capably over the past year and the psychological burden it has placed on you, and his desire to ease that burden."

"Well, I mean . . . sure, he has a professional concern. He's my supervisor. He's my boss. He's the one who encouraged me to come see you. I guess I had PTSD for a while after Grace's death, and Daisy, and the Missing Nine, the Crow Killer case, and . . . fuck. The Violinist. By the way, I hate that the media calls him that. Violinists deserve better. Anyway, I'm getting better. I'm off my meds completely, and that underlying feeling I used to have that there was more going on in Burning Lake . . . something bigger and more ominous . . . those feelings of paranoia and fear are pretty much gone now. I was only kidding about Abby's hex. It was a lame attempt at humor."

She nodded and pursed her lips together. "Well, Natalie, like I told you before, that's a perfectly normal reaction to have. You needed enough time and space to process your grief and all your losses. And you've come a long way. You're at a pivot point in your therapy right now. When I heard the news about Veronica this morning, I was very concerned for your well-being. Not because I think you'd crack under pressure, or anything like that, but because it's a lot to ask someone to bear psychologically. Fortunately for you, your colleagues are stepping up. There's no shame in that. Luke has given you a smaller role, which is exactly what I would've recommended. It's good to know he's protecting you. How do you feel about that? About Luke?"

"How do I feel? Well, it feels like I'm living with Hunter Rose now."

"So you and Luke . . . ?"

"We're on a professional footing."

"So you're colleagues? What about your friendship?"

"We've come to an agreement, sort of," Natalie hedged. "Whenever one of us really needs to talk about something . . . we'll reach out late at night and talk on the phone, but only if it's important and can't be covered at work."

"So Luke has called you under these conditions?"

Natalie shifted uncomfortably in her chair. "Mostly I've called him."

"How often?"

"I don't know. Five times? Six, maybe? Luke puts up with it."

"Why?"

"Because he doesn't want another rift to open up between us."

"And you don't think it's because he's secretly in love with you?"

"No," she protested loudly. She hated it when the doctor inadvertently put thoughts in her head—thoughts she'd banished from her own consciousness. "He's seeing Rainie. She knitted him a winter scarf, for Pete's sake."

"So," Dr. Mazza said, summing it up, "you're secret friends, then?"

"I wouldn't say that."

"What then? Haven't you been friends for a very long time? Why can't you be friends now? What could possibly get in the way of your friendship?" When Natalie didn't answer, she said, "What does this arrangement mean for your relationship with Hunter?"

"Nothing." Natalie frowned. "Apples and oranges."

"Really? So your late-night phone calls with Luke don't bother him?"

"I don't tell him about them."

"Why not?"

"He'd get jealous."

"That won't work for very long. Not if there's no trust in your relationship."

"Bullshit." Natalie felt a little twist in her gut. "Sorry, but I don't believe that. I know how I feel about Hunter. My talks with Luke won't change that."

"And what do you feel?"

"About Hunter?" She smiled and relaxed a little. "He's a very sensual man. Very funny and smart. I like the way he moves, the way he talks. I like him. Whenever I'm with him, I feel insulated from the past."

"Like? Not love?"

"I said love."

"You said like."

"Well, I'm nuts about him, okay? It feels right, as if we belong together. I belong to him, and he belongs to me. It was ridiculously easy, falling for him—almost romance-novel easy, you know? All those dark glances steeped with lust, barely masked in public places, all that epic longing. There's an intense mutual attraction that we almost can't . . ." What she couldn't say out loud, what she didn't say was that her body belonged to Hunter exclusively. All her pulse points would throb when he came close to her. His touch created heat. His kisses left her drenched in pheromones. Their chemistry was undeniable.

And yet . . .

Doubts. Natalie always had her doubts.

She was happy with Hunter—she knew that—and yet she could feel in the outer reaches of her being a certain lack, an itch, a longing for something more. She'd tried shrugging it off as a primitive attribute that had nothing whatsoever to do with her.

But the honeymoon period was beginning to fade, and she sensed that her euphoria was about to peak. She needed something deeper from this man. She was starting to notice a few quirks that bugged her—Hunter's nail-biting, his humming, little habits that weren't important, and yet . . . Natalie understood that she and Hunter were about to enter a new phase in their relationship, one where deeper bonds were required.

Hunter, for his part, wanted Natalie to quit her job and pursue other interests—to move on, to reach higher. She was trying to embrace the new and let go of the old.

"So you're saying there's a strong physical attraction?"

"Yeah, sex therapy does wonders," Natalie joked.

Dr. Mazza listened patiently. She had zero sense of humor. "And he's still pressuring you to quit the force?"

"He's not pressuring me. I'm thinking about it."

"Because of this past year's burdens?"

"You could say that."

Within the span of a single year, Natalie had lost her sister to suicide after finding out that Grace was a murderer. And as if that wasn't deeply shocking enough, Natalie had solved Upper New York's biggest serial killer case ever—the Crow Killer. Samuel Hawke Winston had abducted and murdered dozens of homeless people, along with a handful of tourists visiting the Adirondack Mountains, and his crimes went back several decades. And then, six months later, on the day after Halloween, Natalie discovered a dead body in a dumpster, a naked woman with an inscrutable tattoo and a strange callus under her chin, the tragic victim of an ongoing murder spree by a deranged and troubled young man—this one dubbed the Violinist by the press. Now Veronica Manes, who'd been peripherally involved in Natalie's last homicide case as a witness, had been killed in the most brutal, horrific way imaginable.

No wonder she wanted to quit the force.

"Are you still contemplating quitting your job?"

"Yes. I've typed up my resignation letter. I have a few more weeks to decide."

"And do you find yourself wondering what Joey would say about that?"
Dr. Mazza asked. "What his advice would be?"

Natalie had a flash image of her father's piercing, intelligent eyes. Before
his death eight years ago from a traffic accident, Joey Lockhart had been
the hardest-working beat cop in Burning Lake. Compact and shrewd, like
an ex–football tackle with beefy layers of muscle, he had influenced Natalie's decision to become a cop and shared his street smarts with her for
years, and she missed him terribly.

"I'm more concerned about what Luke will say."

Dr. Mazza raised an eyebrow. "Do you think that's why he's protecting
you? So you won't leave the force? Maybe he understands your situation
better than you do."

"I think you're reading too much into this."

"You do?"

Natalie nodded. "I don't believe he thinks very much about me at all
anymore, except as an old friend who keeps bugging him once in a while.
I think he's moved on. I think he's got something going on with Rainie
Sandhill, and it's getting serious."

"Why is that?"

"I've never known Luke to give in to sentiment, but there he stood, wearing that freaking ugly scarf she made him."

"So you think Luke's in love with Rainie. Are you in love with Hunter?"

Natalie had a physical reaction to the question.

First, she could feel Hunter's hand probing the flesh between her legs,
and her heart began to pound furiously, and she blushed.

Second, she found herself wanting to run away from the question. Was
she in love? What was love? It occurred to her that she was bitterly resentful toward her shrink for even asking her these things. What business was
it of hers?

"I think our time is up," Natalie said, secretly relieved.

Dr. Mazza glanced at the digital clock on her desk. "Five more minutes."

"Sorry, I have a team meeting at two. I have to go."

"You've got plenty of time. But you froze up at my last question."

"I just hate talking about it, that's all," she confessed.

"Why?"

"Because dredging up my feelings about everything is exhausting. Going over the past is exhausting. It makes me want to hibernate for a million years."

"Why is it so hard?"

"Are you kidding? It's like juggling dinosaurs."

"Dinosaurs? Why dinosaurs?"

She laughed, but in a nervous way. "They're huge and dead."

"What, your memories? Or your feelings?"

She nodded. "My memories are these huge, dead dinosaurs."

"And your feelings are . . . ?"

Natalie stood up. "See you next week, Doc," she said as she left.

13

The detectives of the Burning Lake Police Department's Criminal Investigations Unit met inside Conference Room B for today's debrief with their supervisor, Lieutenant Detective Luke Pittman. Natalie and the guys settled into their seats around the polished laminate table—Brandon Buckner, Augie Vickers, Lenny Labruzzo, Peter Murphy, Mike Anderson, and Jacob Smith.

Luke took a seat at the head of the table. "Good afternoon, everyone."

"Afternoon, Lieutenant," came the muffled response.

"I just got off the phone with the chief. He's making this case his top priority. We have authorization for overtime, lab equipment, anything we need to get it done. I'll be asking a lot from you in the coming weeks, but I know everyone in this room is highly motivated to solve this case and seek justice for Veronica Manes. She wasn't just a beloved member of the community, she was a symbol of this town's history and heritage. I want everyone at the top of their game. Understood?"

The detectives nodded in silent agreement.

"Okay. Here's what we know so far," he continued, shuffling through his notes. "Sometime between last night and early this morning, the victim was chained to the tracks on the north side of town. At around six twenty-six A.M., she was hit by an oncoming commuter train. What she was wearing when she died is of concern—a witch costume, including a long black dress, a hooded cloak, and a hat . . . over pants and a blue shirt. She also wore underwear, heavy socks, and winter boots. We didn't find a coat or a jacket. We didn't find a cell phone, a wallet, house keys, or photo ID in the snow. There was a silver necklace with a small silver cross draped around her neck, which may be significant. She was a practicing Wiccan, and not known to wear such a type of item."

The detectives shifted uncomfortably in their seats and sipped their coffees.

"This morning, we got an affidavit to search the victim's house and found her car parked in the garage. We also found her wallet and handbag inside the house. No mobile phone or house keys—those are still missing. The front and back doors were locked, all the windows were locked, and there was no broken glass at the points of entry . . . and so we're assuming someone must've picked her up, but we don't know who or what time. There were no Uber or Lyft requests for that neighborhood. Also, we don't know if she left the house wearing the costume, or if she put it on after she left the house. Or whether she was forced to wear it. Lenny's in the process of gaining access to her phone and cellular records, and hopefully we'll be able to track where she went last night and find out who she may have called.

"Veronica lives alone on an isolated street. None of her neighbors saw or heard anything unusual—the neighborhood has been canvassed. It was snowing, so everyone was hunkered down indoors for the night. There were no reported screams or unusual sights or sounds in the vicinity of her domicile. However, Veronica's house was ransacked, and there were a few potential signs of a struggle. There was a small amount of blood on the front hallway, on the floor—we don't know whose blood yet. Her computers and a few other devices are missing. Boxes of books were overturned, and the desk was rifled through. It's hard to tell what else was taken at this time, but in the coming days, we'll be asking friends and relatives. We did find two different sets of muddy footprints in the front hallway and upstairs hardwood floor, and Lenny is looking into that now.

"We retrieved dozens of boxes of evidence from the house that Murph will be processing in Conference Room C. It's a thankless job and we appreciate him for volunteering. Meanwhile, Lenny's prioritizing the trace evidence we retrieved from the house for anything we can glean as to what went on last night." Luke paused to take a sip of his coffee. He glanced around the table and said, "We're treating this as a homicide but keeping certain details from the public. We aren't revealing to the press what she was wearing, or elements of the costume, or exactly how she died. We don't want to alarm the public, and the chief and the mayor are discussing how they'd like to proceed. Eventually, the news will leak out no matter what we do, but in the meantime, I want everybody on notice . . . do not talk about details of the case to anyone. Loved ones included. Understand?"

Nods. Feet shuffled. Sips of coffee. Throat-clearing.

"We've got officers in the field canvassing for witnesses and grid-searching the railroad tracks for evidence. So far, we know very little about her personal life—lovers, friends, family. We need to explore this aspect more. Basically, from what we've gathered so far, she was a priestess for the Pendleton coven, very active in the community, and she enjoyed mentoring young women who were interested in Wicca. Between the ages of twenty-three and thirty, Veronica wrote several books under the pen name Corvina Manse, but she stopped writing in order to dedicate herself to her religious practice. She was fifty-eight years old when she died. She has no known enemies.

"Like I said, we're treating this as a homicide," Luke continued, "although we're publicly calling it an unknown death. As a strategic measure, we're withholding specific details that only the killer or killers would know. But like I said, this won't last. The media's already receiving leaks." Luke looked around the table. "We've got our hands full, people. The chief wants it solved ASAP. I want all hands on deck. Brandon? Why don't you tell us about your investigation of the railroad company."

"Sure thing, Lieu." Detective Brandon Buckner cleared his throat. At thirty-seven, he was a large-framed man who'd lost twenty pounds recently, and it showed in his chiseled face and tired brown eyes. He used to be enthusiastic about everything, with a puppyish kind of exuberance, but this past year had changed him.

All year long, Brandon had been avoiding Natalie as much as possible, but lately she'd detected a possible thaw in their relationship. The tragic events of last April had torn them apart, but Brandon appeared to be going through some sort of transition. He was turning over a new leaf. Rumor had it he was now mentoring Riley Skinner, the boy he'd mistakenly blamed for Daisy's death. The kid he'd assaulted on the night of Daisy's murder. Brandon had gone to arrest the teenager, who collapsed due to a medical condition, but the family blamed Brandon for putting Riley in a coma. They sued the town for police brutality. Brandon's wealthy father eventually paid a large settlement to the family and basically made it all go away. The Skinners were doing well now—they had their farm, and Riley was doing better, but the entire incident had left a stench over Brandon's reputation.

So this was Brandon's redemption—community outreach and charity work for troubled kids who grew up on the poverty-stricken west side of town, trying to heal his past mistakes and make amends. Maybe there was hope for them all, Natalie thought.

Brandon shuffled through his papers and said, "Commuter trains run along the tracks north of town, from morning to midnight every day. Amtrak, plus two other railroads. Twice a day Amtrak has trips from New York City and continuing points west. The Adirondack Train runs through once a day, from New York City to Montreal, and then we have the Sherborn Railroad Service, or SRS, passing through to points west. So we're served by four passenger trains daily, going both ways, plus we also get an occasional freight train passing through at irregular times.

"According to the SRS, this morning at six twenty-six A.M., a two-hundred-ton commuter train traveling seventy miles per hour along the westbound track struck and killed Veronica Manes. The engineer said it was snowing lightly, it was foggy, and he didn't see a pedestrian standing on the tracks until it was too late. As soon as he was made aware, he hit the emergency brakes and sounded the warning horn, but it took a full two or three minutes for the train to come to a complete stop. By that time, she was deceased.

"I haven't gotten the CCTV from SRS yet, but they'll be sending it to us shortly, hopefully tonight. Meanwhile, the engineer has filled in some details. He said the deceased looked away at the last second, something that will haunt him for the rest of his days. He said the train continued for a half mile after the emergency brakes were deployed, until it came to a full stop approximately five minutes later. Nobody on the train was seriously hurt, just a few minor injuries. The engineer bumped his head. They took him to the hospital as a precaution. All other train traffic has been diverted because of this event. All tracks have been de-energized."

"We've got how many trains going through here each day?" Luke asked.

Brandon shuffled through his notes. "There are trains going through Jefferson Station about ten times per day, so I'm told. Approximately every five hours, between six thirty A.M. and midnight, a train will travel through here, stopping at the station on the west side of town. That's four trains going through both ways—to and from. So it's eight trains daily on these tracks, plus the occasional freight train."

"How occasional?" Luke asked.

"Freight trains have irregular schedules since they might be carrying toxins or other substances that could be used by terrorists, so the information is kept closely guarded. There aren't regular schedules for freight trains posted online, like there are for passenger trains. I've contacted the local traffic department to see if they have a clue about the schedule, since they maintain the railroad crossing gates, but most of the freight trains will pass through town during off-hours, mostly around midnight or later, so I'm told. We have yet to get a timetable, and we're communicating with the companies."

Luke nodded slowly. "So we can estimate that whoever did this must've put her on the tracks at some point after midnight, knowing that an SRS train would be heading west at six twenty-six this morning? But also knowing that no freight trains would be coming through?"

"Sounds about right," Brandon said.

"Or maybe they got lucky," Lenny said. "Regarding the freight trains."

"If a freight train did run through here last night," Natalie said, "then we could further pin down the time line. In other words, if it came through at three o'clock, then Veronica wasn't shackled to the tracks until afterwards. It's vital information."

"I'll try to get an answer after our meeting," Brandon said, jotting it down.

"What was the victim doing as the train approached?" Luke asked.

Brandon looked up. "She was awake and alert. The engineer described her as standing in the center of the tracks, but with seconds to spare she turned her head away. She didn't try to jump or seek safety. Advance word on the video says she turned away at the last second, and didn't seem distressed so much as she was talking to herself."

"Praying," Natalie interjected. "Probably. Whatever Wiccans do to come to terms with their impending deaths, since she knew she couldn't get away."

Luke looked at her and nodded. "Anything else, Brandon?"

"Just that we'll know more once we get the video evidence."

"Natalie, why don't you fill us in on Grimsby's cottage."

She cleared her throat and said, "Reverend Grimsby rents out his cottage on Hummingbird Lane to people he meets at the Narcotics Anonymous or AA gatherings in the church basement. About six months ago, he rented it to Edward and Holly Host, who were attending the NA meetings at the time. She's originally from Burning Lake, Edward isn't. At first the couple seemed interested in improving their lives, but somewhere along the line they got sidetracked and started to mess around with the occult. Looks like they also started doing drugs again. Once their neighbors complained about the partying and the noise, Reverend Grimsby gave the Hosts an ultimatum. He hoped they could still turn it around. But instead of cleaning up their act, they bolted around the end of January. He hasn't heard from them since."

"Do you think they were involved somehow?" Luke asked.

"It's too early to tell," she said. "But when I first arrived at the cottage, I found a set of snowed-over footprints going across the front yard, when nobody's supposed to be there. Shortly afterwards, I followed the barking dog toward an oak tree in the backyard. That's when I found the thirteen glass jars and the animal carcasses. I called Grimsby and got permission to search the property. Then you guys came and processed the scene."

Luke nodded. "Augie, tell us what you found at the cottage."

"Sure, Lieu." Augie sat forward and said, "We're still doing a grid search of the area, looking for more evidence. This is both private and public land, about a hundred yards north of the railroad tracks. The area behind the cabin is messy with beer bottles and assorted debris and other detritus. There's a ravine down behind the house, which is partly an extension of the backyard, and then continues into conservation land. The oak tree in question is approximately eighteen yards north of the house. The dog was digging up animal bones, a squirrel carcass, and various other remains from under the tree. There were also the twelve mason jars full of what appears to be urine hanging from the tree. And there were more animals' bones or carcasses hanging from the branches of the tree. It certainly looks as if rituals were performed. This wasn't some random thing."

"What about the urine?" Luke asked. "Is it animal or human?"

"Lenny just confirmed that, in at least one case so far, it's human urine. We're sending more samples out for DNA testing. Some of the glass bottles had a brown patina, which is the result of aging and decomposition. Inside we found items such as pins and nails, along with a few desiccated, decomposing mice. Once we started to dig under the tree, we found a dozen or so dead animals buried in shallow graves, some with their faces sewn together, or a limb removed from one and sewn on to another . . . it was disgusting. This isn't the result of normal animal scavenging, obviously. So far we found a dead skunk, a raccoon, a couple of squirrels, and a crow. We didn't find any traps nearby. No evidence of hunting implements inside the cottage. Some of the corpses were flattened and could've been roadkill, picked up from the roadside and then transported to the property. Also, those bottles of urine . . . the mason jars, it's like voodoo. There were samples of human hair inside—some with roots, so maybe we'll get DNA."

"I'm working on it," Lenny said. They all knew how overworked their best crime scene specialist was, how quickly overwhelming this case was becoming. The BLPD couldn't afford its own CSI unit. Who could? Only in Hollywood. So the detectives processed the scene themselves, and Lenny was brilliant at everything—photographing, fingerprinting, bagging and tagging, chemical analysis, digital processing, wound diagnostics, polygraph administration, the works.

"So we can assume that the animal remains were part of an occult or satanic ritual, right? Which means they could be Satanists or something," Brandon said impatiently.

"Grimsby told me they were more naïve than satanic," Natalie said. "Apparently they thought that by messing around with the occult, they could somehow fix their lives. That everything would magically come together for them. He tried reasoning with them, but eventually he had to threaten eviction proceedings. About a month ago, they took off, and he never heard from them again."

"They never returned to the cottage?"

"Not as far as Grimsby knows. But they could've come back. The key was kept under the picnic table. Hung from a hook."

"So they could've returned at any point without him knowing it."

"No heat or utilities, but yeah. No one else lives on Hummingbird Lane. It's a dead-end road. The only other residence burned down years ago. It's very isolated and private, surrounded by woods. I doubt the neighbors would've noticed anyone had come back to the cottage, if they kept a low enough profile. At least for a few days."

"So we need to track them down—the couple who lived there," Luke said.

"The Hosts," Jacob interjected. "I can ask my contacts who've been to all the NA meetings at the church. Maybe they'll have some knowledge of their whereabouts."

"Great. You work on that," Luke told him. "Anything else, Natalie?"

She opened her notebook again. "Tabitha Vaughn is a member of Veronica's coven. She's sending me the Pendleton membership list today, and also one for the Carrington coven. Those two groups sometimes have shared activities. Also, I found out that Veronica was writing another book, after a long absence, and doing research at the library. I'll go talk to Patrick and find out what she was researching, any contacts she might've met there."

"We found a stack of library books inside Veronica's house," Luke told her. "We boxed them up and brought them over here. Murph? Could you find those boxes and make sure Natalie gets them?"

"Sure thing," Detective Peter Murphy responded with a mock-salute.

"Natalie, I want you and Augie to split the two membership lists and get all their statements," Luke said. "Find out what they know."

"Right," she said, making a note of it. "There's also the matter of Veronica's will," she said. "Who the beneficiaries are, where she wants to be buried, what becomes of her house . . . who stands to benefit from her death."

Luke nodded. "Murphy will follow up and get back to you on it. Okay, Murph?"

"Sure thing, Lieu," Murphy said, his glance sliding toward Natalie. He seemed to be scowling at her, but it could've been his thick dark eyebrows and that permanently constipated look of his.

"You all have your assignments," Luke said, glancing down at the assignment sheet. "Mike will investigate the origins of the costume and the shackles, man the police tip line, and help out with the media. Murphy will catalog the evidence and follow up on the will. Brandon will continue working with the railroad—collecting witness statements and video footage.

"Veronica had a lot of fans and admirers. She was also involved in the Monster Mash contest last October as one of the judges. Jacob will be talking to his sources and looking into the backgrounds of all the musicians who entered the contest, any rejected witches who might've wanted to join Pendleton, people in town who've been antagonistic toward witchcraft, and anyone found trespassing on her property in the past five or so years." Luke looked slowly around the table, studying them carefully. "This is a bizarre situation that requires out-of-the-box thinking, people. I want everyone working at peak level. Veronica's killer wanted us to find her there on the tracks. They chose that particular costume, including the hat, the broom, and the cross, for a reason. They're sending us a message.

"Anyone who thinks this was a suicide, come talk to me. Because I sincerely doubt it. There are a lot easier ways to die. She wouldn't be out in the cold for hours. Her wrists wouldn't have shown signs of a struggle—meaning she tried to break free. I have a feeling that the autopsy results will indicate she was forcefully taken to those tracks. This was a high-profile, sensational, aggressive act. Someone wanted to punish her and hurt the whole town, or perhaps increase our notoriety. Who stands to gain? I want to know who killed Veronica Manes in such a horrific manner. Let's get to work, people. There's a lot to do."

14

After the meeting, Natalie suited up like an astronaut about to set foot on the moon—sweater, winter coat, boots, scarf, hat, gloves—and took an elevator down to the ground floor, where she left the back way.

Outside, the air had a cold bite to it. The edges of the parking lot were crusted with snow. Her phone buzzed. It was a text message from Tabitha Vaughn. *Here's the list of those members I promised you.* Natalie forwarded the attachment to Augie and Luke.

Brandon came up behind her. "Natalie, can we talk a minute?"

"Sure," she said, surprised to see him. It was the first time he'd put more than two words together in her presence. Usually he grunted or brushed past her in an effort to get away.

"Let's talk in my Jeep, okay?"

"Okay." She was game for anything. He hadn't spoken to her in months, and she welcomed this change of heart. Not that Natalie blamed him. His wife was only three months pregnant when Grace killed her in cold blood. The two girls had been best friends since kindergarten, but in the blink of an eye, Grace Lockhart had taken Brandon's entire family away from him, and Natalie hadn't seen any of it coming. Her own sister had deceived her for years. All that praise from the media, and Natalie couldn't help thinking—what kind of detective was she?

Now the dry winter air crackled with static. Brandon stomped the snow off his boots, while Natalie got into the passenger seat of the black Jeep Cherokee. She closed the door and shivered, watching her breath pool before her.

Brandon slid in behind the wheel and turned on the heater. "Fucking snow, huh? All I want to do in the wintertime is eat macaroni and cheese and sleep. How pathetic is that?"

"I prefer MoonPies, but yeah. Ditto. What's up, Brandon?"

"A lot is up, Natalie. How are you? How've you been?"

"Fine." She looked at him, knowing he could see through the lie. "You?"

"Fucked up these many months."

She nodded. "So here we are. Two fuckups."

He rubbed the condensation off the driver's side window and sighed, creating more condensation. "Sorry for my long silence. It took me a while to process everything, you know? What I'm saying—of course, you know. You've suffered as much as I have. But I blamed you because it was easy, and I wanted to hurt somebody. I care about you, so by hurting you, I was hurting myself. Or some psychobabble bullshit like that. Anyway, it's been a crazy year, hasn't it? And now there's this thing with Veronica Manes, and it's got everyone acting jumpy as hell. This is the *last* thing anyone in this town expected. It's the very last thing we need." He turned to her. "If I believed in God, which I don't, I'd say the devil was fucking with us."

She gave a faint nod. "I know. It's like the town is cursed."

"Exactly what I was thinking," he said. "Remember Abby's hex? She warned us three hundred years ago. Everybody's talking about it, Natalie. We're all thinking the same thing. Once you say it out loud, though, it sounds ridiculous." He stopped talking and just looked at her.

"What?" she said.

"There's a rumor going around you might be leaving us."

"Sheesh."

"So it's true?" he said, sounding upset.

"I don't know. I haven't decided yet."

"Haven't . . ." He scowled and put his hands on the wheel. "Why would you leave us right now, when we need you the most?"

"Because this could be my only chance to save myself."

"From what?"

"The emotional toll."

He nodded slowly. He seemed to calm down. "I get it. You're burnt out."

"It's more than that."

He turned to her and said, "You know this is going to break Luke's heart."

She rubbed her temples, feeling nauseated. "Did he say that?"

"He didn't have to. It's obvious. You two have this weird connection going on."

"Me and Luke?" Her voice went higher than she'd expected it to, and she felt a reactive tightening of her facial muscles. "What the hell are you talking about?"

"Come on," he said, studying her with excruciating honesty. "Rainie's a nice person, don't get me wrong. But the way Luke looks at you . . . actions speak louder than words."

"Shut up, Brandon. That's enough."

"I'm just saying . . . if your name happens to come up at the station, his whole disposition will change. His eyes become alert, and . . ."

"Shut up. I mean it, I'll leave if we continue along this path," she said furiously.

"Okay. Sorry. Enough said."

She listened to the heater blasting more hot air around their feet. "What did you want to talk to me about?" she said with more than a little irritation.

"I've got a lead for you. Jules Pastor knows about the couple who used to live in the cottage. He said something about a drug connection. You should call him. He likes you. He and Jacob aren't getting along right now. Jules thinks Jacob screwed him over. Long story. Yadda yadda. But you should pick his brain."

"I will. Thanks." She looked at him sideways. "Anything else?"

"Yeah. I've been thinking we should all have a drink sometime. You, me, and Luke. Just like old times."

"That wouldn't be such a good look today."

"Not today. I mean when this is all over. In the future."

She nodded, and his unspoken relief was obvious.

"Look, I don't blame you for avoiding me all this time, Brandon. Not even a little bit. I beat myself up for not seeing any of it. How could I have missed it? She was my sister, and I loved her dearly, but I had no idea what she was capable of. And the question I keep asking myself is . . . how did I miss this? All those years? It's one of the reasons I'm thinking about quitting the force."

His eyes narrowed to stubborn slits. "You can't quit, Natalie. That would be stupid."

She couldn't help smiling. "Oh, so I guess I need your permission now?"

"Look, I feel bad about this past year. It was a difficult time for everyone. But no matter how mad I was at you—and that was misplaced anger, Natalie—I didn't let any of the guys talk shit about you. Not in my presence."

"What kind of shit?"

"Like you brought bad luck to the town. You know, small-town gossip and narrow-mindedness. Scapegoating and blame."

"So you defended my honor. Is that what you're saying?"

"What's wrong with that? And I'm not the only one. Luke's out there chewing anyone a new asshole who even looks at you sideways. And he's done that from day one. He won't tolerate haters and other bullshit."

"Oh great. I've got haters now?"

"Doesn't everybody?" He grinned broadly at her.

"Maybe I was happier not knowing. Besides, I don't need you guys out there white knighting for me. I can defend myself."

"You think so, huh? You're tough, Natalie, but you're not that tough."

She gazed out the window at the snow. It was true. She was damaged.

He raked his fingers through his brown, medium-length hair, his eyes ablaze with conviction. "Anyway, what I'm trying to say is, we all need each other. We have to stick together. That's the hard lesson I've learned recently."

"I agree." She smiled. She glanced at her watch.

"Look, I stopped by the house the other day," he said. "Me and Daisy's. It's just sitting there, vacant. No construction, no contractors, nothing. So I went around back and looked in the windows, and I swear to God, it looks exactly the same way it did on the day she died. Nothing's changed. I was freaking out. I'm not a hundred percent certain, but I think there was blood on the kitchen floor. I don't think they cleaned it up. Isn't that weird?"

"It's definitely weird," she agreed.

"The guy who bought my house, the new owner . . . not the owner, I mean the blind trust. I don't know who bought it. They made a big offer, and I was so anxious to get rid of it at the time, that I didn't even clean up the place or take half my stuff. I just packed a few essentials and split. I accepted their offer without thinking about it. They changed the locks as soon as the ink was dry. I asked about the furniture, but my lawyer told me I'd agreed to let them have everything inside the house, and they took it as is. To be honest, I was probably three sheets to the wind when I signed the paperwork. I was drinking heavily at the time." He wore a look of frustration. "Anyway, I've asked my lawyer to look into it, but he says that I have no claim. I regret selling it now, but at the time I just wanted to unload it as soon as possible and buy the farm. Know what I mean?"

"Yeah, I do," she said. "You're saying that sometimes we do things spontaneously without thinking about it, only to regret it later on. We sell our homes and quit our jobs, only to wish we hadn't been so rash."

"Exactly. You need to take your time and consider your options."

"I don't have time," she told him. "The hiring freeze starts in April."

"Fuck that. This decision will affect you for the rest of your life."

"I'll take that under advisement."

"Speaking of which, did I show you my farm in Chippaway?" Brandon swiped through the images on his iPhone. "Check this out," he said, showing her pictures of the old farm. The village of Chippaway was twenty miles west of Burning Lake, two towns over in the back of beyond, and it had been a lifelong dream of his to purchase his grandparents' farm.

"I'm happy for you, Brandon."

"I'm living the dream," he said softly and without conviction.

All of a sudden her phone buzzed.

It was Luke. "I just got a call from Tabitha Vaughn," he said. "The Pendleton coven is about to get together at one of the member's homes as we speak. I want you and Augie to head over there and take down everyone's statement."

15

A brilliant afternoon light poured in through the windshield of Natalie's Honda Accord as she took Route 87 past the frozen lake. The wind had swept the clouds away. She put on her sunglasses and watched as the wind batted scarves of snow across the road, playing cat and mouse games.

Burning Lake was a shaggy midsize town located south of the Adirondack Mountains at the midpoint between Albany and Syracuse. Sort of perfect. Sort of idyllic. There was plenty of hiking, climbing, bike riding, fishing, and cave exploring to attract tourists by the thousands during the warmer months, but when autumn rolled around those numbers tripled or quadrupled for the monthlong Halloween festivities in October. Things died down afterward, and the town celebrated the holidays, then settled in for a long winter, the cheery social events of December and New Year's Eve giving way to a lulling interlude of isolation and self-reflection. This winter had been especially harsh and unrelenting, beginning with an ice storm in November. They still had a ways to go.

The bohemian east side of town where Marigold Hutchins lived was a realtor's wet dream full of charming fixer-uppers. People fell in love with the Victorian-era homes surrounded by lush stands of spruce and hemlock, along with the neighborhood's easy access to the quaint downtown shopping district. Members of the Pendleton coven were meeting at the residence of Marigold Hutchins, whose claim to fame was her pedigree—she was a direct descendant of Sarah Hutchins, one of the three witches who'd been burned at the stake in 1712. Marigold had done her due diligence, tracing her lineage all the way back to a brother of Sarah's, and she proudly proclaimed herself Sarah Hutchins's nine-times-great-grandniece on her website. Her Twitter handle was @9xgr8grandniece.

Natalie hadn't met Marigold in person yet, but she knew quite a bit about her. Just like any small town, everyone knew everyone else's business. Marigold had moved here from Rochester ten years ago to open a boutique called Skeletons in the Closet, where she sold Wiccan-related merchandise and also sold occult items online. A soft-spoken woman in her mid-forties, Marigold had a warm, gentle demeanor, and everyone who came into contact with her seemed to like her.

The east side of town was woodsy and hilly. As Natalie crested Woodpecker Lane, she spotted several dozen cars parked by the side of the road in front of Marigold's house. The drifts were tall on either side of the shoveled driveways, and there was no room for her to pull over, so Natalie continued a few more blocks until she finally found a parking space. Then she got out and walked back to 58 Woodpecker Lane—no sidewalks here— over the ice-crunchy asphalt, past ornate wrought iron fences and sheets of snow sliding off the turn-of-the-century roofs.

The air had a cold bite to it. Marigold's house was an olive-green Gothic with diamond-paned windows, pointed gables, and gingerbread trim, the type of architectural confection that was popular on this side of town. Before she could open the front gate, Natalie's phone buzzed and she answered it.

"Hey, Nat, I'm running late," Augie said. "Are you there yet?"

"I just arrived. Looks like a full house."

"Okay. Be there in twenty."

She hung up and took the narrow, shoveled path toward the front door, where she wiped her boots on the woven-brush welcome mat and rang the bell.

Marigold Hutchins answered the door with a smile of recognition. "Detective Lockhart, please come in!" Although they'd never officially met before, Natalie was probably familiar to Marigold from the tabloids. Her face had been plastered all over the newspapers for months now next to sensational headlines: DETECTIVE CATCHES SECOND FIDDLE, THE VIOLINIST GETS LIFE, COP KILLS CROW KILLER!

"Brrr, you look cold," Marigold said sweetly. "Can I get you some coffee?"

"That'd be great."

"Follow me."

As Natalie stepped into the warm house, she felt the gravity of her winter coat, boots, scarf, hat, and gloves weighing her down. They passed by a crowded living room, where a lot of hugs and teary-eyed greetings were being exchanged. It smelled of woodsmoke from the blazing hearth. Glasses of wine and boxes of tissues were being passed around.

"Have a seat," Marigold said as they ducked into the empty kitchen. "Cream and sugar in your coffee?"

"Thanks."

The renovated Victorian kitchen was spotlessly clean. There were cheery signs on the walls that read HANG IN THERE, BE STRONG, and LIFE GOES ON.

"We're having a potluck supper," Marigold explained, while getting a ceramic mug down from the cabinet. "Both covens are here. Pendleton and Carrington. Mostly it's an excuse for us to drink and commiserate, to remember Veronica and how much we loved and admired her. We also heard that her family, who are Christians, might not allow us to hold a Wiccan ceremony, so that's a big worry. We wanted to discuss how to handle it. Anyway, how can I help you, Detective? What can I do?"

"I hate to barge in like this, but I need to talk to every member of Veronica's coven, and we figured that while you're all gathered together in the same place . . ."

"You'd like to talk to the Carringtons, too, I understand. That's a good idea. We're like one big happy family." She had an expressive face and long dark hair parted down the middle, with wisps of dark bangs fringing her pale brow. Unlike most of the practicing Wiccans in town, Marigold didn't dress like a typical housewife or a working girl or businesswoman. Instead, she embraced "witchy" culture by wearing black all the time and dying her naturally ash-blond hair ebony. She wore Goth makeup and jewelry and seemed obsessed with the trappings of witchcraft as portrayed in movies and TV, whereas some of the other witches in town found it to be a bit much. Or so Natalie had heard.

Now Marigold smoothed a few silky strands of hair behind her ears and smiled inquisitively at Natalie. "Would you like to start with me?"

Never look a gift horse et cetera, as Joey used to say.

"Sure. That'd be helpful." Natalie took out her notebook and pen and launched right into the interview. "Did Veronica have any enemies that you know of?"

"Enemies?" She frowned thoughtfully. "I don't think so."

"Do you know where she was last night?"

"I assume she was at home, bundled up like the rest of us."

"When was the last time you saw her?"

"Last week. She invited me over for coffee, and we spoke about our next meetup."

"What was her mood like? Was she distracted or unhappy?"

Her mouth softened, and her shoulders sagged a little. "I didn't pick up on anything like that. Veronica was her usual self. Friendly, upbeat, generous with her time. You know, there wouldn't be any historic covens if it weren't for her. She fought hard to have Wicca and other pagan religions accepted. Basically she's the heart and soul of the Craft community here in Burning Lake."

Natalie smiled sadly. "That's what I hear."

Her face bunched with pain. "How could this have happened?"

"I don't know. That's why these interviews are so important," Natalie said. "Did she have any disagreements or altercations recently?"

"No. Everybody looks up to Veronica. We all want to be like her. She lives such a modest life. Lived. Oh gosh, I can't get used to that." Marigold's eyes glistened with sadness. "You know, she achieved so much over the years—writing those books and working to get Wicca accepted as a legitimate religion. She never bragged about who she was. She fit right into any conversation. She wanted to be treated like the rest of us. Like nobody special. She had a great sense of humor, when the mood hit her. She could keep us in stitches. I can't think of anyone who'd want to hurt her. Did you say sugar?"

"Thanks."

Marigold stirred cream and sugar into Natalie's coffee, then handed her a mug that read WITCHES BREW.

"So Veronica was writing again after a thirty-year absence? Do you know what the new book was about?" Natalie asked.

Marigold shook her head. "She kept it pretty close to her vest. She called it her WIP, which means work in progress. I figured it was another guidebook about witchcraft."

"What kind of relationship did you have?"

"Me and Veronica?" She seemed startled by the question. "Excellent, I would say."

"What about the others?"

She blinked. "We're all sister witches. We love one another. Why?"

"These are just routine questions, nothing more. We try to be thorough."

"Okay. We're all very close. Very loving. With witchcraft, you can make deep connections to the earth and your ancestral origins. It taps into a powerful energy you've always had right inside you. It gives women nurturing and protective powers. We could use more female power in this world, don't you think?"

Natalie smiled. "It can't hurt, right?" she said automatically, but she didn't honestly mean it. Grace and her friends had sought power through witchcraft, and that hadn't turned out so well. "What about stalkers? Any overly enthusiastic fans?"

"If Veronica had a stalker, she never mentioned it to me." Marigold frowned. "You may want to talk to Belinda or Tabitha. They were both fairly close to her."

The living room was spacious and smelled of roses, a sweet, sad fragrance that made Natalie feel nostalgic for long-ago visits to her grandparents' house, where her grandmother would place rose sachets around the rooms. During the holidays, Natalie's grandfather would stack the firewood in the hearth, crisscrossing the logs and rolled-up newspapers. He would fan the flames until the fire roared, until heat swelled against the firebrick and spilled like a breaking ocean wave into the room, warming their faces.

Inside the living room, Belinda Pickle stood holding her wineglass and staring contemplatively into the fire. There were lovely bay windows and

Victorian-era built-ins, but the rather grand fireplace was the focal point of the room.

"Belinda?" Natalie said, approaching her.

"Oh God. Isn't it awful?" Her eyes were bloodshot. She bit her lower lip, clearly shaken to the core, but trying to hold it together. Dell Pickle's forty-five-year-old daughter had short gray hair and a perpetually worried look on her heart-shaped face. She managed her father's popular bed-and-breakfast, the Sunflower Inn, and was a member of the Pendleton coven. Now she squeezed Natalie's hand and said, "How could this have happened? They're calling it an accident, but there's a rumor going around town that she was . . . oh my God, *chained* to the tracks. Is that true, Natalie? Because if so, this town's in serious trouble. Who would do such a thing? You'd have to be crazy!"

Natalie knew she wasn't supposed to commiserate on a personal level, but she touched Belinda's arm briefly and said, "We don't know all the facts yet, but it's terribly tragic. We're all shaken by this, really rattled down at the station. Veronica was such a strong presence in this town." She smiled sadly, hoping that was enough. "I need to ask you a few questions, Belinda. Can we talk in the kitchen? Do you mind?"

"Not at all."

Once they were settled at the kitchen table, Natalie asked Belinda, "Did Veronica have any enemies or adversaries that you know of?"

"Enemies?" She squinted at Natalie. "I can't even imagine such a thing."

"What about relationships? She never married, right? Did she have any lovers?"

"She had an affair with a married man once, but they broke it off decades ago."

"Really? What was his name?"

Belinda shook her head. "She never told me. She kept it close to her heart."

"It never even slipped out?"

"Veronica was a very private person. If she didn't tell you something, that meant she didn't want you to know." She paused to rub the back of her neck. She kept her voice light and even, but Natalie could detect a growing tension underneath. "There were rumors, of course . . ."

"What rumors?"

"There are always rumors in Burning Lake, right?" Belinda rolled her eyes.

"What kind of rumors?"

"About her and Reverend Grimsby," she said softly. Then she brushed the air with her hand. "It's ridiculous. Besides, who cares? This is the twenty-first century, for crying out loud. As far as I know, Veronica was celibate. She used to joke about it—said she was an involuntary celibate. But I never saw her with anyone, and I never heard her mention anybody special, and she didn't care about the rumors. Veronica wasn't one to gossip. She only mentioned this affair to me once during a summer solstice Sabbat. He was married, and he broke her heart. So that was it for her."

"You don't believe the rumors then?"

"About Veronica and the reverend? No. Why would they keep it a secret? Who cares anymore? This isn't 1712. But they were good friends. Veronica was very close to him. He invited her to give a speech at his Christmas service last December, and she told me it was well received. She sent me a copy."

"What was the speech about?"

"Mostly about natural remedies, the cycles of the earth and the moon, ritual practices, and how closely related Christmas is to the pagan ritual of winter celebration. In the winter, we celebrate decay and death as part of the life cycle. Death makes way for new life."

"Did anyone object to her speech?"

Belinda shook her head. "If they did, she never mentioned it."

"Have you had any trouble with the churchgoers in town?"

"Not in ages. I mean, everyone in Burning Lake knows a Wiccan or a pagan. We're their neighbors, family, friends, co-workers. They know we don't worship the devil. Except of course, there are always a few narrow-minded souls who refuse to tolerate other religions, but that's because they're weak. If you were strong, you'd embrace your brothers and sisters of different faiths. But some people are weak."

"Who, for instance?"

"Occasionally you bump into someone. But we haven't experienced that kind of discrimination in years. Not to our faces, at least."

Through the arched kitchen doorway, Natalie had a good view of the crowded living room and recognized half the faces in that room. These women shared a long history together—divorces, children, promotions, new houses, weddings, funerals. They basked in the glow of their long friendships, their overlapping conversations straining to be heard above the New Age music playing on the sound system. There was plenty of food, wine, and spirits—lots of weeping and swapping stories and getting drunk just to ease the pain.

Natalie spotted Felicity Briggs talking to Val Hastings over by the buffet table. Felicity gave off the air of a turn-of-the-century lady posing for her royal portrait while holding a lapdog. When she saw Natalie watching her, she looked away. Felicity's husband worked at the hospital with Dr. Russ Swinton, and there was a contingent of medical personnel who were still upset that Natalie had suspected Russ of being a cold-blooded murderer. He turned out to be innocent, and Natalie was only doing her job, following the evidence, but people had long memories in Burning Lake. Grudges had sticking power.

Val Hastings, who'd been talking to Felicity, gave Natalie a sour look as well. The manager of a local bank, Val was congenitally nasty. She'd been born that way.

It was surprising to realize that all these women were witches—Tammy Jones was the head stock clerk at the grocery store, Ginny Moskovitz was married to a city councilman, Honey Fitzgerald was the head of a nonprofit organization working on the preservation of historic properties. Modern-day practitioners of pagan tradition didn't dress like Goths or have tattoos and nose piercings—with a few exceptions. Rather, the real witches of Burning Lake wouldn't stand out in a crowd. You'd never guess that they were witches. Right here inside this house was a collection of suburban moms and businesswomen, lawyers, teachers, grocery clerks, middle managers, apple farmers, and boutique owners. Instead of broomsticks, they drove SUVs and Toyotas and Fords. Instead of brooms, they used Dysons and Swiffers.

"Did Veronica say anything else about the married man she was involved with?" Natalie asked.

"Only that it lasted for three or four years. He made a lot of promises he couldn't keep. It broke her heart. For some people . . . I guess that's enough to turn them off relationships for good." Belinda shrugged. "That's all I know."

"Okay." Natalie glanced at her notes. "About this new book Veronica was writing, was she going to use her pen name, Corvina Manse?"

"She told me she wanted to publish under her own name. You know, really own it this time. But her family would've had a fit. So no. It was going to be another Corvina Manse book."

"And her family wouldn't have approved? After all this time?"

Belinda shook her head. "They're devout Christians. They equate witch-craft with devil worship. So no, they didn't approve of her lifestyle choices. But Veronica didn't slam them for it. She empathized how hard it was for them to accept her decision. Such a radical departure from what they'd always believed. She was sympathetic. So she decided to publish this one under a pen name, too, and save them some grief."

"Do you happen to know who's going to inherit Veronica's property, like the house and the rights to her publications?"

Belinda leaned back in her chair. "It would be in her will, I'd imagine."

"She didn't share that information with you?"

"No. Like I said, she was a very private person."

"Who's going to take over for Veronica as the leader of the Pendleton coven?"

"Ah. That's part of the reason we're getting together today, to discuss it."

"She never wrote down her wishes, or spoke to anyone about succession?"

"No, that's not how Wicca works," Belinda said with a shake of her head. "There is no second-in-command. This is a very democratic group. But . . ."

Natalie leaned forward slightly. "But what?"

"Marigold seems to believe that Veronica wanted *her* to head the coven. She claims they had a conversation about it. But no one else witnessed this so-called conversation, and some of us are concerned that Marigold might use the opportunity to lobby heavily for the position. And I, for one, don't want that."

"Why not?"

Belinda drew closer and lowered her voice. "Don't get me wrong. Marigold's a very smart and capable person, but she's a bit of a control freak.

She can be rather bossy. You know, my way or the highway. Nobody wants that. Wicca is a loose and flexible religion, and we all should have a say in what goes on. Also, to be honest . . . Marigold is certainly no Veronica Manes, I can tell you that. Not by a long shot."

Natalie's phone buzzed. "Excuse me," she said, picking up. "Detective Lockhart."

"Autopsy's in half an hour," Luke told her. "I'd like you to be there."

16

The golden hour had faded to dusk. Luke was waiting for her outside the county health building a few blocks east of the police station. He stood with his back to her and his face to the wind. The temperature had dropped about five degrees. It was in the teens, and Luke shoved his hands into the pockets of his parka and stomped his boots on the sidewalk.

"Hey," she said by way of a greeting. "Thanks for the new desk."

"Oh. Right." He blinked at her. "Happy belated birthday."

She smirked. "I still haven't forgiven you for that creepy card."

"I thought they were supposed to be creepy?"

"Corny, tasteless, or ridiculous. Not creepy."

"Oh. I promise to do better next time." He relaxed a little, his face breaking into a beautiful smile. His eyes were so clear. So Luke.

"I just spent the afternoon with a bunch of witches. They all told me how much they loved and admired Veronica. There was a lot of heartache in that house. A lot of grief. Augie arrived a few minutes after you called, so he's completing the interview process."

"What do you think?" he asked, the lines of his face once again taking on the gravity of the case.

She nodded. It was time for honesty. "This looks like a revenge killing, pure and simple. Whoever did this wanted to humiliate her in the worst way possible. To shame and terrify her."

"Why?" he asked, playing devil's advocate. "Who would do such a thing?"

"I don't know. A rival. A fierce enemy. Someone who clearly hated her or was furious at her. It seems deeply personal."

"Right," Luke said. "But who would hold such a personal grudge against her?"

"There are rumors about a love affair with a married man, but that ended a long time ago. There's a more recent rumor about her and Reverend Grimsby being involved, but no one believes it. Belinda told me Veronica used to joke about being celibate, and she thinks it may be true—that her love affair with the married man broke her heart and she turned away from earthly temptations. She devoted her life to Wicca instead."

"Maybe the rumors about her and Grimsby stirred up some negative emotions," Luke suggested. "Maybe one of his congregants or one of the Wiccans was angry about it, or even jealous."

"I thought of that. The witch costume, combined with the silver cross, is a clue. It turns out Veronica gave a speech about Wicca at St. Paul's Christmas service, where she compared Wicca to Christianity, exploring the roots and origins of both. Maybe somebody took offense. And then there are the Hosts, who were attending NA meetings in the church basement. There's definitely a church connection. I need to talk to Grimsby again . . ." Natalie's phone buzzed in her coat pocket. "Excuse me." It was Hunter.

She turned away from Luke and said, "Hello, you."

"Hey, you," he said warmly. "How are you holding up?"

"I'm still standing," Natalie said, glancing over at Luke. "I'll be home late."

"Yeah, I figured," he said softly. "Listen. Dinner will be waiting for you whenever you get here, okay? There will be wine, a blazing fire in the hearth, and a special-discount foot rub waiting just for you."

She smiled. She got emotional. Tears welled in her eyes, but she quickly brushed them away. "You don't have to wait up for me, Hunter."

"Are you kidding? It's the highlight of my day."

"I'll be home around midnight."

"Just remember to pace yourself," he said.

"Thanks. See you." She hung up and turned around.

Luke had distanced himself. He stood with downcast eyes beneath the streetlight, his breath slowly steaming before him in the brittle air. He looked like the kind of guy you shouldn't ever mess with—like the lone antihero in a stark 1960s Western. "Shall we go inside?" he said stiffly. In an instant, his behavior toward her had become cordial, professional, polite, and accommodating. The Luke she knew and loved had disappeared.

Natalie was tempted to tease him and say, "We shall," but she didn't. The moment was grave and solemn. They were about to enter a sacred space.

Down in the basement, the morgue was chilly, full of mechanical sounds and dank dripping pipes. Natalie inhaled the tang of dried blood as she put on her disposable gloves and face mask.

Coroner Barry Fishbeck was in his mid-sixties, a dignified-looking man with a silver goatee. He seemed unusually solemn tonight. "She's over here," he said quietly, escorting Natalie and Luke to the other side of the autopsy suite.

Veronica Manes's ruined body lay on a chrome table. Her shoulder-length gray hair was clotted with blood. Her pale torso had been partially ripped open from the impact of the train, and some of her insides were exposed. The victim's arms and legs were fractured in multiple places. She looked like a rag doll stuffed with crimson yarn.

Another chrome table several yards away held sections of torn black fabric that had been laid out like a jigsaw puzzle, crowned with a Halloween witch's hat. The coroner had carefully reconstructed the witch costume worn by Veronica when she was killed. The small silver cross with its delicate chain were placed on the table above the collar of the dress. The broom was upright in a corner, wrapped in plastic. It looked like an ordinary household broom with corn fiber bristles and a lacquered wooden handle.

"Ready to proceed, folks?" Barry wore the standard long-sleeved coroner's gown, a blue surgical cap, a splash shield, and latex gloves. The harsh overhead lights cast uneven shadows down his weathered, porous face. "This is the autopsy of Veronica Manes on March the eighth, commencing at five thirty in the evening," he said into his digital recorder. "Female Caucasian, five-six, one hundred and thirty-nine pounds, fifty-eight years of age. Gray hair, blue eyes. The body is fixed in rigor mortis. There is some anterior and posterior lividity. Time of death is approximately six twenty-six this morning. CCTV will verify exact TOD once we receive it from the railroad company.

"Clothing found on the torso and body parts, before I removed them, are as follows: a blue Hanes T-shirt, a faded pair of Levi's jeans, white cotton panties, a beige sports bra, and one blue sock. The other sock is missing. Plus a pair of winter boots from Land's End. I've reconstructed the torn pieces of the black dress and cloak, which are part of a Halloween costume the victim was wearing at the time of the incident. It appears to be a classic witch costume with a matching hat, made of polyester-type fabric. Everything else has been bagged and tagged for further analysis."

Luke and Natalie were standing a little too close together, as if they shared a secret. Luke seemed to become aware of this and stepped slightly to the right, making a small space between them. She couldn't help glancing at the gruesome collection of plastic bags on the counter next to the scale, each one containing a body part that had been found at the site. She recognized the reddish-brown liver, the bile green gallbladder, a purplish spleen, a smooth brown kidney, the yellowish bladder, and several yards of bloody intestines. None of it seemed real.

"Several witnesses, including a couple of detectives at the scene, identified the victim as Veronica Manes of eight Plymouth Street," the coroner continued. "This afternoon, I matched the victim's teeth to her dental records and can positively confirm her identity. This morning at six twenty-six, a two-hundred-ton train traveling seventy miles per hour impacted Veronica, who was shackled to the tracks. As a result, she suffered devastating injuries to her body. These injuries are extensive and resulted in the following items being flung and dispersed across the site . . . partial brain matter and skull fragments, intestines, the right kidney, a partial liver, and other pieces of organs and bone fragments. Upon impact, wind from the speeding locomotive ripped the hat and part of the costume off her body and flung it away. Due to the fact that her wrists were handcuffed and chained to the rails, both hands were torn off and flung into the snow on either side of the tracks."

Natalie felt sick to her stomach. Sweat trickled down her neck and underneath the collar of her blouse. She forced herself to look at the bloodless, twisted body on the table. She recalled how pale her sister Grace had been when they fished her out of the lake last year, and the thought of it almost shattered her cop's resolve. She held her breath and studied Veronica's severed hands, which were perched on either side of the table, fingers frozen in repose. The nails were unvarnished. The hands were ashen.

"Notice the abrasions and lacerations to her forearms in an area just above her severed wrists," Barry said, using his scalpel as a pointer. "These are impressions of what I'm assuming were zip ties used to bind her hands behind her back at some point. And then again, closer toward each wrist . . . these repetitive cuts and purple bruising are the result of her trying to escape from the two separate sets of handcuffs that were ratcheted around her wrists."

"She was zip-tied before she was handcuffed?" Natalie asked.

"That's what it looks like. The bruising from the handcuffs is severe, indicating that she pulled on the cuffs, twisting them in an attempt to escape from the tracks, once she realized how dire her situation was."

"What's that small circular bruise on her left thigh?" Natalie asked.

Barry took a closer look at the tiny hole surrounded by circular bruising on Veronica's thigh. "That appears to be a needle mark or a puncture wound. Hold on just a second." He turned the body on its side and studied the back of the victim's legs and thighs. "There are two more needle injection sites. Here and here." He pointed at the left and right buttocks. "Indicating she was drugged. I'll take samples and have the lab run a full toxicological evaluation. I'll pressure them for a quick turnaround."

"It makes sense to inject her with a sedative in order to control her better," Natalie told Luke. "Once she was out cold, they could dress her in the costume and transport her to the tracks. Which would explain why none of the neighbors heard any screams."

"They?" Luke repeated.

"She's a hundred and thirty-nine pounds," Natalie explained. "That's a lot of weight for one person to carry, especially during a snowstorm. Whoever did this also had to carry the steel chains, handcuffs, and padlocks to the tracks. And they had to be holding a flashlight. I'm assuming we could be looking for two murder suspects here."

"Or else one strong guy. Large, muscular, works out, lifts weights."

Natalie nodded. "At some point, she woke up chained to the tracks. She must've known who killed her, and why."

"That all depends," Barry said. "Some drugs produce amnesia or hallu-
cinations."

An eerie silence filled the morgue. This was a professional job. Premeditated, carefully planned and executed. The air was tainted with death. Natalie couldn't stop wondering how it must've felt to die like that. The sheer
terror of it.

"Records show the victim's overall health was excellent," Barry said. "She
had a wellness checkup last summer. Her cholesterol level was slightly el-
evated, but nothing to be alarmed about. Heart rate and blood pressure
were good. No medical concerns. Blood tests and urinalysis were negative.
She wasn't taking any prescription drugs. Despite the obvious injuries to
her heart, lungs, liver, stomach, and other organs, she appears to have been
in very good shape. I conclude that the method of death was blunt trauma
to the head, torso, and spine from the impact of the train."

Veronica's lips were smeared with red lipstick. Natalie fixated on this one
fact, until she suddenly realized it wasn't lipstick. It was blood. Veronica's
nose, earlobes, and fingertips were tinged with a dark purplish color, the
result of frostbite from being out in the cold for so long. Natalie didn't want
to look anymore. What was that awful smell? Disinfectant, grease from the
railroad tracks, bacterial fumes rising off the body.

"Excuse me." She hurried across the morgue, flung the door open, ran
out into the echoey hallway, and headed for the restrooms.

Natalie locked herself in a stall and knelt on the cold tiles, vomiting until
there was nothing left. Another horrific homicide. Another living nightmare. At least she wasn't the lead detective on this one. She pitied Luke.

She could feel her own body heat worming up her chest as she struggled
to put the pieces together. This was a deliberate act of violence, meant to
impact everyone in town with its clever cruelty. The zip ties, the handcuffs, the costume, the silver cross, the broom, the shackles, the snow, the
train. Why? What was the sick message they were supposed to derive from
it all? Even worse, now that Natalie really thought about it, the scene felt
staged somehow. Deliberately misleading. What was she missing? What
couldn't she see?

She washed up at the sink and wiped her mouth on a paper towel. She
tossed the towel away and went outside. Luke was waiting for her in the
chilly corridor.

"Are you okay?" His face was drained of color and full of concern.

"Yeah, fine." She shrugged it off.

"Fine?" he repeated skeptically. "You look exhausted."

"Yeah, well." She crossed her arms. "This sucks."

"It sucks big-time. Are you going to make it through? Because I need you, Natalie. I need your instincts."

"My instincts? You mean, my paranoid delusion that the town is cursed? That we should all get the hell out of Dodge before it's too late? Those instincts?"

He stared at her solemnly. He didn't crack a smile. "Let me know the instant I ask too much of you, okay? Let me know when I cross that line. Sometimes I take your strength for granted, and that isn't fair."

She looked away, hurt by these considerate words. She could feel her eyes slowly begin to well with tears, but that was the last thing she wanted Luke to see. It would only bring out his protective instincts. "You've heard the rumors about me leaving?" she asked.

He nodded reluctantly. "Yeah."

"Great timing, huh?" She took a breath, brushed away the tears, and looked at him with steady eyes. "Now what am I supposed to do? I have the letter of resignation in my pocket."

He nodded, as if he'd been expecting her to say this for a while. Both expecting and dreading it. "Do what you have to do, Natalie."

"Are you kidding me? I can't. Not anymore." She waved her hand at the entrance to the morgue. "Not after seeing that. Now I'm determined to follow through with the investigation . . . and do everything in my power to help you solve this case, Luke. But at the same time, I've thought about it a lot, and I'm totally burnt out, and then there's the hiring freeze . . . it's fucked up."

He nodded, wrinkles stacking up on his forehead. "Let's go back to the station and do our write-ups. Then I want you to take the rest of the night off. Just promise me you'll be back in the morning."

"Well, I'm not about to abandon her now," she said with a furious sigh.

17

By eight o'clock at night, Natalie had finished the last of her reports. She had only a vague sense of time, as if an entire week had passed. She was lost in the details, slipping down one rabbit hole after another.

She and Lenny were the only ones left in the office tonight. Brandon had caught a break-in on Sarah Hutchins Drive, and Augie—who was on call this week—had gone home to catch a few z's. Murphy was cataloging evidence in Conference Room C, while Jacob was out talking to his snitches. Mike was running down the origin of the chains and padlocks, while Luke was fielding calls in his office. They could hear his tired voice drifting down the hallway toward them. His latest conversation sounded like a muffled engine revving and idling.

The Criminal Investigations Unit consisted of seven detectives and a supervising lieutenant detective. They handled homicides, suicides, accidental deaths, rapes, assaults, domestic violence, drug overdoses, armed robberies, burglaries, carjackings, missing persons, hostage situations, and any suspicious incident that resulted in life-threatening injuries. A row of heavy-duty binders lined the bookshelves to Natalie's right, and her active investigative files were spread across her brand-new desk. They had already moved her wobbly old desk into storage, and she wondered if there was a warehouse full of battered municipal furniture, like an elephant's graveyard.

"Hungry, Natalie?" Lenny asked. "I got a meatball sub that ain't gonna eat itself."

She smiled at his kindness. "I had something earlier," she lied.

"When? I've been watching you work for twelve hours straight without a break."

"I'm fine, Lenny. Enjoy your sub." The last thing she wanted was a meal. The thought of a meatball sub repulsed her. The image of Veronica's torn-up body sat like a coagulated lump in her stomach. Everything was a surreal blur.

"You can't keep running on empty, Natalie."

"I have my coffee."

"That's not enough."

"Show me what you're working on," she said, getting up.

He put down his sub on a paper plate and wiped his mouth with a napkin. Lenny had his own whiteboard marked up with a blue marker, and his desk was covered in tidy stacks of paperwork, sticky pads, and a jar of ballpoint pens. He had a system. "Check this out," he told her.

She looked at his computer screen with its 3D reconstruction of the torn-apart witch costume. The label had been cut off. The long black imitation-Victorian dress was a sexier version of the classic Wicked Witch of the West outfit. It had long sleeves, a fitted bodice, silver buttons, and a full tulle petticoat. The matching cloak had a magical, oversized hood, and the pointy cone hat practically cackled at them. *My little pretty . . .*

"The fabric's one hundred percent polyester," Lenny explained. "The hat has wire in the brim edge. Someone deliberately cut the label out—most likely to mask the manufacturer. Size is large." He leaned back and said, "You know, Natalie, when I first started in this job, I'd go home so bone-tired that I could barely help my wife out with the chores—fix the leaky sink, take out the garbage, help the kids with their homework. I'd be too pooped to notice some of the changes that were taking place all around me. For years, I missed out on the daily details of family life because of my devotion to my job."

She nodded patiently.

"Then one day, Joelle and I had a little sit-down. She set my ass straight, and almost overnight I learned how to accommodate my family obligations into my hectic schedule. Once a week, for instance, we'd have a date night. And I made sure not to miss Andy's baseball games or Jackie's dance recitals. Life is a blessing. Your family is a gift. I had to get that through my stupid skull."

"Good advice," she said, although Lenny must've forgotten that she had no family left. Unless he was talking about Hunter. But they weren't a family yet, and might never become one. She didn't know. Still, it was sweet of him to care. To share his own personal battles.

Lenny glanced at his watch. "Anyway, priority one, we need to check out the local costume shops, Halloween outlets, and thrift stores in the area, and find out who bought this particular costume. In the meantime, I found a dozen or so blue fibers on the costume, mainly on the cloak—short dark synthetic fibers made from polymers that could've come from inside a vehicle, like a car mat or upholstery, maybe a seat belt. This needs further analysis. There's a lot of trace to be processed, but that's a significant find." Lenny took a sip of Coke. "There's more. We swept through Veronica's house this afternoon, lifting loose evidence from the furniture and vacuuming the rugs. We found multiple animal hairs inside the residence."

"What type of hairs?"

"Short brown hairs from a cat or a dog maybe. I haven't pinned it down yet."

"But she didn't have any pets."

"No. And we mostly found these hairs on the first floor—living room, kitchen, half bath. We also found some green fibers of unknown origin. I'll be going back to the residence tomorrow to investigate further. In the meantime, I've sent samples of everything to the state lab for testing. Hopefully, they can tell us what type of animal hairs these are, along with the green fibers and the blue polymer fibers we found on the costume— whether they're made of acetate, acrylic, or nylon, et cetera."

"Luke said the house was ransacked," she said.

"Yeah, and it looks like her computers were taken, PC and a laptop, maybe some other devices. We still haven't found her cell phone, there's no signal. On the first floor, books and paperwork were scattered everywhere. Her corner office was tossed. Upstairs in the bedroom, somebody obviously rummaged through the bureau drawers and closet. We don't know what they were looking for, because there was a jewelry box, a silver tea set, and some high-end appliances that weren't taken. No bloodstains so far, but I'm going back there tomorrow with luminol and a black light for a do-over. None of the windows were smashed or open. The front and back doors were locked, although the front door chain was hanging loose. The front door locks automatically behind you, and her car is still in the garage, so it looks like she either left of her own accord, voluntarily, or was forcibly escorted from the house."

"At gunpoint?"

"Could be."

"If somebody tossed the place, what were they looking for?"

"At this point, I'm withholding my guesses."

"Did you find any prints on the doorknob or doorbell?" Natalie asked.

"No, but I did retrieve a few glass fragments from the front hallway near the point of entry. They don't correspond to any other source inside the house, as far as I can tell. Sometimes glass fragments will cling to a person's clothes, gathering in the pant cuffs or shoelaces, only to fall off somewhere else. So the perp could've carried the trace into the house with him—a remote possibility, but you have to follow all your leads, right? It's more probable these greenish glass fragments came from an item of glassware that was broken and disposed of by Veronica herself a while ago. We don't know." Lenny rubbed his forehead thoughtfully. "The good news is, we got footprints. As a matter of fact, we got two different sets of boot prints tracking mud into the house. I vacuumed up some of the soil trace from the hallway carpet. I took photographs and measurements of the partial tracks, then sent them along with the soil sample to the lab. It could be significant, you never know. I did a preliminary on the sole patterns, and they look like a popular brand sold at Walmart. Veronica's boot size and shoe treads were not a match. So that's significant. And the lab might be able to determine within a reasonable degree of accuracy where the soil trace came from, like the woods around her house, or some other area. They'd need another soil sample to compare it to. When it comes to soil evidence, it's difficult to get an absolute positive. The best you can hope for is a might-have-originated-from response."

"So then—we've got blue fibers from a vehicle on the costume itself, plus brown animal hairs, muddy boot prints, a soil sample, green fibers, and a few glass shards from Veronica's house?"

He leaned back in his seat. "That's a pretty good haul."

A scenario presented itself in her mind. "I think there must've been more than one person involved. There are too many moving parts. It has to be someone she knew and trusted, Lenny. Not a home invasion. Whoever the perps are, they didn't break into the house. They parked on the street and rang the doorbell, like visitors. Friendly faces."

"I agree. And the two sets of footprints reinforce that."

"Two people wearing gloves, so they left no prints. Veronica answered the door and invited them in. They tracked mud on the carpet. They asked her to drop everything and come with them. If they were strangers, I doubt she would've opened the door in the first place. And if they drew a weapon or threatened her, she would've put up a fight or tried to run, and we would have found more evidence of a struggle."

"You think she went willingly with them in their vehicle? That late at night?"

"Yeah, I do. She was either asleep upstairs when the doorbell rang, or they called her beforehand—which is why getting her phone records is vital. They waited downstairs in the hallway while Veronica got dressed—T-shirt and jeans, boots and socks—there was a sense of urgency about this. She put on her winter coat, grabbed her cell phone and house keys, and went with them into the snowstorm. No cries for help. No struggles or screams—her nearest neighbor is only twenty yards away. According to her statement, this neighbor was up late last night, reading a book, and she would've heard something. Veronica got into their vehicle, and maybe that's when they injected her. Or they drove her someplace else . . ."

"The cottage maybe?" Lenny inquired.

"Or somewhere nearby. They parked on Mountain Laurel Road, and one of them carried her down to the tracks, while the other carried the shackles and chains—those are fairly heavy—and held the flashlight. It was still snowing. It was pitch-dark. But first they had to remove her coat and take away her cell phone and house keys, before they left her on the tracks to die."

"So when did they ransack the house?"

"Afterwards. That's when they went back to her house, let themselves in—they had her keys—and ransacked the place, looking for something."

"Looking for what?"

"Once we solve that little riddle, we'll know who did this." Natalie's phone buzzed, and she checked the screen. "It's Ellie. Sorry, Lenny. I have to take this."

"Not a problem. Say hi to the cutie for me." He picked up his meatball sub and took a big bite.

18

Natalie took the call out in the hallway. "Ellie?" she said.

"Aunt Natalie, are you okay?" the sixteen-year-old asked with some urgency. "I heard about Veronica Manes, and I can't believe it. What happened? What's going on? They said she was hit by a train, but they didn't say if it was an accident or not. Did she do it on purpose? Because she was one of my role models growing up."

"Oh, Ellie, I'm so sorry, I should've called you earlier."

"That's okay, I figured you were swamped. What happened?"

"I can't go into any details, but we're all incredibly sad about it, and we're doing everything we can to find out what happened."

"They didn't put you in charge, did they?" she asked.

"No, Luke took the lead."

"Thank God."

"Don't worry, nobody wants a repeat of last time. Least of all, me. How are you doing otherwise, sweetie?"

"Pretty good, I guess. Considering that Asher and I broke up last week," she said.

"Oh, no. I'm sorry to hear that."

"Yeah, it sucks. It's taking me a while to process it. He told me that I was becoming overly dependent and needy, and I just . . . what should I do, Aunt Natalie?"

"Do you want my honest opinion?"

"Yes, please. Dad's hopeless. He wants to kill Asher. You're the only one I can turn to."

Natalie sighed and rubbed her tired eyes. "You have to let him go."

"Really?"

"That's it. Let him go and move on." She could feel Ellie's disappointment through the phone line and wished she had better advice to offer. She wondered what Grace would've said. "I know it's a cliché, but . . ."

"What if I don't want to move on?"

"Look at it this way. If Asher sees you as an independent woman, he might come to his senses. If not, then you two simply weren't meant to be together."

"So, like, ignore him? Snub him?"

"More like—get on with your life. Don't be too dependent on any other person to give your life meaning. Find your life's purpose and pursue it. Find the very center of yourself, honey. Love comes afterwards."

"Is that what happened to you?"

Natalie smiled sadly and shook her head. "Don't go by me. I'm a mess."

Ellie laughed. Then she broke down crying.

"Ellie? I'm sorry. I'm no good at this." She hated the self-doubt in her niece's voice. "Ellie? What is it?"

"I feel like such a pathetic loser," she confessed. "I've been secretly stalking him on Facebook, lurking in the shadows. Seriously. I formed this whole phony online identity last week after we broke up, and then I friended him just to see what he'd do without me. So far, he hasn't got a clue it's me. And now I'll never be able to come out and say—'Hey, it's me!'—because it's too creepy. I can't believe I'm catfishing him. Am I crazy, Aunt Natalie?"

"No, just lovesick."

"I've messed up my life. He'll never love me now."

"The guy's a jerk. He has to be nuts to have dumped you."

When Ellie was a baby, she would flap her little arms and flail her way into a sitting position, an effort that was so strenuous and cute, it made Grace laugh. No longer the goofy, funny little kid with the crammed book bag and excitable laugh, Ellie was turning into an intelligent, brave, beautiful young woman. Fortunately, the burns on her body had healed enough not to be a physical problem for her anymore, but the emotional scars remained. Her best friends since forever had utterly betrayed her. And yet, she seldom spoke of it and never complained. Natalie wanted to protect this wonderful person, like a hand curled around a flame.

"We're still on for Mom's deathiversary in April, aren't we?" Ellie asked.

"I wouldn't miss it for the world."

"Me neither."

Last fall, they'd scattered Grace's ashes on the lake, and two months from now, Natalie and Ellie would observe the first anniversary of Grace's death by going back to the lake and holding a remembrance ceremony. It was hard to believe almost a year had passed since that dreadful time. It didn't feel real.

Natalie glanced at her watch. "Listen, I have to go, Ellie. Let's talk this weekend, okay? Saturday or Sunday . . ."

"I'll be fine. Don't worry about me, Aunt Natalie. I'm tough. Like you."

"Don't let anyone else define you, Ellie. Ever."

"I won't. Stay safe, Aunt Natalie."

"You, too." She hung up and thought about herself and Hunter. Was she letting him define her?

19

The third-floor hallway was dark, with stray slants of office light spilling out of open doorways. Natalie went into Conference Room C, where Detective Peter Murphy was seated at the far end of the long polished table, evidence boxes piled everywhere—stacked against the walls, tucked under the table, perched on chair seats and the polished tabletop. Murphy's eyes were spaced wide apart beneath his thick, Muppet-like eyebrows, and he wore the condescending expression of a man who knew everything there was to know.

Tonight, his sleeves were rolled up, his face was sweaty, and he smiled at her with a pained expression. "What can I do you for, Natalie?"

"How's it going, Murph?"

"Oh, you know. Same old same old."

"Right." She nodded and felt an uneasiness around him, based on nothing but the feeling of disappointment she usually got whenever they interacted. Their mutual distrust hadn't always existed. It started last year when Murphy had misplaced a crucial file from the Crow Killer case, and things had only deteriorated since.

"What do you want, Natalie?" he stated flatly.

"Luke mentioned a box of library books."

"I was supposed to get them for you." He smiled at her.

She threw up her hands. "That's why I'm here."

"Sure thing." He didn't move. He was being passive-aggressive.

Her mind toggled back and forth between her diminishing options. "Okay, Murph, out with it. What's up?"

"Up? Nothing's up." He scraped his chair back and pointed at the floor. "There it is. See the box over there? 'Library Books' is written on the top."

"Thanks." Natalie knelt down, picked up the heavy box of books, and carried them over to the door. "You ever want to talk, let me know."

"I'm fine," he said in an exaggeratedly cheerful way, typing something into his laptop.

"Good to hear it," she said, thoroughly agitated with him.

Back out in the hallway, she heard Luke's mellow voice echoing down the hallway. She followed that alluring sound to his office. His door was open, a rectangle of yellow light slashing across the worn carpet. Luke was on his phone. He glanced up and nodded at her. "Yeah, okay, tomorrow then," he said into the receiver. He hung up.

"What you got there?"

"Library books."

"Ah." He stood up and came over, taking the box from her arms. "Let me carry that for you. Where you going?"

"Home."

"Okay. Down to the car then."

"Thanks, Luke. I'll just get my coat."

All the muscles of Luke's face grew slack. His silence didn't trouble her.

She ducked into the Criminal Investigations Unit, gathered up her paperwork, put on her coat, and said good night to Lenny. Then she and Luke headed for the elevators together, a pale light from Luke's office casting their shadows ahead of them down the passageway. A silhouette of two people who seemed to complement each other. A couple. At the end of the hallway, the elevator bank receded into darkness. Funny. Those lights were never turned off.

Natalie hit the switch and the lights flickered back on. Then she pressed the button for the elevators. "I called Jules Pastor earlier today and asked him about the Hosts—who they are, where we might find them. He said he'd ask around and call me back. Did Brandon get the cab view video from SRS yet?"

"Not yet."

As soon as the elevator doors closed behind them, Natalie said, "Murphy's still acting like a jerk. I can't help it if I got pissed at him for losing a vital piece of evidence. Misplaced an entire box of evidence, remember? He found it three days later, but it wasn't the first time his incompetence has slowed things down."

"We've discussed this before."

"I know, but his attitude hasn't changed."

"Did you confront him on it?"

"Sort of," she said. "In my own passive-aggressive way."

Luke's patience soon faded. "You need to talk to Murphy face-to-face. No triangulation. Direct communication."

It frustrated her that Luke seemed to ignore the fact that Natalie rarely if ever triangulated. But in this instance, she really needed his help. "Can't I vent to you once in a while?"

Luke pushed back. "If you can't alleviate the situation on your own, *then* you bring it to me. But not beforehand."

"You're right," she grumbled. "I'll talk to the big jerk."

That did it—a crack in the armor. Luke smiled slyly at her. "It's not my job to smooth ruffled feathers. Give it another shot. Be honest with him. See what happens."

The tension between them was broken.

They got off the elevator and walked out to the parking lot together. It was freezing cold outside, her breath feathering in the air before her. As a child, she used to pretend-smoke invisible cigarettes, exhaling plumes of breath into the wintery air and feeling so sophisticated. So grown-up. But it wasn't the same when you finally got there, to grown-up land.

Luke deposited the box of books in the trunk of Natalie's car, and she thanked him. They said good night. Still friends. She got in her car and drove home.

20

N atalie turned west onto Sarah Hutchins Drive, then took a right at the light and headed north. Hunter lived in an exclusive neighborhood where the mayor, the chief of police, and other bigwigs resided. The northern quadrant of Burning Lake consisted mostly of conservancy lands and wealthy neighborhoods where the estates were passed down from generation to generation. It surprised Natalie to be included among this privileged crowd. She still felt as if she didn't belong.

Now her radio crackled to life. "Calling all available units . . . we've received a report of a disturbance at St. Paul's Church," Dispatch announced.

That was only a few blocks away. She scooped up the mike and said, "This is CIU-seven. Responding to the call. ETA two minutes." She dunked the mike back in its cradle on the dash and took a left at the next light.

The church was eerily lit up this evening, but the parking lot around back was practically empty. Natalie pulled into a space between a forest-green Toyota Camry and a battered pickup truck, then slung her shield around her neck and got out. She could hear several men shouting. She took the shoveled pathway around the back of the church toward the main entrance.

Three men stood in the snowy front yard—Reverend Grimsby, Wayne Edison, and Justin Fowler. They were arguing, their voices raised in anger.

"Burn the witches? Is that what you meant?" Justin tossed a few crumpled pieces of paper in the snow. "What is all this bullshit?"

"I never said that!" Wayne shouted back. "Jesus, can't you read, Justin? That's not what it says!"

Reverend Grimsby gently waved his hands in an attempt to keep the two men from physically attacking each other. "Gentlemen, please, now now."

Justin Fowler wore an old, cracked leather jacket with a hoodie underneath. The gray hood was drawn tightly around his face, and there were coin-sized circles under his eyes. He'd been cleared of murdering Natalie's sister and pardoned by the governor, and now he was a fish out of water, struggling to adjust to life as a free man. He had brought a darkness with him from prison, Natalie thought. He slurred his words. His pain was palpable. His face was gray and tense.

Wayne Edison had once been lean and lanky but had fallen victim to middle-aged spread. He worked at the cider mill west of town, and the skin of his calloused hands was covered in liver spots. "Those women may not worship the devil or perform animal sacrifices, but *some* in the name of Wicca do. The Hosts practiced witchcraft in the most barbaric ways— animal sacrifice was involved. And where are the Wiccans? Why haven't they put out a statement denouncing this behavior? Are we supposed to just give them a pass? How does that help their cause?"

Justin's face turned red with anger. "I want to know one thing, Wayne," he said, pointing his finger threateningly. "Do you know who killed Veronica?"

"No, you idiot! None of my friends would ever dream of doing such a thing."

In a burst of fury, Justin grabbed Wayne by the lapels of his overcoat and dragged him across the snow. A scuffle broke out.

"Stop it!" Natalie shouted from across the yard. "BLPD!"

The two of them were locked together, punching wildly, their fists smacking into hardened flesh. Wayne swung recklessly at Justin's head and missed, punching him repeatedly in the shoulder instead.

Justin wobbled a little, absorbing the blows, before releasing himself from Wayne's grip. Then he lowered his head and charged forward, head-butting Wayne so hard he fell over backward.

Natalie grabbed Justin by the arm and twisted it around behind his back, barely able to hold him still. When you sensed your life was in danger, everything inside of you tensed. You became primed for fight or flight. Her police training gave her an edge—alerting her to her own physical reactions, teaching her how to counter the adrenaline with rational decision-making. You learned protocols and approved methods for handling any situation imaginable. But Justin's superior physical strength was a factor she couldn't ignore. She needed to use psychology in order to counter it.

"Justin, it's me," she said. "Natalie."

He turned and gazed at her with unfocused eyes. To her shame, she'd been avoiding him since his prison release a few months ago. She hadn't kept track of his progress. This was the first time they'd met outside of the courthouse twenty years ago.

"What's going on, Justin? What's the problem?" she asked.

He studied her with haunted eyes. "Wayne and his friends at the church are distributing nasty flyers about the Wiccans."

Wayne Edison stumbled to his feet. "That's a misrepresentation. Justin's been threatening me and my friends," he asserted loudly.

"Only because you threatened *my* friends."

"What friends? You mean Veronica Manes?"

Justin raged forward, and Natalie could barely contain him. "Tell me who did this!" he shouted at Wayne. "If you know anything about it, anything at all, you'd better tell me now before I kill the whole lot of you!"

"Kill us? What the hell are you saying?"

"All right, back off." Natalie managed to pull Justin away from the brink of his outrage and wondered where backup was. She'd called in her request a few minutes ago. She could hear the drumming of her heart. Her hands were trembling. She wanted to be stronger than this.

Wayne looked to Natalie for understanding. "You know what I'm talking about, Detective, don't you? A lot of folks in this town are deeply Christian, and then you have others who are Wiccan, and we've all resided peacefully together for years. Side by side. But recently something evil has infected this town, and it ain't weed, it's a whole lot darker. I'll tell you right now, there's a battle going on for the hearts and minds of the people of this town."

"Fuck you," Justin spat.

"Justin, I would never hurt Veronica," Wayne said, looking him straight in the eye. "She came to our church and spoke about healing, and that was a welcome message. My friends and I are just concerned about folks like the Hosts who practice devil worship, not anyone else in town. You've got to believe that."

The wind began to blow, making the treetops writhe and creak. Natalie could feel Justin's raw, jangling energy. He was practically bucking in her arms—not hearing Wayne's message of unity, refusing to accept the olive branch.

Before she could say anything else, a squad car pulled up to the curb, and two muscle-bound law officers got out. "It's okay, Detective, we'll take care of this."

Natalie released the two men into the custody of Officer Keegan and Officer Marconi. Justin and Wayne were given Breathalyzers and arrested for public drunkenness and disorderly conduct. Her heart beat sick and tight as she watched them being taken away. She tried to shake off the sense of the surreal that had enveloped her today.

"Two stubborn gentlemen," Grimsby said, "with very different points of view."

She nodded. The reverend wore an unzipped parka, jeans, and a red sweatshirt with black lettering that spelled out 10,000 Kids a Year—Can You Help? She wanted to do nothing more than to crawl home and fall asleep for about a million years.

"How much does bail cost nowadays?" he asked her, taking out his wallet.

"Bail?" She frowned. "Who are you bailing out of jail?"

"Justin. He works for me."

"Justin Fowler works at the church? I didn't realize . . ."

"After he was released from prison, we tried getting him a job, any job, something on a construction site or maintenance. He's had a tough time of it. Nobody would hire him, despite the governor's pardon. Here at St. Paul's, we like to give ex-cons a chance, just as long as they're clean and sober. Some folks pay lip service but don't get personally involved, except for tossing a few bucks into the collection plate. So we gave him a job cleaning up the church. He's a good man, Natalie. He works hard."

She nodded. She could feel her face flushing. Of course, Justin Fowler was a good man. Her sister had done this to him—Grace and her friends set him up to take the fall for Willow's murder, and he'd served twenty years for the big lie. Twenty long years. "I'd be bitter too if I were him," she said. "It's unforgivable what Grace and the others did to him."

"Oh, you'd be surprised at the power of God's love to forgive. Don't blame yourself, Natalie. It wasn't your fault. He's doing okay. He's gradually pulling his life together, living at home with his mom. But this job will afford him the opportunity to set down roots in the community. I've already seen big changes in him, for the good. And he's eager to prove himself. He's never missed a day so far. This is an old building. There's a backlog of repairs to worry about. Something's always breaking down."

"I'm glad to hear it. I wish I'd done more."

"You did what you could. I haven't forgotten."

Shortly before Christmas, Natalie had donated more than she could afford to the church fund that was set up to help Justin transition back to civilian life. Reverend Grimsby knew about her generosity, but he hadn't shared her secret with anyone else, especially not Justin, per her request. She was an anonymous donor. The fund helped him buy that battered truck in the parking lot, job training, some new clothes, and a few necessary devices, like a cell phone and a computer.

"I gather the fight was about something Wayne wrote?" she asked the reverend.

"He sent around flyers to the congregation. Wayne considers what Holly and Edward did to the cottage an affront to the church. He wants to hear the Wiccans step up and condemn their behavior. Justin, on the other hand, has taken this reasonable reaction as an admission of guilt, or at least bias. He's heartbroken about Veronica's passing, and he's searching for answers. I told him that he needs to let the police do their job. But he's bereft and grieving."

"I didn't realize he knew Veronica."

"Oh, they were very close. I introduced them shortly after he joined the NA meetings in the church basement," Grimsby explained. "He was a troubled soul. Lost in the wilderness. He wasn't sure what he believed in anymore. And this being Burning Lake, he decided to find out if Wicca was right for him. That's how he and Veronica became friends. She took him under her wing and was trying to help him heal. Veronica and I consider ourselves shepherds of the town's flocks. She ministers to the Wiccans, and I minister to the Christians. Justin was undecided. Veronica and I both believed we were saving souls."

"Is that why you decided she should give a speech?" Natalie asked.

"Yes," he said brightly, as if recalling happier times. "She suggested it, and I thought it was a splendid idea. Most of my stauncher congregants, like Wayne, have their limits, but they try to be open-minded and charitable. What the Hosts did stretched people's tolerance to the breaking point. It's better they left town when they did."

"Sounds like temperatures are pretty high right now."

"Oh, they are."

"And you don't have any suspicions yourself as to who might've done this to Veronica, Reverend? None of your congregants, not the Hosts—no one in your sphere of influence?"

He thoughtfully shook his head. "Good Lord, no. It's unthinkable. Holly and Edward were two troubled kids, but are they capable of such evil? Maybe I'm naïve, Detective. But I can't think of anyone who would do such a thing. It's monstrous. And especially her. Veronica was such a kind, caring person . . ." His eyes filled with tears. "She wouldn't have wanted this to happen—all these divisions and anger and scapegoating. It's the opposite of what she'd hoped to achieve."

Natalie hesitated. "I hate to say this, Reverend, but there's a rumor going around that you and Veronica were closer than friends. Can you comment on that?"

"Lord give me patience." He scowled and brushed away the tears. "It's based on ignorance. If two adults of the opposite sex can't be friends in this day and age, then I don't know what to say." He shook his head wearily. "Veronica would've known how to shut those rumors down." He smiled at the thought, then said, "I've known about the Pendleton and Carrington covens for years, of course. But we only met officially a few years ago in the cemetery behind this church. She was looking for her ancestor's grave. Thomas Bell, the judge who condemned Victoriana Forsyth to death in 1712. Manes was his daughter's married name. Veronica confided in me how guilty she felt about that sad heritage, and that was the beginning of a beautiful friendship, to quote Bogart."

"Did she confide anything else that might have some bearing on the case?"

"Sorry. I wish she had. If by any stretch of the imagination she'd left some sort of clue . . ." He shrugged. "I only know she was working very hard on her new book."

"When was the last time you spoke to her?"

"Oh, let's see." He paused to reflect. "Last Wednesday afternoon. We had tea."

"How did she seem?"

"Fine. In high spirits. Excited about her writing. She was telling me about the Witching Tree, how fascinating it was to her, its mysterious history . . . I think she was going to write about it in her book."

"Anything else?"

"Only that." He shook his head slowly. "I sincerely hope you find Veronica's killer before Justin does."

21

Blackthorn Park on the south side of the lake was a vast white landscape of snow and ice. Tonight, the sky was clear and dark, with just the sliver of a moon to light the way. From the parking area, Natalie got her heavy-duty flashlight out of the trunk, then took the entrance past the old gatehouse and crumbling carriage house. She proceeded over the footbridge and entered the woods, the dry, crisp snow crunching underfoot. The trail was spectrally still, surrounded on both sides by leafless beeches, majestic elms, and weeping willows that swayed gently in the wind.

The path wound through the forest for forty yards or so before coming to a large clearing, dead weeds sticking out of the drifts like bleached straw. A faint light from the waxing moon slanted through the conifers and birches, casting bluish shadows over the snow-covered ground. A child's rhyme rang in her ears.

Don't stare too long at the Witching Tree,
Defile it not, or cursed you will be.

In the middle of the clearing was the Witching Tree of Burning Lake, an ancient two-hundred-year-old oak with tortuously twisted branches that clawed at the sky. This mythical-looking tree was surrounded by an 1879 ornate wrought iron fence that protected it from vandals. There was a brass plaque on the fence explaining the tree's history.

In 1825, a local witch named Nettie Goodson lived on this very spot in a cabin in the woods. When her nearest neighbors' cattle began to get sick and die, the village turned against her, accusing her of witchcraft and eventually burning down her house with Nettie inside it. As legend had it, a few months later, an oak tree began to grow on the deserted spot. None of the villagers dared touch the tree out of superstition, but when the farm animals started dying again, people believed that Nettie had returned from the dead in the form of a sapling oak that was growing on the site of her burned-down cabin. One year later, in 1826, farmer Moses Youngblood attempted to chop down the tree and was struck by lightning and killed on the spot.

Over the years that followed, dozens of other arrogant locals tried to get rid of the tree, and each time they met with bad fortune or unexpected death. From 1835 onward, it was declared that anyone who tried to destroy Nettie Goodson's Witching Tree would come to an untimely end. Those who disrespected the tree by urinating on it or carving their initials in the bark would come to great harm. After the last victim succumbed to smallpox in 1835, people left Nettie's tree alone. Some claimed it was the portal to hell.

The forest grew over the property, but the legend persisted. New generations wanted to tempt fate and leave their mark. In 1879, the town council passed a law making it illegal to carve graffiti into the Witching Tree. They put up the wrought iron fence in order to prevent the town drunks and daredevil teenagers from giving in to temptation. But even that didn't stop some folks, so in 1883, the town declared the Witching Tree to be a historic landmark and cleared the area around it, then planted thirteen beech saplings in a large circle around it and let it be known that people were allowed to carve their initials and other symbols into the bark of the thirteen beeches, just as long as they left Nettie's Witching Tree alone.

To this day, a hundred-plus years later, the thirteen beech trees encircling Nettie Goodson's Witching Tree were full of tree carvings—birth dates, death dates, hearts, pentagrams, half-moons, spirals. At some point, they were dubbed the Witch Trees. As legend had it, if you carved your deepest desire into the bark of a Witch Tree, then over time, as the tree grew larger, the bark would gradually swallow the carvings until they became dark swollen patches with ingrown ridges, and only a witch could read them. Natalie and her sisters had each carved their adolescent wishes into the bark of these very trees. So had half the town.

Inhaling the frosty air, she crossed the clearing and walked briskly around the fence and into the woods on the far side, past the moss-covered stones delineating the pathway. A few yards in was the one-hundred-and-forty-year-old beech tree where Natalie had carved her and Luke's initials many years ago. The tree had grown to an impressive height and had withstood well over a century's worth of rain, blizzards, and blistering summer heat.

Beech trees were fairly common in these parts, with their stout limbs and rounded crowns. The bark of the beech made a pretty good canvas. All you had to do was scratch off the outer layer of bark with a knife. As the tree grew and the bark slowly healed, the carvings would become darker and more corrugated around the edges, making them stand out against the pale, untouched bark. A few places where the knife cut especially deep, it left strange scars that looked like little lines of crumpled burnt sawdust.

When Natalie was a child, she'd mistakenly called these thirteen beeches the "Wish Trees." Her sister Grace thought it was cute and didn't correct her. Grace brought nine-year-old Natalie to the park one day so that they could carve their initials into the Wish Trees. Natalie was told to make a wish, and eventually it would come true. So she carved what was in her heart.

Now she found the tree—her favorite Wish Tree with the wind-twisted branches and the gnarled root sprouts. Occasionally, things were found in the crotches of these trees—poppet dolls, locks of hair, burnt offerings. Natalie ran her fingers over the craggy bark. The initials she had carved were still there, but they were almost illegible. *NL + LP,* inside a big heart. She had scratched them herself using a penknife. The markings had grown deformed over time, as the tree grew and healed.

A few years ago, an archeologist from NYU had come to Burning Lake in search of the world's oldest arborglyphs—ancient markings carved or painted onto the bark of a tree. Arborglyphs were rare and fleeting, since their life span was limited to the life of the tree. What interested the professor about the Witch Trees were the concentric circles and double V's, protective charms against evil spirits dating back a century or more. He called them "witch's marks," and said their purpose was to ward off evil spirits.

Native Americans and colonists also communicated by carving directions, warnings, and stories on the local trees, but most of the oldest ones had already devoured these ancient messages.

Natalie could feel circles of numbness on the tips of her fingers. Many of the symbols were sacred in these parts. The pentagram, a five-pointed star inside a circle, was a Wiccan symbol, mostly protective in origin—misinterpreted as evil by some. Winding spirals were thousands of years old and symbolized the life force. They were said to have a profoundly energizing effect. The Golden Spiral connected the earth to the heavens—it mirrored the pattern of a sunflower or the branches of a tree. The Vesica Piscis was drawn from sacred geometry and represented the union between men and women, light and dark, heaven and earth.

Natalie took out her phone and snapped as many pictures of the arborglyphs, new and old, as she could find. There were plenty of initials carved inside hearts, birth and death dates, biblical references, sexual imagery, curses and mockery, and even a witch's knot.

She went from one to the next, taking pictures of the markings on the trunks while the beeches creaked and rubbed together in the wind. Something had brought Veronica here—was she interested in the trees and their mythology, or was she perhaps interested in one of the arborglyphs that had been carved there?

Natalie angled her phone and snapped a picture of a hexagram next to a six-letter word that was difficult to read, since the carving contained too many overgrown ridges. The hexagram was a six-pointed star, the sign for dark magic. The letters seemed to spell out "m-a-l-l-o-w," but it could've been "w-a-l-l-l-m" or "w-o-l-l-i-w." Then Natalie realized with a horrific start that it was Willow spelled backward, or "w-o-l-l-i-w."

"No," she murmured, running her hand over the scarred trunk, dark notches interrupted by swollen patches. Hexagrams were evil. Forbidden. Six-pointed stars also represented 666, the sign of the devil. She sensed a shifting in the wind and ominously thought about Grace and her friends coming here as teenagers. Perhaps they'd left this dark message behind before they'd gone and stabbed Willow to death? She wondered why the police hadn't found it, then realized there were hundreds upon hundreds of carvings on these trees, as well as many more going farther back into the woods. Tree carvings were ubiquitous in this town. If you took the time to look, you could probably find hundreds of pentagrams alone carved into the trees in this forest. The older they were, the harder they were to read or recognize, and the higher up they were situated on the trunk.

She shuddered as a gust of wind buffeted the snow at her feet. The wind stirred her hair. Fear flared inside of her. The last thing she needed was to dredge up the past. It felt like a bony finger tapping her on the shoulder. She was afraid to turn around.

Just then, another carving drew her attention—a very fresh carving of an Awen, which resembled three rays of light inside a circle. It was an ancient Druid symbol meant to represent creative awakening and divine inspiration. This one looked brand-new. Perhaps a few days old, Natalie guessed. That was odd. Not only were there fresh cuts in the bark, but a wetness seeping from the cuts had frozen over, meaning that the tree was trying to heal itself. Natalie took a few pictures, wondering what the Awen was supposed to mean and who could've done it so recently.

She spent the next hour taking as many pictures of the tree carvings as she could, until she was exhausted and on the verge of hypothermia. When her phone buzzed, her fingers were so frozen she had trouble activating it. "Hello?"

"Detective Lockhart, it's Jules. Jules Pastor. You still want to get together?"

"Only if you've found out where Holly and Edward Host are staying."

"Not yet, but I've got a promising lead. I think it'll pan out. How's tomorrow morning sound? Same place as usual? How's nine o'clock for you?"

"Sounds good, Jules."

"See you then."

She hung up.

The moon was a sliver in the black, starry sky. They called it the waxing moon. For Wiccans, it was the maiden phase, or the "naïve" phase of the moon, when the goddess was at the very beginning of her journey. Veronica was killed during the waxing moon phase, and someone had recently carved an Awen into one of the Witch Trees. Why? Was it a coincidence or intentional? What was the message?

Natalie pocketed her phone, then aimed her flashlight at the beech tree she'd started with. Once again, she found the old carving of her and Luke's initials inside a scarred heart. *NL + LP.* When she was young, Luke was the most comfortable person to be around in her life. They talked and laughed all the time, at ease with each other. They shared private jokes. Scenes from the past flickered through her head like a silent movie. Luke climbing a tree to pluck an empty bird's nest out of the branches, then scrambling back down to show her the beauty of the woven nest. How he'd taken her hand before leading her into the police station when she was nine years old, after she'd been attacked by an older boy in the woods. And how afterward he'd walked with her to school for the rest of the year. Only Luke's presence had calmed her.

When he was a scrawny kid, all of Luke's T-shirts had holes or rips in them. His sneakers were threadbare. He couldn't wait to get his driver's license, and as soon as he did, he bought a beat-up Buick Skylark for $500 and got lost on the back roads of Burning Lake while blasting the B-52's "Dirty Back Road" on his crummy RadioShack speakers. He was proud. He was vengeful. He kept score. He was a misunderstood superhero. He was Deadpool. He was Wolverine. She cut off these thoughts so she wouldn't start crying. The pain she felt was deeper than anything she'd experienced since last year. No one ever made her feel the way Luke did—not really. Not exactly. Her wish from so long ago—the wish she'd carved so carefully into her favorite Wish Tree—was obvious.

She wanted to marry Luke someday.

Now she turned and headed back up the path, out of the woods, and toward the parking lot. It was time to go home.

22

She made it home around midnight. "Hi," she said from the kitchen doorway.

"Hey, you." Hunter's voice was self-consciously upbeat, and she knew that he'd been worried about her. She could feel his vulnerability pulsating toward her through the air. "How'd it go?" he asked.

"It was intense. Upsetting."

"I'll bet." He glanced at her. "Have you eaten?" he asked, licking his fingers. "You look beat. Go have a seat, Natalie, I've got this."

The dining table was elegantly set with a centerpiece of fresh flowers. The drippy white candles in their tarnished bronze candlesticks had been lit. There was a basket of sourdough bread next to a serving dish of oil and balsamic vinaigrette. The balsamic vinegar looked dark and slimy. The crusty bread had a leathery texture.

"I made something hearty on this cold night," he said. *"Poulet en croûte de sel* with a side of *galettes de pommes de terre."* He wore Armani and Zegna with careless indifference, and his hands were impeccably manicured. He kept in shape by regular morning swims in his indoor heated pool in the east wing of the building.

"I need to take a shower," she said, and he gave her a worried look.

Upstairs, Natalie stripped out of her clothes and stood under the showerhead, hot water beating down on her, steam slowly filling the room. She attempted to scrub off today's grit and horror. Then she stood very still under the showerhead, waiting for tears that never came. Why couldn't she feel anything? What was wrong with her?

She dried off and got dressed in fresh, comfortable clothes, and then rejoined Hunter downstairs. He was seated at the head of the table, politely waiting for her. He served her a large helping of chicken and potatoes onto an earthenware plate and handed it to her. "I canceled the dinner party next weekend," he told her. "I figured that was probably the last thing you needed."

"I don't fit in anyway," she said. "All your friends hate my cop stories."

"Fuck my friends. I don't care what they think."

Hunter had two different sets of friends—a large group of local friends, and a scattered group of college friends who lived mostly in New York, Miami, and Denver.

Here in Burning Lake, instead of the vast and glittering social circle she'd once envisioned, Hunter belonged to a solid, stuffy group of wealthy business associates. Some of them had been his father's friends. Lots of gray and silver hair, lots of business and investment talk. At these dinner parties, she met older men with Goyard briefcases and second wives, and younger bearded computer geeks wearing Yeezy Boosts. These parties were subdued and rather dull, and the men drank port and smoked cigars after dinner, while the wives polished off their desserts with a glass of wine and plenty of gossip.

At the first fancy party she'd gone to in Manhattan to meet Hunter's college friends, everyone treated Natalie like their best friend. These sophisticated thirtysomething women fawned all over her, stroking her long dark hair and holding her hand, squeezing it and exclaiming that she looked like a young Natalie Portman. They teased Hunter, saying things like, "Do you mind? I'm talking to Natalie, and she's *so* much more interesting than you." Then they'd laugh flirtatiously and toss their five-hundred-dollar haircuts. It made Natalie jealous. She couldn't compete with these trust fund kids with their creamy complexions, designer jeans, and quips about microprocessors and terabytes. If you peeled away the false flattery, Natalie sensed that they disapproved of her. The thirtysomething men were kinder, but she couldn't keep up with their patter about obscure French movies and computer technology and cutting-edge longevity breakthroughs.

At least they were polite enough not to bring up the Crow Killer or Violinist cases. Perhaps Hunter had warned them not to. Only one of his friends asked Natalie if she was "carrying," and she had to explain that detectives only armed themselves in specific circumstances, and the young man seemed gravely disappointed.

In Miami, Hunter knew a lot of cool, successful people—an Italian diplomat's daughter, the son of an oil-industry titan who was big into antiques, a tech CEO, a photo editor from a glossy fashion magazine, a futurist who'd given a TED talk. Staying at a fancy hotel, ordering room service, going to private clubs, tipping everyone for every little thing—Hunter handed out twenties like breath mints—Natalie had been overwhelmed. The people she met during their jaunts to New York and Miami struck her—for the most part—as shallow and giddy, like children who were staying up way past their bedtime. And sad underneath. Hiding their desperation behind the martinis they were constantly drinking, posing in prestigious bars or clubs where the big argument—like an old James Bond flick—was shaken or stirred.

But Natalie didn't want to dis them simply because she didn't fit in. There was a young artist couple in New York who seemed genuinely welcoming and sincere, not at all judgmental, and very curious; there was an older couple from Syracuse whom she liked very much. Oliver Chabert and his wife, Serena, now in their sixties, had taken an interest in Natalie, and the first thing Serena said to her was, "Oliver and I admire the police. What you do is profoundly important, and I can't imagine how difficult this past year has been for you." She had won Natalie's heart in an instant with her frank, makeup-free face and her sensitive observations about life.

Now Natalie looked over at Hunter and said, "Some of them are very nice."

"And some try to hide how nice they are," he said with a nod. "They expect everyone to have a tough skin, because they've hardened themselves to the world."

"You mean they're rude to the world."

He shrugged. "It's a coping mechanism."

"I suppose it's easy to be rude when you have fuck-you money."

He put his fork down. "Does that include me? Am I supposed to apologize for inheriting what I have? And starting a successful business, and hiring a bunch of employees and paying their salaries plus benefits? Are my charitable donations simply not good enough? Should I grovel? Should I give it all away and become a monk? Would that make you happy?"

She put down her fork. "There's a tower room in the west wing of the building that you use as an observatory. You have a five-thousand-dollar telescope for viewing the stars. There are five bedrooms and eight bathrooms, not including the master suite. The garage holds six vehicles. Do you actually need all this space?"

"No. But it's my home. Do you need all the space in the house where you grew up? There's only one of you. And you're never there anymore."

She smiled irritably. "You could turn this place into a museum."

"Maybe I will." He stared at her over his glass of wine. "What if I did that . . . what if I turned my childhood home into a museum and handed it over to the historical society, and left Burning Lake. Would you come with me? We could downsize together."

She smiled at him. "I thought you wanted me to quit my job and become a lady of leisure."

"You make it sound so boring." He picked up his fork and took a few bites of chicken. "Besides, that's not what I said." He wiped his mouth on a linen napkin. "I don't want you putting yourself in danger like this. I've seen how much flak you've gotten over the past year—all those haters on social media, all the tabloids full of misinformation, that reporter guy who stalked you for an exclusive. I'm bothered by the very public aspects of your career, because I'm a private person, and I don't think it's healthy or safe for you to go on living this way." He went back to eating. He ate with zest. He attacked his *poulet en croûte de sel* and *galettes de pommes de terre,* and if she didn't know any better, she would've thought he was angry at her.

"The truth is, it's a seductive idea, and I'm seriously considering quitting my job."

He wiped his mouth again. "I'm not trying to seduce you away from anything."

"I know," she said gently, because he looked so wounded.

"Do you somehow imagine that life with me is like living with the Kardashians? I work, play, eat, fuck, and sleep. That would make a very boring reality series, pre-Natalie."

"Pre-Natalie?" she repeated. "What about post-Natalie?"

"Private. Not for sale. Not a TV series at all. Just a beautiful reality."

She was disarmed by this. "Sometimes, Hunter . . . just when I think you're full of shit, you prove me wrong."

"Do I?" He smirked. "Good."

The minutes ticked past. The dining room smelled of cherrywood smoke and roasted potatoes. The walls and wide plank floors had been oiled for decades so that they retained every square inch of patina. The room was situated to catch the setting sun, but tonight it was heavily overcast.

Natalie took a bite of bread and stared at the chicken dish on her plate. She was reminded of torn flesh, and her stomach turned sourly. She chewed on the bread and tried to swallow, but her mouth was too dry. She sipped some pinot noir. "You know what," she said, resting her fork on her plate. "I'm not very hungry."

"Are you okay?" he asked with genuine concern. "What can I get you?"

"I need to lie down." She stood up and swayed on her feet.

Hunter stood up. "Come sit in the living room. I'll make you some tea."

"No, I'm okay," she insisted, but he escorted her into the living room and made her sit on the antique Victorian sofa with its overstuffed blue velvet pillows.

"Just relax," he told her before disappearing into the kitchen, where he prepared a cup of tea as if it were a coronation.

Natalie settled against the sofa and sighed.

And then something happened. The world grew fuzzy. There was a blurring of reality, a gradual distancing and diminishment. She looked at her own slender hands, at the dimming away of herself, and was overcome with grief. She sobbed so hard she wondered who was making that awful racket. Her stomach was in free fall. She let the tears flow.

"Natalie, what's wrong?" He came back into the room.

She looked at him and said, "I can't quit my job. Not now."

"I know." He pulled a chair over to the sofa and held her hand. "Do whatever you have to do. I'll support whatever you decide. It's not up to me. It's your decision."

She wiped away her tears. "You should've seen it, Hunter. It was awful. I'll never get that image out of my head."

"Can you blame me for not wanting you to do this anymore?" he asked softly.

She shook her head sadly. "I'm going to catch whoever did this to her."

"That could take years."

"Not years. Months, maybe. We have a few promising leads."

Hunter leaned forward. "Did I ever tell you about this sofa?"

She shook her head numbly.

"It once belonged to Clark Gable. Many years ago, the estate held an auction, and my father—who was a big fan of *It Happened One Night*—flew out to Hollywood and bought this sofa, along with a few other pieces of movie memorabilia." He ran his hand over the velvet cushion as if it were something organic and naked. There was no denying he was a sensual man.

Natalie gazed at him. He had her full attention now.

"My father forbid my brother and me from sitting on this sofa, or going anywhere near it. It was one of his most prized possessions. After our mother died, he became obsessed with owning things. Things were more important to him than people." Hunter slid his hand under the carved wooden skirt of the sofa. "One day, I watched our maid stick a wad of chewing gum . . . right here. Dad was at work, and she was taking a break. She sat on the sofa, where she wasn't supposed to sit, and read a magazine and peeled a stick of chewing gum and popped it in her mouth—another thing my father had forbidden Nesbitt and I from ever indulging in. Magazines and chewing gum.

"Anyway, our maid didn't realize she was being watched. She didn't have a clue that I was looking at her through that window, right over there." He pointed. "And because she didn't know she was being observed, she was completely, one hundred percent herself. I was mesmerized. Here she was, doing all the fun things my brother and I couldn't do. It amazed me that this older woman—she was about thirty at the time, with long red hair she pulled into a tight bun—that she could actually have fun and be herself. I didn't know how to be myself. I was always Gunther Rose's oldest son." He leaned forward and kissed her. He stroked Natalie's damp cheek. "When my father found out that someone had stuck a piece of chewing gum underneath his precious sofa, he blamed Nesbitt. He screamed at him. I was in the room, and I never defended my brother. Because my father would've turned his wrath on me, and I didn't want that. I was selfish. I wanted an easy life. I wanted the kind of life that our maid appeared to be having. I mean, I understood that her choices were limited—that she had to work, that she had to get up every morning at a certain time and do her job, that her life was difficult and not carefree. But I was still envious, because she seemed freer somehow. Free in a way that I've never been. I don't know how else to describe it. She was pissed off, and she expressed her anger. She had a right to be angry, but I don't have that same right. Look at me. I've gotten everything I ever wanted. I have a five-thousand-dollar telescope and a six-car garage. But I was jealous of her, and I still am, in a way. Jealous of that memory. She was funny and cool, and ultimately she could get away with stuff. Chewing gum and reading magazines and leaving little fuck-you messages to her boss. I liked that attitude of hers. I preferred it. So I let my brother take the heat. And I'll never forgive myself for that. Because it was my job to protect him. And that isn't the only time I failed him."

Natalie felt like crying again. She touched his face. "Don't blame yourself."

"I should've protected my brother, and I didn't. But I'm not going to make the same mistake with you, Natalie." His clothes rustled as he leaned forward to kiss her.

He didn't understand how obvious he was in his desire for her. It was written all over his face and embedded in his body language. Some nights, he liked to sit and watch her get drunk. He delighted in her stories and her laughter. He refilled her wineglass and asked her questions about herself, and caught her whenever she was about to tip over like a dizzy child. He watched and waited, sitting on his desire for her. Their lovemaking on those nights was like having a prolonged fever, hallucinatory and thirsty.

She wanted him. She was wildly in love with him. She pushed the guilt aside, chased it away. She shed every last doubt and fear. Lust took over. She shed everything for him until she was totally naked. Vulnerable and hurting. It felt like a dive off a high cliff into a clear dark pool of water. A deep pool. One smooth dreamlike plunge that sliced off the present from the past. Cutting the cord forever.

They ran their hands over each other's body. They couldn't get enough. They ended up in a long, dark hallway with brass sconces barely lighting the way. There was a museum-like quality to the walls with their austere eighteenth-century portraits of thin-lipped men and ruddy-cheeked women. They fucked by the ghostly light of the main staircase. They lay sprawled across the carpeted floor where Hunter's brother, Nesbitt, used to ride his tricycle, and Natalie could see the scuff marks on the walls. So much history inside this house. Just as much as was harbored inside hers.

She wrapped her arms around his neck and clung to him.

Nothing else mattered but this moment. Natalie would ignore all the rest, because she knew that, waiting for her on the other side, there was a crushing burden she could never wish away.

23

That night, Natalie couldn't sleep. It was two A.M., and Hunter was snoring softly beside her. She gently peeled back the covers and snuck out of bed. She put on her robe and slippers and went downstairs, where she grabbed a bottled water from the fridge, plopped down on the living-room sofa, and opened her laptop. She used her iCloud app to import the pictures she'd taken at the park from her mobile phone to her laptop, then scrolled through the digital images of the tree carvings.

Just then, her phone rang, and she checked the number. It was Luke.

"Can't sleep?" he asked.

"My mind's going a mile a minute," she admitted. "You?"

"Not a wink."

She glanced at the clock. "It's two in the morning. You're aware of that, right?"

"Painfully."

She smiled. It was the first time he'd called her in the middle of the night since before the holidays. Usually, she called him, and even though she had a lot she wanted to say, she gave him the space to express himself. "What's up?" she asked.

Luke let out a long sigh. "I'm pissed off. This elusive thing we're chasing. This evil. All we can do is collect little bits and pieces of evidence. A thumbprint on a fender, a cigarette butt in a ditch, a stain on the carpet. It's bullshit."

It soothed her to know she wasn't alone. She needed to hear that sometimes. "My father once said that evil was an anagram for 'vile,'" Natalie told him. "It's also an anagram for 'live' and 'veil.' He said, 'Evil lives behind a vile veil of lies.'"

Luke chuckled softly. "Joey knew how to reduce things to their basics."

Natalie smiled. Her father, Officer Joey Lockhart, had short-cropped salt-and-pepper hair, an angular face, and a calculating gaze. His uniform shirt was crisply pressed beneath his dark blue jacket. Every morning, he meticulously put himself together. Only his smile was sloppy—it revealed his inner kindness and compassion for others less fortunate. His smile betrayed a forgiving nature that all his years of training as a police officer had never erased.

"Listen, I followed another lead tonight," Natalie told Luke. "It might be nothing, but Veronica was interested in the Witching Tree, so I went to the park and took pictures of the tree carvings, and one of them stood out from the others. It was carved more recently—maybe a day or two ago. Three rays of light inside a circle. It was much fresher than the others."

"What kind of symbol is that?"

"An ancient Druid symbol called an Awen, which stands for creative awakening and divine inspiration. Last night there was also a waxing moon, which means she was killed during the maiden phase of the moon, also known as the 'naïve' phase, when the goddess is at the beginning of her journey. The Awen and the waxing moon both represent an awakening, something new and just beginning."

"Do you think the killer is following the lunar phase?"

"I don't know. It could be a coincidence."

"Because it was snowing heavily outside, and whoever did this must've known that the snowstorm would cover their tracks—tire marks and footprints. That would be smart. In any case, I talked to the chief this evening about assigning extra patrol cars to the neighborhoods where members of Veronica's coven live," Luke said tiredly. "He's approved the overtime, and a couple of extra officers will be patrolling the area tonight. They'll be doing that for a couple more weeks, at least."

"Good." She closed her eyes.

"In the meantime, the chief's going to officially meet with the two historical covens in the next couple of days, where he'll offer his assurances and advise everyone to be cautious. Best we can do for now."

A heavy silence followed. Their relationship was full of deep understanding, the kind of solid connection Natalie could feel in her bones. Their silences never bothered her. She drew her knees up to her chest and listened to his steady breathing.

"Luke?" she finally said.

"I'm still here."

"Should I quit the force?"

"That's not for me to say."

"You told me this afternoon that you take my strength for granted. But I don't feel strong. I feel overwhelmed. I feel weak and scared. I'm not sure what I want to do. I'm not sure who I am. All I know is that I'd give my last dying breath for this town, but this job has taken a huge emotional toll. I'll be lucky to leave the department with only emotional scars."

Luke weighed his next words carefully. "I don't blame you for what you're feeling. You've had an amazingly difficult time of it. You may think that your sacrifice and commitment haven't been appreciated. But they are. You're appreciated more than you'll ever know."

"I don't think I can be the detective you want me to be. Maybe it's time for someone with a fresh perspective to step into the job."

"Natalie, this is a crucial decision. There's no turning back."

Tears stung her eyes. "I realize that. Which is why I haven't handed in my letter of resignation yet. Because I also know that if I don't stay and chase down whoever did this to Veronica, then I'll really be lost."

"You know who you are deep down. You simply have a choice to make. And nobody else can do it for you."

Natalie smiled sadly. She would have to be fearless.

24

The following morning, she got up early, took a shower, and got dressed for work, then left Hunter snoring with his face buried in his pillow and went downstairs. Last night, Natalie had brought the heavy box of library books in from her car, and now she pried off the lid and got a big whiff of mildew courtesy of the Dewey decimal system.

One by one, she took out the musty-smelling books—a 1923 leatherbound hardcover on witchcraft with gold embossed lettering on the front, called *Maledictions for Beginners;* a jacketless hardcover printed in 1941 called *The Devil in Burning Lake;* a well-thumbed 1990s paperback full of blackand-white etchings of pagan rituals titled *Ceremonial Magick for Wiccans;* two slender paperbacks from the 1970s called *The 1712 Witch Trials* and *Abby's Hex.* There were a dozen or so softcovers on the history of Burning Lake. And at the bottom of the box, she found a 1995 hardcover entitled *The Witching Tree* by Garwood Padgett. The jacket was illustrated with a dramatic graphic of a twisted, scary-looking tree silhouetted against a bloodred sky. Natalie experienced a déjà vu feeling, a blurry memory she couldn't summon up. She sensed she had seen this book before, but couldn't remember when or where.

Natalie flipped through the pages. It was all about the history and legend of Nettie Goodson. She placed the book in front of her and felt a prickling sensation across her scalp as she flipped to the back cover. The library loan card was missing from the pocket. Under the old-fashioned system, library loan cards used to contain the names and dates of every single patron who checked a book out of the library. At some point in the past decade or so, the Burning Lake Public Library had switched to an automated checkout system using barcodes for digital record-keeping—swipe and go. Sort of like pumping your own gas. You got a paper receipt, which most people used as a bookmark.

Natalie checked all the books, flipping through the pages, but couldn't find a single library receipt. Perhaps Veronica had kept them tucked inside her wallet or stashed away in her desk. A bookmark or two would've been helpful to indicate how far she had gone in her reading. There were no bookmarks in this stack of library books, no folded-over pages, no hastily scribbled notes or yellow stickies. Just a box of old books. It was odd. Something was missing from this picture.

Natalie checked her watch. She didn't want to be late for her appointment with Jules. She put everything back in the box, grabbed her keys, and left.

When she got to Pioneer Memorial Park, Natalie took the winding pathway past the eighteenth-century tombstones and mausoleums, a thin layer of compacted snow crunching underfoot. The old headstones had historic family names chiseled into them—Pastor, Goodson, Bell, Buckner, Grimsby, Clemmons. You could sense the mossy history of the graveyard in the chipped stone markers. Everything was cracked and falling to ruin. Grace had always feared cemeteries, whereas Natalie took comfort in them somehow. It was nice to have a place where your loved ones could come and remember you. Where they could add up their losses. Now she paused to read a carefully crafted epitaph carved into granite: LOVE IS ENOUGH.

Jules Pastor stepped out of the shadows just then, startling her out of her reverie. Thin and pale, this one-hundred-and-sixty-pound man had a sly instinct for self-preservation. "Did you know that I was a local baseball hero in high school?" he said.

Natalie shook her head. It was hard to believe—his flesh was crisscrossed with tats and tracks, and his face had been ravaged by narcotics.

"Back in the good old days, ho hum," he said. "Now I'm a shit magnet."

He rested his hand on a limestone angel. In his mid-twenties, he had a surprisingly deep voice for such a young guy. He was distantly related to Jeremiah Pastor, the town elder who'd famously sentenced Abigail Stuart to death. A few years ago, Jules had gotten caught for dealing pot, and as a consequence had been turned by detectives Jacob Smith and Brandon Buckner into a confidential informant for the Burning Lake PD. He was their bitch. Their CI. She felt sorry for him.

"We all have those roads not taken," she said.

"Oh yeah? What was the fork in your road, Detective?"

She smiled at him, unwilling to tell him about the fork in the road she was facing. "What've you got for me, Jules?"

"The Hosts were definitely into witchcraft. They sacrificed a few squirrels and shit like that. Word on the street, they left town last month and nobody's heard from them since. Not a peep. They came here from Utica, but their address is bogus and their phones have stopped working." He studied her with his overbright eyes. "You know Holly's from Burning Lake originally, don't you? I sort of knew her."

"You did?"

"We saw each other around town, but then she went away to college and moved to Utica and got married to this guy, Edward. Anyway, we reconnected at a party last Fourth of July. We got wasted together. We had a good time reminiscing about the good ole days or whatever. Then she started acting a little weird . . ."

"Weird how?"

"Moody. Paranoid. She told me her ex had followed her from Utica."

Natalie frowned. "Edward?"

"Turns out they were separated, but he couldn't let go. They'd been together for three years and split after he lost his job in June. He was an auto mechanic or something. She was going to file for divorce. Anyway, he dogged her from place to place, and they finally got back together in August and rented out Grimsby's cottage." Jules glanced guardedly around the graveyard. "They joined NA and met a few people, then they started holding séances at their place. I was at this party once when someone found a dead raccoon in the woods, and Edward decided to use it in a ritual. Things escalated from there. Anyway, I told them how dangerous it was to mess around with the occult, but nobody listened."

"You tried talking them out of it?"

"Yeah, animal sacrifices, that's some evil shit. Anyway, they stopped going to their meetings. They stopped paying their rent. They were running out of money. So they figured that by getting into witchcraft, it could help them somehow. I tried talking some sense into them, Holly in particular," he explained. "Here she is, this smart, beautiful woman, getting into something she knows nothing about, hoping her life will somehow magically get better. Just by wishing it was true. Pixie dust and bullshit. I told her it didn't work that way. That didn't go over so well. They kicked me out."

"They didn't want to hear it?"

"No. Look, I know all the local practitioners. Wiccans do not worship the devil. And they'd never kill or mutilate an animal. According to the Wiccan creed, 'If it harms none, then do what you will.' My aunt was a Wiccan priestess, and I'm telling you, these folks are *not* into harming any living creatures. That isn't what their religion is about. But a lot of these self-proclaimed, pseudo, so-called witches out there these days don't do their homework. They disobey the rules and start coloring outside the lines. Anyway, Holly and Edward just up and left the cottage in late January and haven't been back since. Nobody's seen or heard from them." He tipped his head. "Is this about Veronica Manes? That cottage is pretty close to where she got hit by the train."

"We're not sure. That's why we need you to keep digging for us."

"Yeah, sure." He nodded congenially enough. "But if you're looking for a suspect, Edward Host is a walking billboard for angry weirdo paranoia syndrome. I'm almost positive he's got an arrest record."

"Yeah, we're looking into that."

"The guy's a true cunt. He harbors grudges. Rumor has it he attacked a buddy in Utica with a samurai sword. He fires at people with an air gun. He brags about blowing up a cow."

"Sounds charming."

"Sheesh, right?" Jules let out an ironic chuckle.

"Did they own any pets? A dog or a cat? The Hosts?"

"Ha, no. That poor thing would've been dead from starvation and neglect. Or else it might've disappeared, you know . . . as one of their sacrifices."

"Did they ever talk about the phases of the moon?"

"Maybe. I dunno." He shook his head slightly.

"Did they visit the Witching Tree?"

"Not that I know of. Why?"

"Somebody left a fresh carving in one of the Witch Trees. An Awen."

He shrugged. "I could ask around."

"That would be helpful."

"Detective, I can sense you're a skeptic, but you should arm yourself if you're going to continue dealing with this shit."

"Arm myself?" she repeated blankly.

He dug his fingers into his coat collar and pulled out a ceramic pendant on a cheap chain with a large red eye painted on it. "Evil is real. This is protection. It's an anti-curse charm. I got it on eBay. I wear it around my neck at all times to ward off the evil eye, because you never know. This one's specifically designed to block any curses that can cause bad luck or injury. When it comes to curses, it's best not to take any chances. Just think of a counter-curse as a security system, like those signs on the lawn that say—this property is alarmed by So-and-So Security, right? That's what it's for." He tucked the pendant back under his coat collar. "In the meantime, I'll ask around and get back to you." He slipped into the shadows and was gone.

25

Natalie spotted Luke's Ford Ranger parked in Veronica Manes's driveway. The house was a handsome two-story colonial built in 1698 by Thomas Bell, who'd sat in judgment of Victoriana Forsyth during the 1712 witch trials. Judge Bell had raised his six children here, and one of his daughters married Minister William T. Manes. It was only fitting that their great-great-great-great-great-granddaughter had become a witch, taking history full circle.

There were a couple of unmarked cars and police cruisers parked on either side of the road. Natalie got out and took the shoveled walkway across the front yard, past a grove of snow-covered spruce trees. The house with its vine-softened walls and spidery wrought iron gate had a spectral aura about it. She could feel herself tensing up as she rang the doorbell.

Officer Andrew Marconi answered. He was six-three and by the book. They had just seen each other last night, but he wasn't into chitchat. "Detective."

She nodded crisply. "Hi, Andy. I'm here to see the lieutenant."

"He's upstairs."

She stomped the mud off her boots and followed him into the oak-paneled hallway. There were orange evidence cards everywhere, preserving two sets of muddy boot prints that crisscrossed the hardwood floor. The mud had dried and crumbled. She could make out a partial boot print or two, but no full ones. Through an arched doorway to her right was the living room—white walls covered with framed photographs, antique upholstered chairs, and capricious side tables. The corner office had been ransacked. The desk had been rummaged through, the bookcase had been overturned, the filing cabinet drawers were open, and there were books and paperwork scattered across the floor. On the other side of the hallway was an antiquated parlor that appeared to be relatively untrammeled. Straight ahead was the sun-filled kitchen where—five months ago—Veronica had made Natalie a cup of tea. They'd spoken about Morgan Chambers, a lost soul and one of the Violinist's victims. Veronica had been extremely forthcoming and helpful, and Natalie had left with a good impression of her.

There were other voices inside the house now. Lenny and Augie were working their way through the first floor—photographing, fingerprinting, spraying the walls and furniture with luminol, vacuuming for trace. Luke didn't want them to leave a single stone unturned, and so they were using extra care. She noticed that the front door, hallway walls, and staircase banister were coated in red-and-black print powder.

"He's upstairs, the last door at the end," Officer Marconi told her before returning to his post.

Careful not to touch anything, Natalie took the creaking staircase to the second story, where she could hear Luke's voice drifting down the colonial hallway. He was on the phone. She slipped on a pair of latex gloves and continued walking toward the end of the hall where the victim's bedroom door was open.

She paused in the doorway and gave the room a quick look around. Half the room was in disarray. The bureau drawers had been pulled out and overturned, leaving a messy pile of clothing on the floor. Family pictures had been knocked off the bureau top along with discount beauty products. The closet had been rummaged through. Perhaps they were looking for a safe, or maybe something small that a person would tuck inside their underwear drawer. But Lenny had told her no jewelry or other valuables were missing.

It was odd, because not everything had been overturned. A glass of water sat untouched on the nightstand. There was a rocking chair over by the window next to a side table and lamp. The side table held an undisturbed clock and a stack of magazines. It looked as if someone had slept in the four-poster bed. The covers were peeled back and pushed aside. A pair of slippers were on the floor. The old-fashioned radiator hissed steam into the stuffy room.

Luke put away his phone and stood gazing out the window at the snowy backyard. "Veronica's sister is on her way from Pennsylvania," he said. "I didn't know what to tell her. We don't know anything yet. The place was obviously ransacked, but there are no signs of forced entry. Both doors were locked. No scratch marks around the keyholes. The windows were locked from inside, with the blinds and curtains drawn for the night. Her jewelry's still here, as far as we can tell. There's money in her wallet. Credit cards. Audio equipment downstairs. A few valuable-looking antiques. Nothing else was taken. Just the computer, the hard drives, a tablet, and her mobile phone. Maybe some flash drives and paperwork, we can't be sure."

"Which means they were looking for information, rather than material goods. Something she was writing about or researching?"

"I don't know." He turned to look at her, and it startled her how vivid blue his eyes were from the sunlight coming in through the windows. "It's frustrating as hell. We have very few leads."

"What about phone records?" Natalie asked.

"She had no calls last night."

"Nothing incoming or outgoing?"

He shook his head. "She did leave the house, though. Lenny was able to track the location of her cell phone to the general vicinity of the northern quadrant of town that includes the McKinley Forest and Mountain Laurel Road, but there the signal stops."

"Well, that's where the cabin is. That's where Edward and Holly Host used to live. It's where Jerry Duckworth and Tabitha Vaughn and Aimee Dreyer live."

"Why would she go anywhere with any of them in the middle of the night?"

"She'd go with Tabitha Vaughn. Not Jerry Duckworth, and Aimee doesn't know her well. Maybe the Hosts kidnapped her? According to Jules, they were out of money and out of luck. Edward Host sounds like a very troubled guy. Jules said he and Holly were practicing occult rituals and dark magic in the delusional belief that it might somehow turn their lives around. Maybe they wanted Veronica to help them out?"

"And then what? When she wouldn't cooperate, or something went hinky, they killed her? In that manner? That took some planning." He shook his head. "First officers to arrive at the house didn't smell any gunpowder. We haven't found any bullet holes, cartridge casings, bloodstains, knives, or any other weapons at the scene. The place was tossed, but there are no signs of a struggle. No blood spatter, scuff marks, ripped clothing, or bloody hand-prints. Under the costume, Veronica wore her own clothes—jeans, T-shirt, boots. If they abducted her, she'd be bootless, right? She wouldn't have taken her keys and cell phone with her. The landline cord wasn't yanked out of its socket. The bed looks slept in. The water glass is upright. Her slippers are neatly placed on the floor. She hung her bathrobe up on the back of the closet door. Her winter coat appears to be missing. It looks as if she got dressed voluntarily, grabbed her keys and phone, and went with somebody in the middle of the night. Most of the furniture downstairs remains upright. The ransacking was confined mostly to her desk, her computers, books, paper-work, and the like. The ransacking in her bedroom looks methodical, but nothing of value was taken. That doesn't make any sense."

"What about her social media accounts?"

He shook his head. "She didn't have any, just a website that hasn't been updated in months. In the meantime, Lenny's checking with her inter-net service to see if we can gain access to her online accounts—banking, phone plan, medical, online vendors. We'll have to wait and see what he comes up with."

Natalie knew enough not to look too directly at Luke, since doing so might violate some hidden contract between them. But occasionally, against her will, their eyes would meet for a lingering moment, reminding them both who they really were. She didn't like the anxiety in his voice. It reminded her of her own growing frustration.

"Everything had been put away for the night," he went on. "The dishes were neatly stacked in the dishwasher, the leftovers are in the fridge, the laundry's in the dryer. There's a place setting for one at the kitchen table. The coffee was set to the morning timer. The outside lights were on, including the porch light. The interior lights were all turned off, except for the front hallway."

"She wouldn't leave the outside lights on if she was going to sleep, would she? Those are pretty bright, they might keep her awake. Leaving the outside lights on and no inside lights except for the front hallway is something a homeowner would do if she left her house voluntarily in the middle of the night. Indicating it was someone she knew, and not a stranger."

Luke nodded. "Any word on the whereabouts of the Hosts?"

She shook her head. "No one has been in contact with them, according to Jules, and the address they gave the NA organizers was fake. He's going to keep digging."

Luke nodded. "Mike's investigating Edward Host's background for arrests and police reports. We've got an APB out for them, and I've spoken to the Utica PD. We're looking statewide. What else did Jules say?"

"The Hosts don't have any pets, but those roadkill animal sacrifices, or whatever they are, might link us to the brown animal hair trace that Lenny found."

"I'll ask him about it. Jesus. That would be pretty definitive." Luke rubbed the bridge of his nose with his thumb and index finger, leaving two red spots. "Anything else?"

"Well," she said, "Reverend Grimsby denied having an affair with Veronica. He said they were just friends. He admitted there's been some tension between the Wiccans and churchgoers, but nothing so bad that it would drive someone to homicide. That's his opinion, anyway."

"What about the cross around her neck?"

"I've been thinking, it could be a form of misdirection," Natalie said. "I mean, this homicide was so outrageous. Maybe it was staged to look like a ritualistic killing over religious differences, in order to deflect from the killing itself. Maybe whoever did this wants the police to focus on the churchgoers and the Wiccans. Maybe we're looking in the wrong direction? Maybe the robbery was the whole point?"

He studied her face. "I find that hard to swallow, don't you? You said yourself that such a brutal type of murder is usually personal, intended to punish and humiliate."

"Right." She nodded. "Maybe it's all of those things?"

"You'll have to convince me of that. Because so far, none of the pieces fit."

She ticked through the facts they knew so far. "This was a carefully planned murder, premeditated, and it was meant to humiliate and punish the victim, while at the same time . . . the house was ransacked in a professional, methodical way. They were after something specific, something on her computer hard drive or her phone, something written down, perhaps in a journal or a diary or some sort of paperwork, maybe copied onto a flash drive. Something related to her new book?"

"So you're suggesting that she stumbled across something her killer wanted to keep hidden. Meaning she overstepped a boundary." He looked at her with concern. "Let me see that tree carving you mentioned."

"The Awen?" Natalie handed him her phone, and he swiped through the images she'd taken in Blackthorn Park—occult symbols, initials, hearts, dates—then stopped when he came to the Druid symbol. An Awen—three rays of light inside a circle.

"Looks a lot fresher than the others, for sure."

"We need to find out how fresh," she said. "I know a couple of people who've studied the Witch Trees over the years. The town historian for one. He might have a connection to an expert in tree carvings. Somebody who can tell us exactly how recently that Awen was carved into the tree."

Luke handed back her phone. "Okay. But even if whoever killed Veronica also carved an Awen into the tree—so what? Where does that lead us?"

"It symbolizes a creative awakening. The beginning of something. Perhaps the beginning of creative destruction . . ." Her phone buzzed. It was Max Callahan texting her. "Sorry. I'd better take this. I forgot about this appointment."

"Natalie," Luke told her firmly, "there are other detectives involved in the case. You don't have to do everything yourself. I'll have Mike find us an expert in tree carvings, and Brandon can pursue the information from Jules. Go take your meeting. Don't burn yourself out. And if you come to a decision, call me. Anytime. I'm here for you."

26

N atalie drove back to the place where she'd grown up on Wildwood
Road, the sunny, drafty hundred-year-old farmhouse she'd inherited
from her parents. Max Callahan was waiting for her in his father's company truck, Callahan & Son.

"Sorry I'm late," she said as they went inside.

"Not a problem," Max said cheerfully, breezing into the house and taking
a seat on the living-room sofa. The early-afternoon sunlight slanted down
through the windows, highlighting his optimistic, laissez-faire presence.

"Want some coffee?" she asked, peeling off her coat.

"No thanks, I'm trying to quit. Although it isn't working, obviously. I've
had three cups already. Hey, I'm surprised you didn't cancel our meeting,
Natalie. With such grim news and all."

"Sorry, I should've called, Max. We'll have to cut this short."

"No worries." He had aged a bit since their high school days—a paunch
over his belt buckle, gray hair, crow's-feet around the eyes—but he was the
same old Max she'd known since they were kids. Jovial, inquisitive, and
comfortable anywhere. He'd repaired her leaky roof last summer and was

currently helping her renovate her house to be put on the market soon— maybe. She wasn't sure. "Hey, there's a rumor going around town that Veronica Manes was chained to the tracks by a group of Satanists," Max said. "Some type of devil-worshipping cult. Is that true?"

Natalie sagged a little. Where there were rumors, the media wouldn't be too far behind. "I can't talk about it, Max. We're in the middle of the investigation."

"Yeah, but is it true?" His smile contained an unguarded sweetness. "Jesus, Natalie, your silence speaks volumes right now. Was she really *chained* to the train tracks? Are you serious?"

"Like I said . . ."

"Nuff said." He made an absentminded gesture with his hand. "Okay, let's get down to business. I've run the numbers, and if you're going to renovate the place yourself, then you need to focus on the big picture, starting with curb appeal. I can recommend a landscaper who'll do it for cheap. Fortunately, your front door's in good condition, so it just needs a coat of paint and a brass knocker."

"Okay, well, that's not so bad."

"Nope." Max wet his thumb and turned the coffee-stained page of his notebook. "Switching to the interior, I'd recommend we paint everything white. No colors. Those awesome sky-blue or salmon color schemes you might like will lower any offers, since most people are finicky and will want to repaint. On the other hand, too much white can overpower a space, so I'd recommend we go with different shades of white on the walls, ceiling, and trim—cream, marble, ivory, porcelain, gray. The contrast—subtle as it is—will open up the place. We can put in some pinpoint lighting to give it a sophisticated look. Rearrange the furniture, add some plants. All that plus an overall decluttering will do a lot to boost the price."

"What if I don't want to sell?" she asked. "Maybe just fix it up a little?"

He frowned thoughtfully, then brushed the air with his hand. "That's a whole other kettle of worms. On a low budget, you can DIY your interior with a repaint and a plaster. You can replace the kitchen cabinets and storage space using recycled materials. Put in new windows to make sure you're getting enough light into the house. Maybe a basement reno to provide more living space."

She glanced around the old-fashioned living room. She'd taken a stab at renovating a couple of years ago, sanding and repainting the walls herself, but the end results had been pretty awful—the hallway was yellow, the living room was beige, the kitchen was supposed to be pale blue but looked London fog gray. She'd donated some of her parents' ugly-ass furniture to Goodwill and had moved the rest of their belongings up to the attic, piles of boxes and scarred sticks of furniture that she couldn't bear to part with. If she proceeded with her plan to put the house on the market, she would have to get rid of everything.

At first it had been liberating—thinking about renovating the place. She imagined stripping off the ugly wallpaper, maybe knocking down a few walls. She badly wanted to flip this house. But unless she bought another property, the only place to go would be to Hunter's mansion. And that was quite a commitment. She wasn't even sure Hunter wanted her to move in with him, although he'd mentioned it once or twice when they were both pleasantly drunk and basking in pheromones. Natalie figured that didn't count.

"Sounds like you're undecided."

"I am," she admitted.

"That's fine." Max stood up. "Let me know when you've made up your mind."

"Thanks, Max." She escorted him to the door. "Hey, listen, you don't happen to know anything about tree carvings, do you?"

"Nope. Why?"

She smiled. "You seem to be an expert on lots of things involving wood."

He laughed. "Not really. I mean, I know building construction and stuff. Why?"

"Don't worry about it."

"You look tired, kiddo."

She crossed her arms and smiled. "I am, a little."

"You aren't going to move in with Hunter Rose, then?" he asked bluntly.

"Haven't decided," she told him. "My life is kind of up in the air."

"What happened? The bastard doesn't know a great thing when he sees it?"

"Stop. You're making me blush."

"Yeah, well." He looked around. He rapped on the hallway wall with his knuckles. "This one's solid. Built to last. She has good bones. You could do worse."

"Thanks, Max."

"See you later, Natalie. And stay safe."

She closed the door, then went into the kitchen and grabbed a Pop-Tart for lunch. Joey and Deborah Lockhart had had an old-fashioned marriage with clearly defined boundaries and a cemented sense of duty. Just like the furniture in this house that wasn't pretty but lasted forever. Her father was a beat officer, and her mother was a housewife, always doing laundry or shopping or housework, and three times a day, seven days a week, Deborah bought, planned, and cooked meals for four hungry mouths. To make life simpler, she'd assigned each girl a color: Willow was pink, Grace was purple, and Natalie was blue, like her father's uniform. They all had plastic dishware in their own color, socks and pajamas in their color, headbands and sweaters. Even the walls of their bedrooms were painted pink, purple, and blue. Willow wanted to be a ballerina, Grace a writer, and Natalie an artist, since she'd shown talent for it early on. When Natalie eventually chose Joey's dangerous profession over Deborah's own preferences, they'd stopped talking for weeks.

Regardless of her decision, the old house needed a lot of work. The gray paint was peeling off the siding, and you couldn't tell what color it had once been—white or green or yellow—who knew? The windows were drafty and the frames were warped. She needed to replace them with updated energy-efficient windows. The house bled heat. She couldn't stand the thought of going through another winter hopping from electric heater to the stove, crouching over inefficient heating vents and warming her hands on the toaster, for fuck's sake.

Deep down, Natalie wondered if she'd ever leave Wildwood Road. This modest plot of land was fairly isolated, bordered on three sides by thick woods. The house contained countless little mysteries and memories. The sun slanted down hard in the morning, finding the kitchen's cubbyholes full of knickknacks her mother had collected over the years. Out back, just beyond the overgrown garden, was the pet cemetery for the girls' deceased goldfish, hamsters, and guinea pigs. In the winter, Grace, Willow, and Natalie used to make snow angels and snow forts, and one of her first memories of Luke was of him teaching her how to keep her bare hands warm in the winter, just in case she forgot her mittens at home, by folding her thumbs under her other fingers. Natalie cherished these memories and couldn't imagine a life without them.

Once, she'd had a dream about tearing it all down, like a haunted house, except that afterward, in her dream, the grounds were haunted. Natalie's childhood home felt like a haunting companion. Sometimes she could sense it stunting her growth, pulling her back, weighing her down. She occasionally felt punished by it. She knew she would never be free of her demons until she could walk out and shut the door behind her. Being with Hunter provided her with a distinct alternative to this interim place of being stuck between worlds.

This place was a touchstone. It was important to her. It contained all her secrets, all her failures and successes, and she knew that if she didn't let it go, then one of these days, it would swallow her up like the rest of her family. However, if she went ahead and sold it, then Natalie would lose a vital connection to her roots and her past that could never be replaced.

After Max had driven away, Natalie settled on the sofa and looked at the pictures she'd downloaded to her laptop earlier that morning. She studied the images of the tree carvings one by one, finally stopping at a digital photo of a carved heart with two names inside: *Dottie C. & Tommy G.*

The only Dottie C. Natalie knew of was Dottie Coffman, Grace's eighth grade teacher, the one who'd inspired Grace to teach biology. Back in the 1990s, Mrs. Coffman was a slender, dark-haired fortysomething woman who wore tailored pants and jackets. She was a sharp-witted teacher who quoted nineteenth-century poets and twentieth-century philosophers. Grace had always raved about her.

When it came time for Natalie to have Mrs. Coffman for English, all she did was talk about what a terrific student Grace had been. How smart and talented she was. It had irked Natalie, constantly being compared with her older sister like that.

Natalie also recalled that her best friend, Bella Striver, was infatuated with Mrs. Coffman. She was always referencing Mrs. C., but Natalie never liked her. She was too friendly, too interested in their lives. A snoop.

Back in high school, the popular girls would snicker at Natalie's hand-me-downs, so she hid behind her shades and ill-fitting clothes until she was able to find her own tribe—a small group of "gifted" kids who excelled academically and rebelled against their parents' hopes and dreams by listening to Nine Inch Nails and dying their hair funny colors. They prided themselves on standing up for the underdog. Their weapons of choice were snark and derision. They called themselves the Brilliant Misfits—an exclusive group that included Natalie, Bella Striver, Bobby Deckhart, Adam Fontaine, and Max Callahan. They were five smart, gifted kids who felt like total losers, but their club made them feel like superheroes.

Adam eventually died of a drug overdose. Bobby was married now, working as an accountant in Syracuse. Max worked for his dad, and Bella Striver had disappeared on the night of their high school graduation, never to be seen or heard from again. It had shocked the whole town.

Bella used to play the violin, and her biggest dream was to become a famous musician and travel around the world. All hell broke loose twelve years ago when she disappeared on the night of their high school graduation. Natalie's father, Joey, was involved in the extensive search for the missing girl, and at one point Mr. Striver himself came under suspicion. But the prime suspect was Nesbitt Rose, Hunter's younger brother, who'd had cognitive problems since birth and was allegedly the last person to see Bella alive.

Hounded by the media, with the town in an uproar—three weeks after Bella's disappearance, on a drizzly rainy night—Nesbitt sucked on the nozzle of a vacuum cleaner and put an end to his misery. It broke Hunter's heart, and he'd never gotten over the loss. He was supposed to protect Nesbitt, and somehow he had failed him.

Three months later, Bella's father started to receive letters from his missing daughter containing Polaroid pictures that "proved" she was still very much alive. She was fine, she wrote him. She just had to get away and become her own person. Natalie also received a few letters from Bella, explaining why she ran away. Mostly she blamed it on her ambitious, overbearing father. She said that since she could never measure up to his demands for perfection, she no longer wanted to be a violin soloist. As a consequence, the police labeled her a runaway, and the missing persons case was closed.

Eventually, the notes and snapshots from Bella stopped arriving, and no one ever heard from her again. Natalie still missed her. There was a hole in her life where Bella belonged. And even though the police had closed the case, it remained an enduring mystery for Natalie and Max, who were part of the close-knit group that had once believed it could conquer the whole world.

Back in the eleventh grade, carrying her scuffed and battered violin case with her wherever she went, Bella would linger after class to talk to Mrs. Coffman, while Natalie waited impatiently outside. She could hear Bella's musical laughter—more jazz than classical. And afterward, Natalie would ask her what they talked about, and Bella would say, "Mrs. C. thinks this," or "Mrs. C. says that," and now Natalie remembered that Mrs. C. was something of an expert on witchcraft, and that she'd encouraged Bella to form a coven. And in fact, Natalie and Bella had briefly formed a coven of their own that year.

Now Natalie turned her attention to the other name inside the carved heart. Who was Tommy G.? Could it be Thomas Grimsby? Hard to believe, although they were around the same age. Mrs. Coffman had retired from teaching years ago and lost her edge. She was in an assisted-living facility now, Natalie vaguely recalled.

She decided to go upstairs into the attic and look through Grace's belongings in the hopes of finding something that might connect Grace to Mrs. C. Before Natalie's niece, Ellie, had moved to Manhattan to live with her father, she and Natalie had gone through Grace's belongings and divvied everything up. Burke Guzman, Grace's ex-husband, didn't want to pay for storage, so Natalie agreed to take all Grace's childhood toys and books and things she'd had since she was a baby, and Ellie took Grace's jewelry, her photo albums, a sheath of handwritten poems, and a few items of clothing. Natalie promised to store the rest in her attic until Ellie was ready to decide what to do with it.

Now Natalie climbed the narrow stairs and flicked on the overhead bulb. It was freezing cold up here—no insulation. She'd have to add that to her reno list. She stood at the top of the narrow stairs, already overwhelmed. There was way too much stuff up here—trunks full of clothes, stacks of old photo albums, outdated CDs, well-loved dolls, corroded kitchen appliances, furniture that was more nostalgic than useful. Tucked underneath the rafters were too many storage boxes to count, shoved away and forgotten about. Fortunately, most had been labeled and dated in her mother's careful handwriting.

Natalie found a dozen of Grace's high school–age boxes and pulled them out. They were full of old yearbooks, scrapbooks, sweaters and scarves, tangled clumps of costume jewelry, dolls, and books. In one box, she found a paperback on spell-casting and vaguely recalled that Mrs. Coffman had given it to Grace, but there was no inscription inside. It wasn't much to go on.

Nothing but an uneasy feeling.

As she was stuffing everything back into the last box, Natalie found her old St. Jude's medallion on its long silver chain, the one Joey had given her on her eighth birthday. She thought she'd lost it. What was it doing in Grace's stuff?

She studied the silver pendant. St. Jude was the patron saint of lost causes. Joey used to call her a lost cause, but he meant it in the very best way—he meant that she was stubborn and headstrong, like her dad. That she never gave up. He was proud of her achievements, but even prouder that she relied on her conscience.

As the years passed, Officer Joey Lockhart became circumspect about his occupation. After a lifetime of encouraging his youngest daughter to follow in his footsteps, Joey changed his tune. Shortly before Natalie graduated from the police academy, her father suddenly pleaded with her not to go into law enforcement. It was dangerous, he said. There were too many things that could go wrong. He didn't want her risking her life for a paycheck and a pension.

"Dad, it's okay," she told him. "I have your St. Jude's medallion to protect me."

"But that's not real, kid."

Her fingers closed around the medallion, and she told him, "Of course it's not real. But everything you've drummed into my head all those years . . . *that's* going to protect me," she said. "You're my St. Jude's medallion, Dad."

Now, remembering Jules's warning about curses and counter-curses, she looped the medallion on its long silver chain around her neck. It wasn't so much that she believed in counter-curses as she believed in her father's love.

Joey liked to share stories about his adventures with his wife and children, but there were some things he couldn't reveal. Secrets. One night, when Natalie was ten, she found him shredding documents in his den. He glanced up, pale and drawn, and told her to go back upstairs. He shut the door quietly, and Natalie could hear him continuing to shred the paperwork behind the closed door.

This memory triggered other memories. Natalie felt a prickling sensation across her scalp. Around the same time, when she was ten or eleven years old, she remembered seeing a hardcover book on her father's desk with a striking cover—she recalled staring at the distinctive cover and asking him about the book, before Joey quickly shooed her out of his office. It was the same book she'd found in Veronica's box of library books—*The Witching Tree* by Garwood Padgett. A gnarled ancient tree with wind-twisted branches against a bloodred sky. Déjà vu. That's where she'd seen it before.

What this all meant, she didn't have a clue.

But her instincts were telling her to find Tommy G.

27

The church's lacy wrought iron door opened with a cranky whine. St. Paul's felt immense inside, with cold sweeps of wind echoing through the rafters. Early-afternoon sunlight shone through the tall stained glass windows, casting rainbow prisms on the far walls and pews.

Natalie found Reverend Grimsby downstairs in the basement, which was both festive and melancholy, as if you'd arrived too late at the party and everyone else had gone home. There were banners and colorful posters encouraging sobriety, a table with a coffee machine, Styrofoam cups, and plenty of sugar packets. There was a large half-empty box of donuts sitting open like a yawn. Only the lemon cream and powdered sugars were left.

"Detective Lockhart, we've got to stop meeting like this," the reverend joked. He had a strong, dry handclasp. "Have a donut and cup of coffee. You just missed our weekly A A meeting. Oops, watch your step." There was a mop bucket on the floor, and little puddles of melted snow around a grouping of winter boots. "Another lawsuit waiting to happen. Sorry about that. Hold on." Reverend Grimsby took out his phone. "Justin? You left a mop and bucket downstairs, could you come get it, please? Thanks."

He hung up. "Let's go upstairs to my office where we can have some privacy."

They passed Justin Fowler on the stairs. Natalie and Reverend Grimsby were going up, and Justin was going down. He looked more gaunt than he had the night before, and he eyed Natalie warily. There was a wad of chewing gum tucked into a corner of his mouth. "Excuse me," he said politely. "After you."

She didn't know what to say, so she said, "Thanks."

"Sorry about last night," he added.

"That's okay."

It was an awkward moment.

Upstairs, Natalie and Reverend Grimsby stepped into his cluttered office, and he closed the door behind them. He sat down and clasped his hands together. His eyes contained a vacuum-sealed quality that told you he would never reveal any of the many secrets he knew. "How can I help you, Detective?"

"Well, your name is Thomas, but did you ever go by Tommy?"

"A long time ago, when I was a kid. Why?"

She took out her phone and showed him pictures of the tree carving—the one that read *Dottie C. & Tommy G.* "Are those your and Dottie Coffman's initials?"

He drew back, startled. "Why, yes. My goodness. We were in a religious club back in junior high. My gosh. Dottie's the one who did that . . . carved our initials into the tree."

"A religious club?" she repeated. "But I found these initials carved into one of the Witch Trees."

"Oh, I see what you're saying. Right. We were in our early teens. Dottie rebelled and went through an occult phase, like pretty much everyone else in this town. Am I right? Anyway, I didn't know about the tree carving at the time. She only showed it to me after the fact, and it ticked me off. Had I known beforehand, I would've stopped her."

"So you didn't go through an occult phase as well?"

"Me?" He shook his head and laughed self-consciously. "Goodness, no."

"I hear she's in an assisted-living facility now. Have you seen her?"

"Not in ages." He sat back. "Like I said, we were good friends in junior high before we sort of drifted apart. After high school, we headed off for college and went our separate ways. She got married, came back, and started teaching. I devoted my life to God. We both care about this community. It's hard to leave Burning Lake."

Natalie nodded sympathetically. "So you drifted apart in high school? Did her interest in witchcraft have anything to do with that?"

He glanced at her curiously. "Well, we all do foolish things in our youth, like I said. I can see the appeal in it for young people."

"But Dottie maintained her interest in the occult," Natalie persisted.

"Yes, she did. For her, it was all about female empowerment."

"Were you ever in a coven together?"

He gave her a patient smile. "Now you're drilling down. No, I certainly wasn't. Dottie joined a coven when she was fifteen or sixteen, but I don't know anything about it," he admitted. "She was fourteen when she carved our initials into that tree, if I remember correctly. We broke up not long afterwards. Needless to say, I wasn't happy about it."

"As a teacher, Mrs. Coffman influenced Grace and her friends to form a coven. And I remember her talking quite a bit to my friend Bella, too, before we formed our own coven."

He studied her as if he were trying to read her mind. "She did? I wouldn't know about that."

"So the two of you really did drift apart?"

"Yes. Sadly. I liked Dottie. And I try to be open-minded. As you know, Detective, those who follow Wicca are as dedicated to their religious beliefs as most of the Christians I know. That's what Veronica and I were attempting to do—build a bridge between both communities. Showcase the similarities."

Natalie nodded and put away her phone. "Are most of your parishioners that open-minded, Reverend?"

He rubbed his chin thoughtfully. "We have a lot of pious people in our church, worshippers who are staunchly opposed to pagan religions like Wicca, but they wouldn't dream of harming anyone. If that's what you're getting at."

"Your parishioners confide in you."

"Yes, they do. All I can tell you is . . . I have no idea what kind of person could've done something like that. Veronica was beloved in this community. It's beyond my comprehension."

"So . . . no hints? Any gossip or rumors of discord when it came to Veronica—besides Wayne and Justin last night? Anything at all?"

"Nothing from my parishioners. You'd be surprised how tolerant most of them are. We live side by side here in Burning Lake. As a matter of fact, Veronica's sister called me this afternoon. As a Christian, she doesn't relate in any way to Wicca, but she's honoring her sister's wishes by holding a joint Christian-Wiccan remembrance ceremony before the funeral. Veronica had requested such a ceremony in her will, for her family's benefit, along with a separate, more private Wiccan funeral. I put her sister in touch with Tabitha Vaughn. They'll be organizing the memorial gathering on Abby's Hex, where Wiccans will preside, but where I'll also be present, along with anyone else who wants to honor Veronica's memory. The tentative date is March twelfth. I hope you'll be there."

"Of course."

"Meanwhile, some of my parishioners have started a prayer chain for her, by email or by phone. Can I add you to the list, Detective?"

She hesitated for a moment. "Sure. That's very thoughtful."

"Wonderful."

Natalie supposed her reluctance to associate with prayer on a personal level had occurred when she was ten years old and in desperate need of comfort after Willow died. Where had Willow gone? Lovely Willow? Her mysterious, wonderful big sister? Gone.

After Willow's body was discovered by the police, Natalie's father turned to stone. She remembered the dead silence between them at the dinner table, and the silence on the many nights that followed. His stony face and grief-hollowed eyes.

Her family wasn't particularly religious, but Natalie's mother used to pray fervently to herself, near tears and pacing back and forth if word came that a cop had been shot, or if there was a car crash and one of Natalie's sisters was out driving that night. As soon as she learned that everything was okay, Deborah would say, "Thank God!" As Joey used to say, "There are no atheists in foxholes." The Lockharts went to church on Sundays and thanked God for their food, until Willow died. Then they didn't so much as turn their backs on God as they tried to ignore him. In high school, Grace got heavily into the power of witchcraft, chanting strange things to herself in front of an altar of burnt hair or figures made out of twigs. And

Joey's buddies on the force would say things like, "Stay safe out there," and "Be mindful," and "Sorry for your loss," but no one ever said, "God will protect us" or "She's up in Heaven with the angels." Rather, there was a grudging respect for God, who didn't seem to care about the residents of Burning Lake very much. Or perhaps he was too busy to remember them all by name.

And even though it was painfully obvious, it took Natalie years to recognize how her sister's death had impacted her family. The Lockharts were never the same again. Sometimes she'd watch old Super-8 movies and marvel at the difference between Before Willow and After Willow. The joy was gone. The optimism was gone. Cynicism had risen up in its place. Caution prevailed.

But none of that mattered anymore. You had to forgive.

And you had to ask the dead to forgive you.

She would pray for Veronica Manes.

She would add her name to the reverend's email list.

Whether it was real or not, God would at least know she was trying.

28

Behind the church was an old burial ground full of moss-covered headstones and cracked brownstone urns with Gothic motifs. Natalie spotted Justin Fowler smoking a cigarette over by a centuries-old stone wall that was half-buried in the snow.

Taking high steps through the drifts, she joined him underneath a stand of pine trees, saying, "It's pretty out here."

He squinted over at her. "You think cemeteries are pretty?"

"Snow makes anything look pretty."

"I guess that's true," came his emotionless response. He was powerfully built from all those years in prison—lean and mean, prison tats, greasy long hair tucked behind his ears. Struggling to adjust to life as a workingman. Natalie empathized.

"How close were you to Veronica Manes?" she asked.

He took a deep drag of his cigarette. "When I first got released, I was confused. I thought I could fit back into my old life, but it was gone. Completely disappeared. Twenty years later, coming home felt like falling into a black hole. I didn't know anything. First couple of weeks, I hid from the world. Holed up in the basement, drinking and doing drugs. Then one day,

Reverend Grimsby came by for a visit. He helped me get into a church program. I started attending weekly Narcotics Anonymous meetings and got myself off the drugs. But I held on to a bitterness in my heart. I couldn't let go of all the terrible things that had happened to me."

"I understand," she said quietly.

He squinted critically at her, his head cocked to one side. "I found it nearly impossible to forgive your family for ruining my life. I held a lot of hatred in my gut and in my heart, but the reverend helped me see how all that negativity can eat you alive. It can rot you from inside. Grimsby told me how, after the witch trials in 1712, the relatives of the victims went on living side by side with the relatives of the judges who'd executed their loved ones. Ultimately, the families of the victims had to forgive the families of the accusers. *Forgive* them—can you imagine that? Forgiveness is hard, it's a difficult path. But the reverend assured me . . . stress is released when you finally let go."

"I'm grateful if you've achieved that, Justin," she said carefully. "Because I carry the guilt around with me everywhere I go. The knowledge of what my sister did to you."

He fell silent, shifting his weight from foot to foot. There was a smattering of pine cones on the snow underneath the trees. Justin stepped on one, and it emitted a loud crunch. "Maybe that's not reality," he said, looking at her. "Maybe forgiveness doesn't exist. Maybe it's wishful thinking. Maybe what's wrong in the past is what's wrong in the present."

"What do you mean?" she asked, listening intently.

"I mean those judges did a bad thing . . . a very bad thing . . . and maybe they can't be forgiven. Not their children, or their children's children . . . that's what Abby's hex is all about, right? Those three witches who were burned at the stake, they were judged and killed for no reason. It's a crime. And consider that maybe their families could never forgive what was done to their loved ones. Not really. Not deep in their bone marrow. Because those innocent lives were taken from them forever. So maybe forgiveness is impossible. Maybe it's a lie."

Natalie sympathized, but it made her sick to think she might never be forgiven.

"When Grimsby realized how much I was struggling with the issue, he suggested that I talk to Veronica Manes, since she was the great-great-whatever granddaughter of Thomas Bell, the judge who'd condemned Victoriana Forsyth to death. Now, think about that. Victoriana was seventeen and very religious. She was a good girl. She proclaimed her innocence, and nobody believed her. They didn't believe that poor, beautiful child. They were out for blood. And so here you have an innocent girl, only seventeen years old. It was said you could hear her screams for miles around. It was said she died of shock and smoke inhalation before the flames fully engulfed her. Thomas Bell watched her die. He watched her body burn. Then he went home and slept soundly at night, and had a pack of kids and grandkids, and the Forsyths were just supposed to forgive and forget. Forgive this pitiless man who ruined their lives."

Natalie couldn't help reacting emotionally. She felt a burning shame at the core of her being, but she didn't interrupt him. She let him talk. She wanted him to tell her everything he was feeling—all his pent-up fury and rancor. Maybe that was the path to self-forgiveness.

"But Veronica explained to me that it's possible to forgive even the worst evil over time. She talked about white magic, how it could help me heal. How powerful it was. She said that Marigold Hutchins, who's related to Sarah Hutchins, is one of her best friends. They're both witches, and they've let go of the past, and it's much better that way. She told me that time heals all wounds—cliché but true. She set up a meeting with me and the two of them, so that I could listen to their story, and it helped. I wanted to believe that the families of those who were harmed, and the families of those who did the harming, could get along and be friends. That's a world I can live with. Because if those two parties can honestly forgive one another, then I can forgive you and your family for your sins against me."

Natalie nodded, feeling a spark of hope.

"But it didn't work out that way," he said, dashing her hopes. "Veronica's dead. And I'll *never* forgive the person who did this to her. Forgiveness is off the table." He shook his head calmly. "She gave me hope. She was my friend. And they snatched that away from me."

"So you think she was wrong about forgiveness and healing?"

"It doesn't matter whether she was right or wrong," he explained, glancing across the snowdrifts toward the church. "I feel utterly betrayed." He dropped his cigarette in the snow. "Anyway, I have to go."

"Were you in the same NA meetings as Edward and Holly Host?"

"Yeah. Why?"

"Did Veronica know them?"

He shrugged. "Veronica knew a lot of people."

"I know, but . . . did she ever mention them? Did you ever see her with them? Maybe they visited her house?"

"They came to one of the workshops she was giving in town."

"When was this?"

"About mid-January."

"How well do you know the Hosts?"

He shrugged. "I met them when I joined the NA group in church. They had me over to their place, and we got high a couple times. They were a bad influence. So I cut off ties with them. But Veronica had a healing influence, and I thought it might help them sort their shit out. Why are you asking me this?"

"Veronica's workshop? Where was this?"

"At one of the occult shops on Sarah Hutchins Drive."

"Did the Hosts talk to her? Interact with her?"

"I don't remember. Why?"

"Do you think Veronica would've tried to help them if they'd asked?"

His fingers trembled slightly. His woolen coat hid the prison tattoos on his arms. "Why? Did the Hosts have something to do with her death?"

Natalie shook her head, but his eyes pushed back.

"Because I'd crawl through broken glass to find out who killed her. If those two dirtbags had anything to do with it . . ."

"No, these are routine questions, that's all," Natalie told him firmly. "We have to chase down every lead. That's why I'm talking to you."

He nodded politely, but his eyes shone with skepticism. She could tell he wasn't buying it.

"Where was this workshop in mid-January held?"

"At a boutique called Skeletons in the Closet. She introduced me to Marigold Hutchins, who runs the place. Marigold's cool. Maybe she knows more about it than I do," he said and headed back to the church.

29

S arah Hutchins Drive had a cozy Victorian feel to it, with its worn brick sidewalks and turn-of-the-century wrought iron streetlamps. The storefronts were warm and welcoming—boutiques, pubs, bookstores, cafés, art galleries. Occasionally classical music piped out onto the street and twinkle lights adorned the doorways.

Natalie kept heading east past the alleyway where she'd found the victim of her last homicide case, Morgan Chambers, dead in a dumpster, and felt a little twist in her gut. Across the street was Heal Thyself, a New Age boutique owned by Luke's current girlfriend, Rainie Sandhill, a slender blond businesswoman with a wry smile and a big heart. A few blocks farther down, Natalie was startled to find that the violin was still in the window of Bertrand Antiquities. The shop had been sold to a new owner, but nothing had changed yet. The sign hadn't even been replaced. Natalie shuddered. Around every corner was another troubling memory.

Skeletons in the Closet was located on the first floor of a Queen Anne–style brick building sandwiched between a bike rental shop and a feminist bookstore. Marigold Hutchins's occult boutique was popular with tourists and locals alike. The bell above the door jangled as Natalie swung it open and stepped inside. The boutique was cozy and full of good smells—incense, fresh-baked croissants, brewed teas. They sold everything from smudging herbs to crystal balls here. The store appeared to be empty at this hour. She headed down the aisle toward the register. "Hello?"

Marigold came scurrying out from the back room. "Hello, again. Welcome to my store." Her face was flushed. Her long black dyed hair framed her valentine-shaped face, and her dramatic eyebrows were raised in confusion. She was wearing another Goth outfit—a black-and-purple tie-dyed skirt, a button-down black blouse beneath a black velvet jacket. There was a silver pentacle pinned to her lapel.

Natalie had done a little online research before driving over this afternoon. The occult boutique sponsored psychic readings every Tuesday. They offered workshops on tarot cards, Reiki, and lunar meditation. They featured monthly guest speakers. The store website debunked myths and rumors about Wicca. According to her biography, Marigold had majored in the socioreligious historical cultural context of witchcraft, whatever that meant.

"I was wondering if you had time to answer a few more questions for me," Natalie said, knowing that people rarely refused.

"Sure. Come sit at the bar. It's the slowest time of day. I usually sit here reading a book."

There were four small tables arranged in front of a mahogany herbal tea bar. Natalie took a seat at one of the tables, while Marigold poured them each a cup of aromatic tea and brought them over. "So? How can I help?" She sat next to Natalie and smiled.

"Did you sponsor Veronica's workshop in mid-January?"

"Yeah, she was great."

"What did she talk about?"

"It was an introduction to Wicca as a religion. Mostly she spoke about how spirituality intersects with witchcraft. You know, pagan rituals and Christian holidays, stuff like that. It was mostly a beginner's guide."

Natalie nodded. "Were Holly and Edward Host there?"

"Yeah, they were very interested in Wicca."

"How well did she know them?"

"I'm not sure. But after the workshop, they hung around asking her questions."

"How well do you know the Hosts?"

She made a face. "I know Holly better than Edward. Holly's the daughter of an old friend of mine, Jodi Stewart. She passed away four years ago in a car accident. I don't know Holly that well, but she's been to the shop a couple of times. We've talked over tea. She was very interested in becoming a witch. I didn't like her husband, Edward. He gives off a weird vibe. I'd call it a dark energy. She apparently loves the guy. Bad boy syndrome?"

"So Holly came to your shop several times? What did she buy?"

"Oh, I'd have to look it up. I honestly don't remember. She and Edward were dabbling in black magic. I told Holly she should focus on white magic instead. Wicca is nothing to fool around with. Seriously, though, her husband seemed like trouble. He came in here once and stared at me. It gave me goose bumps. It's a good thing they left."

"Do you know where they went?"

"No idea. They just up and split."

"Veronica was helping Justin Fowler adjust to life out of prison, wasn't she?"

Marigold nodded. "He didn't know how to handle the transition from prison to newfound freedom, and who can blame him. So Veronica and I presented ourselves as an example . . . two people whose ancestors had once been enemies. Thomas Bell and Sarah Hutchins. We told him it's possible to forgive and forget. We wanted to present him with a good role model. You know, like—hey, look at us. Anything's possible."

"Would you say that you and Veronica were very close?"

"She's one of my favorite people in the world. She helped me come to terms with my own life."

"How so?"

"Long story." She rolled her eyes. "My father was abusive. He used to hurt my mom. Veronica helped me deal with it. I've come to terms with my past, but I don't necessarily like to talk about it."

Natalie nodded. "I can respect that."

Marigold grimaced and heaved a sigh. "My father would threaten us. He'd rant and rave. He used violent language that sometimes turned physical." She blushed a darker shade of pink. "Look, my father ruined my life. He was a congenital liar. He'd get drunk and beat up my mom, and she'd be screaming so loud the neighbors would call 911, but then my father would lie so convincingly to the police . . . I learned early on that the system was rigged."

"I'm so sorry."

"Oh gosh," Marigold said with dramatic irony. "I'm babbling. But the point is . . . we ran away when I was little. Mom and I. We ran away and changed our last name. After her experience, my mother was paranoid about everyone and everything. She didn't know who to trust. So she changed our last name to Hutchins. You can legally do that, you know—change your name and identity, just as long as you're the victim of abuse and want to evade your abuser, then it's perfectly legit to file a petition with the state and legally change your name. But Mom didn't want to just pick a name at random. So she spent time looking up her heritage on one of those ancestry sites and got me involved. I was the one who discovered the direct connection to Sarah Hutchins."

"I'm so sorry you had to go through that," Natalie said, full of empathy for her.

"No, it's okay." She seemed a little nervous. She used a paper napkin to wipe the sweat off her face. "I look at it this way—because of the hardship, as a direct result of my father's abuse, I discovered my true heritage. We learned who we were. I mean, to be related to Sarah Hutchins . . . how cool is that? I find a lot of comfort in it. Serendipity. Destiny. I cling to my history, and I'll never let go of it, because I know that if we hadn't run away at the time, my father would've beaten my mom to death. And if we hadn't run away, Mom and I never would've found out we were related to a real witch. And it makes perfect sense, actually, who my ancestor was, and who I am. I'm the direct descendant of a witch. And so, ten years ago, I became a witch in my own right, because I know that good and evil truly exist. My father was the embodiment of dark energy."

Natalie smiled sympathetically—although Sarah Hutchins wasn't really a witch. She'd been falsely accused of witchcraft and had been executed for this so-called sin. But it was clear how important this interpretation was to Marigold, who'd embraced the myth as part of her healing process, and Natalie wasn't about to correct her.

Marigold's eyes filled with tears. "We don't really know what happened to Veronica, but all these terrible rumors keep circulating around town. Someone said she chained herself to the tracks. I can't imagine her doing anything like that, although they say you don't really know people, even the ones you care deeply about."

"It wasn't suicide."

"No? Then what was it? Oh my God, what a gruesome way to go. Some people think *we* had something to do with it, us Wiccans, can you believe it? That's so Middle Ages. Wiccans don't advocate ritualistic killings. And even if we did—why would we kill Veronica? We loved her. It's insane, the things people believe."

Natalie reached out to touch Marigold's hand. "I'm going to ask you something that might be upsetting, but it's a routine question. I have to cover all the bases. Is it possible Holly and Edward Host could've had something to do with Veronica's death?"

Her jaw dropped. She shook her head. "I don't believe that. I mean, he's creepy. But you should've seen Veronica talking to them. She had a calming effect. She was so wise and such a good listener. Holly seemed to really take to her."

"Maybe just Edward then?"

"I don't know anything about him. But I doubt Holly herself would've participated in something so evil as that. Do you?"

"I don't know her."

"Well, I seriously doubt it."

The bell above the door jangled, signaling another customer had arrived.

Marigold grabbed a couple of paper napkins to blot away the tears. She blew her nose and wiped the runny mascara from underneath her eyes. "Oh, gosh. I don't know."

Natalie stood up. "I'm sorry this was so upsetting. But if you think of anything else, please let me know." She handed Marigold her card.

"Be careful out there, Detective. And thank you for your service."

30

O utside, Natalie's phone buzzed in her coat pocket.

"I found the Hosts," Jules Pastor told her. "Believe it or not, they're still in town, staying with this girl I know on the west side. It's an old farmhouse, looks abandoned. She thinks it's haunted."

"What's this girl's name?"

"Topaz Revelli. Just to warn you, her boyfriend is the ultimate hustler, Nyle Hockney. Once a week or so, it depends, you'll find him at one of his chosen locations . . . cash transactions only. He'll show up dragging around a trash bag full of stolen goods or dex or what have you, like an anorexic Santa Claus. Topaz inherited her grandfather's run-down farm last year, and he crashes there sometimes. He's been known to carry. Let me give you the address."

The west side of town reeked of marijuana and boredom. There was never anything going on unless you created it. Many of the pot farms had gotten busted in the past couple of years, but there were still a few cannabis gardens lingering undetected out this way—tucked-away homes owned by paranoid men with guns, their basements fitted with hydroponic systems and LED lights.

There were neighborhoods on the west side where people knew Natalie from her police officer days, back when she walked a beat before joining the CIU. She could go into certain parts of town where she knew the families, and people would tell her things. She learned that if you approached them without an agenda, they'd open up and talk to you. The west side, despite its problems, was a point of pride. It was home—this was where they'd grown up and raised their kids and gone to school and made lifelong bonds. Poverty and drugs had merely complicated their lives.

She crested the top of a hill and descended a series of switchback curves through dense woods of wintergreen and birch. After ten minutes, she drove into a valley where the land flattened out and the old orchards flourished. She dug her shield out of the glove compartment and slung it around her neck as she drove past snowy fields where cattle grazed in the warmer months. Now they huddled together near the barns.

Natalie found the old Revelli farmstead and got out. There were two pickup trucks parked in the driveway—one silver, one red—and she called in their license plates. One of the trucks belonged to Topaz Revelli, and the other was registered to Edward Host.

Natalie unbuttoned her coat and unfastened the safety strap of her shoulder holster, just in case. Beneath the layers of winter clothing, despite the shivery cold air, her body grew clammy and damp.

There were several rusty hulks of rotting cars in the yard, weeds growing through the broken windshields. Nobody answered the door. She waited on the porch. She checked her watch. Almost four o'clock.

Natalie knocked again. "Open up. It's the police."

Finally, a young woman opened the door. Her face was shiny and moist, pale strands of hair sticking to her forehead. She stood on the threshold, bathed in the golden light of late afternoon. "Can I help you?" she asked tightly. Eyes pinwheeling.

"Topaz Revelli?"

"Yes? Who are you?"

Natalie could see past her into the kitchen, where the table was cluttered with dirty dishes and liquor bottles. A distinct marijuana-and-piss aroma drifted out of the house. "My name is Detective Lockhart. Can I come in?"

"No. What's this about? Do you have a search warrant?"

"Are Edward and Holly Host here?"

"Who?" She stared at Natalie with hardened, bloodshot eyes.

"I'd like to talk to them."

Topaz shrugged. "Sorry, never heard of them."

"Isn't that their truck parked in your driveway? You don't want to be an accessory, do you?"

"An accessory to what?"

"Yo," a male voice said loudly from the interior of the house. "What's up?"

A hushed tension filled the air. A man came to the kitchen doorway. Natalie recognized the T-shirt through the unzipped white hoodie: Bohemian Falls Brewery. He was of average height and weight, and he gazed at her blankly. His hoodie was coffee-stained, and his jeans were baggy at the knees.

"Detective Lockhart." She flashed her badge. "I'm here to see Edward and Holly Host."

"You got a warrant, Detective?"

"No. I'm not here to arrest anyone. I just want to talk to Edward and Holly."

Nyle Hockney stepped out of the shadows, favoring his left leg. He winked at Natalie as if they were old friends. "Okay. They aren't here. Sorry, should I call you Detective?"

"Detective Lockhart's fine."

"Cool. Look, I know my reputation precedes me," he said. "I'm so evil, right? So greasy and shifty, selling lemons to innocent dopes who think it's lemonade."

"Can I come in?"

He shook his head, then glanced beyond Natalie's left shoulder.

All of a sudden, one of the trucks parked in the driveway roared to life.

Natalie turned around, fear coating her throat. "Stop! Police!" she shouted.

Edward and Holly Host had snuck out the back way, and now the silver Dodge pickup truck drove off in a cloud of kicked-up snow and gravel.

Natalie felt her heart beating at the base of her throat as she ran across the yard to her Honda Accord, dug the keys out of her pocket, started the engine, and pulled away from the curb. She accelerated hard, squinting into the late-afternoon light as she tore down the road after them.

She radioed the dispatcher. "This is CIU-seven, in pursuit of a silver Dodge pickup truck heading east on Cedar Grove Road toward Redwing

Circle. The driver failed to stop and is driving to endanger. License plate is . . . hold on . . ." She picked up her notepad and rattled off the numbers. "I need backup now," she said.

"Where are you?" Dennis asked through crackling static.

"Northbound on Redwing Circle, heading for Route 17."

"Received," Dennis responded. "Calling for backup now."

She plopped the radio back in its cradle on the dash, while her adrenaline spiked. The sun came down hard through the windshield, and Natalie's cheap sunglasses failed to block the glare. She grabbed the portable beacon, slapped it on the roof, and switched on the siren. Her hands choked the wheel as she sped after the truck.

Natalie clocked their speeds at seventy-five or more miles per hour. When they reached ninety miles per hour, Natalie thought for sure someone was going to die. Sweat beaded on her neck as she took a left onto Daniel Boone Lane, a lonely stretch of hills that eventually connected to Route 17. Soon the establishments gave way to the woods, gray trunks tapering into a swirling blue on either side of the road. Her discount tires hugging the asphalt.

The chase came to an end when the silver pickup truck went off the road after Edward failed to navigate the turn. Natalie swallowed a scream as she watched the vehicle careen into the woods, bucking wildly over the underbrush, and finally crashing into a tree. There was a loud *bang*, and the driver's side door flapped open. Then Edward Host fell out and landed in the snow. Holly was screaming in the passenger seat—an intense wide-eyed girl with scruffy reddish-brown hair.

Natalie drew her weapon and approached the vehicle, saying, "Get up, Edward. You're under arrest."

The young man smiled at her from a fetal position on the snowy ground. A twitchy grin lifted the flesh of his face. His hair was black and as thick as guitar strings. His eyes narrowed critically as he stumbled to his feet.

"Put your hands up where I can see them," she said.

He raised his hands in the air. He didn't appear to be injured. Fortunately, the underbrush had slowed the vehicle way down before the tree had finally stopped it.

"Holly, show me your hands."

The girl stopped screaming and raised her hands.

"Keep your hands up and *slowly* get out of the vehicle, please."

Holly edged her way out of the truck, while keeping her hands in the air.

"Edward, clasp your hands behind your head."

"Why am I being arrested?" he asked with exquisite politeness.

"Fleeing and eluding. Driving to endanger. Hands behind your head." Natalie did a pat down search, looking for weapons and making sure he wasn't bleeding. Then she slapped on the cuffs. "You have the right to remain silent . . ."

31

I don't know why you're arresting us," Holly Stewart Host complained. She was an awkward twenty-six-year-old in a tweed jacket with elbow patches, dressed in black from head to toe, and wearing UGG boots. She had scruffy reddish-brown hennaed hair, smudged mascara, and resentful, smoky eyes. "Justin came to the farm, like, an hour ago . . . and he wouldn't stop banging on the door and accusing us of killing Veronica Manes. Like he believes we would actually do that. He's crazy! You should be arresting him instead of bothering us. We haven't done anything wrong."

So Justin had in fact known where the Hosts were staying. He'd lied to Natalie. She tucked this bit of information away for later contemplation. Right now, the Hosts were being separately interrogated at the police station.

"I'll talk to Justin about that," Natalie said. "Do you know why you're here?"

Holly's lean body was slumped over the table—slumped with despair or boredom, Natalie couldn't tell which. "Do I know why I'm here?" she repeated dully.

The light gray walls and medium gray venetian blinds of the interrogation room were as oppressive as the gray twilight outside. Luke was interviewing Edward in a similar room down the hall, while Natalie questioned Holly.

Holly sat up and shrugged. "Something about obstruction of a police officer."

"Eluding, evading, failing to stop, leading to a chase with speeds reaching ninety miles per hour. Our Breathalyzer test shows that Edward was driving while intoxicated. You owe your landlord back rent. Edward has several outstanding warrants for burglary and theft by unauthorized use of property back in Utica. He'll face additional charges once the investigation is complete."

Holly leaned back in her seat and crossed her arms. "Okay," she said sullenly. "But what about that low-sperm-count loser living at home with his mom? When are you going to arrest him?"

"Justin Fowler? I said I'd talk to him."

"Edward and Nyle had to chase him off the property."

"In the meantime, I have a few questions for you," Natalie told her. "You left Grimsby's cottage five or six weeks ago, isn't that correct?"

Holly glanced at the ceiling. "Umm. End of January."

"And you never went back to the cottage, even though the key was accessible?"

"No, we haven't been back there. I figured he'd changed the lock."

"How long have you been staying at Topaz's house?"

"About a week now."

"Where were you before that?" Natalie asked.

"Different places. You know, you touch base with your cousin Claire once in a while on Facebook, and that's kind of enough for me. But when I explained we needed a place to crash, she invited us to stay with her. Until she kicked us out."

"Why did she kick you out?"

"She called us freeloaders. We were on our very best behavior, but I guess that wasn't good enough for her."

"Where does she live?"

"Syracuse."

"How long did you stay with her?"

"A week and a half, I think."

"And after your cousin?"

"We stayed with friends here and there. You want a list?"

"Yes." Natalie slid her pad and pen toward Holly. "Write it all down, please. Names, dates, and any other details."

Holly's tongue poked out of the side of her mouth as she wrote everything down.

"I know you're struggling," Natalie said gently. "It's hard in your twenties."

Holly glanced up. "We owe about fifty thousand in student loans. When Edward was working, all our money went to rent and food and utilities and cable and credit card debt and student loans. It all went away, and there was nothing left for us. It's like 'Merry fucking Christmas' every single day," she muttered sarcastically.

"How well did you know Veronica Manes?" Natalie asked her.

"Not very well. I mean, I met her at this boutique called Skeletons in the Closet. She was giving a speech about witchcraft. She explained how it was all about empowerment and self-love. Afterwards people got to ask questions, so I went up and talked to her for about fifteen minutes."

"What did you talk about?"

"Like . . . how witchcraft could help turn your life around."

"And what did she say?"

"She was really nice. She explained all about Wicca, what it can and can't do for you. Why?" Holly studied Natalie curiously. "Is this about her getting all chained up and hit by that train? Because, I mean, clearly some psycho did that."

"Holly, did you or Edward have anything to do with Veronica's death?"

"What? No!" She recoiled. "No way. That's insane, what you're implying." Her demeanor changed. She sat up straighter. She pushed the pen and notepad away. The tendons in her neck stood out. "Fuck that shit."

"Okay. But what about those bottles of urine we found hanging from the tree behind the cottage? Some people call that dark magic. And what about the animal sacrifices?"

"They were already dead. We found them in the woods, roadkill and dead stuff. Besides, we got the idea from this book on witchcraft . . . it's called *Exploring the Dark Side*. You want me to write that down, too?"

"Yes."

She snatched the pen and wrote it down. "Look, this is highly disturbing, okay? Don't you think it freaks me out a little bit? I knew Veronica. I liked her. Just the thought of it sends shivers running down my spine. There's no way Edward could've had anything to do with it."

Natalie looked at her sharply. "Do you suspect him?"

"What? No." She shoved the pen and notepad across the table toward Natalie.

"Where were you and Edward two nights ago?"

"Monday night? We were at a party."

"All night long?"

She shrugged. "As long as there's drugs, sex, and alcohol . . . you know."

"Where was this party?"

"Topaz and Nyle's place. We partied, and then we crashed there."

"So you have witnesses who can place you inside the house for the entire night?"

She scowled. "Maybe not the whole night."

"Why not? Where else did you go?"

"Outside."

"In the snow?"

"Yeah, there's a barn on the property."

"So you left the party to go into the barn and do what?"

"Fuck."

"Could you write down the names of the people who saw you that night?"

"Who saw us fuck?"

"Sure. Saw you at the party. Went into the barn with you. Whatever. Just give me the names of everyone who can vouch for your alibi, wherever you were that night, all the way through to early Tuesday morning."

She picked up the pen, and then paused. "You know, it's hard getting off drugs. Pulling your life together. Nobody needs drugs, but you want them."

Natalie nodded. "It is hard, and it won't necessarily happen on one try. You have to keep trying over and over again."

"Look at you. Dispenser of wisdom."

Natalie shrugged. "Is that why you got into witchcraft?"

"Aren't we all on a journey? I don't know about you, but I'm totally lost and confused half the time. And I keep looking for land. I just want this freaking journey to end. I want to shout land ho."

"So you're seeking answers?"

"You bet I am." She had a tight, tired look around her eyes. There were reddish spots of color on her cheeks. "I know I have a bad attitude. It's dogged me my whole life. I was picked on as a kid. I was this skinny, shy nerd. I tried basketball once, but I quit after one season because the other girls seemed to be dead set on knocking my teeth out. So yeah, I come with an attitude. But when I met Edward, we both knew—this is it. It was like a thousand-watt bulb going off inside your head. He's the only member of the Holly Stewart fan club, and that's all I need. He sees things in me nobody else does."

Natalie nodded mutely.

"All my friends from college moved away to distant locations, and so life wasn't the same anymore in Utica. All my friends are busy with their big-city careers or breastfeeding their babies and nursing their lattes in Starbucks. Edward and I are pursuing our own adventures. Edward doesn't want to be a corporate hack. But then things sort of spiraled out of control, and we thought that maybe she could help us . . ."

"She?"

"Veronica. Anyway, before we crashed the truck, Edward told me to ask for a lawyer. I'm not supposed to talk to you. He said to ask for an attorney, so that's what I'm going to do. I'm putting this pen down and telling you I've got nothing more to say." She slid the lined pad with names and dates on it over toward Natalie and folded her hands primly on the table.

Natalie scooped up the pad and pen. "Okay, then. Wait here."

32

Luke's office door was open, yellow light spilling across the worn carpet. He was on his phone. He glanced up and nodded. "Yeah, okay,
talk later," he said into the receiver, then hung up and waved her inside.

She took a seat and said, "Holly drew up a list of everyone they've been
staying with since they left the cottage at the end of January. She claims
they were at a party on Monday night at Topaz Revelli's place. It should be
easy enough to verify."

"Great. I'll have Augie follow up on her alibi."

She handed him the lined pad with the list of witnesses. "My gut tells
me Holly had nothing to do with it, but she might know who did. What
about Edward?"

"He refuses to talk. Asked for a public defender. In the meantime, we got
the toxicology results back." He picked up a printout of the lab report from
his desk and handed it to Natalie. "Intramuscular ketamine confirmation."

Natalie rifled through the pages. "Ketamine?"

"A fast-working sedative. Other than that, there were no other positive
findings—no alcohol, cocaine, opiates, or other metabolites in her system.
Barry confirmed the injection sites—one to the thigh and two to the

buttocks. The first injection was delivered to the thigh muscle, most likely five to seven milligrams per kilogram. Once the initial injection wore off, a second injection to the left buttocks was given, and finally a third injection of approximately nine to thirteen milligrams per kilogram or more, which would've lasted a couple of hours."

"So whoever did this sedated her with a shot of ketamine and drove her to an isolated location, where they removed her coat, phone, and keys, then dressed her in the costume and gave her a second shot. Then they transported her to the tracks, where they injected her for a third time, leaving her there to die." Natalie crossed her arms tightly. "How long do you think it took them to chain her to the tracks? And how did they know they wouldn't get surprised by a freight train operating on an off schedule?"

"Freight train companies don't share their timetables for security reasons," Luke said, rubbing his chin, "since they transport a lot of hazardous materials. I'll ask Brandon to find out whatever he can about the off schedules for that night. And I'll have Lenny re-create the shackling, see if he can come up with a time estimate."

"What do you want me to do?"

"Go home and get some rest."

"I've got reports to fill out."

"You can fill them out just as easily at home."

She put the tox report down. "Was any trace found under Veronica's nails?"

"Only dirt from the gravel bed. Besides that, nothing significant."

Natalie sighed with frustration. "What about the broom?"

"It's a common household broom you can buy at any Walmart or Costco."

"And the costume?"

"Mike's following up on that."

"We both know this town attracts a lot of sickos. But whoever did this knows the area," she said. "They know about the back roads abutting the railroad tracks. And it happened during a snowstorm, which means they had to be comfortable enough with the area to get around at night during a winter storm."

"Or they could've just been lucky," he suggested, playing devil's advocate.

Natalie shook her head. "This wasn't a disorganized crime. It has to be someone she knows, since she left the house voluntarily, taking only a few things with her. You said so yourself—the doors were locked, the outside lights were on, the inside lights were off except for the front hallway. She was asleep when someone rang her doorbell in the middle of the night. She got up and answered the door. She got dressed. She stepped out of her slippers and hung up her bathrobe. She put on a pair of boots. She fetched her phone and her coat and her keys, then turned off the lights and locked the door behind her. The ransacking must've taken place later on, when she was unconscious. I believe she trusted this person. And they utterly betrayed her."

An awkward silence enveloped them. On his desk was a framed photo of his teenage daughter, Skye, looking bored at Universal Studios. She lived with her mother in Los Angeles now. Luke's ex was a documentary filmmaker. Seventeen-year-old Skye had inherited his piercing smoke-blue eyes. Natalie used to sometimes wonder what their children might look like. Hers and Luke's.

"What about Edward's vehicle?" she asked, shaking off this distraction.

"We've impounded it. Lenny and Augie will be processing the truck for hairs and fibers tomorrow, so we should know something soon."

She rubbed her face and tired eyes. "This is an in-your-face crime, Luke. It happened right underneath our noses, as if the killer or killers wanted to shock the whole town. To create widespread fear and attract media attention."

"I'd say they succeeded."

"But why? What's their motive? To intimidate Wiccans? To create a holy war? To let the town know that real evil exists in a way we never quite understood before?"

He sat shaking his head slowly.

"Veronica must've stumbled onto something quite dangerous," Natalie went on. "I'd like to look at everything that's left inside the house, all her paperwork and research, her notebooks and library books . . . whatever wasn't taken during the ransacking."

He nodded. "I'll have Murphy gather it up. In the meantime, Lenny's trying to find out if Veronica had iCloud storage. We can't find her passwords, so we're playing catch-up here. It's possible that whoever took the computer and other devices has already scrubbed them clean and deleted her accounts."

"That would suck."

"Indeed it would." He cleared his throat. "Anyway, the guys are working overtime to solve this thing. Go home, write up your reports, and get some well-deserved rest, Natalie. Don't burn yourself out. Tomorrow you'll thank me."

"Just stop it, please. Will you stop worrying about me?" She stood up. "I'll make a compromise with you, Luke. I'll work at home tonight, just as long as I can take the evidence with me. Can you ask Murphy to get me those boxes, please?"

There was an unmistakable tension between them.

"Natalie," he said quietly, "you mentioned the killer did this to create fear."

She rested her hands on the back of the chair. "Yes."

"What's your worst fear?"

Her face grew hot. "That this keeps happening. That there's never an end to it."

He nodded thoughtfully.

"Why?" she said. "What's your worst fear?"

His gaze drifted to her lips. "That I'll lose you."

This stunned her—his confession. She'd assumed it was all behind them.

He held her eyes for a moment too long, then picked up the phone. "I'll ask Murphy to help you carry those boxes of evidence down to your car."

"Thanks, Luke. Good night," she said and left.

33

Back in high school, Natalie used to hide her growing body under bulky layers of clothes in order to look less attractive. She wanted to be respected for her mind and her accomplishments. She worked desperately hard to be the funny girl or the courageous girl or the drama club girl or the artist—anything but the pretty girl all the boys lusted after. And so she adopted a layered look, which meant plenty of sweaters and jackets and untucked Annie Hall shirts. She covered her swanlike neck with her sister's scarves, wrapping them around her neck three or four times, and the smell of Willow's peach perfume had lingered on the material forever. She never thought she'd become one of those girls who lusted after boys. The more deeply invested she was with Hunter, the more her desire seemed to spread and branch off like a river flooding its banks.

Winter's potholes and patched asphalt were rough on the Accord's suspension. The flickering neon lights of Sarah Hutchins Drive were reflected in frozen puddles of ice. Natalie left downtown behind and headed north into the woods. She took the covered bridge across Swift Run Creek and recalled the time, only five months ago, when she'd lost control of her car and swerved into the river. Her smoke-gray Honda Pilot had been totaled.

She'd replaced it with the silver-gray Honda Accord. There was a moment in the water when Natalie stopped fighting. She stopped resisting and re-laxed her whole body, as if she were dead. She stopped struggling. She surrendered. She gave up. She gave in. A warmth suffused her body. She became lighter than water. Lighter than air. She saw a brilliant light all around her. This was how it would end.

But then someone grabbed her and pulled her up out of the river. Her rescuer. She popped to the surface like a cork—coughing, choking, sputter-ing. Air. At last. Great gasps. Deep breaths. We took breathing for granted. We didn't know how lucky we were.

She took the next right past the bend in the river and felt the skipped heartbeat, the momentary shift of reality, as if the universe had slipped off its axis. Strange how you could carry the trauma around with you. Certain sights triggered a physiological reaction, and Natalie would feel the emotional echoes resonating in her body. Death waited just out of range, impatient for her to make one fatal mistake. Fortunately, Natalie had survived, and the Violinist had been put away for life. Still, she couldn't go anywhere in this town without being reminded of her past mistakes.

On the way home, she rolled to a stop at an intersection, and a dark se-dan pulled up behind her, its brilliant headlights blazing in her rearview mirror and momentarily blinding her. Natalie flashed her taillights, but the driver didn't lower his high beams.

Natalie squinted into the glare, and then continued driving. The sedan dogged her down this lonely wooded road, its high beams obscuring her vision. Her heart began to pound. It felt menacing. It felt like a threat.

She finally twisted the wheel sharply and veered off the road, braking hard. She watched, frozen, as the sedan quickly pulled a U-turn, its high beams splashing across the interior of her car. Then the vehicle sped away, taillights receding quickly into the night before she could identify the make and model, let alone the plates.

She thought about chasing after the sedan, putting on her shield, slap-ping the portable beacon on the roof and switching on the siren. Maybe it was nothing. She told herself to calm down. She tried to shake it off. If she saw the vehicle again, she would pull the driver over. For now, she just wanted to go home and put up her feet.

Burning Lake was the beneficiary of a state park and plenty of nature preserves, sanctuaries, and conservation areas. On these long winter nights, it got spooky dark way out here in the wilderness. Occasionally a pair of eyes would stare at you from either side of the road—raccoons, foxes, hawks, coyotes, mountain lions. Nocturnal creatures roamed the woods at night, hunting for food or love, trying to survive until the next day. She took a left onto Harvest Lane and found herself in Hunter Rose's upscale neighborhood.

Hunter's nineteenth-century mansion was nestled on twenty acres of rugged wilderness. She pulled into the gravel driveway, parked her car, and stepped out of the warm interior into the freezing cold March night. The eerie-looking stone mansion was a Romanesque Revival folly constructed in the late 1800s by a Boston steel magnate, who had turned it into a luxury resort. In the 1920s, it became a sanitarium for tuberculosis patients. In 1935, it was abandoned and left to rot until the mid-1980s, when Hunter's father bought it and restored it to its former glory. Hunter and his brother had grown up here, which was still something Natalie had a hard time believing. It looked like a haunted castle.

It was almost ten o'clock. The outdoor lights were on, and the landscape lighting gave shape to the snow-covered bushes and fountains. She let herself in, then unlaced her boots and took them off, little sparks of static electricity snapping from her socked feet. She left her wet boots along with her coat and gloves in the mudroom.

It was cold inside the house—the kind of dry cold that made you want to bundle up and eat a pizza and skip the after-work shower. But Natalie couldn't skip the shower. The house smelled of lavender and orange, but she smelled of death.

"Hunter, I'm back," she said to the empty first floor, then took the sweeping staircase up to the master bedroom at the end of the hall. "Hunter?"

Sometimes he worked late.

Natalie charged her phone, took off her shield and weapon in its shoulder holster, then peeled out of her static-prickly clothes and tossed everything into the laundry hamper. After a hot shower, she looked in the mirror and was surprised to see that two small crescents of eye makeup had collected under her eyes. She plucked a tissue out of the box and wiped the smudges away, then got dressed and went downstairs. She found Hunter in his study, listening to music through his earbuds.

She lingered in the doorway for a moment, gazing at the nape of his neck and the little cowlicks of dirty blond hair. He was one of the most discreet people she'd ever met. She trusted him with her life. He was extremely smart—freakishly smart, a genius—and yet he seemed to be in a trance half the time, thinking about how to expand his business or planning new ventures. His eyes were often restless behind his dark-framed glasses—restless gray mystical eyes.

She watched him nod his head to the beat. "What're you listening to?"

He smiled and pulled the earbuds out. "'Dancing Queen.'"

"Seriously?" she said. "We're listening to Abba now?"

"It's cool, right?" He bobbed his head to the beat. "The harmonies. The way it kind of rocks gently. Kind of echoey, you know? Like all the way back in time."

She smiled. She felt happy. They shared odd and ironic observations. He made her laugh. They were on the same wavelength. He got her.

She said, "We'll still be friends after this is over, right?"

"You mean, 'Dancing Queen'?" His broad shoulders went up and down. "Maybe."

"You say that now, but just wait," she said with a laugh.

"Come here." He opened his arms wide, and his Icelandic sweater crackled with electricity. He was exquisitely handsome, lean and muscular, like an Olympic runner, only perfectly relaxed. He wore his woolen crewneck pullover sweater and faded, slightly frayed jeans with the artfulness of a fashion model. He made the most casual outfits look expensive. When they kissed, a magical spark touched her lips.

"A little birdie told me to feed you," he said.

She drew back. "Luke called you?"

"Luke? No." He seemed crestfallen. "Your friend Augie. You remember him?"

"So they're all spying on me. Monitoring my nutritional intake."

"If by that you mean they care about you, then yes. They do."

"And you believe it's your task to feed me?"

"My assignment. Yes. I am at your beck and call, milady." He bowed his head and smiled. "You are hungry, aren't you? Please say yes. It will make my job that much easier."

They headed for the kitchen together, walking through a maze of hallways. The living room was full of rose tones and lots of polished wood—an antique cherry cabinet and sideboard, a Regency bamboo-patterned tilt-top table, an antique walnut mirror, a set of four carved-mahogany hall chairs, a George III tulipwood wine cooler.

The kitchen was equipped with the latest appliances, like a slick brochure come to life. Stainless steel and teak, sleek and immaculate. The walls were almond-colored, and it was snowing outside, icy white specks falling from the sky and plinking against the windowpanes.

"Have a seat. Enjoy the show."

She smirked and sat down at the marble-and-oak kitchen island.

He fetched a frying pan and took the eggs out of the fridge. A spatula. A plate of butter. He took a fresh loaf of sourdough out of the bread basket and gazed at her. "What can I do to help you through this, Natalie?"

"Besides make me dinner?"

"All kidding aside," he said, giving her a solemn look.

Natalie thought about it for a moment. Out of all the things she'd dealt with over the past two days, there was only one thing Hunter could really help her with. Everything else was beyond the pale, too difficult to explain or too dreadful to describe. She recalled what Brandon had told her about his and Daisy's house. "Do you happen to know how a blind trust works?"

"A blind trust?" he repeated. "Well, let's see. If you want to protect your privacy, then you can establish a trust and a limited liability company, or LLC, to buy a specific property. Because otherwise, it's too easy for anyone to pull up the records online."

"So it's mainly for privacy?"

"There are other reasons, such as conflict of interest, if you happen to be a politician or a wealthy businessman. You can establish a blind trust, but you'd need to hire a good lawyer, because it can get complicated, what with living trusts and grantors and other choices. But the most obvious advantage to a blind trust would be privacy. Home purchases are made public nowadays." He studied her. "Why?"

"Just curious."

"What's the property in question?"

"Brandon was telling me that a blind trust bought his and Daisy's house."

"Huh. So you two have mended fences?"

"Yeah, Brandon and I are friends again, I guess."

"Really?" A satisfied smile spread across his face. "I'm glad to hear it."

"Anyway, I think it's a little strange . . . because an anonymous trust also bought Bella Striver's childhood home."

"What's so strange about it?"

"Two properties where tragedies occurred."

"It's probably just a coincidence. Upstate New York, especially the area around the Adirondacks, has a booming real estate market. And Burning Lake is pretty hot, too."

"Brandon said her blood was still on the kitchen floor. He looked in the window."

"He did what?" Hunter grimaced. "Well, I'm not an expert on blind trusts, but I'm pretty sure they'd want to clean the blood off the floor. Maybe Brandon is having seller's remorse."

"Yeah, you're probably right."

"He saw a shadow and thought it was blood. Anyway, I'd be happy to ask around, Natalie, but it could take some time, and I can't guarantee anything. If certain individuals feel the need to protect their privacy, they aren't about to go around boasting about it."

"Don't bother your friends," she said, wishing she hadn't brought it up. The people Hunter knew tended to be a tight-lipped group, who didn't reveal a whole lot about themselves.

He glanced over at her. "Gossip spreads fast in this town. You share your secrets at your own peril. Take my father, for instance," he said, cracking an egg into a large mixing bowl. "He was a powerful man, and I suspect he was involved in some dicey dealings, to gain all that wealth and power so quickly like he did in his twenties and thirties. It makes me sick to my stomach, wondering how he came into all that money. Which is why I try to lead a purposeful life. To give back to the community. But there are powerful people here in town with the same mind-set, who are very ambitious. They aren't satisfied just being rich. They want power and control, which is why I mostly stay out of it. They'll ask me to come in with them on this or that deal, and I've done pretty well on my own, but there's constant pressure to join in on certain projects, or to put my name on this or that charity. It seems harmless. I suppose it is harmless. But deals go on behind closed doors, agreements are made, not everything is aboveboard and transparent. I try to avoid it as much as possible. But as a favor to you?" he said, cracking another egg into the bowl. "I'll do whatever I can. In the meantime, I realize the timing is lousy, but have you thought any further about quitting your job?"

"Not really." She looked down at her hands resting on the marble countertop.

"I thought you had a deadline. The hiring freeze." He waited for her answer, as if it were urgent.

"Now's not a great time to talk about this, Hunter. Veronica's death has torn everything wide open."

"I realize that. I don't expect you to give your notice tomorrow. But I'd like to take you away from all this bullshit, Natalie. Just the two of us. A trip to Ibiza. We'll wake up to massages and spend our days hiking and swimming. We can sip Frigola on the rooftop overlooking the ocean. I'm serious. I'm concerned about you. I mean, we've gone over this before, and I thought you were on board . . ."

"On board?" she said with distaste. "This isn't a business deal, Hunter. Could you give me a little space tonight?"

"Sorry. I shouldn't have brought it up." He studied her carefully.

She tried not to look at him. Sometimes, he quickly apologized just to get it over with. She resented these "sorry"s because they weren't sincere, and because it meant that she would have to explain why his apology wasn't good enough, which would lead to another fight. Two or three arguments in one night was too much. That was when Hunter would collapse in bed with his back to her and turn off his light and pretend to fall asleep. Later, in the dead of night, one of them would reach for the other and say, "I don't want to fight." And the other would say, "Me neither."

If the argument hadn't resolved itself, it would crop up again the next day or the next week. They built up little splinters of unresolved issues, and occasionally Natalie would snag herself on one of these.

"I can't help it that I'm in love with you," he said.

It was the first time he'd said those words out loud.

34

The following morning, Hunter groaned in his sleep before his voice shied away to nothing. He was dreaming. Not a good dream, apparently. Natalie rested her hand lightly on the back of his head to soothe him, and he grumbled and rolled away. Their clothes were strewn around the room. An empty wine bottle lay on the floor next to the bed.

Downstairs, Natalie spread the contents of the evidence boxes Murphy had given her across the dining-room table. Then she stood there sipping her coffee, wondering what she had here. How to fit the puzzle pieces together. She sorted through a voluminous amount of Veronica's handwritten research notes, but nothing struck her as particularly significant until she picked up an old John F. Kennedy High School yearbook from 1975 with a handful of dog-eared pages.

She relished the quiet of early morning, but today there was a chill in the air. She felt the hairs rising on the back of her neck as she flipped through the yearbook's pages and studied the grainy black-and-white photographs. The seventies fashions were distracting. Miniskirts and paisley shirts. Earlobe-length hair for the boys and cat's-eye glasses for the girls. There were pictures of "Class Favorites"—best looking, biggest flirt, best dressed, most spirited, most fun to be with—along with separate sections for clubs, class trips, sports, activities, and awards.

Some of the pages had their corners folded over in place of a bookmark. On page fifty-two, Natalie was surprised to find the class photo of a pudgy senior she recognized—Ned Bertrand—scowling at the camera. His yearbook quote said: "They told me to write something. Something."

On page seventy-one, she found a skinny, pimple-faced eighteen-year-old Thomas Grimsby, smiling awkwardly into the camera. His yearbook quote said: "We are God's handiwork."

On dog-eared page one hundred twenty-six was the Young Christians Club, consisting of eight kids. Thomas Grimsby stood in the center, surrounded by seven others. There was Ned Bertrand again, and Natalie didn't recognize the rest of them, except for sophomore Dottie Coffman who beamed out from the grainy photo, looking innocent and wide-eyed, not yet into her occult phase, apparently. She wore a flowered minidress with a pixie collar and her long dark hair was parted down the middle.

One of the last earmarked sections of the book was called "Student Life," and it consisted of candid snapshots of various groups of students hanging out together. There were no names listed in the captions, just funny sayings, like "We're way cuter in person" and "We are going to cure cancer and walk on Mars."

Natalie turned to the last folded-over corner, on page one hundred sixty-nine—among a couple of other candids, there was a snapshot of four students posing in front of the Witching Tree. The photograph was of poor quality, and it was difficult to make out their heavily shaded faces, but she recognized Dottie Coffman among them. The other three were girls. The caption read: "Witches in Training."

35

No matter how modern the building was, no matter how much they tried to spruce up the place, nursing homes were depressing. There was a dormlike feel to the large, airy main lobby and adjacent cafeteria, to the broad carpeted stairs and the large-print posters.

Dottie Coffman shared a room on the third floor. The other bed was empty. The windows were narrow and hermetically sealed. The bathroom had lots of handrails and grips for seniors.

Natalie found a frail, elderly woman seated in front of the TV with the volume blaring. A quiz show. There was a beige pocketbook in her lap, and she stared not so much at the TV screen as into space.

"Hello?" Natalie said. "Mrs. Coffman?"

The woman looked up. Her face had settled into deep lines of sorrow, despite her best efforts to smile. Her sorrow-baked wrinkles told the truth, whereas her smile tried to mask her grief. It was the smile of a prisoner—trapped in this sorry place, but also inside her own mind.

"I'm sorry to bother you. May I turn this down?"

"Why, yes, that would be fine." She had a delicate, rusty voice.

Natalie turned the volume down on the TV, pulled up a chair, and took

Dottie's cold, age-speckled hand. Her heart went out to this woman. How many visitors did she get? How many of them did she recognize? It felt as if she'd been abandoned here by busy relatives who wanted her safe and sound but not around. Not underfoot. So fucking sad.

Dottie put her fist to her mouth and began to cough—a weak, phlegmy sound.

"Would you like some water?"

"No, where is the . . . what's your name?"

"Natalie."

"Do we know each other?"

"We've never met before. I work for—"

"Patty . . . may I call you Patty?"

"I'm Natalie. Detective Natalie Lockhart. I work for the Burning Lake police."

The woman tried to sit up straighter by repeatedly and hopelessly clawing at the vinyl-upholstered arms of her chair. She reminded Natalie of an injured bird, and it brought out her protective instincts. She got up and adjusted the pillow that was propping the older woman up. "Better?"

"Yes, thank you."

"Dottie, I wanted to ask you about my sister, Grace. Do you remember Grace Lockhart? You were her teacher several decades ago. Do you remember talking to her about forming a coven?"

Her eyes widened a bit. "No."

"You don't remember Grace?"

"I've had so many students over the years."

"Perhaps you remember Bella Striver then? She played the violin."

"No, I don't remember." She grew upset, her frail breastbone heaving with panic.

"It's okay. Calm down."

She tried to speak, and her breath whistled. She patted her pocketbook as if it were a dog sitting on her lap. Her eyes were the color of accumulated dust.

Outside in the corridor, people hurried past the doorway—nurses, doctors, trained senior-care staff. Natalie sat patiently, as if she could somehow redeem herself for the impatience she'd once felt while sitting with her sick mother, all those long-ago chances lost to time and death.

Dottie regained her composure and said, "We don't talk about that."

"You don't talk about what? Bella?"

"We don't speak of it anymore."

"Speak of what?" Natalie asked.

"I like to listen to the wind. I like to watch the stars and the moon. I wasn't supposed to say anything . . . I'm not supposed to say anything." There was a hushed urgency to her voice that gave Natalie goose bumps. "They will pass judgment."

"Who will pass judgment?"

"The thir—" The word broke off abruptly into a hacking cough.

"Third?"

"No," she gasped. "You can't . . ."

"I'm not passing judgment," Natalie said. "I'm simply asking questions."

"There aren't very many of us left."

"Many of who?"

"Us," she hissed, suddenly clear-eyed.

It startled Natalie. "Do you mean you and Thomas Grimsby? The boy in your school? You and Tommy G. and Ned Bertrand were in a religious group together, right?"

"Ned . . ." Dottie's eyes narrowed as she focused on Natalie's face. "Ned Bertrand is here. He's right here in this loathsome place."

"He's in this nursing home?"

Dottie blinked. Her eyes lost their focus. She was growing tired and weak. Natalie had pressed her too hard. "I don't know. How am I supposed to remember? Life rushes by so quickly . . ." She tugged randomly at her clothes and pulled anxiously on her arthritic hands.

"Are you all right? Do you need anything?"

"I'm tired. No more talking."

Natalie stood up. "I'll come back some other time."

The agility and strength with which Dottie reached out and grabbed Natalie by the arm was startling. Then her gnarled fingers tightened around Natalie's wrist. "Time is short." She wheezed. "The birdbath . . ."

Natalie sat down again. "What birdbath?"

"Behind my house. It's buried there. Under the birdbath. You need to find it for me. In the backyard. You need to get rid of it for me. Burn it."

"Burn what?" Natalie asked breathlessly. "What is it I need to find, Mrs. C.?"

"It's buried there in the backyard. It needs to be destroyed—please do this one last thing for me. Look underneath the birdbath. That's where they buried it."

"They who?"

Dottie's eyes widened with terror, as if she'd awakened out of a nightmare into another one. She shook her head, muttering, "I'm not supposed to say anything . . . no more talk."

"But you just said—"

"No more talk!"

On her way out, Natalie stopped at the reception desk to ask about Ned Bertrand. Even though the place looked clean and tidy, the air smelled stale and the staff came across as overworked and grumpy. They ignored some of the seniors seated in their wheelchairs in the corners of the common room. They ignored people asking for help and seemed to chalk it up to various diseases of the mind. There was the taint of giving up in the air, of the uselessness of it all.

"Yes, Ned Bertrand is one of our patients here," the busy smiling receptionist said. "Would you like to see him, Detective?"

"Thanks. Which way?"

A staff member escorted Natalie to Ned's room. The sight of him lying there half-paralyzed sent chills rippling through her. His son, the Violinist, was in prison for murder. Five months ago, he'd almost killed Natalie.

It was obvious that Ned Bertrand had had a stroke. One side of his face sagged. He looked terribly ill, with a jutting jaw and greasy white hair—a far cry from the dapper antiques dealer she used to know.

Natalie slowly crossed the room. A few hazy rays of late-morning sunlight filtered through the gaps in the blinds. There was a medicinal smell in the air. She scrutinized his wrinkled face, the sharp lines of pain around his mouth.

"He's slowly improving," the staff member told her. "He can't speak or communicate, but he's getting better, bit by bit. We've seen some progress."

It was an optimistic prognosis, at best. He seemed worse than when she'd last seen him—alone in his room with an armless corpse, at the mercy of his sociopathic son.

Something sparked behind Ned's eyes—he recognized who Natalie was and grew agitated, focusing on her with great intensity. His tongue rolled around as he tried to form words with his half-paralyzed mouth. He struggled with the syllables and consonants, but all he could manage was a disgusted hiss. It sounded like "Get out."

36

Natalie drove past the ugly billboards, obsolete factories, and old family farms on her way to the south side of town. Dottie Coffman's former house was set back from the road, an English country cottage with dark red shutters and a rooster weather vane. Today the entire structure was coated with glistening snow and bathed in a pretty noontime light. A green Subaru Forester was parked in the driveway.

Natalie got out and took the shoveled path to the front door. She'd already called the owners and had gotten their permission to come see them. She heard a confusing blur of voices inside as she rang the front bell. It was coming from a television set. The show's theme music sounded familiar.

A woman in her late twenties answered the door. Astrid Conway had chocolate-colored curls that teased her rosy cheeks. Her face contained an uncomplicated warmth. Her husband was a UPS driver. She was a secretary at an insurance company. She was pregnant. She rubbed her shivering arms and said, "Detective Lockhart?"

"Thanks for agreeing to see me on such short notice."

"Not at all. Your call intrigued me. Come in."

The house was full of comforting smells—cinnamon buns and melting chocolate and fresh-brewed coffee. You could tell Astrid was four or five months along. She virtually glowed, as if she'd brought her own inner light source with her.

"When are you due?" Natalie asked.

"Around the end of July."

"How exciting."

"I feel too young to be anybody's mother. I'm afraid I'll get it all wrong."

"I'm sure you'll do fine." Natalie smiled.

"Long as I don't drop the baby, right?" Astrid escorted her down a central hallway past the country kitchen and into the mudroom at the back of the house. An assortment of boots stood in puddles of melted snow. Astrid grabbed a gray wool coat from the rack and put it on, then wrapped a plaid scarf around her neck and opened the back door. "We bought the place five years ago. We felt so lucky. We love the backyard. We didn't realize the neighbors would be such a pain in the ass, though."

They headed into the backyard, past the barbecue pit and weathered picnic table. It was only when you stepped out the back door that you got a real sense of separation from the rest of the community. To the right of the house was a tall cedar fence. To the left of the house stood a thick pine forest. There were two stunted, snow-covered apple trees and a vegetable garden. In the approximate center of the yard was an old birdbath.

"Behind that fence are our lovely next-door neighbors, the Fergusons," Astrid said in a mocking tone. "They seem to think that their fence will protect them from us 'drooling maniacs' next door." She laughed. "My husband and I enjoy getting drunk and playing volleyball, or staying up late to look at the stars and philosophize. They think we're nuts." She waved a dismissive hand at the cedar fence.

The pedestal birdbath was made of cast stone concrete with an olive-green patina. It was very old, cracked in places, and covered with a veil of moss. It must've weighed about a hundred pounds. There were cattails carved into the base, a large water lily engraved on the underside of the bowl, and two frogs perched on the perimeter of the bowl. The water inside the basin was frozen solid.

"Would it be possible for us to dig up the area directly under the birdbath?"

"Sure, but what for?" Astrid asked.

"We have reason to believe there's something buried underneath it."

Astrid frowned and studied the birdbath. "What could possibly be buried there? Are you talking about a dead body?"

"No," Natalie said—but she really didn't know.

"Okay, but when you're done, you'll fill in the hole and put the birdbath back in the same place, right? Because I really love it."

"Yes." Natalie had no idea if that was possible.

"So you'll replace it as soon as you're finished digging?"

"Yes," Natalie repeated, without having any solid basis to make such promises. But the owner had agreed to the basic principle of the thing, so she said, "Let me call my supervisor. I'll be right back."

She walked a few yards away and called Luke. It took her several minutes to explain the situation.

When she was done, he said, "What are you talking about, Natalie? We'd need a warrant, and there's no basis for it, except for the word of an elderly woman suffering from Alzheimer's. Besides which, we don't have the funding for a wild-goose chase."

Frazzled by his tone, Natalie snapped back, "It's more complicated than that, and besides, it's a lead. What other leads do we have right now?"

"Debrief is soon. You need to come down to the station. We'll talk about it then." He hung up.

"Shit," she said under her breath, then turned toward Astrid, who was pretending not to listen. "Okay, there's been a little snag. I need to talk about this further with my supervisor, but just so we're straight. As long as we put the birdbath back, you'll give us your permission to dig in the ground back here?"

Astrid nodded. "You know, it's funny, this reminds me," she said, "a month after we moved in, a man dropped by. A stranger. He said he was Dottie Coffman's nephew. I've never seen him before or since. But anyway, the house came furnished with boxes of stuff. Lots of junk. And he wanted to know if we'd found a lockbox in the house. A metal box about yea big that was locked. We said no. Carl and I never saw anything like that. There were a lot of things in the house when we bought it, boxes of crap, piles of old clothes and furniture. But my husband and I never found anything like a lockbox. We would've opened it immediately. We're curious that way. And this guy . . . he grew sort of upset, and so we invited him in and told him to have a look around. By that point, we'd stored most of her stuff down in the basement. He was lucky, because we hadn't donated it to Goodwill yet. He spent quite a bit of time rummaging around down there, searching for something. Going through boxes. He left empty-handed."

"Do you remember his name?"

"Nope."

"What did he look like?"

"Pretty average. Maybe forty-five. Maybe younger."

"Balding? Big ears?"

Astrid laughed. "I don't remember. He was kind of rude. When he didn't find what he was looking for, he just left. Walked right past us without saying thanks or anything. The asshole."

It alarmed Natalie. Maybe there was some truth to Dottie Coffman's claim, despite her frail health. "Thanks," she said. "I'll figure something out and get back to you."

37

A honey-colored afternoon light slanted through the mini-blinds in Luke's office, highlighting the skepticism on his face as Natalie explained her reasoning. She tried to connect all the dots for him, but it came out muddled.

"Veronica Manes earmarked several pages in JFK's 1975 yearbook. I found a picture of the religious club Dottie Coffman was in with Thomas Grimsby and Ned Bertrand. Ned Bertrand! What are the odds? I believe Veronica visited Blackthorn Park, where Dottie Coffman carved her and Thomas Grimsby's initials into one of the Witch Trees. I confirmed it with the reverend. Dottie taught English at JFK High and was a huge influence on both Grace and Bella, and maybe many more female students. She encouraged them to explore Wicca and form covens. Veronica was looking into all of this."

"What you've described sounds pretty harmless, Natalie." His shoulders were squared. His eyes were direct. "You said so yourself, Dottie Coffman can't remember anything about Grace or Bella. Regarding the birdbath, she might be delusional, or else whatever's buried there could be unrelated to the case. Who knows? You're spreading yourself too thin."

"But I saw the birdbath. It's right there in the backyard."

"Okay, I have a question for you. Is now the right time to pursue it? First of all, the ground is frozen solid. We'd have to pay for a special excavation, and we don't have the funds for that. If you want to pursue this lead on your own time, and if you find enough evidence for an affidavit, then come to me. In the meantime, the case you're assigned to is Veronica Manes. Let's keep focused on the task at hand. We've only begun our investigation, and there's a ton of stuff to do."

"I understand." He was right. She needed more evidence. She would have to find it on her own. She reluctantly shifted her focus. "What's next?"

"Brandon got the train video from SRS. Do you want to see it?"

She nodded.

He opened his laptop, and Natalie walked around behind his desk, where she stood looking over his shoulder. He hit play, and the train's cab view CCTV began to play. Visibility was poor. From the engineer's point of view, you could see the snow-covered tracks directly in front of the train, up to a distance of about fifty yards. After several minutes, the fog lifted and you could see a person standing on the tracks—the silhouette of a witchlike figure, dressed in black with a tall pointy hat.

The engineer hit the emergency brakes. The train horn sounded. The train's air brakes hissed. The person standing on the tracks appeared to be struggling to get away, twisting and turning and waving her arms at the train.

As the locomotive relentlessly approached, Veronica Manes finally stopped struggling and faced the train, which was in full emergency stop mode by now. She stared wide-eyed at the engineer and put her arms up, as if to protect herself from the beast barreling toward her. In the last few seconds, she turned her head away, squeezed her eyes shut, and whispered something—a Wiccan prayer, perhaps.

The train impacted the woman dressed as a witch, and in a heartbeat she was gone. The train kept barreling forward along the tracks, while the brakes screeched and screamed, and the engineer could be heard shouting, "Oh no! Please no!"

Natalie could feel the dull thudding of her heart as she stood behind Luke, experiencing all sorts of emotions—grief, shock, disgust. The video was far worse than she'd expected. "I can't imagine what it must've been like for her," she whispered.

Luke pinched the bridge of his nose between his fingers. "Clearly this was intended to punish and humiliate her, or else the Wiccan community as a whole." He turned to her. "You were right on the money about that, Natalie."

Her psyche was covered with tender spots, like a land mine of little bruises. She ran her fingers through her hair and looked away, feeling the pressure of his gaze. Too much pressure. He was expecting her to help him solve the case—but what if she couldn't do it this time? She walked around to the front of his desk and took her seat. "What else do we have?"

Luke picked up a report. "Lenny and Augie did a second sweep of both sites, and this time they found a few green glass fragments with a small quantity of blood on them in Veronica Manes's kitchen. It tested positive for the victim's blood type, so he sent it to the lab for a DNA match. But Veronica could've cut herself on some broken glassware. There's no way of knowing whether it occurred on Monday night or not."

"What about the soil samples?"

"Nothing definitive. They said it could be potting soil. However, the two sets of boot prints tracking mud into the house look as if they belong to an adult male and either a younger male, or a female. Sole patterns indicate they're a popular brand of boots sold at Walmart. Men's size eleven for one set of prints, and men's size seven and a half for the other. Veronica's boot and shoe treads are not a match. So that's significant."

"Meaning there are two killers. Not just one."

"Or a killer and his accomplice."

"What about Edward's shoe size?"

"We're trying to get him to cooperate," Luke said. "I've been on the phone with Edward's lawyer. Holly seems to have disappeared."

"Are you serious?"

"We put out another APB . . ."

"We had them and we let them go," Natalie said angrily.

"These things happen."

"That's what people say when they mess up."

"We'll find her," he said confidently. "Trust me. And Edward's lawyer will cooperate. It's just a matter of negotiations . . ."

"Jesus, Luke. The boot prints? We should've thought of that before."

"What do you want me to do? Dwell on the negative? Regret all the mistakes I've made over the course of the past seventeen years?"

It was odd, because she had memorized Luke down to the freckles on his shoulders and the gentle lines around his intelligent eyes, and they knew so much about each other, and yet it felt as if they were complete strangers now.

There was a knock on the door.

"Come in," Luke called out.

Peter Murphy greeted them with his Muppet-like eyebrows furrowed. He wore a heavy tweed overcoat, a blue woolen cap, and calfskin gloves. "Sorry to interrupt, but I just got back from the impound lot, and you wanted me to relay the info to you pronto, Lieutenant."

Luke nodded. "What'd they find on the pickup truck?"

"Nada so far. That's a big fat zero." Murphy winked at Natalie. "But they're in the middle of the process, so maybe we'll get lucky."

"Okay, thanks, Murphy."

"How's the hunt going, Natalie? You find anything interesting in those evidence boxes I gave you?"

"Nothing to report yet," she said. It was odd, how chummy he acted in front of Luke, when they both knew he'd turn into a stone-cold jerk behind Luke's back.

"All right, folks, don't work too hard." He smiled and closed the door behind him.

Luke picked up another report. "Lenny finished his analysis of the costume. Here's a print copy of the three-dimensional reconstruction." He handed it to her. "I emailed you the digital images. Lenny says it's above-average quality, made of a hundred percent polyester."

She studied the reconstructed costume. It had a timeless Victorian feel about it—a full-length, long-sleeved black dress with silver buttons and a fitted bodice, a black tulle petticoat, a classic pointed cone-shaped hat with a broad brim edge, and a Renaissance-inspired cloak with an oversized hood.

"We're in the process of checking out the local thrift shops and costume outlets, to see if anybody recognizes this one." Luke checked his watch. "I'm due for a meeting with the chief. I need you to start with Murray's Halloween Costumes on Route 151."

"Yeah, I know the place."

"Lenny says the label was cut out, so we need to identify who manufactured it. If Murray Gallo sells this costume in his shop, I want you to go through his sales records and find out who purchased it in the past handful of years. Mike's also looking online." He checked his watch again. "Any questions?"

"No, I'm good." She stood up.

His warm smile was back. Her familiar Luke was back. "Hold on, Natalie, one more thing . . ." The tenderness in his voice was jarring. They were friends now, nothing but friends, and they were supposed to have left all the tenderness behind. "I don't mean to pry into your life. I want you to take all the time you need before coming to a decision. But it would be helpful for me to know if you've made a decision. In other words, should I keep on handing you assignments?"

"As of right now, I'm all in. But I'm considering my options. I wish I could give you a more definitive answer."

"That's all right. Take your time. Just keep me apprised."

She turned to leave, then said, "Sometimes it feels as if I have no other life besides the police station, you know? Do you ever feel that way? Like you were born here, and you're going to die here between these four walls?"

His smile hardened into a cynical smirk. "All the time."

"I almost can't imagine having any other kind of life. How do I separate myself from Burning Lake? From my childhood, my family, and all my friends? My biggest dream was to become a cop like my father, but then I think about all the horrific things that have happened, and I wonder if I did the right thing. Grace and Willow and I grew up in that house, and I didn't see any of it coming. How is that possible? How can I lay the dead to rest for other people, when I can't even do it for myself?"

He nodded thoughtfully. "Just know you aren't alone. We all feel the same way. It's a tough job. We've all made mistakes. We all have regrets. Comes with the territory, unfortunately."

She smiled sadly. "Thanks for indulging me, Luke."

He waved it away. "My door is always open. You know that."

"I'll let you know what I find at Murray's," she said and left.

38

Natalie drove to Murray's Halloween Costumes on Route 151 and parked in the sprawling lot behind the sooty brick warehouse. She unbuckled her seat belt, but before stepping out of her silver-gray Honda Accord, she got on the phone with Max Callahan.

"Hey, Lockhart, what's up?" he said, slightly out of breath.

"Hey yourself. I need an estimate for an excavation. It's in someone's backyard. I don't know the depth. I'd need to act soon."

"You're talking frozen-ground excavation? Are you digging up a coffin?"

"No, just . . . looking for something. I don't know how big or how small."

"Okay. Either way, those can be a challenge. This time of year, it's like digging through concrete," he told her. "Depending on ground density, moisture content, and surface temperature, you've got your excavation equipment and trenching machines that can generate enough force to penetrate frozen ground, but that's a blunt instrument if you don't know the depth and size of the object. You also have to watch out for gas lines, water pipes, and electrical lines. You'd have to consult with local utilities companies if it's a big job. They'll come out and check the area for a fee."

"Okay, let's say we've done all that. How would it work?"

"First, you dig out the snow over the site and heat the ground with several self-contained heaters. You'd probably use a hydraulic ripper, which breaks up frozen ground fairly significantly with minimal stress on the machine. Then you'd use a dig bucket with sharp teeth designed specifically for excavating frozen ground. There's some other equipment, too, but it would depend on the requirements."

"How much would it cost?"

"Well, considering labor and equipment, plus any replacement parts if there's breakage, plus the likelihood of delays due to bad weather, it'll cost you."

"How much?"

"Five thousand bucks or more. I'd need the variables to pin it down."

"Thanks, Max." She hung up, feeling deflated but not defeated. As she got out of her car, a frigid breeze blew her coat open. It flapped in the wind. She yanked it shut and crossed her arms.

A sign on the redbrick building read "Prices Slashed!" Murray's Halloween Costumes was an 80,000-square-foot outlet store. The large, high-ceilinged lobby was full of mannequins dressed as gangsters, clowns, pirates, vampires, werewolves, and superheroes of every stripe. From there, the store branched into separate wings leading into many other rooms, and you could easily get lost in the mazelike corridors if it weren't for the giant red arrows pointing the way toward the exits. Even then it was fairly easy to get lost at Murray's.

In the lobby, there were three cashier stations with computer registers, credit card machines, and orange plastic bags with MURRAY'S HALLOWEEN COSTUMES printed on the side. The place appeared to be empty this afternoon, which wasn't unusual for March. She doubted that anyone in Burning Lake needed a costume right now.

Just then, Murray came bustling out of his office to greet her—once again, she'd phoned ahead. "Natalie Lockhart, as I live and breathe. I remember when you were yea big." He held a hand up to his mid-thigh to demonstrate. "You and your sisters would come in here every Halloween, so excited, and Grace always wanted to be a princess, Willow wanted to be a ballerina, and you wanted to be a cop, or else Wonder Woman."

"I remember it fondly," she said with a warm smile.

In his early seventies, Murray Gallo was a stout, ginger-haired man with a stately Italian face and a fastidious mustache. Always ready to reel you in with a new sales pitch, he offered Natalie a stick of gum. "Look at this, my new customized promotional chewing gum. This one's peppermint. Would you like a piece?"

She shook her head.

"No?" He popped the stick of gum into his mouth. "Okay, down to business. How can I help you, honey? I'm sorry. Detective?"

She took out her phone, swiped through the images, and showed him a digital copy of the computer-reconstructed witch costume. "Have you ever seen this before?"

"Oh, that's a beaut," he said, leaning so close she could smell the peppermint on his breath. "Nice and classic. I recall purchasing a few dozen of those maybe six years ago. I don't know if they make them anymore. They were quite expensive, and that affected sales." He chewed his gum thoughtfully. "You know, our biggest problem is chasing trends. Once a popular costume becomes obsolete, you're stuck with it. Then what do you do? Which is why we offer such a big selection, Natalie. We keep abreast of all the new trends. It's basically a guessing game. We've got thousands in inventory, but once a costume stops selling, we'll never order it again. Out with the old, in with the new."

"So this costume—you never ordered it again?"

He shook his head. "Too expensive, and probably too refined. It didn't sell well, which is too bad, because I like quality costumes. But I'd go broke if all I did was sell quality costumes. The whole trick to running this business is flexibility. Halloween comes once a year, with merchandise flying off the shelves, but by November it's over. Which is why we also rent costumes to high school productions, theater groups, churches, and musicians. We do pretty well in that department, what with the summer music festival and the spring and fall events . . . that keeps us busy year-round. We also supply decorations for birthday parties and princess parties. Bottom line—people trust us for their costume needs. Which explains why we'll outlast the competition. Murray's is forever, Natalie."

She smiled briefly, acknowledging his pride in his shop and his business acumen, then said, "The label was cut out of this one. Do you happen to remember who the manufacturer was?"

"Well, let's see. I deal with thousands of manufacturers, maybe tens of thousands. So not offhand, but I can look it up."

"While you're at it, can you get me your sales records for this costume?"

"Sure, although it may take a while. In the meantime, can I get you anything, Natalie? Cup of tea? Coke? Lemonade?"

"Thanks, I'm good, Murray."

He gave her an indulgent, softhearted grin. "You want to sit in the office?"

"I think I'll have a look around, if you don't mind."

"Help yourself. We got some new stock in last week, including Wonder Woman."

The floor space was disorganized, with dusty corridors leading into rooms full of costumes, wigs, hats, face masks, fake beards and mustaches, makeup kits, and jewelry. There were lawn decorations for Halloween and Christmas. There was a whole selection for period-costume colonial attire, which was used in theatrical re-creations of the witch trials during the month of October.

The smell was a mixture of floor wax, dry-cleaning fluids, and damp wool. There were Walking Dead costumes, medieval plague-doctor masks, Sponge-Bob, baby Yoda, Spider-Man, Captain Marvel, Princess Leia, E.T. phoning home, Michael Myers, the Coneheads, Teenage Mutant Ninja Turtles, and ThunderCats.

She picked up a mask and studied the transparent piece of molded plastic with two eyeholes in it. The material was soft and pliable, but you couldn't see any details behind it. It was barely there, and yet when she held it to her face and looked into one of the wall mirrors, it distorted her face like a shape-shifting device.

She shuddered and put the mask down, thoroughly creeped out by it. She walked up and down the aisles, then paused in front of a bulletin board full of snapshots of the outlet's employees throughout the years. The handmade banner above the collection of Polaroids proclaimed: "Murray's Minions." His employees were dressed in a variety of costumes, and they all looked fairly upbeat. Then something caught her eye. Natalie spotted a woman wearing the same kind of witch costume that Veronica had died in—same long sleeves, same bodice with the unusual silver buttons, same hat and cloak.

She went to get Murray, and a few minutes later, they were standing in front of the bulletin board together.

"Oh yeah, that's Jodi Stewart," Murray explained. "She worked for us for fifteen years. An excellent employee. She was never late, hardly ever sick, and she was such a kindhearted person. These are all Murray's employees, past and present. Every year, we show off the inventory for the entire month of October."

Natalie recognized the name—Jodi Stewart was Holly Host's mother. "She's wearing the witch costume we were just discussing."

"Yeah, what a coincidence, huh?" Murray shook his head. "Jodi passed away four years ago. Such a tragic loss. She was like family."

"Can I see the picture?"

Murray took down the Polaroid and handed it to her. "I was looking through my records, and I found the manufacturer, a small company in California called Crystal Mystic Design. They do good work, but it wasn't a moneymaker for us. Anyway, once I had the name of the manufacturer, it was easy to locate the itemized sales records. A handful paid cash, the rest used credit cards, so I'm compiling the information for you."

"Thanks, Murray. Could you send it to me at this number when you're finished?" She handed him her card.

"Of course. May I ask what this is all about?"

Natalie shook her head. "We're in the middle of the investigation."

"Such a terrible tragedy."

"Can I keep this?" She held on to the Polaroid.

"Only if you promise to return it. Sentimental reasons."

She nodded. "This particular costume—do you have any left?"

"I doubt it. We would've sold them off as part of our overstock."

"Sold them to who?"

"Various boutiques in town. We do bulk sales for things that are no longer moneymakers. Basically, you have to keep your inventory moving. Nowadays we're competing with online merchandise, as well. For-sale items are tricky because most folks can get it cheaper on Amazon. You've also got pop-up stores to worry about. That's why we invest most heavily in our rental costumes. High-end, high-quality, very detailed outfits made of good material. Regional high schools and theater production companies will order their costumes from us year after year, because we're solidly reliable. You can make money off your reputation, but only if it's A-plus."

"Are you positive you sold all of these costumes?"

"No. I'd have to keep checking my records."

"Do you mind?"

"Not at all. But again, it may take some time."

"Call me when you're done, Murray. And thanks. You've been incredibly helpful."

39

It was late afternoon by the time she got to the public library. The main reading room was deeply silent. She found Patrick Dupree behind the circulation desk. The thirty-five-year-old associate director was intelligent, fair, and compassionate—words you wouldn't find on his résumé, but which certainly belonged there. He had a friendly round face and wire-rim glasses, and today he sat shivering in his forest-green corduroy jacket with the leather elbow patches.

"How are you, Patrick?"

He peered at her over his eyeglasses. "Not great."

"I'm sorry to hear that."

"I think this town is cursed," he whispered, looking around. "We've become a serial-killer magnet."

She winced a little. The library was sparsely occupied today, chilly and hushed. People were scattered about, holding books in their hands, sitting or standing, some as motionless as mannequins in a diorama.

"Cursed," he repeated with gentle melancholy. "I'm considering applying for a job in Syracuse and moving there. I mean, why does this keep happening? What's going on? It goes deeper than random coincidence, don't you think? Like we have to pay for the sins of the past. I know that's not factual—I'm a librarian, I deal in facts—but still, you have to admit it makes sense to start thinking that way. Don't you?"

Natalie leaned against the circulation desk and said, "I need a list of all the books that Veronica Manes checked out in the past year or so."

"Listen," he said, hesitating. "One of the biggest clichés about librarians besides the whole 'hush' thing, is First Amendment rights. If the government asks you to rat out a reader, that's cause for concern. But I get it. She's dead. I'm assuming you don't need a warrant for this?"

"I could get one," Natalie replied.

He drew a sharp breath. "Okay." He typed a few commands into his computer and said, "So the good news is . . . we use a barcode system with an automated checkout that keeps tabs on everyone's withdrawals. When I first started working here, we used good old-fashioned library loan cards. You wrote your name and date by hand. We hand stamped each loan card pocket. Now there are barcodes instead, and no one talks to us, and we don't talk to them. Modernization has come to the public library. Big whoop. Now all the digital information is stored online. No need for eye contact or personal connection. We might as well be robots. Anyway . . ." He typed in a few more keystrokes and squinted at the screen. "Here's the list of Veronica's checkouts. There are dozens and dozens of books."

"Can you print that out for me?"

"Sure." He typed in the command. "You know, I don't know if I should mention this or not, but she used to come in here regularly to write and do research. She was a peach. She'd spend hours on her laptop or perusing the stacks for certain books. She cleaned up after herself, unlike some people. She always had a smile for everyone. Always said hello and good-bye. There were never any issues. Then one day Marigold Hutchins comes in and walks over to where Veronica is sitting and starts arguing with her."

Natalie raised an eyebrow. "When was this?"

"About a month ago. I mean, I know they're friends, and friends can disagree, but still. This is a library." He took the two-page list from the printer, stapled it, and handed it to Natalie. "It was odd to see Veronica involved in an altercation like that. She was such a professional person. I think she was mortified. They had to go outside to the courtyard, and even then you could hear Marigold yelling."

"What was the argument about?"

"I don't know. I only heard raised voices, and maybe a few words, but it didn't make sense. Something about a name. I mean, it's not like our patrons never misbehave or anything. There are a lot of—how can I put this without sounding like a jerk?—mentally unstable people coming into the library. I don't mean to be cruel, but it's the truth. Pierre LaPointe comes in all the time with his imaginary friend, who isn't very nice. Some days they'll get into a squabble, which can escalate into a screaming match, and when that happens, we have to escort *both of them* out of the building, if you get my drift." He rolled his eyes and shrugged. "You know. Typical day at the library."

"What happened between Marigold and Veronica?"

"They were in the courtyard for a good five minutes or so, and then Marigold stormed off, and Veronica came back inside and continued working on her book. She seemed very composed and in control, as if nothing unusual had happened. She never mentioned it to me. And it would have been impolite to ask."

Natalie picked up the list. "Would you do me a favor and get me as many of these books as you can?"

He nodded. "That's a lot of books. It'll take a couple of hours."

"I'll come back for them later," she said. "And Patrick . . . please don't move to Syracuse. The town needs you."

He smiled. His eyes welled up. "You, too, Detective. You're awesome."

40

Everyone was out buying food or gassing up the car, getting ready for the next storm to roll through. A light snow was falling, dusting the freshly scraped windshields. The winter blues had descended upon the town. The month of March felt like one big hangover, with no end in sight.

Natalie parked on Sarah Hutchins Drive and walked to Skeletons in the Closet, where the bright-eyed young clerk behind the register explained that her boss had gone home. So Natalie got back into her car and drove to the east side of town, where the bushes growing by the roadside were full of plump red berries, the kind you weren't supposed to eat. The poisonous kind.

She found the olive-green Gothic at the end of Woodpecker Lane, a waft of bluish smoke drifting from the chimney. Marigold Hutchins answered the door, looking surprised. Her long dark hair was pulled into a ponytail, and she wore casual clothes—jeans, sneakers, and a Marilyn Manson sweatshirt. "Hello again. What are you doing here?"

"I have a few more questions if you don't mind."

"Sure. Okay."

They sat in the living room. The fire had gone out. The wine bottles and Kleenex boxes had been put away. The house was clean and quiet.

"I've just come from the library," Natalie explained, "and Patrick Dupree told me that you and Veronica had an argument about a month ago."

"Really? Patrick said that?"

"Why? Isn't it true?" Natalie asked.

"No, I mean . . . we had a discussion. But that's all."

"What was the discussion about?"

Marigold blushed. "Would you like some coffee?"

"No thanks. I'm all coffeed out."

She sighed and rubbed her forehead. "Patrick said we had a fight?"

"Yes."

"Gosh, how embarrassing." Marigold wrung her hands together. She looked around as if she were trying to find an escape route. Then she dropped her hands and said, "Veronica had a big heart. Maybe too big. She felt sorry for Justin—everything he lost, his youth, all those years behind bars. It happened so subtly, I didn't notice at first. And then I realized they were sleeping together."

Natalie sat forward slightly. "Veronica and Justin Fowler?"

"Yes." Marigold nodded. "As soon as I sensed there was something going on between them, I asked her about it. This was back in late January. She admitted they were sleeping together, but she begged me to keep it confidential. She felt sorry for Justin, he was struggling. It just happened. So I didn't tell a soul. I figured they'd get tired of each other eventually. I mean, look at the age difference."

"So what caused the argument?"

"It was Valentine's Day when I got a frantic call from Veronica. She asked me to come over. She'd cut her hand. She and Justin had apparently had a fight—she didn't tell me what it was about, but he threw a glass at her, it hit the wall and broke, and she cut her finger on the shards. It was bleeding pretty badly, so I took her to the ER. I told her to call the police, but she insisted that he'd done nothing wrong. She didn't want him getting into trouble. She said he'd had enough trouble in his life. So I respected her wishes. After a couple of stitches and a tetanus shot, I took her home."

"And you didn't tell anyone about this?"

"No. She asked me not to."

"Not one single person?" Natalie pressed.

Marigold stared at her. "Look, if you want to keep a secret, tell a witch.

Okay? Witches don't judge. We like our privacy. We keep our rituals out of the public eye."

Natalie nodded—it was interesting. She'd never thought about witches that way, that they might be good at keeping secrets because of their history of persecution. "So the argument at the library . . . ?"

"Happened the next day. After sleeping on it, I realized I had to say something. I didn't want my friend getting hurt. I've lived through domestic violence myself, as you know, so I understand the instinct to want to protect your abuser. I watched my father brutalize my mother, and I swore I'd never let a man do that to me. I wanted to empower myself. That, combined with my ancestry, made me realize that I wanted to become a witch, which is how I met Veronica. So I wasn't about to let some guy hurt my friend."

"What did Veronica say?"

"She told me to mind my own business. Imagine that? She insisted she was fine, that she'd spoken to Justin and he'd apologized. I told her I've heard that song and dance before. But she didn't want to hear it."

"So you left?"

"Yes."

"And then what?"

"We never talked about it again. I assume she and Justin remained close. You couldn't really tell with Veronica. She kept her cards close to her vest."

"Why didn't you tell me this before?"

Marigold heaved a weary sigh. "Because Veronica's a private person, and she asked me to keep my mouth shut, and so I did. For her sake. For her reputation around town. Besides, I didn't think it was relevant."

"Why not?"

"Because I find it very hard to believe that he would've done something like *that* to her. Chained her to the railroad tracks. He really did love her. He was like a puppy around her."

"That's not your decision to make," Natalie said. "I still don't understand why you never mentioned any of this to the police."

"Are you kidding me? And make her a laughingstock? Here's this fifty-eight-year-old woman, a self-proclaimed witch, and she's sleeping with a thirtysomething ex-con who's living at home with his mother? How pathetic does that sound? The media are all over the place, looking for salacious tidbits like that. Veronica asked me to keep it quiet, and for Pete's sake, I didn't want to drag her name through the mud." Marigold glared angrily at Natalie. "But I guess the cat's out of the bag now."

41

Ever since Natalie was a little girl, her father, Joey, used to take her to food banks and shelters to see how real people managed to survive against great odds. To strengthen her character. "This isn't some abstract theory about poverty and homelessness for you to feel fleetingly guilty about," he told her. "This is for your soul, Natalie. There is no homework. All you need to do is listen."

And it had served her very well all these years. She'd learned a lot from their stories of survival. But lately, the lessons eluded her.

Natalie found Justin Fowler behind the church, smoking a cigarette. He wore his janitor's T-shirt with its embroidered name patch underneath his wool coat. He wore jeans and rather new-looking camouflage boots. He was standing in front of Thomas Bell's gravestone. The three-hundred-year-old limestone marker was cracked in a dozen places. Eventually it would fall away to dust.

"Veronica's ancestor," Natalie commented, coming up behind him. "Thomas Bell. The judge who condemned Victoriana Forsyth to death during the witch trials."

He glanced over his shoulder at her and nodded. "Veronica told me how guilty she felt about it. I asked her why? What for? She said because it's karma. Bad karma worms its way through the generations." He drew slowly on his cigarette, then blew out an exhausted plume of smoke. "Veronica had a beautiful soul. She's the only one who welcomed me home and made me feel safe. When Veronica took me under her wing, I didn't feel like such a freak anymore."

Natalie felt terrible. It was true. She should've reached out to Justin after he'd left prison, but she was too embarrassed and ashamed about her family's complicity in his incarceration. "It sounds like you were more than just friends."

"What are you talking about?" he snapped.

Natalie decided to be blunt about it. There was no use dancing around the subject with a hardened ex-con, even if he was an innocent ex-con. "A witness told me you two were sleeping together."

He leaned in threateningly. "Who told you that?"

"The same witness who took Veronica to the ER after she cut her hand on some glass shards."

"Marigold," he snarled.

"What was the fight about? Between you and Veronica?"

He drew on his cigarette and glanced at the overcast sky. "I would never hurt her. And it's true, we were sleeping together. So what? It's a free country."

"What was the fight about?" Natalie repeated.

"Veronica was helping out this person, and I thought it was a bad idea. She fell for this person's innocent act, and if there's anyone who can see through bullshit, it's an ex-con. I wanted Veronica to cut off all connections, but she had a hard time turning Holly down."

"Holly Host?"

"Yeah, Veronica was letting her stay at her place for the weekend, and I told her that was crazy. She let this girl, who's clearly a drug addict, have the key to her house and everything. Veronica felt sorry for her. Holly and her husband had a fight, and Holly needed a place to stay. So Veronica let a drug addict have the run of the house. She could've done anything— snooped around, read all her emails, copied files, stolen shit. I don't know. I couldn't believe Veronica would trust her like that."

"So you threw a glass at her?" Natalie asked.

"No, that's not what happened. We were talking, I became agitated, I have a nervous tremor that sometimes flares up, like PTSD, and I dropped the glass . . . maybe I was shouting at the time. She told me to leave, so I left. I found out the next day what happened . . . that she'd gone to the emergency room for stitches. I felt terrible about it."

"Were there any altercations between Holly and Veronica that you know of? Or between Veronica and Holly's husband, Edward Host?"

"Edward's a piece of shit. But no . . ." He shook his head. "I was upset that Veronica put her trust in this person for some reason, but she told me Holly had important information she was trying to verify."

"Information? Like what?"

"I don't know. She wouldn't say. At the time, I thought it might've had something to do with her book. Veronica was interested in the Witch Trees and the connections between past and present, how it all braids together. But I'm not sure."

Natalie nodded and asked, "Did Veronica know that Edward and Holly owed the reverend rent money? And that they'd performed occult rituals with animals?"

He frowned. "Yeah, like I said. They're bad news. But Veronica was an amazing person. She wanted to help Holly get out of her troubled relationship. She didn't want to give up on her."

"And she told you Holly had important information? But she didn't say what?"

"She just said it would affect the coven."

"The coven? So it wasn't about her book?"

"I don't know. She wouldn't tell me. And believe me, Veronica knew how to keep a secret. You could trust her with your most private thoughts."

Natalie paused a moment, then switched gears. "What were you doing on Monday night?"

He looked at her suspiciously. "I was at home with my mother. Why?"

"What's your shoe size?"

"My shoe size?" He tossed his cigarette in the snow. "Ten. Why?"

"Is there anyone who could verify your whereabouts on Monday night and early Tuesday morning?"

"Yeah, my mother." He shoved his fists into his pockets. "Look, I was home with my mother. You can check it out. Whoever did this to Veronica? They're dead."

"How do you know that?"

"Because. I'm going to kill them. As soon as I find out who they are."

"Jesus, don't say that. It can be taken as a threat."

"Good. Because it is a threat," he said and headed back to the church.

42

The case was like black smoke wandering around in Natalie's head as the facts continued to elude her. On her way back to the police station, she stopped by the library to pick up the books. There were three boxes' worth, mostly hardcovers, and Patrick helped her carry them out to her car.

When she got back to the station, Natalie went directly upstairs to Luke's office. He was on the phone. He held up a finger. She waited with growing impatience, her hopscotching emotions giving her a jumpy stomach. When he hung up, she blurted, "We need to find Holly Host."

"We're looking for her. We put out—"

"An APB, I know. Listen, I'd like to interrogate Edward Host."

"We can't. Not without his lawyer present."

"Fuck."

"Stop pacing, Natalie, you're making me dizzy. Take a seat, would you?"

She sat down.

"What's this all about?"

She handed him the Polaroid photograph. "That's Jodi Stewart," she explained. "Holly's mother. As you can see, she's wearing the same costume

Veronica died in. It's made by a California design company called Crystal Mystic. Jodi Stewart worked at Murray's for fifteen years before she passed away four years ago. Murray says they bought dozens of these costumes six years ago, but they eventually sold them off with some of their unwanted bulk inventory. He's checking on it for me. He's also going to send us the sales records for the costume."

"Okay, as soon as you get them, forward them to me. I'll have Mike follow up. This is a great lead, Natalie."

"That's not all," she said, and Luke leaned back and loosened his tie. "I stopped at the library to get a list of all the books Veronica checked out over the past year or so, and Patrick Dupree told me he overheard an argument between Veronica and Marigold Hutchins. He said the dispute got so heated, they had to step outside. So I went to see Marigold, and according to her, they were arguing about Justin."

Luke raised a quizzical eyebrow.

"Apparently, Veronica and Justin were having an affair. And Marigold suspected that Veronica wasn't entirely safe in the relationship. She said they had an altercation where glass was broken—perhaps those green glass shards Lenny found in the kitchen—and that Veronica cut her hand. She asked Marigold to take her to the ER. Marigold was concerned that Veronica was falling into an abusive relationship, but she didn't tell the police about it for reasons of her own. So then, I went to get Justin's side of the story. I asked him what he and Veronica were fighting about. Apparently, Veronica had invited Holly Host to stay with her for a short while, and Justin didn't like the idea. He believed Holly was trouble, but Veronica didn't heed his advice—that's what their fight was about. Justin claims he didn't throw the glass. He said he has tremors and it slipped out of his hand. It turns out that Holly gave Veronica some important information that she believed would affect the coven. Justin has no idea what the information was."

"Affect the coven how?" Luke asked.

"Nobody knows. Veronica was very good at keeping secrets."

He studied her closely. "So what's your conclusion?"

She stiffened a little. She understood what he wanted from her. A cold reading. "Well, so far we've got a growing list of circumstantial evidence, but nothing concrete. We have a link between Holly and Veronica, and also a link between Holly's mother and the costume. We need to find Holly and sit her down and talk to her before she lawyers up again."

"What about Justin?" he asked.

"We need to verify his alibi. He says he was at home with his mother on Monday night. I'd like to take a look at his phone records and credit card purchases."

"Did you believe him about the tremors?"

"It would surprise me if he didn't come out of prison with PTSD. His medical records would tell us more. But he does seem to have a problem controlling his temper—that fight with Wayne Edison, for instance. His shoe size is ten, but that doesn't necessarily rule him out."

"Why not?"

"This crime was meticulously planned, down to the last detail," Natalie said. "Why would the killers leave their muddy footprints all over the house without a care in the world? Don't you think they're smarter than that?"

"So how do you change a size ten to a size eleven?"

"I don't know. Maybe they wore layers of socks to increase their shoe size. It's a possibility, right? After all, we've been eliminating suspects because their shoe sizes don't match."

"I'll consult with Lenny and see what he thinks. In the meantime, I'll ask Mike to start working on an affidavit for Fowler's phone and other records," Luke said. "This afternoon, we received Veronica's phone records. There were no calls between her and Holly or Edward. So unless Holly was using a burner phone . . ."

"She probably was . . ."

"We're looking into it. There were plenty of calls between Veronica and other members of the coven, a few to her agent, and a bunch of calls to various friends and business acquaintances around town. There were also dozens of calls from the church, and we figured it was Grimsby, but now we need to consider the possibility that some of those calls may have been from Justin. That puts a whole new spin on things. There were a few unlisted numbers, and that's problematic. Augie's tracking it all down. In the meantime, Jacob and Brandon are rounding up the usual suspects and conducting witness interviews, Murphy's sifting through piles of evidence, Mike's following up the most promising hotline tips and tracking down chain manufacturers, I'm fielding press calls and trying to prevent the chief from having a meltdown, and Lenny's got his plate full."

"So what can I do?"

He took off his reading glasses, and his gaze caught hers and glowed for an instant. She had no idea how Luke felt about her anymore, because he hid his feelings so well behind a wall of professionalism. Whenever they got too close, he would emotionally withdraw from her. The signals were pretty clear, but she kept trying to read between the lines, like an insecure teenage girl deconstructing a boy's "Hello." It made her feel dumb and self-destructive. She was incredibly happy with Hunter. Wasn't she? So why this childish need to be loved by the very man she had rejected?

"These are good, solid leads, Natalie. We'll take it from here," he said. "Write up your reports and go home. Your shift's almost over. I'll see you tomorrow."

"But I want to keep going. I'm not at all tired."

He put his glasses down and rubbed his eyes. "Look, I saw what those two previous cases did to you. I understand you want to solve this case. We all do. We're all working our asses off right now. But I'm not going to let you catch any flak for this one, Natalie. I won't let you become tabloid fodder. I'm telling you to write up your reports and clock out. Let it go for the night. It'll be here in the morning."

"Go ahead, be a little more condescending," she said angrily.

He nodded. "Duly noted."

"I don't need your protection, Luke."

He eyed her skeptically.

"If all the guys are busy, then give me the next assignment on the list. I can handle it."

Hesitation played across his face, and she could sense him withholding his response, as if he wanted to tell her something very badly, but it was clear that once he said this thing, he might not be able to walk it back. "Okay," he said softly. "I'll stop arguing with you. We're all overwhelmed here."

"You'll stop babying me? Is that what you're saying?"

"No one is babying you."

"Coddling? Overprotecting?"

"Fine." His face flushed with anger. "I'll take your well-being out of the equation, Natalie. All the guys are busy, so I was wondering if you'd go over to the Sunflower Inn and talk to Veronica's sister, who arrived last night. She's staying there for the duration. See if you can get a statement and find out if she knows anything."

"Okay," Natalie said.

"When you're done, you can write up your reports wherever you fucking please."

"Sounds good," she said and left.

43

Outside a freezing wind pummeled against Natalie as she made her way across the lot toward her car. She didn't want to argue with Luke. It upset her to see him so frustrated and angry. She needed his friendship. They both needed this connection, but she couldn't let him suffocate her, either. Then again, what did it matter? She'd be leaving the force soon enough, wouldn't she? Wasn't that the plan?

Her head felt foggy. She got in her car and started the engine. Winter was still very much with them. There was a grinding overcast to the sky, with more storm clouds embedded along the horizon. On her way across town, vehicles rolled past, their tires kicking up annoying sprays of muddy slush.

The Sunflower Inn was located on a quiet side street on the eastern end of downtown. Built in 1820, this quaint bed-and-breakfast was owned and operated by seventy-year-old Udell Pickle, whom everyone loved. Short, stooped, and balding, Dell was always willing to update you on the current goings-on in Burning Lake. He'd bend your ear and offer you a fresh-baked cookie.

As soon as Natalie rang the bell, the front door popped open, as if Dell's forty-five-year-old daughter, Belinda Pickle, had been standing there waiting for her. "Oh, Detective Lockhart!" she said with obvious surprise. "I wasn't expecting you."

"Hi, Belinda, how are you? I'm here to talk to Veronica's sister."

She nodded. "She's upstairs unpacking. Want me to ring her up?"

"Would you mind?"

"Not a problem, come on in and make yourself comfortable. There's coffee and tea in the dining room."

The bed-and-breakfast was spacious and welcoming, with built-ins full of bric-a-brac and comfortable chairs and sofas. The living room had speckled eggshell carpeting, large blocky furniture, and impressive views of the snow-covered gardens. The adjoining dining room's long pine table was set for dinner. Alongside the far wall was the beverage buffet.

Natalie poured herself a fresh cup of coffee, adding too much cream and sugar, then took a seat in the living room. A few minutes later, Lorna Manes came downstairs and greeted her. In her early sixties, Lorna had silver hair and papery skin drawn tight across her grieving face. "I thought Detective Pittman was in charge of my sister's case?" she said.

"He thought it would be a good idea if I spoke to you first."

Her mouth grew tremulous. "Yes, certainly. Anything to help."

"Have a seat."

Lorna took a seat on the beige sectional, while Natalie sat in a sand-colored armchair so monstrously comfortable, she could've disappeared into it and been perfectly happy. "Is there anything you can tell us about Veronica that might shed some light on her death? Did she have any enemies? Any run-ins or arguments that you know of?"

Lorna's body sagged under the weight of these questions. "We didn't talk much, maybe once a month. Sometimes three months would pass before she checked in. When we did speak, we kept it light. Veronica's my little sister. I've always been worried about her. I didn't like it when she got involved in witchcraft. I warned her that it might attract a very dark energy. I wish I wasn't right about that."

"Is there anything else she mentioned during your phone calls?"

Lorna shook her head. "I loved my kid sister. We were honest with each other. She knew about my concerns, and she spent time explaining to me what a coven really is. How they gathered in circles, sometimes in the nude. How they use wands to guide energy and cast spells—but only white magic. She said the nudity wasn't about sex, it was about empowerment. It was about capturing the earth's natural energy or something like that. She emphasized that they weren't out to hurt anybody. That they didn't worship the devil, or any nonsense like that. I know she was sincere in her beliefs. I always hoped that, in the end, she might return to Christ's loving embrace. Maybe she did. Do you think it's possible? At the very last second?"

"Anything's possible," Natalie said warmly, "but I can't speak for Veronica."

"No, I understand. Anyway, I wanted to hear from her more often, but Veronica set the terms. She's stubborn, like our mom. She's always had an independent streak, ever since we were kids. But she sounded happy the last time we spoke. She was meeting people, living her life. She seemed okay. I wasn't overly concerned when I didn't hear from her in several months."

Natalie opened her notepad in her lap. "When was the last time you heard from her?"

Lorna gazed out the window at the snow-covered trees. "We spoke a few days before Christmas. And then again on New Year's Eve. That was the last time."

"And you can't think of anything she said that might be pertinent to the case?"

"No. Just the usual." Lorna's eyes welled with tears. "We never said 'I hate you' the way some sisters do. We were best friends. We were there for each other. Veronica could master anything she took on. I envied her that ability. I can't stay focused. I used to feel stupid around her. I thought—someday I'll figure out what it is I do best. But Veronica was my baby sister. I'm five years older than her, and I love her like crazy. I watched her grow up. I diapered her, for gosh sakes."

Natalie gave Lorna the space to feel hurt. Then she said, "I understand you're the executor of Veronica's will. Can you tell me what it says?"

She folded her hands in her lap. "Veronica left a few special items to some of her friends—Marigold Hutchins, Belinda Pickle, Ginny Moskovitz, Tabitha Vaughn. She also left some historical items and antiques to the Witch Museum here in Burning Lake—"

"Wait," Natalie interrupted, "nothing for Justin Fowler?"

Lorna shook her head.

"When was the will dated?"

"Three years ago."

"And she didn't update her will more recently?"

"No. I'll be inheriting her estate, including the rights to her published books. I was surprised by that, but I'll honor Veronica's wishes. I won't let her down."

"Did you know she was writing a new book?"

"Yes, and I'm considering finding a publisher posthumously. I think Veronica would like that. I'm grateful she trusted me with her estate, and I want to do right by her. I plan on following her wishes, including a Wiccan burial. Thankfully, she says in her will that we can also perform a simple Christian remembrance ceremony alongside the Wiccan ceremony. I want her to be happy. I want her to know she was right to trust me. She can see us right now, so I know she's at peace with all this."

"I understand what you're saying, that you two were very close despite your differences. And that's why she left you everything, as opposed to one of her friends who's a practicing Wiccan, which some might think would've made more sense."

"Yes," Lorna said, a little defensively. "Because she's my sister, and blood is thicker than Wicca. We used to joke about that once in a while."

"Blood is thicker than Wicca," Natalie repeated.

"We refused to let our religious beliefs get in the way of our love for each other. I hope you'll be joining us at the remembrance ceremony, which will be open to the public. It's separate from the funeral, which will be more private. From what I've heard, half the town will be at the remembrance ceremony. We've gotten permission to hold it on Abby's Hex Peninsula."

"I wouldn't miss it," Natalie said sincerely.

"I'm glad the Witch Museum will be getting some of her most treasured possessions. I wouldn't know what to do if she'd bequeathed it to me. Frankly some of it frightens me—a silver altar chalice, a ceremonial knife, a collection of poppet dolls, a pentacle brooch." She gave a brief shudder. "So it was the perfect solution. I also met with Belinda, Marigold, and Tabitha this morning, and we had a good talk. They're open to a double ceremony and were relieved to find out that Veronica had requested it in her will.

They're very nice people. They made me feel welcome, and I wasn't sure what to expect. It's been a pleasant surprise."

Natalie stood. "Thanks for your time, Ms. Manes. I'm so sorry for your loss."

She clasped Natalie's hand between her thin cold ones. "Just promise me you'll find out who did this to her."

"We're trying our hardest, believe me."

"Don't stop until you've solved it, please? For Veronica's sake. How can we have any peace otherwise?"

After Lorna Manes went back upstairs, Natalie stopped by the front desk, where Belinda Pickle was busy taking reservations and managing the bed-and-breakfast.

"Excuse the mess," Belinda said. "Busy day."

"Phones are ringing off the hook!" Dell shouted from his office, which was located directly behind the reception area. His office door was open, and Natalie could see him sitting behind his desk. He gave her a little wave, and she waved back.

"Dad, Natalie is trying to talk to me," Belinda told her father.

"Yes, I can see that!" he shouted through the open doorway. "Natalie, guess what? We're booked solid for Halloween already. Can you imagine? The entire month of October is already booked. In March! Now that's a record, and I've been in this business for fifty years."

"Okay, Dad, don't be ghoulish," Belinda said with a frown.

"What's so ghoulish about it?" Dell Pickle got up and stood in the doorway. He was smartly dressed in a camel's hair sweater over a white shirt, pressed black trousers, and a pair of suede loafers. "It's just a fact. Hello, Natalie," he said with a wink. "Would you like a cigarette?" He offered her one from the pack.

"No thanks, Dell, I'm good."

"Dad, she quit months ago!"

He shrugged. "Suit yourself."

"Dad, stop it . . ."

"Stop what?"

"Don't be so happy about everything, for God's sake."

"I've never seen anything like it! People are bribing me to kick somebody else off the guest list so they can steal their reservation. That's how badly they want to be here for next Halloween. I guess you're right, sweetheart, it is a little ghoulish. But great for business! On the back of such a despicable tragedy. Life is strange."

"Okay, Dad, thanks for your two cents," Belinda said.

"I'm sorry, honey."

"Just because the media's out for blood," she told him, "I don't think we should be, too."

"What do you want me to do? Turn them down?"

"No, just don't crow about it."

"Was I crowing? I'm just saying how ironic it is that all this bad publicity ends up being good for the town. Interest in Burning Lake has skyrocketed, internationally as well. Henry Morbinder, the town clerk, told me the town website was getting a ton of hits! We're *trending*, as the kids say. That this terrible thing turns out to be great news for the tourist bureau and local businesses, I don't know what to tell you." He went back into his office and left the door open so that he could eavesdrop.

"Don't mind him," Belinda said apologetically. "This is just terrible. Veronica never wanted to be in the spotlight. I don't care what my father says, it's bad for the whole town. Wiccans are already mocked nationwide. It's awful for our image. Another sensational murder case—that's the last thing Veronica would've wanted." She leaned forward and said softly, "We're all scared, Natalie. We feel targeted. I mean, it could happen to any of us, right? Somebody's coming after witches. We keep asking each other—who's next?"

"We're doing everything in our power to resolve this," Natalie assured her. "We're putting all our budget and manpower into this case. We've got extra police patrolling the neighborhoods. The chief has approved plenty of overtime."

"Thanks. I can't think straight. Maybe I should've said yes to taking over the coven. But it scares me, you know? They asked me to take over for Veronica, but look at me, Natalie, do I look like the kind of person who has any spare time on her hands? I'd like to see Sequoia or Honey or even Tabitha take over. Not Marigold, which it looks like that's the way it's going, unfortunately."

"Why is that?"

"Like I said before, she's not right for the role. I know for a fact that Veronica wouldn't have wanted Marigold in charge, but nobody has the balls . . . pardon my expression, to confront her and tell her this. We're all afraid of our own shadows—can you imagine? Witches cowering in the corner? I've heard rumors the two historical covens are going to merge, but that wouldn't work. We want to maintain Veronica's policies, her leadership goals, her stamp on the coven. Not blend in with the Carringtons."

"Can you elaborate on how Veronica felt about Marigold?"

"Pretty much the same as me. I've heard Veronica say that Marigold's too needy. She's too insecure, she'll drive us all crazy. They were good friends. But you could tell she sometimes got under Veronica's skin, just like she gets under everybody's skin."

"So you think Veronica would be against the idea now?"

"Absolutely. But Marigold keeps pushing it. My friends and I are appealing to the goddess to tell us what to do, because Marigold feels she's ready to take up the reins, and we don't think it's right, so we've been appealing to Veronica's spirit to guide us. If it comes to a vote, and if we lose, we may break off and create a new coven of our own, but Veronica wouldn't want that, either."

Natalie nodded. She could see Dell in his office, tilting his head and straining to listen, so she lowered her voice and asked, "Do you know anything about Veronica and Justin Fowler?"

Belinda blushed and glanced away. "I should've mentioned it earlier . . ."

"Why didn't you tell me, Belinda?"

"Rumors are rumors, you can't believe everything you hear."

"So it was just a rumor? Veronica didn't tell you directly?"

"No, it was part of the scuttlebutt going around."

"Thanks, Belinda."

"You take care, Natalie."

"Good-bye, Natalie!" Dell shouted through the open doorway.

"Bye, Dell." She waved.

"Stay safe, darling! We care about you!"

This hit her in the heart. Sometimes people surprised you in the most devastating ways.

44

B efore heading home, Natalie made an unscheduled stop at Blackthorn Park, where she got her flashlight out of the trunk and took one of the public walking trails into the woods. Her footsteps were so quiet.

Don't stare too long at the Witching Tree,
Defile it not, or cursed you will be.

Her heart rate soared as she came to the clearing. Most of the towns-people avoided going anywhere near Nettie Goodson's cursed tree. There were no carvings in the bark, no desecrations. The towering oak scared her tonight. It had that twisted evil look—writhing in pain as if it were burning in hell forever.

Surrounding the infamous tree, beyond the clearing, was a large circle of thirteen beeches, planted by the town one hundred thirty-eight years ago in an attempt to give the local scoundrels a canvas for their mischief. Thirteen gray trees in a winter landscape beneath a dark sky. In contrast with the Witching Tree, these thirteen beeches were scarred with decade upon decades' worth of graffiti.

Natalie swept her flashlight beam across the defaced, scarred trunks. There were hundreds of scratchy initials carved into the bark, and "I love you"s from a hundred years ago. There were unique-looking "witch marks" made to ward off evil spirits alongside crosses, pentacles, concentric circles, and ancient Druid symbols.

On her previous trip to the park, Natalie had taken many pictures of the carvings, and one of them stood out in her mind. The Awen, meant to symbolize new beginnings. The freshest-looking carving on all of the trees.

Natalie found it again, and stood before it. She studied the Awen, and then looked above it. There was an odd, misshapen grouping of very old carvings about a foot and a half above the Awen on the tree. These scarred arbor-glyphs were so old, Natalie could no longer tell what they were supposed to be. Circles? Pentacles? She couldn't make out the shapes. They were just de-formed lumps or knots of healed-over bark. She stood and counted—there were thirteen of them, grouped together. Thirteen scarred symbols.

Natalie wondered what they were meant to represent. Thirteen hearts? Thirteen trees? Thirteen crosses? Thirteen pentagrams? She honestly couldn't tell. The bark's scar tissue had slowly overgrown and devoured the symbols over time, until they were unrecognizable.

The wind picked up, carrying with it a distinct howl. Natalie shivered and turned around—the woods were silent and dark all around her. You could easily get lost in this fairy-tale forest, she thought. Just like the old carvings, the trees would swallow you up alive.

She took the footpath back to the main entrance of the park, kicking up autumn leaves that had been frozen under the snow. She hurried back to her car, imagining something was chasing her. A shadow. A hovering presence. The trees were good at keeping secrets, just like Veronica.

Twenty minutes later, Natalie parked her car in Hunter's long gravel driveway, got out, and stood for a moment gazing at the trees as they tossed in the wind, her eyes adjusting to the clambering darkness. The slender moon had taken on a sinister ash-gray hue. Her body felt clammy beneath her winter clothes. The thought of seeing Hunter again after such a trying day set her blood vibrating. It had been a long winter, and as the snow fell outside and a howling wind had blown through the rafters, they'd spent most of their days fucking inside his big empty mansion. Over the past few months, Natalie had lost her stubborn sense of self in the lust-buzz of their passionate coupledom. She had sanded down the hard edges of her identity and become blurry with love. Fuzzy with desire. But now, with this new case, reality had crashed down on everyone's heads, and her detective nerve endings were tingling, and her investigative senses were sharpening like the claws of a werewolf.

She turned toward the house and headed inside, her every footstep becoming heavier and more burdensome. Hunter must've heard her key in the lock, because he swung the door open and said, "Hey. You're home."

"Hello." She stepped inside and kissed him, peeling off her outer garments and kicking off her boots. He took her coat and scarf and hung them up on the old iron coatrack. He placed her boots neatly side by side on the antique boot rack. Then, with intense concern, he drew her inside. "How was your day, sweetie?"

"Hellish all the way to the bone."

Hunter had perfected a look of intense introspection, which he could turn on and off at will, but now he looked at her sheepishly, letting his boyish vulnerability show. He was worried about her. His piercing gray eyes and elegant face made her heart skip a beat. She had a fleeting desire to lose herself entirely in him, or perhaps just misplace herself for a little while. "Would you like a drink?" he offered.

"I'll take a white wine, thanks."

So polite. Such a strained, awkward civility between them.

They were standing together in the living room, where the dark varnish, ornate trim work, and heavy drapes felt oppressive between hopeful islands of light—table lamps, recessed lighting, mini-spots to highlight the artwork he collected.

"Is there anything I can do to help?" he asked.

She shook her head, grateful for his concern but all out of words.

"Well, I hope you're hungry. We're having shrimp tartlets, roast duck, and hot lava cake for dessert."

"Sounds yummy." She mustered a smile. "But first, I need to take a shower." She kissed him again. "Be right back."

Upstairs, the master suite featured a large fireplace flanked by two Victorian upholstered benches, a customized walk-in closet, deep bay windows, and teak-paneled walls. Hunter's bed—a massive four-poster mahogany yacht—seriously belonged in a Mary Shelley novel. The canopy and drapes were made of royal-blue velvet, and the old bedsprings squeaked when they made love.

The master bath had a cornered spa tub, dual pedestal sinks, Chinese marble, and stained glass. She took a hot shower, as hot as she could stand it—so hot, tears sprang to her eyes. But they weren't tears of grief or frustration or anger, they were merely a physical reaction to the blistering heat splashing down her body. Instead, she felt numb inside as she breathed the thick warm steam into her lungs.

When she was done, Natalie towel-dried and got dressed for dinner. Before she'd moved in with Hunter, her evening attire consisted of T-shirts, boxer shorts, sweats, and slippers; and her dinner typically consisted of a microwaved meal and a diet soda or an ice-cold beer. Maybe a glass of wine, if she was feeling fancy.

Now she actually got dressed for dinner. Hunter had insisted—it was a tradition in his family, and she didn't mind honoring that tradition, just as long as he ignored her dietary habits, like her occasional cravings for Pop-Tarts and MoonPies. Certain areas were off-limits for judging each other. She ignored his habit of self-grooming (plucking at his tousled ash-brown hair, chewing on his fingernails while watching sports on TV, rolling his shirt-sleeves up in careful increments, and then smoothing them down again).

The one thing Hunter insisted on was this dress-up thing for dinner every night. It was their time to connect in a formal, habitual way, he explained, saying how important he felt it was for their relationship. Almost like having a "date night," only this one happened every night. She'd finally caved in January and let him take her clothes shopping for her birthday, an extravagance Natalie could ill afford—in time or money. But she secretly enjoyed these frivolous, expensive items—silky pantyhose and Italian designer pumps and pretty blouses and skirts and tailored pants. It made her feel like a spoiled child, while at the same time it made her feel like a desirable woman.

She descended the staircase, careful not to miss a step and tumble down the rest of the way, thereby spoiling the illusion.

Hunter smiled at her. "You look beautiful." He handed her a glass of chardonnay. "Shall we step into the dining room, milady?"

"That's getting a little old."

"Milady? What should I call you then? Babe?"

"Babe's fine." She smirked.

"Okay, babe. Have a seat."

She plunked herself down and drank the entire glass of wine.

Hunter sat next to her and watched, amused. "Another glassful?" he offered.

"Please."

He refilled her glass, and she drank that one down, too.

"Feeling better?" he asked—sincere this time.

Natalie nodded.

"Do you want to talk about it?"

"I don't think so."

"Okay."

He ate his meal with relish, as if he were starving—and maybe he was. It was almost ten o'clock. It made her feel loved and cared for, that he'd waited for her to come home before having a bite to eat himself.

She ate her shrimp tartlets with exquisite politeness, chewing every mouthful, and patting the edges of her lips with a white linen napkin. Hunter cleared the appetizer plates himself and refilled their wine and water glasses. He performed every task with a rakish, sarcastic smile, as if he enjoyed nothing more than making fun of himself. "Ah, look at me, the lord of the manor, and I have to do *everything* myself, ha-ha." He didn't enjoy being waited on. He had a chef and a housekeeper, but the chef prepared their meals and then left in the afternoon, with specific instructions on how to prep, warm, and serve the food. The housekeeper came early the next morning to clear everything away.

Now Hunter brought out the entree, and Natalie looked down at her duck à l'orange, then set her fork on her plate with infinite care.

"Everything okay?" he asked, sitting down beside her and wiping his mouth with a linen napkin. "Because I can fix it, you know."

"Hunter . . ."

"Or at least I can try."

"I'm just tired. And numb. And distracted. All those things."

He nodded, watching her carefully. "I found out who's handling the blind trust for Brandon's former property. It's Timothy Cochran's law firm. I have no other information."

Great, Natalie thought bitterly. Timothy Cochran, Esquire, was known as Burning Lake's super lawyer, a diminutive man who planted his intellectual weight into every step. Not only that, but his daughter India used to be best friends with Natalie's niece, Ellie—until the very moment when India decided to set Ellie on fire.

It happened over a year ago. The two girls had been best friends forever and, as curious sixteen-year-olds, had formed a coven together. There were jealousies over boys and more specifically their English teacher, Ethan Hathaway. They dabbled in dark magic and got in over their heads. Most teenagers left the Craft after a few thrilling months. They either got scared or grew tired of it. But the Sisterhood could also lead to darker things, like self-harm and black magic. Ellie and her friends had gotten into something monstrous. One night, India Cochran and Berkley Auberdine dragged Ellie down to Abby's Hex with them, where they sought their revenge by attempting to light her on fire. Fortunately, Natalie had found them in time.

Ellie spent the next few months undergoing multiple operations to treat her injuries at the Albany burn unit, but her long-term prognosis was excellent. In July, she went to live with her father in Manhattan, and Natalie had kept in touch with her. All was well. Ellie was safe and in therapy. They rarely spoke about what her friends had done to her, but when they did, Ellie spoke in confused, hurt whispers. The two girls, India and Berkley, had been convicted of aggravated assault and were currently serving time as juveniles. They'd both be out before their twenty-first birthdays, but rumor had it India would be out much sooner than that, thanks to her father's behind-the-scenes wrangling. In the meantime, Ellie had healed better than expected and was doing fine.

"The law firm is handling the trust for an individual or group of individuals, but there's no way of finding out who that person or persons might be. Anyway, I hope that helps," Hunter said with a sweet eagerness.

"Yes, it does." She reached for his hand and squeezed. "Thanks."

"You're welcome." He leaned forward to kiss her, his warm lips lingering on hers. He tasted of shrimp tartlets and expensive wine.

When he let go of her hand, Natalie was shocked by how naked and abandoned her skin felt. It made her realize how much she depended on him.

"Anyway," he told her, "I've got a business meeting in Albany tomorrow that I can't get out of. I'll be leaving early in the morning."

"How early?"

"Catching the six thirty train."

"They're running again?" she asked, feeling suddenly nauseated.

"Yeah. They must've cleared the tracks," he said distractedly, forking away tender pieces of duck. Then he looked up and caught her eye. "Oh God, I'm sorry. I didn't mean to sound so casual about it. Are you okay? Want me to cancel?"

"No, don't do that. Go to your meeting."

"Because I will. I don't care. Conference call. Zoom, whatever."

"No, I'll be fine."

"Are you sure?"

She nodded, not sure at all. Not certain about anything in her life right this second. He took her at her word, however, and shoveled down the rest of his food.

Natalie grew cold inside, watching Hunter eat. He really appreciated his food—you could tell by the way he occasionally sniffed his food before popping another forkful into his mouth, chewing contentedly, and gazing at her. Smiling with his mouth closed. She hadn't considered that the trains would ever run again. Now an image flashed through her brain—a shocking splash of crimson on virgin snow.

When Hunter was done eating, he said, "I've got something for you." He reached into his jacket pocket and took out a small designer gift bag, which he placed on the table beside her.

She gave him a blank look. "What's in the bag?"

"Open it and find out."

She hesitated. She wasn't ready for any more drama tonight, like a marriage proposal. He'd been hinting around about "making it official" lately. But surely he knew that would be a mistake right now. She was in too dark a mood to tolerate any surprises.

With great reluctance, Natalie picked up the bag, reached inside, and took out an elegant black-and-silver embossed jewelry box. She opened the box and held up a gold watch. "It's beautiful," she said, looking at him starkly.

His face fell. "But what?"

"But I don't need another watch, Hunter. I love the one I have. You know that." She showed him the old Baume & Mercier stainless steel watch her father had given her as a graduation gift.

"I'm not asking you to give that one up. I just thought you might like this one, too. I saw it in the window and thought of you, Natalie."

"So now I have two watches."

He laughed and shrugged. "I have five. One for each mood."

"You only have five moods?"

"Dopey, sneezy, sleepy, grumpy, and horny. Am I missing anything?"

Her shoulders fell gently earthward as she studied him with equal parts amusement and pity. "It's very sweet of you to give me such a dazzling gift, especially one so . . ."

"Expensive?"

"But I don't need another watch."

He scowled. "All or nothing, huh?"

She put it back in its elegant box. "You don't have to impress me."

He crossed his arms. "Yeah, I get it."

"What?"

"I'm the stinking rich moron who owns more watches than he could ever need."

"I didn't say that."

"I feel especially insulted because I never try to flaunt it. I don't even think about it half the time. I have friends who are Prada poor . . ."

"What's that?"

"Prada poor? They're out there slumming it in their Prada pants and Prada shoes, but everything is deliberately wrinkled and scuffed and rumpled, as if they'd picked it up at the Goodwill. Their frayed overcoat is Armani. Their wrinkled shirts are by Behar, and their whole entire *look* has been carefully calculated to project poverty and despair. They're all messy and scruffy and unshaven, but in reality, they've got more money than they could ever want. Me, I never try to hide it. I don't flaunt it, but I don't hide it. I am who I am. Sorry about that."

"You don't have to apologize."

He stood up and walked away from the table. He gazed out the window at the snowy backyard. "How can you talk to me with all that contempt in your voice when you don't really know me?" he asked, turning around. He wasn't smiling anymore. "Like you're the virtuous one. You're the only one who's suffered, and I haven't. You're the middle-class girl from Burning Lake," he said with an angry snarl. "And I'm like . . .

what? The prom king gone bad? Some rich tyrannical shithead buying you gold watches you don't need? Christ." He frowned at her. "Do you want me to give it all up? Because I will. I don't care. What is it all really worth, anyway?"

"It's worth a lot. If you've ever struggled with your bills, you'd know that."

"So I'm not allowed to complain? Ever?"

"Stop putting words in my mouth."

"What are you saying then?"

"Just that . . ." She reached for meaning. "Just that I'm not sure how this is all supposed to work."

"How what is supposed to work? You mean us?" He looked deeply wounded. "I thought it was working, Natalie. I thought it was working beautifully."

A heavy silence filled the living room. It filled the entire house. She exhaled as if she'd been holding her breath forever. Her thoughts grew as stagnant as a muddy pond. Love was powerful. Love was heartbreaking. Her future was standing right there in front of her, only she couldn't imagine it. She didn't know why. She jiggled her foot. She wanted to scream. She wanted to grab Hunter by the hair and bash his brains out. Brutality was maybe something a man could understand.

"It is. Working," she admitted. "You're right. I'm sorry."

Without hesitation, he bent down to kiss her. He cupped her face in his hands as if she were an angel. His salvation. She felt his warmth like a low painful fire and drew him closer. His breath was scented with fine wine. His fingers stroked her cheek and circled her ear, then touched her earlobe. "So delicate," he whispered, as if he were an archeologist on the brink of discovery, and she was this rare, precious object he had unearthed. He would dust her off and keep her forever.

She started to peel off her brand-new clothes, one item at a time. She dropped her shoes on the floor, then reached for her sweater. She wanted to be naked and vulnerable in his arms, to forget about everything else. To be swept away.

"Wait." He stopped her. He took her hands and kissed them. "Let's finish our meal and talk," he said. "Okay? I want to look into your eyes."

45

After Hunter helped Natalie carry the three boxes of library books into the house, he went directly to bed. She took her cup of peppermint tea into the living room with her, where she sat on the sofa and turned on the art deco lamp. It cast a soft, stained glass glow. The backyard was a stretch of moonlit snow, ending in a dark silhouette of woods. She preferred this time of night, while the rest of the world was asleep.

Natalie opened her laptop and picked up the list of books Veronica had checked out of the library—mostly historical books about Burning Lake and the origins of Wicca. There was another high school yearbook—this one from Rochester, New York, circa the 1990s. Curious. She settled the yearbook in her lap. Once again, there were a couple of folded-over corners marking specific pages.

Natalie sipped her peppermint tea and set it aside. She opened the yearbook to the senior class photographs and studied the faces. The girls had such big hair back then. There were lots of chokers and mood rings. Each of these high school seniors had big plans. Their eyes sparkled with their hopes and dreams. Even the cynical ones looked sweet as hell. She didn't recognize any of the students, but as she turned to the next dog-eared page, she noticed that one of the photographs had a pencil mark next to it. A small arrow. Natalie's gaze lingered on the high school portrait of an eighteen-year-old Goth girl with chubby cheeks named Cindy Templeton. Cindy seemed vaguely familiar. She would be in her mid-forties by now.

Natalie frowned. The next earmarked page contained a photograph of someone Natalie recognized, but again there was a faintly penciled arrow. Jodi Johnson, a slender doe-eyed senior, looked just like her daughter, Holly Host. This must be Holly's mother, Jodi Stewart, before she'd gotten married. Johnson was her maiden name.

Natalie picked up the Polaroid from Murray's Halloween Costumes and held it next to the yearbook photograph—they were the same person. She was sure of it. You could see the familiar lines of Jodi's face in the curve of her nose and those surprisingly large ears, partially hidden behind her long hair.

Jodi Johnson and Cindy Templeton were in the same class together. So who was Cindy Templeton? She looked remotely familiar, but like a lot of teenagers, she'd buried her youthful prettiness under so much unruly hair, Goth jewelry, and cheap makeup that Natalie couldn't envision who this person was twenty-seven years later.

She thumbed through the rest of the yearbook, but there was nothing to connect the two girls. Not even a candid of the two students hanging out together. It appeared that Jodi and Cindy had been part of that overlooked crowd of invisible kids, unpopular and unnoticed. It made Natalie sad.

The copper pipes clanged somewhere inside the house, creating a cranky lullaby. She listened to the wind as it brushed against the stone exterior of the building. She closed the yearbook and felt oppressed by something dark and ugly. If Veronica was onto something here—and Natalie still had no clue what that might be—it could be the reason she was killed in such a pitiless, horrifying manner.

So what did Veronica know? What great secret had she stumbled across?

Did Holly know?

Did Justin know?

Tabitha? Marigold? Belinda?

What about Reverend Grimsby?

Natalie carried her mug of peppermint tea back to the kitchen, where the pendant lights cast pools of warmth over the Victorian tulip wallpaper and polished wood trim. It was snowing outside. Sheets of fluffy snow flapped against the windows, leaving clumps of snowflakes on the glass.

She felt a strange energy surround her. She moved closer to the windows overlooking the backyard. The frost on the glass panes reminded her of miniature ice cities. Life was so fleeting. She ran her finger through one of these ice cities, melting it. More frost formed in its place. How easy it was to destroy things. How easy to fall in love. She drew a heart shape in the condensation, then rubbed it out with her fist. She felt a bittersweet sadness that wouldn't go away, like the aftertaste of a good gourmet chocolate.

Her phone rang in the living room, and she hurried to answer it before it woke Hunter out of a sound sleep.

"You're up," Luke said, unsurprised.

As soon as she heard his voice, she felt reassured. There was something very grounded about Luke that went deeper than friendship—he was a primal force for Natalie, like the earth or trees or the sky.

She plopped down on the sofa. "Yeah, I'm majoring in sleep deprivation."

He laughed.

"What about you?"

"Can't sleep. I keep thinking about Ned Bertrand. Why Ned Bertrand?"

"You mean, why were he and Dottie Coffman and Thomas Grimsby in a religious club in high school together? And why was Veronica interested in that?"

"It's definitely strange."

"Well, I've got something else for you to chew on." She opened the Rochester yearbook in her lap. "Veronica took another high school yearbook out of the library, only this one's from Rochester, New York. It's twenty-seven years old. She marked two of the pictures—Jodi Johnson, who later became Mrs. Jodi Stewart . . ."

"Holly's mother?"

"And a girl named Cindy Templeton. They were in the same class together. No idea what that's supposed to mean. I couldn't find anything else inside the yearbook to indicate how the girls are related. Maybe they were friends. But there are no other hints."

"So how old would they be now?" Luke asked.

"Forty-five."

"Who else is forty-five?"

"Marigold Hutchins. Tabitha Vaughn. Belinda Pickle. Some of the other women in the coven."

"Okay. What do you think it means?"

"All I know is Veronica was onto something that spans decades."

"I'll have Augie do some digging into Dorothy Coffman's background. Also Jodi Stewart and Cindy . . . what's her name again?"

"Templeton."

"Cindy Templeton," he repeated slowly. Even in this digital age, Luke kept a notepad by his bed and scribbled down the ideas he got in the middle of the night. Funny that she knew this about him.

"While you're at it, ask him to find out who the girls are under the Witching Tree, the one with Dottie."

"Okay." He paused.

"Hello?"

"I'm still here."

"What are you thinking?"

Another pause. Then he said, "Rainie proposed tonight."

Natalie sat bolt upright. Her heart began to beat so fast, it was an effort to keep her voice steady. "Really?" she said as casually as she could.

"Yeah. Funny, huh?"

"I can think of another word for it," she said. "Sweet. Cute. Charming."

"So you approve?"

She exhaled sharply.

"Is that a yes?"

"No." She could hear him breathing. "It doesn't matter what I think, Luke. Well? What did you tell her?"

"Nothing yet. I was hoping you'd have some advice for me."

Her face flushed, and she sank down into the velvet cushions, feeling physically ill. "Advice? From me? With my great track record?"

"Who else can I turn to?" he said bluntly.

"Rainie, for one."

"Natalie . . . come on."

The tenderness in his voice was alarming. She thought they'd both made their peace with it, but things had just gotten real. It awakened in her equal feelings of tenderness.

"Luke . . . don't even go there," she said softly, keeping her voice down.

"Why not?"

"It's too late."

"This is the last chance we'll have to talk about this, Natalie."

Another mothlike flutter touched her heart. But she was pissed at him, too. He could've taken his chance months ago when there was still time. Her feelings for Luke were complex and spanned decades, going back to their childhood. Their shared history felt like a handicap sometimes, like an impediment to true happiness. A speed bump. A road not taken. "We're friends for life, okay?" she said.

"That's bullshit. You know how I feel about you. And I know how you feel about me."

"Stop it, please," she whispered. The last thing she wanted was for Hunter to wake up and catch her talking to Luke at three in the morning. "Don't you dare tell me how I feel, Luke. For *months*, there's been this awkward silence between us. For *months*, you've said nothing. And now you call bullshit?"

"Yeah, I call bullshit. So let's get it all out on the table, while there's still time." His tone was softly insistent, with a salty urgency to it. "I'm serious, Natalie."

She was falling apart. It was more than she could handle. Because it was true, he was right, she still longed for something she couldn't describe. An ambiguous something. Wasn't this exactly what she wanted? A commonplace but lovely contentment? To be happy with life's simple pleasures? To bask in someone's love and respect and desire? To finally be with Luke? To make a life with him?

"Talk to me," he said.

She glanced up at the ornate molded ceiling and whispered, "I've been thinking about quitting my job, but I honestly don't know what to do. Hunter has mentioned marriage and kids, and sometimes I think it would be so nice . . . to live here forever in this beautiful old house with him. Sometimes I'm so tempted. I almost gave my notice twice. But I didn't. I don't know why. He says if I quit my job, I can spend all my time painting and drawing and following my dream of being an artist. But it's an old dream, Luke. I don't know what I feel or think anymore." Her voice sounded very small to her as she said, "Tell me what to do."

There was a long silence. Then he said, "I can't make that decision for you. I can only support whatever you decide."

"You know what I mean," she told him. "You said we should be honest."

"Okay. You want honesty? I love you, Natalie."

She froze.

"And therefore, I think you should do whatever is best for you."

The truth was revealed to her at last. She loved them both for different reasons. Luke and Hunter.

"Natalie?"

She didn't respond. She could tell it was killing him. She opened her mouth to speak, but no words came out. It would've been obscene—to tell Luke that she loved him, too, while Hunter was asleep upstairs. It appalled her.

But the truth was she sometimes imagined herself and Luke making love in his office, and other times Luke's body would replace Hunter's body in her mind. She would feel the heat rush up her chest toward her face, and she would furiously try to cast it aside, to bury these obtrusive thoughts, but every once in a while they'd rise to the surface again. At the oddest moments.

"Natalie?" he said calmly.

"I can't . . ."

"All right. I understand."

"No, you don't! I just can't . . ." She couldn't get the words out.

"Natalie. I don't want this to be painful."

"No, Luke, listen to me. I can't say it. I can't say the words out loud. Not here. Not now." Tears sprang to her eyes. "Don't you get it?"

"Okay, look," he said gently. "I'll make it easier for both of us, since I brought it up. I'll always have real feelings for you, Natalie. But I think the universe is trying to tell us something. Because every time it looks as if we're about to get together, something interferes with those plans. And at this point—let's just roll with it. For whatever reason, this thing we have between us, maybe it was never meant to be."

Tears rolled down her cheeks. She almost laughed, she was so upset. "You can't just rip this whole thing wide open, and then decide you're going to shut it down."

"Okay," he said. He waited.

Natalie wiped away the tears with her hand. She sniffled. She looked around for a tissue, but there weren't any. She used the sleeve of her blouse.

"Why'd you wait so long?" she asked him accusingly. "Why didn't you tell me this months ago?"

"It makes me sad. But here we are."

"That's it?"

"What do you want? I'm at your mercy here."

She clasped a hand over her mouth, shuddering for breath.

"Thank you for being honest with me. I have a feeling this was long over-due, but you're right," he said. "Maybe it's too late. Maybe this is the way it has to be. But once we shut this conversation down, we can't reopen it again. You understand, right? This is the final word. We can't keep yo-yoing back and forth."

"I don't buy that," she said bitterly. "Human beings are flawed. We yo-yo."

They were silent for a good long while. She tried to think of what their options were, but they were extremely limited. She was committed to Hunter. How could she ever break his heart? As far as they'd traveled? "Luke, I . . ."

"Yes?"

"I . . ."

"Yeah?"

"I guess . . . just as long as we can always be friends," she said at last. "I need you in my life. I can't imagine my life without you, Luke. We have to promise each other . . ."

"Okay," he said sadly. "Now it's time to stop talking about this."

"Wait."

He waited.

She wiped the tears from her face and sighed. She didn't know what else to say.

"Look, I love you, Natalie. And this breaks my heart. But I think we should stop calling each other. We can talk at the office, we can even go out for coffee to talk business, but no more late-night calls. I know Rainie wouldn't like it, and Hunter won't be happy about it."

She reluctantly agreed. She didn't see any other way around it.

This, in a way, was good-bye.

46

In her dream, Natalie had a bloodied mouth. She couldn't speak, because her throat was clogged with blood. A jolt of adrenaline woke her up.

She sat bolt upright, gasping for breath, expecting some fresh danger to appear before her. Hunter's side of the bed was empty. A pink-gray dawn was visible through the windows. It was 5:45 A.M.

She went into the bathroom and splashed cold water on her face. She winced at the memory of her conversation with Luke—it was humiliating. How could they have spoken so casually about love? They were both in committed relationships. If only this conversation had happened six months ago. But now a small darkness sat in her heart. It felt as if a door had been slammed shut.

Downstairs, Hunter was busy rearranging things in his briefcase and making his delicious espressos. He turned to her and smiled, looking very handsome in his London mist Zegna suit. He handed her a perfect latte. "In Burning Lake, it's always pumpkin spice latte time."

She laughed and took a sip. "Mmm." She drank it down greedily.

He gave her an irrepressible grin. "We're going to need a bigger cup."

Her heart seized with emotion. On an impulse, she grabbed him reck-lessly around the neck and pulled him close, then relaxed in his arms, feel-ing his warmth and strength all around her. She sighed deeply, pockets of tension loosening inside of her. Maybe everything was going to be all right.

"Hey, what's all this then?" he said with a wry smile. His face had an old-fashioned grandeur to it, as if he were descended from royalty. He knew how to hold himself erect, how to move around with exquisite grace, what to say and not say. His manners were impeccable.

Natalie often felt like a complete klutz around him, even though she con-sidered herself to be fairly athletic. Hunter hardly ever said "fuck." Some-times she swore just to remind herself of how different they were. She liked to believe their relationship was solid and beyond danger, but in fact she had no idea. Did anyone?

"Do you love me?" he asked bluntly. "Do you?"

"Yes," she said. "Very much."

"Aha. Thought so," he joked.

"Stop teasing me. I'm serious."

"Me, too." He took her hand and cupped it between his, as if it were something precious. Nobody had ever held her hand that way, although Luke had come close, occasionally cupping her in his gaze. But the thing with Luke was finally over, and she shouldn't be thinking about him in the same breath as Hunter.

He licked her cheek. It made her laugh. She pushed him away. He did it again.

"Stop it. I've already had my shower."

"You have? Is that why you taste so good?"

His unusual gray eyes contained many colors, along with a predatory look, as if he'd been born a wild, feral creature who belonged in the woods and not inside this grand mansion with its velvet drapes and mahogany cabinets and inlaid antique side tables.

"Unfortunately, I'm late." He checked his watch—one of his five exorbi-tant timepieces. "They're taking me out to dinner. If I catch the ten forty-five, I'll be home by midnight."

"What happens at midnight?"

"I turn into a pumpkin."

"Hmm, there's a pumpkin theme going on today."

He moved in close. She tilted her head, ready to be kissed. He obliged. She liked his smell. She liked his touch.

"You're beautiful," he whispered. "I love you, Natalie. So fucking much."

47

The sun was out this morning. A big sheet of snow slid off the turn-of-the-century roof, making an avalanche sound as Natalie got in her car and turned the heat on full blast. She shivered, waiting for the car's interior to get warmer. She watched the roof's icicles melting and dripping. Her phone buzzed, and she answered it. "Detective Lockhart."

"Good morning, this is Astrid Conway. You told me to call you if . . ."

"Yes?" Natalie said, encouraging her to go on.

"Well, last night, my husband, Carl, dug up the backyard and found something buried under the birdbath."

Fifteen minutes later, Natalie drove through a neighborhood of melting snowmen on her way to Dottie Coffman's old residence. She parked by the side of the road and got out, the winter sun hitting her in the face like a cold slap.

The Conways lived on a shady tree-lined street in a century-old neighborhood, a cheerful enclave full of smoking chimneys and dogs bounding around in the snow. She rang the doorbell and waited.

Twenty-eight-year-old Astrid Conway answered the door. Her hair was pulled into a curly dark ponytail this morning, and her face was flushed and fragile-looking. She wore layers of clothing for warmth. "Detective Lockhart, come in!"

"So he just decided to dig up the yard?"

"After I told him what you said about the birdbath, his curiosity got the better of him, I guess."

"How did he do it? Isn't the ground frozen solid?"

"I'll let him explain. It's this way."

The pregnant woman took measured steps as they walked down the narrow central hallway, out the back door, and into the snowy yard. The air smelled of applewood smoke. The birdbath had been removed and placed on its side in the snow. There was a deep hole in the ground where the birdbath had been. The hole was approximately five feet wide and three feet deep. A man with a square head and broad shoulders was standing next to the hole. He smiled and waved at Natalie.

"This is my husband, Carl," Astrid said.

"Hello, Detective Lockhart." Ragged-around-the-edges Carl Conway was bundled up against the cold. He swung around slowly, muscle-bound as a bear, to shake her hand.

"Nice to meet you," Natalie said. "How did you manage all this?"

"Well, Astrid told me about your dilemma, and I figured I could probably do it myself. It's not rocket science. First you remove the birdbath off to one side. Then you build a charcoal fire over the area where the birdbath was. The fire will melt the frost layer and thaw out the dirt underneath. Then you boil gallons of hot water and keep pouring it over the area until it saturates deeper into the ground, softening the earth some more. Then you use your pick to dig into the ground, and eventually you can use a shovel."

Natalie smiled. "That's brilliant."

Astrid tucked an unruly curl behind her ear. Her fingers were adorned with cheap rings. "Come back inside and see what we found." She led Natalie back into the house.

Carl followed.

Inside the Conways' kitchen, there was a rectangular box wrapped in waterproof polyethylene and sealed with soiled duct tape on the breakfast table. Astrid picked it up and handed it to Natalie.

Natalie gently shook the lightweight box and could hear things rattling around inside.

"Can we open it?" Astrid asked. Her face was soft all over, like a cat's.

"Wait here. Don't touch it." Natalie got her crime kit from the trunk of her car and put on a pair of latex gloves. She took pictures of the wrapped box from every angle. Then she took out a pair of scissors and carefully cut through the heavy plastic sheeting. She peeled back the polyethylene and unwrapped a metal lockbox, identical to the kind used for storing documents.

The lockbox weighed a pound or two and was made of gunmetal-gray steel. There were scratches on the surface and a few dings, but otherwise it was in fairly good condition for being underground for years, possibly decades. A vintage red plastic sticker on the front said, "Protect your documents from sticky little hands."

Natalie's sticky little hands trembled as she turned the box over—there was a key taped to the bottom of the lockbox.

"I don't believe it," Carl whispered.

"This is so exciting," Astrid said.

Natalie got a large see-through evidence bag out of her kit. "I have to take this back to the station with me."

"You can't show us what's inside?"

"I don't want to destroy any potential evidence." She turned to them and said, "Is that okay? May I take this?"

"Yes, of course," Astrid said. "Anything to help."

Her husband was more reticent. Natalie took his silence as consent.

She placed the lockbox, along with the polyethylene outer wrapper, inside the evidence bag. "You've both been a great help. But I need to follow protocol. I'll give this to our tech expert."

Astrid nodded. "We understand."

Carl looked frustrated. "Not even a peek?"

"I'm sorry," Natalie said.

"Glad to help out," Astrid said, glancing disapprovingly at her husband.

Natalie didn't blame him. She was dying to find out herself.

48

As she was driving the lockbox over to the police station, Natalie called Luke and explained what had happened at the Conways'. He told her to meet him down in the basement of the station where the evidence storage room was located.

Access to the storage area was restricted. There was an intrusion alarm for the doors and vents, but no infrared motion sensors. They couldn't afford it, since theirs was a small department with a limited budget and a limited amount of space.

An entry code got Natalie into the security hallway that led to the evidence room with its bulletproof transaction window. She found Luke and Detective Peter Murphy arguing through the thick panes of glass, using the two-way intercom.

"You told me yesterday you brought those boxes down here, Murph. So where the hell are they?" Luke demanded to know.

"Hughie has his own fucking system, Lieutenant," Murphy said defensively, picking up a clipboard and pointing at the sign-out sheet with a damp finger. "Fill out the request form, and I'll go look again."

She could feel a palpable tension in the air as Luke wrote down the case number, along with the date, time, location, and his signature, then handed it back.

"Hughie's so-called system has a lot to be desired. Just find it," Luke barked. "I don't want a repeat of the Crow Killer case."

It was the first time he'd ever mentioned the incident to Murphy, as far as she knew—and Murphy seemed surprised by the rebuke. An average-looking guy in his early forties, Peter Murphy could sometimes be an arrogant jerk. He was a mediocre detective who'd been promoted over Luke's objections by his superiors, but up until now, Natalie had never heard Luke say an unkind word about him. As a matter of fact, Luke rarely bad-mouthed anyone.

"Right, Lieutenant." Murphy pressed his lips together, holding back a rising tide of resentment. He gave a curt nod before he ducked around back where the lockers and shelving units were full of criminal evidence.

"What's up?" Natalie asked Luke.

He gazed at her with raw anger. "Another evidence box has gone missing."

"Really?" She glanced at the transaction window. "Where's Hughie?"

"Out sick. Murphy's trying to find it for me. It's the blind leading the blind."

She frowned. The storage rooms were supposed to be organized according to specific type of evidence—firearms, drugs, trace, digital. Each piece was tagged and stored away inside a property envelope or box, which was then placed on a shelf or in a locker until it was needed for court proceedings or further lab analysis.

It should've been easy to find any given piece of evidence, since each item was assigned a case/date/location number on Hughie's computer. But for some reason, retrieving evidence was always an ordeal. Hughie Siskin was in charge, and that meant things were often stored in a seemingly haphazard fashion, dust rising wherever you poked around. A large box might contain a single item, whereas a small box might be jam-packed with crucial evidence. Occasionally, evidence would go missing for a few days, while everyone came down to the property room to search for it. Usually, the missing box or bag would eventually be found, but some said Hughie had designed the system to hide his own incompetence.

"Any luck, Murphy?" Luke asked impatiently.

"Still looking, Lieutenant."

They'd been through this bullshit before. Luke had complained about Hughie's overly complicated system on numerous occasions, but his superiors hadn't acted on it yet. It wasn't high on their list of priorities, and that drove Luke nuts.

"What's the evidence?" Natalie asked him now.

"Another box of writing and research from Veronica's house," Luke told her.

"I thought we'd gotten all of those."

"Murphy gave you three boxes, right?"

She nodded.

"There were four boxes of research and paperwork listed on the manifest."

They could hear Murphy shuffling things around in one of the back rooms.

"Need any help?" Luke shouted.

"Nope, I got this," came the terse response.

Luke folded his arms and blinked numbly at her. The look. The voice. The attitude. He had obviously accepted their situation and decided to be thoroughly professional about it.

Still, it was awkward—she could read his thoughts, his body language, his silences. And she heard him loud and clear. There was nothing special about her anymore in his eyes. He'd killed off his feelings for her last night and buried them far, far away, where he would never find them again. He'd murdered his feelings for Natalie.

Not that she blamed him. She would have to do the same.

"Got it!" Murphy said, returning to the window with a heavy-looking storage box in his arms. "It was on the wrong shelf." He slid the box across the counter toward Luke. "This is not a well-designed system, Lieutenant. When are we going to fix it?"

"Never," Luke said. "Hughie is the master of his mini-universe, apparently."

Natalie accompanied Luke back upstairs to her third-floor office, where he set the box down on her worktable and said, "Debrief, my office."

She followed him down the hallway.

"Did you bring it?" he asked.

"Right here." She handed him the lockbox and took a seat.

Luke put on a pair of gloves, took the lockbox out of the evidence bag, and carefully inspected it. "So the homeowners dug it up themselves? How?"

"He explained the process to me. A charcoal fire and lots of hot water. Then he used a pick and a shovel."

"Jesus. Well, I guess he saved us a lot of money. Let's take this down to Lenny's lab, we'll open it there."

Detective Lenny Labruzzo did his most important work in the crime scene lab, which was situated across from the property room down in the basement. His workbench was crammed with state-of-the-art equipment, test kits, and chemicals. He sat in front of his computer, which had three video monitors.

"What's this, Lieutenant?" Lenny asked, putting on a pair of gloves and examining the lockbox.

"It belonged to Dottie Coffman. It was buried in the backyard of her former residence."

"The English teacher?" Lenny looked up. "Isn't she in a nursing home now?"

"Yes. This was Natalie's find. She got the homeowners to comply."

Lenny had a receding hairline and a perpetual constipated look. He'd been threatening to take an early retirement from the department for fifteen years now. He was in charge of processing all trace evidence from the crime scene, since the BLPD couldn't afford its own CSI unit. Now he handled the lockbox gingerly, turning it over and carefully peeling off the tape that held the key to the bottom. He set the tape aside for print processing, then attempted to unlock the box, but the key wouldn't go into the keyhole. He examined the key. "It's slightly bent. I need a hammer."

"A hammer?" Luke repeated.

"Sometimes old school is the way to go."

They waited while he got up and looked around his messy lab for a battered ball-peen hammer. Then he placed the key on a cutting board and gently tapped it with the hammer, until it was straightened out.

Lenny inserted the key into the lock again, jiggling and twisting, but it only went part of the way in. "Looks like a cheap piece of hardware to me," he muttered, turning the key blade this way and that.

He tried again. All of a sudden, a pebble popped out of the keyhole and rolled across the table. They all just stared.

"A pebble?" Natalie said.

"A damn pebble in the lock," Lenny said.

Luke crossed his arms.

Lenny tried again. This time, the key fit perfectly.

Natalie felt a solid hit of adrenaline as the metal lockbox popped open, its rusty hinges creaking. Inside was a disturbing collection of occult miscellanea: there was a scary-looking vintage poppet doll with a straight pin through her head; a folded sheet of paper with five bloody, smeared fingerprints on it; a torn four-by-six-inch piece of pink polyester fabric with a bloodstain in the center; a desiccated leather coin bag full of what looked like ashes; a pair of black lace mesh spandex panties with scalloped edges; a bottle of nail polish called Pretty in Pink; a black-and-white snapshot of a youthful-looking Dottie Coffman, Ned Bertrand, an unknown girl, and a boy who was halfway out of the shot, all of them holding on to what looked like a cow's skull. Finally, there was an old, discolored Polaroid photograph of a girl whose back was to the camera, her hands tied behind her, her mouth gagged with a narrow band of black cloth. You could see only the back of her head and her baggy blue sweatshirt, with the exception of a small portion of her face as she peered over her shoulder at the camera, one terrified eye looking straight into the lens, staring bleakly into a future without her, beyond her own death.

At least that was Natalie's chilling interpretation.

"What the hell is that," Luke drew back, clearly disgusted.

Lenny gingerly picked up the Polaroid. "It's deeply disturbing, is what it is."

"When was it taken, Lenny?" Natalie asked.

"I can't say. Unfortunately, it looks like someone took a pair of scissors and cropped the picture, cutting off the margins along with any identifying numbers on back."

"So there aren't any other identifying marks on this photo?"

He turned it over and showed them. "Not that I'm aware of. On the back of every Polaroid, you'll find a digit code. Pre-2018, it was a ten-digit code. Post-2018, it's eleven digits. In this case, someone wisely cut out the numbers that would've given us a wealth of information—type of film, precise date of production, what kind of machine was used for production, et cetera."

"So we'll never know?" Luke asked.

"Every Polaroid is unique. There are no copies. But there are still a few things I can do." Lenny carefully handled the photograph, holding it by the edges and slipping it into a protective sleeve. "I can test for prints and scan the image for digital enhancement. I can also try to identify the chemical composition. Before 2008, when Polaroid wound down their analog business, different types of chemicals were used. We may be able to pin it down to post- or pre-2008. Let me see what I can do." He squinted at the picture. "In the meantime, do we know who she is?"

"It's impossible to tell," Natalie said. "She's got her back to us, and you can only see one eye, the tip of her ear, and part of a nose. The rest is hidden behind her shoulder and long dark hair. The eye color is hard to read. Which is why the date is crucial. Once we narrow it down to pre- or post-2008, we can at least focus on missing persons cases and homicides during that time line."

"Yeah," Lenny said, squinting, "looks like a blue sweatshirt, and the gag is a narrow piece of black cloth, like a necktie. Long dark hair, scared-looking kid. I can hopefully provide us with more details once I've digitally enhanced the image."

"It could be a child or a young adult," Luke said. "Hard to tell. The photo quality sucks. Discolored, blurry, poorly lit. You've got your work cut out for you, Lenny."

Natalie couldn't help herself—she thought about her old friend Bella. Still absent after all these years. Bella with her long dark hair, only eighteen when she went missing. But the case had been closed, and she was deemed a runaway.

"Yeah, it's hard to see any defining characteristics," Lenny said. He put the Polaroid down and picked through the other items in the lockbox. "This definitely has ritualistic overtones. If we get lucky, I might be able to lift a few prints from the interior of the lockbox or one of these items. There's an abundance of evidence here." Lenny picked up the lace mesh panties.

"Maybe we'll get a semen sample. Hold on." He plugged his handheld laser into an outlet, put on a pair of yellow goggles, and waved the laser light over the panties. The fabric glowed neon green in small patches. Laser examination often revealed things you couldn't detect under ordinary light, like hair and fibers, semen, and other valuable trace.

"We might have a semen sample. And here's something else." Lenny used a pair of tweezers to pluck a curly, dun-colored fiber that was stuck to the panties' elastic band. "A pubic hair." He gingerly teased the curly fiber out of the fabric. "With a root attached. We should be able to get DNA off of this." He switched off the laser light. "Is this related to the Manes case?"

"Could be," Luke told him. "Or it might be another rabbit hole. We aren't sure."

Lenny put everything back inside the lockbox and tucked the whole thing into the large evidence bag, then set it aside on his workbench. "One other thing, Lieutenant. Augie and I processed the hell out of that silver Dodge pickup truck and found a whole lot of useless trace that appears to be unrelated to the case. However, during our second sweep of the truck bed, we found some significant trace—a few green fibers and short brown animal hairs. I just tested everything, and it's a match for the fibers and hairs we found inside Veronica Manes's house. So I can definitely say we've found evidence linking the Hosts to the crime scene."

"That's great news, Lenny."

"We got lucky. We only did a second sweep of the truck because Augie insisted on it. Him and his OCD. I was ready to move on. Don't ask me how we missed those fibers and hairs the first time around."

"Since the Hosts have been staying with Topaz Revelli, I'll have Augie type up the affidavits for a warrant to search the Revelli farm. Good work, Lenny," Luke said, then he gestured for Natalie to follow him.

Out in the hallway, Natalie spoke first. "We need to confront Edward Host about the trace we found in his truck bed. Get a confession."

"He posted bail this morning through his attorney, Timothy Cochran."

She threw her hands in the air. "Where the hell did the bail money come from?"

"I don't know. Maybe someone in his family. Or maybe a GoFundMe. I'm assuming Cochran's representing him pro bono for the publicity."

"Where did Edward go after he posted bail?"

Luke glanced at his watch.

"You lost him?" Natalie said, incredulous.

"We weren't tailing him."

"What the fuck, Luke? We need to find them. They're at the epicenter of this swirling pile of dog shit. At least let's stake out Topaz Revelli's house and ask Jules—"

"Natalie," Luke interrupted. "It's all right. I've got this. We're doing everything we can. We've got an APB out for Holly and Edward. They're listed as 'wanted for questioning.' There's no sign of them so far, but we'll find them. And we're going to get a search warrant for the Revelli farm, so there's no need to set up a stakeout. I've asked Brandon and Jacob to start working their CIs, see if we can track those two down."

She gazed into his face. "Holly told Veronica something she didn't want anyone close to her, including Marigold, to know. We need to find out exactly what that was. It seems to be at the crux of this whole thing."

"Are you sure she didn't confide in Justin Fowler? They were having an affair, after all."

"I'll go talk to him again." Natalie nodded. "But first I want to go through this new box of Veronica's writing and research, see if there's anything else we can link to the Hosts."

Luke glanced at his watch. "I have to go prep for my meeting with the chief. Let me know if you find anything."

"Wait, Luke," she said, stopping him. "I can't help thinking this is what Veronica was looking for—the lockbox. She was interested in the Witch Trees and the yearbooks and Dottie Coffman, and it led us here."

"Okay, but let's not put too much stake in it. All it proves is that Dottie Coffman and Ned Bertrand were part of a coven when they were young and naïve," Luke countered. "The blood on the fabric could be cow's blood, for all we know. The Polaroid could've been staged as part of a hazing ritual for new members."

"Hazing?" Natalie repeated skeptically. "That girl looks scared to death. Besides, Dottie told me to destroy it. She wanted me to burn it for her. Why would she say that, if it's so harmless?"

Luke lifted an eyebrow. "Because she's got Alzheimer's."

The fluorescent lights made everything in the hallway look sterile and flat.

"We don't know anything yet, Natalie. But all the evidence is with our best man. Lenny has a lot of work to do. Let's give him the time and space he needs to do it right." Luke looked at his watch again. "I have to go . . ."

"Let me know the instant they locate Holly and Edward," she said. "I want to be there when you question them."

49

When Natalie was a little girl, she wanted to be a superhero. She pinned a bath towel around her shoulders like a cape, and every Halloween she wore a different superhero costume. She told her mother that the soggy vegetables Deborah served for supper were kryptonite, and therefore Natalie couldn't eat them. She liked to pretend that she could fly like Superman. She made believe that her flashlight beam was the Bat-Signal. She flopped down on the couch and imagined that she was walking across the ceiling like Spider-Man. She used a garbage can lid for a Wonder Woman shield.

After she outgrew her superhero phase, Natalie decided she wanted to be a cop, just like her father. She didn't understand yet that police work wasn't anything like it was depicted on TV. There wasn't a lot of drama every day. You were on your feet twenty-four seven, gathering evidence and interviewing witnesses. You did a lot of online research and rummaged through dusty evidence boxes. You typed up your reports and drank a lot of coffee. Once in a while, it could be dangerous. Sometimes you got shot at. Sometimes an officer you knew would be killed in the line of duty. Toward the end of his life, Joey had warned his youngest daughter against joining the force because he no longer wanted that kind of life for her. Now she wondered—what had made him change his mind?

Back in the Criminal Investigations Unit, Natalie took the documents and paperwork out of the fourth evidence box and spread everything across her workbench. The box was stuffed to the gills with Veronica's writings, journals, old maps, historical records, photographs, and similar items. Everything had been packaged according to protocol, sealed inside plastic evidence bags for safekeeping and signed off according to the chain of custody. Natalie put on a pair of gloves and began to sort through the voluminous material.

There was an early draft—about fifty pages—of Veronica's new book, which Natalie skimmed through. It was a rather dry recalling of Burning Lake's history, beginning with the witch trials in 1712, and also a recounting of the development of Wicca as a legitimate religion. She set the draft aside. Next there was a stack of fourteen ink-stained steno notepads full of Veronica's scrawling handwriting. It appeared to contain the author's musings, along with research notes and interviews with various experts and people in town who knew certain aspects of Burning Lake's history. Again, no red flags.

There was a two-inch-thick bundle of newspaper clippings and photocopies of old articles from local papers, dating from the early 1900s through the present day, including dozens of articles about the Crow Killer case and the Violinist from various websites and online national news outlets. The local papers had the craziest headlines: PLUCKY DETECTIVE SNIPS THE VIOLINIST'S STRINGS, POLICE CHIEF CROWS ABOUT CLOSURE FOR THE CROW KILLER CASE. Every angle of the story had been exploited by the media—the authorities' reactions, the shock of the townsfolk, the sorrow of the victims' families. Reporters had swooped into Burning Lake like a pack of vultures, consuming all the news that was fit to print, every last crumb, and now they were ravenous for more. She didn't want to be standing center stage under the spotlight ever again. Luke was right to protect her. She should be grateful for his concern.

Now she dug a little deeper into the storage box. There was a stack of articles detailing corruption from the early 1920s and 1930s, including a local politician arrested for rape, and a few other scandals involving prominent citizens of the time. One of the most unusual articles in this pile was about a woman in her mid-twenties named Clarissa Dawkins, who claimed to be a witch. The year was 1926, and the newspaper was *The Salem Times* in Salem, Massachusetts. There was a black-and-white photo of Clarissa looking like Morticia Addams in her black flapper's dress, with her sleek black hair and heavily lined eyes. It was captioned MEET A MODERN-DAY WITCH! Later in the article, it explained that Clarissa had been institutionalized in Boston's McLean Hospital after a "public display of vulgarity" and for having "grandiose ideas."

Next came a four-inch-thick collection of photocopied, stapled articles spanning a gamut of research topics relating to witchcraft, and the history of witch trials in both America and England, going back to medieval times; there were articles on the colonial graveyards in Burning Lake; articles on various museum collections focusing on dark magic; and the biographies of various figures like Aleister Crowley and Marie Laveau.

At the bottom of the box was a very musty collection of cabinet and carte de visite photographs from the 1800s. Some of these antique photographs had the subject's name written on the back—Forsyth, Grimsby, Pastor, Hutchins, Bell, Goodson. These old-fashioned portraits included a couple on their wedding day, a brood of children in their Sunday best, and in one sad instance, a mother holding her dead infant. Many of the people in these pictures had disturbingly blurred-over eyes, as if they'd tried their very best not to blink, but instead had blinked over and over again until their eyes became the surreal eyes of the dead. The descendants of the victims of the witch trials were all jumbled in together with descendants of the judges or magistrates.

At the bottom of the box was a USB flash drive in a plastic sleeve. Natalie inserted it into her computer. Veronica had been working on a spreadsheet with information from Ancestry.com. She appeared to be tracking the lineage of many of the key players in the 1712 witch trials. Once again, Natalie recognized the names of the accused, along with many of the witnesses and judges.

Included in the spreadsheet was Thomas Bell, one of the harshest judges at the witch trials, along with his family tree. In 1742, one of Bell's daughters married William Manes, and Veronica had traced her lineage all the way to the early 1960s, when she was born.

Natalie copied these files onto her laptop, then returned the flash drive to its evidence sleeve. Everything would have to be filed away for later rumination. She straightened up and could feel her head beginning to throb, steel blades jabbing into her temples. The world wobbled for a second. She looked around the office with its seven work cubicles. The Criminal Investigations Unit was empty. What time was it?

She checked her watch. One o'clock.

There was one last item waiting to be examined—an old blue vinyl journal whose cover was peeling like old wallpaper. She opened it up and began to read. It was full of Veronica's observations about the residents of Burning Lake—how they interacted, how they felt about one another, the tribes they'd formed, the grudges they held, the rumors they spread. Some of the pages were missing—not just missing, they'd been torn out.

Alarmed, she leafed through the journal and found three separate times where an unknown number of pages had been ripped out, leaving only the ragged torn edges. It was possible that Veronica had done this herself—but very doubtful. She was writing a book. This blue journal was in her private possession. Nobody would ever see it unless she wanted them to.

So who tore out these pages? The killers had been inside Veronica's house—but wouldn't they simply take the journal with them? Rather than selectively ripping out various sections?

Whoever had initially collected the evidence from Veronica's house was responsible for preserving and protecting the scene as much as possible, including documenting all of the items that were confiscated by the police. An inventory list of the evidence was carefully curated, along with accompanying photographs of where said evidence was found. If any single piece of evidence was moved or tampered with prior to being photographed, the fact should've been noted in the report.

Natalie began checking each item of evidence against the detectives' reports, the manifest, and police photographs—both overviews and close-ups. A photograph had been taken of the blue journal on Veronica's desk where it had been found, closed and off to one side of the desk. It was impossible to tell from these pictures whether the pages had been torn out before or after the police photographs were taken.

Next, she reviewed the handwritten police notes by Detective Augie Vickers, written at the time the evidence had been recovered from the house. Signed and dated by Augie. There was no mention of any pages missing from the blue journal, but it could've been an oversight. They were only human, after all. There were so many hours in a day. Augie was meticulous in his methodology, but he may have merely skimmed through the journal and missed those torn-out pages in his preliminary examination of the evidence. He also might've placed the journal into an evidence bag without opening it in the first place.

Next, Natalie compared all the items in the storage box with the manifest, and found two serious errors. Two pieces of evidence were apparently missing from the box—the first was another journal, described as a small red diary with a brass clasp; the second error consisted of two steno pads—the numbers didn't match. The manifest said there were sixteen steno notebooks, but Natalie counted only fourteen. She looked all around her work space, just to be sure she hadn't accidentally misplaced anything.

After reviewing her findings one more time, she went to share the disturbing news with Luke. Any searches for physical evidence had to be thorough and systematic. Once a piece of evidence was determined to be recoverable, then a full accounting and documentation of the chain of custody was necessary.

Luke was in his office, typing up a report after his meeting with the chief. He invited her in, then checked his watch. "I've got five minutes," he told her. "What's up?"

She explained about the missing evidence and the torn-out journal pages.

Luke grew visibly alarmed. "Do you have the chain of custody for the missing items?" he asked.

Natalie handed him a copy of the manifest she'd made for him. "Augie collected the evidence and signed off on it. Then Officer Goodson transported the boxes to the station house, where Dennis took possession. Then Dennis handed it over to Murphy for sorting, labeling, and documenting into the system. Finally, it was transferred downstairs to Hughie for storage. Then you and I collected it and brought it back upstairs. That's the chain of custody for these items."

Luke's face grew pale. He said in a grim tone, "I'll take it from here. In the meantime, don't say a word about this to anyone."

She nodded. They both knew that Augie, Officer Goodson, and the dispatcher, Dennis, were beyond reproach.

"I'll deal with it." He put his copy of the manifest in a desk drawer and stood up. "I have to go now. Are we good?"

Natalie sort of bristled. The brusque manner in which he'd said this to her didn't sit right. "I don't know," she said sarcastically. "Are we?"

"Sure," he said, finally looking at her—really studying her face. "Natalie, I'm trying not to complicate my life."

"I'm pretty uncomplicated. Once you get to know me."

He didn't respond. He didn't smile. His face was unmoved.

"I thought we said we'd still be friends."

"We are."

"And this is your friend face? This stern, disapproving scowl?"

Again, he didn't respond. Didn't even crack a smile.

Natalie tried again. "There's no need for animosity, right?"

"After my wife took our daughter away to California," he confessed, "it felt like a piece of my heart had been ripped out. But then, gradually, I got used to it. I'll get used to this, too. Eventually. But right now, I need a little space from our friendship. Okay?"

Back in her office, Natalie put everything back in the box, following protocol. She paused to straighten out the fifty-page draft of Veronica's book. As she tapped the loose stack of pages on her worktable, an envelope fell out and slipped to the floor.

She picked up the envelope with Veronica's name and address handwritten on the front. No stamp, no postal marks. There was a folded piece of typing paper inside. She opened it and read the handwritten note. It was dated about a month ago. Her head was spinning. This didn't make any sense. It left her with a feeling as slithery as snakeskin.

50

Justin Fowler lived with his mother in an old farmhouse with a rotting front porch that was covered in dead vines. Mrs. Fowler raised rabbits and had an apple orchard. In the fall, you could drive out to the farm and pick your own apples for twenty dollars a bushel.

Natalie rang the doorbell, and Mrs. Fowler answered.

"Yes?" Short and stooped, wearing a curly bronze wig, she stood squinting up at Natalie. "Can I help you?"

"Hello, Mrs. Fowler, it's Detective Lockhart." She flashed her badge. "May I come in?"

The older woman's face held on to a perplexed look. "What do you want?"

"I'd like to speak to your son. Just a few questions."

Justin's mother thought about this for a moment, her eyes turning inward. Natalie could see her wrestling with it. Then she pinched the doorknob and edged sideways, leaving a narrow space for Natalie to enter through. "He's down in the basement."

"Thank you."

"Don't thank me," she muttered. "My son may have forgiven your wretched family, but sure as heck I haven't."

Natalie could feel the hot bitterness emanating from the woman's eyes—not that she blamed her. In fact, she was surprised Mrs. Fowler hadn't slammed the door in her face.

"The entrance to the basement is at the end of the hallway."

Natalie could detect an overwhelming animal-like odor as she opened the door and descended the creaky wooden stairs. She paused at the bottom to let her eyes adjust to the darkness. The casement windows were painted over so that no natural light came through. There were a few lamps inside the carpeted space. There were tools hanging from a pegboard and a workbench in one corner. A water heater and other mechanical equipment hummed behind the nail-studded walls of Sheetrock. Thirty-nine-year-old Justin sat slumped in a plaid armchair in one corner. He had salt-and-pepper hair and dark blue eyes set deep in a pale, haggard-looking face. He removed his dark-framed glasses and put his book down.

"I'm here on official business." She flashed her badge. "Your mother let me in."

The ex-con was patting a rabbit in his lap—a brown bunny with long brown ears. Natalie felt a prickle of alarm. *Brown animal hairs.*

He nodded at the other armchair. "Have a seat."

She glanced around the cavernous basement. Several rabbit cages were stacked double-tiered against a far wall. The furniture was comfortable-looking, blocky pine bookshelves and upholstered armchairs, a teal-colored sleep sofa and pine side tables stacked with video games. The air smelled dense—of mildew and rabbit fur.

Natalie took a seat and said, "I found a letter among Veronica's possessions."

"Okay," came his emotionless response.

She took the envelope out of her coat pocket and unfolded the piece of paper. "It's from Holly to Veronica. She claims you threatened her."

"Threatened?" He shook his head calmly. "I don't think so."

"It says, and I quote, 'Thanks for the book on white magic, Veronica. I loved our talk the other day, and I value our friendship. I hope I've proven to you how good I am at keeping secrets. I hope I've earned your trust. So I'm writing this letter to warn you about some of the people you've surrounded yourself with. I didn't tell you about it before, because I didn't realize how serious it was between you and Justin. Now that I know, I felt the need to warn you. Last September, Edward and I had a party at the cottage, and we invited Justin over. He somehow got a gun and climbed up onto the roof of the cabin and shot randomly into the woods. When the guys tried to talk him down off the roof, he threatened to kill them, but no one seriously thought he'd go through with it. Then he started shooting at them, so everyone hid and spent the next hour trying to get him down off the roof. Finally, he came down, and they took the gun away, and he apologized. He said he'd had too much coke and thought we were all using black magic against him. He finally left. We never invited him back. Veronica, I care about you. Please be careful. Think about what you're doing. Just because he was innocent years ago, doesn't mean he's innocent now. Much love, Holly.'" Natalie put the letter away and looked up.

He was watching her quietly, patting the rabbit.

"Where were you Monday night and early Tuesday morning?" she asked.

He seemed surprised by this. "I told you. Right here."

"Down in the basement? The whole night?"

"I was watching TV upstairs with my mom for a few hours."

"Why don't you walk me through the events of that night?"

He squinted at her. "I just told you . . . we were watching TV upstairs."

"What shows, may I ask?"

He shrugged. "Monday-night stuff. Then I came downstairs to bed. I had to go to work the next morning." The rabbit in his lap gave a precise little shiver.

"What time did you go to bed?" she pressed.

He thought for a moment. "Right after the late-night show."

"So around one o'clock?"

Justin nodded.

"Did you call anyone that night? Text anyone?"

He shook his head sideways.

"Who else besides your mother can support your alibi?"

"My *alibi*?"

Natalie nodded. "Did you order a pizza? Talk to the neighbors? Go out for beer and cigarettes?"

Justin's spine wilted forward. "Look, when I got out of prison, I was having trouble sleeping. I was self-medicating, to use a euphemism. I didn't trust anybody. One thing you learn in prison, most people have ulterior motives. I dealt with killers, con men, drug dealers, white-collar criminals, religious guys, thieves, first-timers, folks of all persuasions. And when I returned to civilian life, I was a marked man, even though I'm innocent. My pardon proves I'm innocent. Your sister's confession proves I'm innocent. But I look like an ex-con. I've got that hundred-yard stare. Most people recoil from me as if I were a hardened criminal. It sucks. It hurts. It feels like I'm still lying in my bunk, watching the sunset beyond my barred window."

"So you're saying you've had a difficult transition. Is that why you climbed on the cottage roof and shot off a gun? Because of a sense of alienation?"

"Let me put it this way. In prison, you're on a strict schedule. Meals are served at the same time each day. Laundry, mail call, phone privileges, visitors. Everything happens at a specific hour on a given day. Lights out at ten. Day starts at five. While serving my sentence, I was confined to my cellblock, the mess hall, the yard, and my job. That was my entire world.

"Then, all of a sudden, I'm pardoned by the governor and set free. Great. So now what? My schedule was how I got through every damn day for twenty years. Now what am I supposed to do? It feels like I'm free-falling. I can't get a job. Meetings get canceled, people flake on you. But I cling to my old schedule like a life raft, because it's all I have.

"So then, Veronica Manes comes along and says—wait. She offers me an alternative. She gives me a shoulder to cry on. She explains the concept of forgiveness. She opens my eyes and gives me hope. She becomes my friend in a sea of indifference. Bottom line. I would never hurt her. Not in a million years."

Natalie believed he genuinely loved her—but it was also true that we sometimes hurt the ones we loved. "Where did you get the gun?"

"A guy at the party was showing it off. He passed it around. I was wasted, like everybody else. Holly's a liar. No one was in danger of getting hurt. I was goofing around. I thought it was funny—and I guess nobody else got the joke. And I learned my lesson. Those people are bad news. A bad influence. I didn't go back there."

"You said you were self-medicating at the time. But you got off the drugs?"

"Shortly afterwards." He nodded, patting the rabbit's long silky ears. "I've been sober for six months now. Got a job. Turned my life around. I have Veronica and the reverend to thank for that."

She glanced around the basement. On the side table nearest her was a church advertisement welcoming new parishioners and a schedule of NA meetings. Opposite them was a kitchenette with a coffeemaker and a mini-fridge. There were several closed doors, behind which was the rest of the basement, including a back entrance and a bathroom, she guessed. Except for the rabbits, the place was clean and tidy. No ashtrays, no liquor bottles, no syringes, no prescription drugs. Nothing out in the open, anyway.

"Justin, did you ever ride in Edward Host's truck? A silver Dodge pickup?"

"No."

"You never hitched a ride with them or sat in the truck bed?"

He shook his head firmly. "No, I didn't. Why?"

"I'm looking for them. Holly and Edward. Do you know where they are?"

"I just told you, I never went back there. Those people are into dark magic. They're garbage people. I can't believe Holly went to all that trouble to write Veronica such a pack of lies. Thank God Veronica didn't listen to her."

"But she invited Holly into her house. She trusted her that much."

Justin scowled at the memory. "She was a trusting person. A sweet woman. I think that's why she's dead. She trusted the wrong person, and look what happened."

"Before, you told me that Holly had information that might affect the coven."

He nodded curtly, losing patience with her.

"And you have no idea where they might be? It's urgent that I find them."

"The Hosts?" He studied her carefully. "Why? Are they suspects?"

"I just need to find out where they are."

"Why? What'd they do?" he asked, the anger rising inside him.

"I just need to ask them some questions."

He carefully put the rabbit down on the floor. Then he leaned back and asked, "Did they hurt her? Do you suspect them of killing her?"

"We don't know anything yet. I simply need to find them."

He rubbed his chin. "They'll be looking to buy, if they aren't already holding. You should find out who they get their drugs from. Maybe that's where you'll find them."

"You don't happen to know who their dealer is, do you?"

"No. Like I said, I'm six months sober."

Somewhere inside the house, a teakettle began to whistle.

"I'll need a list of names of everyone at that party you attended."

"You want me to snitch?" he asked moodily. "You're asking an ex-con to rat out his friends? Or even his acquaintances? Because I don't play that game."

Natalie looked down at the chair arms—the rabbits had shed their fur all over the upholstery. She wanted to collect some and take it with her. "Look, I'd appreciate your cooperation. It would be faster to get a list of names from you. Can't you do that for me?"

"I'll think about it."

"Don't you want me to catch whoever did this?"

He held her eye. "Are you saying that they did this?"

Upstairs, the teakettle was shrieking.

Natalie ran her hands over the upholstered arms of the chair, gathering rabbit hairs under her nails and between her fingers. She stood up and transferred the loose fur into her coat pockets. Finally, the teakettle stopped whistling.

He sat there studying her, his face holding on to its repressed anger. "There's true evil in this world, Detective. It surrounds us every day. I wish it didn't exist, but it does. People like Veronica are very rare. It's not fair that she's gone. Not at all."

"If you change your mind, let me know." She handed him her card.

"You have to decide which side you're on, even if you end up paying for it."

She hesitated before saying, "I'd like to be clear about something, Justin. I want to apologize on behalf of my family. I know it's too little, too late. I don't expect to be forgiven. But I want you to know how sorry I am for what happened."

He sized her up, judging her harshly. Then he nodded. "Thank you for that."

Back upstairs, Natalie bumped into Mrs. Fowler. "Do you have a moment?"

"Oh." The older woman went still all over, wrinkles forming on her pale brow.

"Please. It'll just take a minute."

Mrs. Fowler gestured toward the kitchen.

There was a messiness to the place. A comfort to the clutter. Bills, baked goods under domed display cases, crumbs and used coffee cups on the countertops. Brick-colored tiles on the kitchen floor. Little chipped figurines on a painted shelf. A window garden—clay pots holding herbs.

"My mother grew an herb garden," Natalie commented. "What are those?"

"Oregano, chives, parsley, mint, and thyme."

"Nice," Natalie said. "My mother grew basil, mint, sage, and rosemary."

Over in one corner was a long wooden table with bags of potting soil, packets of seeds, stacked clay pots, and glass jars of varying sizes. Some of the soil had spilled to the floor. Natalie moved a little closer and noticed there were clay pot shards on the table. She was tempted to reach down and nab a soil sample.

"Did something break?" she asked.

The older woman stared in confusion. "Why do you ask? What do you want?"

"Justin told me he was at home on Monday night with you. Is that true?"

"Well, I should say so." She folded her arms, looking highly suspicious.

"He said you watched television together."

"That's right."

"What shows?"

"This and that."

"And he went to bed . . . when?"

"Shortly after midnight."

"You're sure?"

"I was still up. I don't sleep so well nowadays."

"And he didn't leave the house all night long?"

"No," she said angrily.

"I noticed there's a back entrance to the basement. He could've slipped out, and you wouldn't have known. Right?"

The older woman frowned, her withered cheeks sprouting red spots. "All I know is . . . my son was here the whole time. He never left the house. End of story."

Natalie nodded politely. "Does Justin have any guns?"

"No. But Ford did."

"Who's Ford?"

"My husband, Ford Fowler. Passed away eleven years ago. He owned a couple of handguns and a hunting rifle. Fully licensed. Why? Who wants to know?"

The basement door popped open. "Mom, don't talk to her," Justin said firmly.

Mrs. Fowler clammed up.

"You should go now," Justin said.

On her way out of the house, Natalie noticed damage to Justin's green Chevy Blazer that was parked in the driveway behind his mother's white Kia Soul. There was damage to the back fender and the hubcap was scraped, as if the driver had backed into a guardrail, but she was no expert. She covertly took out her phone and snapped a few pictures. She peeked inside the Blazer and noticed that the car's interior was also green. *Green fibers, short brown animal hairs.* She got in her car and drove farther east. Once she was out of sight, she parked by the side of the road and studied the Fowler residence through her rearview mirror.

The old farmhouse looked perfectly normal at first glance, suitable for life in these parts. The creep factor wasn't an issue—lots of homes out this way were centuries old and relatively run-down. The Fowler residence wasn't isolated from the community—there were neighbors across the road and on either side. The property itself wasn't conspicuously disorganized. Nothing to indicate psychosis or neuroses. Nothing to indicate that a murderer might be living there. Nothing to prove he was innocent, either.

51

Natalie got her evidence kit out of the trunk and transferred the rabbit hairs from her coat pocket into an evidence bag. These weren't the most ideal circumstances for evidence gathering, but it was the best she could do.

She put the kit away, then sat behind the wheel and observed the house again through her rearview mirror. It began to snow. A light afternoon snowfall. She called Luke and told him what she'd found.

"It's circumstantial at this point, but if you add it all up," she concluded, "the rabbit hairs, the green fibers, the potting soil and shards of glass . . . Holly's warning to Veronica."

"Yeah, but what's his motive?" Luke asked.

"That's the big question. I don't know. Maybe Veronica broke up with him?"

"Do you think he could've done it?" he asked.

She chewed thoughtfully on her lower lip. "Not really. He seems more intent on finding out who did this to her. I believe he genuinely loved her."

There was silence on the other end.

"But there could be another explanation for the green fibers and animal hairs that were found in the Hosts' truck bed. If the Hosts killed Veronica, and it's looking more and more like that's the case, then when they walked inside her house, they would've picked up a cross-transference of trace from Justin's basement apartment. Since Justin was having an affair with Veronica, it's pretty clear that he could've carried trace from his house and car into her home. That might explain how the trace implicating him got into the Hosts' truck."

"Right. Another explanation is that Holly stayed with Veronica for a few days."

"Shit. Good point. So we're back to square one."

"Did you get anything else from Justin?"

"Only that he was trying to forgive my family. Veronica was trying to help him. In some ways, this comes back around to me and my family."

"Natalie," Luke said quietly. "We've talked about this."

"I know." She changed the subject, brushing it aside. "Anyway, his mother confirmed his alibi, but she couldn't possibly know whether or not he left through the basement entrance. And I noticed his vehicle was damaged, although I can't tell how recently. The left rear fender is dented and the hubcap is scraped."

"Let's get those rabbit hairs to Lenny as soon as possible. He can either make a match or rule it out. Then we can at least get a warrant."

"Okay." Natalie tensed behind the wheel. "Wait, Luke. Justin walked out of the house. He's getting in his car. I'm going to follow him. Call you later." She hung up and put on her seat belt, then waited while Justin brushed the snow off his car and got in. Then he backed out of the driveway and drove away.

The hardest part of any surveillance was remaining anonymous. There was hardly any traffic this afternoon on the residential street, so her Honda Accord would've been conspicuous to someone as sensitive as Justin Fowler. If she followed him too soon, she might as well put a sign in her windshield that said STAKEOUT.

The Chevy Blazer's taillights winked at the end of the street before taking a right turn. Natalie followed cautiously, keeping at least a hundred yards between herself and the Blazer. It was snowing lightly, a good thing. The lower the visibility, the better.

He drove across town to the east side of Burning Lake. There was plenty of traffic on Sarah Hutchins Drive, and the shops were open for business. Art galleries, cafés, antiques stores, upscale restaurants, a yoga center, a vintage movie house, a "fair trade" coffeehouse. It was easy to keep at least two or three cars between them at all times.

After several more miles, the Blazer turned south into a hilly residential community full of charming homes and smoking chimneys. On Woodpecker Lane, he pulled up in front of Marigold Hutchins's house. Marigold was in her front yard, bundled up in a rose-colored winter coat with a matching hat and gloves, and a long dark red scarf. She was busy shoveling her walkway. She looked up when Justin got out of his Blazer and headed up her inclined driveway.

Natalie parked by the side of the road several blocks away and observed the two through her windshield, which kept fogging up at the corners. Her defroster didn't do such a great job. She couldn't hear anything over the blast of her heater, but she could see perfectly well that Justin and Marigold were arguing about something.

Justin waved his arms angrily at Marigold, who clutched the handle of her shovel. They were talking back and forth, their breath clouds blossoming before them. Their faces were rosy with anger or the cold. Natalie took pictures of the heated discussion with her phone. After several minutes, as the argument escalated, Justin shouted something and left, half stumbling back down the driveway, then getting in his Chevy Blazer and tearing away from the curb, his tires kicking up clouds of loose powdery snow.

Natalie waited to see what Marigold would do next. Astonishingly, she continued to shovel out her walkway.

Natalie released the emergency brake and drove the rest of the way to Marigold's house, where she parked by the side of the road and got out of her car.

"Good afternoon," Natalie said and waved.

Marigold waved back uncertainly. "Hello!" A bright spark of alarm in her voice.

Natalie trudged up the shoveled driveway, which was fairly steep. She almost slipped on a patch of ice. She could hear the neighborhood dogs barking, and across the street, a child's bike was half-buried in a snowdrift.

"Detective Lockhart, what a surprise," Marigold said. Her voice was shaking. "You're a busy bee."

"I was on my way to see you," Natalie lied, "when I suddenly noticed that you and Justin Fowler were having what looked like an argument."

"You saw that?" She blushed and suppressed a nervous laugh. "Oh gosh."

Despite the falling snow, the air was very cold—a dry cold, the kind that hurt your lungs whenever you breathed. Natalie looked around at the pine trees in the front yard. They gently creaked in the wind. Snowflakes collected on the shoveled walkway. Ice-blue twinkle lights framed the front door.

"Is something wrong? The discussion looked heated," Natalie said.

"Oh, he does that. Loses his temper. Probably from being locked up all those years . . . him being an innocent man and all."

Natalie gave a curt nod—she couldn't help perceiving this as a dig. "Why did he lose his temper this time?"

"He accused Holly Host of killing Veronica. Can you believe that?"

"Funny. I was just over at his house. It's interesting that he came to see you directly afterwards. What else did he say?"

"He asked me where Holly and Edward were."

"Why would he ask you that?"

"Because Holly and I are old friends."

"You are?"

She seemed a little nervous. She used one end of her scarf to tamp the sweat off her face. "I knew Holly's mother, Jodi. And so I knew Holly, too."

"How long have you known Holly's mother?"

"Oh, umm . . ." She looked around blankly. "When I first moved here, ten years ago, Jodi befriended me. We met in yoga class. She was the sweetest person you'd ever want to meet, especially if you were a stranger in town."

Natalie remembered something. "You're from Rochester, aren't you?"

"Yes, that's right. But we didn't know each other then. Funny, huh?"

"Do you know a woman named Cindy Templeton?"

Her mouth hung open. She stared at Natalie. "Why do you ask?"

"No reason. She went to school with Jodi Stewart."

Marigold blushed a darker shade of pink. "I wouldn't know about that. I attended a different high school."

Natalie nodded slowly. "But you and Jodi had that in common, being from Rochester?"

"Yes, and I know Holly, and she's not capable of murder, or anything like that. Edward's a little strange, but Holly is a good person. But now Justin seems to think they had something to do with Veronica's death."

"And you don't know where they are? The Hosts?"

She shook her head. "Not a clue."

"What else did he tell you? He looked angry."

"He was ranting and raving about the Hosts. Just venting. He does that sometimes. He loses it."

"Does he lose his temper often?"

"Mostly when he's triggered by a bad memory, like what your sister did to him. First taking away the love of his life, Willow. And then Grace and her friends framing him for her murder. And then his incarceration—everything he lost, including his self-confidence and his youth, all those years behind bars. And how Ellie was his only friend—except that now she won't even acknowledge his existence. How the town treats him like an outcast when he did nothing wrong, and how unfair it is. How he couldn't hold a job for the longest time. How people look at him funny sometimes, even in church. How he tries to forgive others, but he isn't forgiven. How he feels invisible. How he can't sleep . . . I could go on."

"Did he ever threaten Veronica? Verbally or otherwise?"

"Justin? No. It's only natural that couples will disagree, but that's all I heard—a few disagreements. Nothing major. No threats or curses. He didn't lose his temper with her. She had a way with him."

"Did you know that Holly had sent her a letter?"

She drew back a little. "A letter? Really?"

"She warned Veronica about Justin. There was an incident with a gun."

"Oh." She almost seemed relieved. "What happened?"

"He got drunk and swung a gun around, shooting it into the woods."

"Justin Fowler is a broken man. Veronica was trying to help him. She never told me about a letter, though. That's unacceptable. If I'd known about it, I would've spoken to him for sure." Marigold looked around and sighed heavily, her breath chasing before her in the crystalline air. "Can I say something?"

"Yes, of course."

"The truth is, Wicca can sometimes attract people who are troubled," she said in a hushed voice. "And I know Holly was into some dark shit for a while." She gripped her shovel and looked around nervously. "As good a person as she is . . . she may have been involved on the fringes somehow. They were staying with Nyle Hockney, who's a bad dude. It's just a hunch, but Holly might know who killed Veronica. I don't know. That sounds ridiculous, doesn't it?" She covered her mouth as if to shut herself up. Tears sprang to her anxious eyes.

Natalie nodded slowly, taking it all in.

"But she couldn't have been involved herself, could she? How could it possibly be true? I can't believe she'd do that to Veronica, of all people. She'd have to be a monster."

Natalie's phone buzzed just then. It was Luke. "Hello?"

"Natalie, I just got word. Holly and Edward Host are dead."

52

Natalie drove back to the police station, where Luke was waiting for her in the parking lot. She got into his midnight-blue Ford Ranger, and they headed north to Chaste Falls.

"I just spoke to Sheriff Dressler," Luke explained. "It looks like a drug overdose. That's the way he's leaning. They were found inside the vehicle with the doors locked and drug paraphernalia strewn about. Needles and a small quantity of heroin. They've been dead for several hours."

"So Justin Fowler couldn't have done it," Natalie said.

"Why do you think he might've killed them?"

"He's been threatening to kill whoever did this to Veronica. He didn't suspect the Hosts until I questioned him about an hour ago. As soon as I left, he drove over to Marigold Hutchins's place and demanded to know where they were. But it sounds like the Hosts were already dead by then."

"Marigold Hutchins? How is she connected to the Hosts?"

"She was friends with Jodi Stewart and knows Holly. She told Justin she didn't know where they were, so he drove off. She doesn't think Holly is capable of murder. She doesn't believe Justin did it, either."

"Great," Luke said sarcastically. "Everybody's innocent."

The bustle and activity in downtown Burning Lake was a little startling. People were resuming their lives. Holiday music played from the loudspeakers and twinkle lights adorned the storefronts. The holidays had come and gone, but the festive spirit lingered on, despite the recent tragedy. It was odd, how quickly we forgot.

Fifteen minutes later, they were driving north past snowy fields and equipment-strewn farms. A stale heat pumped into the vehicle from the vents at their feet. Luke's boots were muddy, and his pants were soaked at the hems from walking through the snow. She wondered where he'd been. He looked ruggedly handsome with his wind-burnt face and piercing blue eyes. He wore the same parka he'd had for seven winters, beneath which was the same suit he'd worn yesterday. Gray jacket and pants. His tie was dark blue. His shirt was white with a small coffee stain on the front. The Ranger was outfitted with all the latest equipment—police radio, video surveillance system, portable data terminal mounted on a swing arm. He kept his travel mug in his cup holder and a holstered sidearm under his jacket.

"Where was the vehicle found?" she asked.

"On an abandoned farm on the outskirts of Chaste Falls. State police called it in. Dressler found the victims' ID cards in their wallets. This wasn't foul play. No theft. The doors were locked. Keys in the ignition. They died with the engine idling and the heat on. The battery was still running. He thinks it's open-and-shut."

"Did you tell him why we were looking for them?"

Luke nodded. "I filled him in."

"And?"

"He said the facts on the ground don't indicate foul play. There were no other tire tracks or footprints in the area when the first officer arrived at the scene."

"How long have they been dead?"

"Coroner estimates at least three hours." Luke glanced at her. "Why? Do you think they were murdered?"

"Doesn't sound like it."

"But you aren't convinced. Why?"

"Holly told Veronica something that Veronica believed would adversely affect the coven. Veronica was looking into it. Now Veronica and Holly are both dead. Which makes me highly suspicious. Holly was the link to everything, and now she's gone."

"The fact that it's a possibility doesn't mean the odds are in your favor. We have to go by the facts on the ground. But I hear you. This whole thing's a shitstorm."

"We know that Holly's mother wore the same costume Veronica was wearing the day she died. Jodi Stewart passed away four years ago. I'd like to know how she died."

Luke nodded. "I'll have Mike dig into her background."

She pulled a small see-through evidence bag with about a dozen rabbit hairs in it out of her coat pocket. "I gathered up some of those brown rabbit hairs from Justin's basement. I'll get them to Lenny as soon as we get back. In the meantime, we need an affidavit for a warrant—I want to do a thorough search of Justin's house. Even if he didn't kill the Hosts, he was actively looking for them. He has access to guns. And we should check out the road and curbside in front of Veronica's house, along with her driveway. Justin may have damaged his vehicle there. We can match paint samples and scrapes or dents to the property."

Luke nodded. "I'll get Brandon working on that." As soon as they stopped at the next light, Luke picked up his phone and texted Brandon and Mike with instructions.

Chaste Falls was located thirty miles north of Burning Lake, about a half-hour drive past barren winter woods, sprawling snow-covered fields, and gray stone walls. They followed the GPS to an abandoned dairy farm, FOR SALE signs stuck in the yard. The Ranger bounced over potholes as Luke pulled into the driveway.

Natalie noticed dozens of crisscrossing tire tracks in the snow from the police response. They drove past a dilapidated farmhouse and a weathered barn that reminded her of a pair of gray, neglected relatives you'd almost forgotten about. Half a dozen police cruisers and sheriff's vehicles were parked behind the barn.

Luke and Natalie got out of the Ranger and headed for the yellow crime tape cordoning off a twenty-by-twenty-foot area around Topaz Revelli's red Nissan Frontier pickup truck. Edward's damaged silver Dodge pickup truck was back at the impound lot, and it looked as if the Hosts had either borrowed or stolen their friend's vehicle. The red truck was parked in a field, snow falling gently over everything, covering up evidence.

The law enforcement officers who'd responded to the scene stood around examining pieces of trace and studying the small details, checking their watches with preoccupied faces, calling their voicemail and listening to their messages. Dignified, cool, relaxed. Comfortable with tragedy.

Sheriff Dressler approached them and shook their hands. "Detective Lockhart, we meet again. Lieutenant Pittman, it's good to put a face to a familiar voice."

Dressler and Natalie had met five months ago while working on the Violinist case. He was an older man with silver-streaked hair, craggy features, and a friendly demeanor who'd been instrumental in helping her nail the killer of Morgan Chambers.

"It's this way, folks." He cordially lifted up the crime scene tape and held it for them as they stepped inside the perimeter. Then he escorted them over to the Nissan pickup, saying, "One of our state police officers noticed a vehicle parked where it shouldn't be and came to investigate. There were no other tire marks visible on the driveway when he arrived, besides those Nissan treads. Of course, he left his own tire tracks and footprints in the snow upon discovery of the vehicle. I'll copy you his first officer's report. He said the doors of the vehicle were locked and the windows were rolled up. The keys were inside. He could see the two victims through the windshield and felt it was imperative to jack the door lock, just in case they were still alive. He opened the passenger side door and realized both victims were deceased. He backed away immediately and called the sheriff's department."

Luke nodded. "Thanks, Sheriff."

"No problem," Dressler said with a seasoned wink. "Take your time."

Whenever she entered a crime scene, Natalie's sense of smell, taste, and touch became heightened. She could smell the ozone in the air from the falling snow. She could smell the diesel fuel. Everything was dusted with a fresh coating of snow. The tires were speckled with sediments of mud and gravel from the driveway and the field. Under the back of the truck, a puddle of oil leached into the ground.

They followed a well-worn trail around the side of the vehicle where the other officers had forged a single path of footprints in an effort to preserve as much of the scene as they could. The passenger door was propped open. They leaned forward and peered inside.

Natalie tasted a crisp metallic tang mixed with something sour and acrid—the victim's vomitus. The couple sat together inside the sleek cab of the truck as if they'd fallen asleep there. The scene was like a snippet of a black-and-white film—long ago and far away. Like a glitch in reality, it shouldn't have happened. Natalie needed to talk to Holly. Out of all the people she'd interviewed, Holly was the one person who seemed to hold many of the answers. A lingering scent of decay clung to the air. She fought off her rising nausea.

Holly wasn't wearing her seat belt. Neither was Edward. Holly had taken her boots off and was curled like a cat next to Edward. Her eyes were half-closed, like a sleepy child trying to stay up past her bedtime. Her slender arms crawled with bruises and injection marks from longtime narcotics addiction.

Edward's frozen facial expression was one of interruption and surprise. He had a head of messy black hair and such an innocence about him, you'd barely imagine he had a juvenile record and rap sheet yea long.

The Hosts were a perfect snapshot of the wasted promise of youth—just two skinny kids in bargain jeans and sales table T-shirts who'd chased their dreams into a ditch. The car heater was running when the first officer had arrived and switched it off. Their hair curled damply across their foreheads. Edward's eyes stared softly at nothing. Holly's sleepy face was placid and accepting of death.

Natalie experienced a pang of fright. Maybe the Hosts had given up. Or maybe this was an accidental overdose, like Dressler believed. Or quite possibly, it wasn't what it seemed. Regardless, this was a uniquely American tragedy—a Romeo-and-Juliet-gone-wrong story, about a dead couple locked in romantic solitude inside a Japanese-manufactured pickup truck on an abandoned farm in upstate New York after overdosing on illicit drugs from across the border.

Natalie glanced at Luke, whose lips were pressed tightly together. He wore a look of concentration, his gaze sliding from one victim to the other, assessing everything.

"So far there's nothing to indicate foul play," Sheriff Dressler told them. "We want to be absolutely thorough in our coverage, given the circumstances, but it looks as if they found an isolated place to shoot up, miscalculated, and passed out, with nobody nearby to get help. We believe they were in the vehicle with the windows rolled up and the engine running for a long enough period of time to die of carbon monoxide poisoning. If so, we should be able to see a cherry-red coloring to the muscles and organs during the autopsy. I'll let you know what we find out, but this looks like a classic overdose situation to me." His lips twisted with disgust. "One other thing. A minor detail, but I wanted to share. Somebody wrote 'Wash Me' in the dust on the vehicle."

Sheriff Dressler walked around to the back of the vehicle and pointed at the windshield. "We processed the glass for prints, but whoever did this most likely wore gloves. It could've been Edward or Holly doing it as a joke, but here in Chaste Falls, we like to cross all our t's and dot all our i's."

"Thanks, Sheriff," Luke said.

"Also the lab results, once we get them back."

Natalie swung her attention forward. "What about their shoe size?"

"Pardon me?" Dressler said.

Luke nodded. "Long as we're here, Sheriff, could you have one of your men check their shoe sizes for us?"

"Sure thing. Whatever floats your boat." Dressler snapped his fingers and called one of his men over. "We need to check the victims' shoe sizes."

The officer put on a pair of gloves, bent into the car, and picked up one of Holly's boots from the passenger seat footwell. "Size six," he called out. Then he went around to the other side of the vehicle and took off one of Edward's boots. "Size twelve," he called out.

Natalie jotted it down on her notepad. "Thanks, Sheriff," she told him.

"Not a problem," Dressler said. "Any questions, you've got my direct line."

They all shook hands and parted ways.

53

Luke drove Natalie back to Burning Lake, where he stopped at one of her favorite places, Salvino's Roadside Diner. As the door swung open, a few snowflakes drifted in with them. The 1950s-era diner was smaller than you thought it would be, with a jukebox playing rock music from the fifties and sixties. It was warm and comforting. The ponytailed waitress nodded at them from behind the counter.

They slipped into a back booth. Their table was set with fresh paper place mats, napkins, silverware, and ceramic coffee mugs. Natalie took off her gloves, unwrapped her scarf, and unbuttoned her coat, while snow swirled against the plate glass windows, blurring her view of the gas station across the street.

Luke picked up the laminated menu.

The waitress came over to their booth holding a coffeepot. "Coffee?"

"Thanks," Luke told her, while Natalie nodded.

The waitress filled their cups. "Ready to order?"

"Nothing for me, thanks," Natalie said.

Luke glanced at her over his menu. "You like the French toast here, don't you?"

"Not today," Natalie said with a strained smile.

"How about a piece of their mud pie?" he pressed.

"I've got a mother already, thanks," she joked, just wanting him to stop.

His smile broadened. "I'll have the mud pie. And keep the coffee coming."

"Sure thing," the waitress said and walked away.

He put the menu down, his face falling into gentle lines. "I'll stop nagging you now."

"That's okay, you're good at nagging. It's part of your skill set."

He shook his head and smiled. Then he grew serious. "The remembrance ceremony is tomorrow morning at Abby's Hex. The funeral's tomorrow afternoon at St. Paul's. You don't have to be there for either one of them, Natalie. We've got enough guys to cover it."

Her cheeks grew warm. "I want to be there."

"You realize there are going to be reporters swarming all over the place."

She nodded. Her hands had turned a dusty red from the cold and were fisted shut. Behind the counter, a busboy stacked the dirty dishes in the dishwasher, making a clatter. She wiped her nose as if to erase the smell of death and meth.

"The shoe sizes aren't a match," Luke said. "Not even with layers of socks. So now what?"

"Now we talk to Topaz Revelli and Nyle Hockney. Find out what they know."

"Nyle won't talk to us."

"Maybe she'll talk to me. Topaz is close to Jules. I'll make the call."

Natalie went to use the restroom, then stood outside in the foyer, and called Jules. By the time she got back to their table, Luke was digging into his mud pie. There were two forks. She slipped into the booth.

"Help yourself," he told her.

She ignored him. "Jules says he'll call me back."

Luke put down his fork. He'd left half a piece of pie on the plate. "So what do you think, given what just happened? Where are we in the case?"

The waitress returned with the coffeepot, saying, "We're closing early. They say we'll get another five or six inches overnight. Would you like a refill?"

"We're all set," Luke told her.

The wind knocked a street sign against its metal post outside, and Natalie listened for a moment to the *tap-tap-tap*. "I can't help thinking there's a bigger story here. Veronica knew too much. It's something I can't define, not even in the vaguest terms, but the horror of the possibility scares me. Because for some reason, it reminds me of something my father did a long time ago. I told you about it once. I must've been ten or eleven, and Joey was shredding documents in his office. He looked terrible. The memory stays with me. Much later, he told me not to become a cop. He said I shouldn't risk my life for a pension and a paycheck. He balked right when I was about to graduate from the academy. It was so strange. And I can't help thinking—what if Joey knew something, like Veronica did, and they killed him for it? What if my father's car accident wasn't really an accident?"

Luke's lingering look made her feel nervous—but all she read in his eyes was genuine concern. No need to be nervous. A lock of brown hair had come loose and hung down over his forehead before he unconsciously brushed it away. "If I thought that, I'd be the first one demanding an investigation," he told her.

"I know, but what about Dottie Coffman and Ned Bertrand and the lockbox full of stuff. What about the Polaroid of the girl? And the fact that Veronica was digging into the past. Maybe she unearthed something, maybe she threatened to expose someone very powerful, and so she was made an example of."

"An example? Like the mafia?"

"I'm just saying . . ."

"It's okay," he said. "I get where you're coming from. I even understand your need to weave everything together into one shiny package. That's only natural. I've been there myself. But, Natalie, you're way ahead of yourself. Usually, the simplest answer is the most likely one. I think what's happened in this past year is contributing to a stressful environment for you. You won't even take a single bite of your favorite pie. I'm concerned that you look so pale and thin lately. That you haven't been sleeping. I'm concerned that you're going to the funeral tomorrow and will quickly be overwhelmed by a demand for comments from the very press you despise. That this case is taking a heavy toll on you. Look," he said, reaching for her hand and holding it briefly, "I think the brain—especially smart brains, curious brains, brilliant brains—they make connections all the time and see patterns that aren't really there, because we're only human and we try so hard to make sense out of things. We're hardwired that way. Some of those connections and patterns are real. We just have to find out which ones."

She knew he was right, but it didn't make her feel any better.

"You're emotionally drained. There's no shame in that, Natalie. We've all reached our limits at some point or other. I think you should take the rest of the day off. You're on background, and you're doing an amazing job. But the guys and I . . . we've got this. We'll find Justin. We'll get our warrants. We'll search both properties and we'll get to the bottom of this horrendous tragedy, once and for all. That I can promise you."

Fat icy snowflakes were hitting the picture window with a persistent *rat-tat-tat-tat*. Another storm was headed their way. The movement of the snowfall was mesmerizing, twirling and shimmering before her, with a dark sky in the distance. Grief burned. Grief stabbed. The more you wept, the harder it solidified in your gut. Crying was no release. It was a trap.

54

Luke drove Natalie back to the police station, where he escorted her to her car. He checked his watch and said, "There's something I need to take care of. Are you going to be all right?"

"Yeah, I'm feeling much better now. Thanks for the coffee."

He nodded, but the reluctance in his expression told her he wasn't convinced. He glanced at his watch again. "I'll take those rabbit hairs upstairs to Lenny, unless you're going in."

"No, I'm not." She dug the evidence bag out of her pocket and handed it to him. "I want to follow up with Topaz and see if there's anything she's not telling us about Justin or the Hosts. Jules said he'd call me back within an hour, so . . ."

He studied her closely. "We're going to solve this thing, Natalie. And you're going to make the right decision. Trust yourself. See you later." He turned and went inside.

Only after he was gone did she realize that he hadn't explained what was so pressing. She got in her car and turned on the heat, then sat for a moment gathering her thoughts. The next step was to talk to Topaz and record her statement. She rummaged through her bag until she found her digital recorder. She took it out and checked the batteries. Then her phone rang, interrupting her. "Hello?"

"Detective, how ya doin'?" It was Jules Pastor. "Topaz says she'll talk to you. She says she might know something about Holly. She's at the farm."

"Tell her I'll be right over."

Ten minutes later, Natalie pulled into the Revellis' driveway, her tires kicking up annoying sprays of muddy slush. She parked and got out. She took the shoveled pathway to the house and rang the doorbell.

Topaz answered. She had a meth-ravaged face and tangled dyed blond hair. She was like a poster child for hard drugs—emaciated, haggard, gaunt. Natalie felt sorry for her. "Come in," the young woman said softly.

The front foyer angled awkwardly into a large, high-ceilinged living room, where the furniture was a grab bag of styles and the lovely old hardwood floors had been covered up with cheap gray carpeting—charcoal gray to hide the stains.

Topaz sat heavily in an armchair and began to cry. "Holly cared about people. She was sensitive to a fault and way too trusting."

Natalie shivered as she glanced out the window at the falling snow.

"I should've taken better care of her," Topaz went on. "I should've warned her that Edward was trouble. Anybody could see it. Holly was too generous in her opinions of people. She gave them too much credit." She broke down sobbing. "Is she really dead?"

Natalie sat awkwardly for a moment, tempted to console her, but that would've been a trap. This young woman had information she wanted to share, and Natalie didn't want to knock her off the subject. "Yes," she responded in a warm but professional tone. "I'm so sorry for your loss."

Topaz pressed her hands to her face and shivered violently. Then she pulled herself together and said, "Holly loved Edward. She would do anything he asked. He had her completely under his control, and she never did anything without checking with him first. She liked his stoned-out attitude. She said they were two freaks in a jungle full of normals. I tried to warn her." She looked at Natalie and her eyes welled with tears. "But how do you help someone who refuses to be helped?"

"That's a good question. I wish I knew."

Topaz shrugged and wiped the tears from her cheeks. "Anyway, I hate talking to the cops usually, but I want to clear my friend's name. Holly and Edward were here with us on Monday night. We were all partying together. So they couldn't have done it . . . you know, to Veronica. The thing that happened to her." She shuddered.

"They were here the whole night? They never left once?"

Topaz nodded. "The whole time. Both of them. But now I'm a little freaked out, to be honest. Because I'm worried that maybe they didn't OD. That it wasn't an accident. Because Holly confided in me something she and Edward were scheming. Edward mostly, I'm sure she just went along."

"What kind of scheme?" Natalie asked.

"They were going to blackmail somebody. Holly told me that her mother and Marigold Hutchins had gone to school together back in Rochester, and Marigold was lying about her ancestry. She's not a descendant of Sarah Hutchins. She changed her name right before she moved to Burning Lake, and the only person in the world who knew about this was Holly's mother, and she was a good person, so she never breathed a word about it to anyone except for Holly. But then, about a month ago, Edward caught wind of it, and he decided to blackmail Marigold. Get some money out of her. I mean, she's built a booming business on her fake reputation, right? The boutique, her online merch, her subscription podcasts, everything."

"Okay, so they blackmailed her? Did Marigold give them any money?"

"Not yet. They were going to confront her soon. But I warned Holly how stupid it was. Marigold could just deny it all, or . . . keep lying. Who's going to believe a couple of meth heads? So Holly told Veronica about it, and Veronica was really concerned, because it would hurt the coven. It would've embarrassed them to have a fake witch in their midst, because they all believed her. They all bought into the bullshit. So Veronica decided she was going to confront Marigold about it before Edward did anything. She asked Holly to stall him for a week or two. Veronica thought it was awful, that Marigold had been lying to everyone the whole time. She was about to rip off the whole façade."

"Do you know what Marigold's name used to be?" Natalie asked.

Topaz wiped the tears from her eyes. "Cindy something."

"Templeton?"

She shrugged. "Sounds about right."

55

Natalie's heart wouldn't stop pounding as she drove home. It was absurd to think that Marigold Hutchins could have killed Veronica over such a minor offense. Okay, so she'd gained notoriety for her fake lineage and made plenty of money tapping into the lucrative Craft industry. But she could always leave town and start over, or else claim she didn't know it had been a lie. Good liars could lie their way out of trouble, couldn't they? Besides, why would Marigold kill Veronica in such a horrific way? Why not make it look like an accident? Why not poison her with the red berries that grew in abundance in her neighborhood? You didn't need to kill someone in such a spectacular fashion just to keep the truth from being discovered, did you? She could have bargained with Veronica somehow. But then she would've had to deal with Holly and Edward.

On the other hand, Marigold could have deep psychological problems that she'd managed to keep hidden from everyone. Perhaps she'd had a psychotic break? Or maybe she wanted to scare the living crap out of Edward and Holly to prevent them from blackmailing her? But that was a reach, wasn't it?

Natalie needed to do some more digging.

She was crossing the yard when she bumped into one of Hunter's security guards walking the grounds. His name was Bill Finley. "You're back early," he said, taking out his phone. "Mr. Rose said to let him know when you return."

"It's just a pit stop. I'll be going out again soon."

"Good to know."

Private security guards cost hundreds of thousands, maybe over a million dollars per year. Hunter had hired a team to work rotating shifts so the house would always be protected. Bill had the Hulk's physique. He was nice. He had a wife and three kids. He talked about his family with sentimental affection, and yet Hunter had explained that Bill wouldn't hesitate to kill anyone who threatened either one of them.

"Why are you doing that?" she asked him now. "Texting Hunter? Is he concerned about something?"

"You get death threats," Bill told her bluntly.

"What?"

The security guard nodded stiffly. "We're just being cautious, for your own protection. So we keep tabs."

"What about when I'm away from the house?"

"We track your GPS via your phone."

"Excuse me?"

"Sorry," Bill said, glancing up from his phone. "I thought you knew."

"No. What the fuck."

"You should talk to the boss about it."

"Jesus, that's ridiculous."

"Not really. All it takes to stalk your prey is patience and observation," he told Natalie, a wad of chewing gum tucked into a corner of his mouth. "The more patient the predator, the more vulnerable his prey becomes. But guess who's more patient than even a predator?"

"You?" she said. Easy guess.

"That's right." He touched his sidearm, hidden under his overcoat, and smiled. "I'm watching the watcher."

"Thanks for watching over me, Bill," she said resignedly and went inside.

It left her feeling confused and angry, but also grateful. She was furious that Hunter hadn't mentioned it to her. Death threats? She forgot to ask Bill if that was him tailing her in his car the other night. Because if it wasn't security, then who was it? And maybe Natalie should be more grateful than angry?

It was true of detectives and their prime suspects, too—the more patient a detective was, the more vulnerable the suspect became. Only she had run out of patience. She wanted to solve this case now. Fucking now.

In the front hallway, Natalie kicked off her boots, hung up her coat, and dumped her bag, gloves, and scarf on a side table. Then she went into the dining room, where she'd left Veronica's boxes of library books and paperwork on the polished table. She rolled up her sleeves and got to work, spreading out the books and notes and various writings across the table. Then she turned on her phone and placed it next to the yearbook with Jodi Stewart's class picture in it.

Natalie studied everything, trying to mentally untangle the knot of this mystery. She found a Sharpie and wrote down the names of persons of interest on seven pieces of printout paper: Holly Host, Edward Host, Justin Fowler, Marigold Hutchins, Topaz Revelli, Nyle Hockney, and Reverend Grimsby. On a separate piece of paper, she wrote down the names of all the members of the Pendleton coven, including Tabitha Vaughn and Belinda Pickle.

Next, she jotted down whatever circumstantial evidence they had, listing it under each name. For Justin, the list was long: his possessiveness of Veronica, his violent temper, the damage to his vehicle, no solid alibi, his access to guns, the brown rabbit hairs, the green fibers, and soil samples. He'd had an altercation with Veronica during which a glass was shattered. His shoe size was ten—if you added thick socks, you could wear a size eleven boot. He'd spent twenty years in prison. Sometimes we hurt the ones we loved. The boyfriend was always a person of interest.

For Holly and Edward, the list was promising but mixed: some of the trace from Veronica's house had been found in their truck, but Holly had spent a weekend with Veronica and it could've come from that; the cottage where they'd lived for six months was easily accessible; they were into dark magic and animal sacrifice; they were drug addicts, which meant they were always in need of their next fix; Holly's mother had worn the witch costume Veronica had died in; they were planning to blackmail Marigold; Holly told Veronica about Marigold's deception, and Veronica was deeply concerned about the information; Holly and Edward had died from an overdose or possible suicide. Perhaps they had seen their grand scheme crumbling in front of their eyes and decided to end it before the law caught up with them? Then again, their shoe sizes were all wrong.

From the pile of stuff on the table, Natalie found the Polaroid of Jodi Stewart dressed as a witch six years ago. Then she opened the Rochester yearbook to the page with Jodi Johnson's class photo. Jodi Johnson was Jodi Stewart. In this same yearbook was a class picture of Cindy Templeton—she would be forty-five years old now. Natalie finally recognized Marigold Hutchins in the old black-and-white yearbook photo. Same chin, same ski-slope nose, the same wariness to the eyes.

But there was a problem. The time lines didn't add up. Marigold had told Natalie that her mother changed their names when Marigold was a little girl after running away from her father. But here was Marigold, a senior in high school, listed as Cindy Templeton. So what was the real story here?

Natalie's phone buzzed. She swiped through her messages. True to his word, Murray Gallo had sent along the list of sales transactions she had requested. She opened the files on her laptop, then sat down to study the information.

There was a list of credit card transactions for those who had purchased the costume five or six years ago. There were copies of receipts for a handful of cash transactions, but the buyers were unknown. And there were bulk sales to various boutiques in town who'd purchased Murray's overstock within the specific time frame. These bulk sales included the witch costume Natalie was interested in. She scanned the list and stopped at a familiar name. Skeletons in the Closet.

According to these records, Marigold had purchased a bulk sale of Murray's Halloween Costumes five years ago, which included several of the witch costumes by Crystal Mystic Design.

Natalie recalled that Veronica had been working on spreadsheets with information from Ancestry.com, tracing the lineage of key players in the 1712 witch trials. Natalie had made herself copies of these files. Now she opened one containing Sarah Hutchins's family tree. Listed on the tree were Sarah Hutchins's parents, her two brothers and four sisters, twenty-five cousins, and numerous aunts, uncles, and grandparents. No other details were given besides the relatives' names, birth dates, and death dates.

Veronica had traced Marigold Hutchins's lineage all the way back to a younger brother of Sarah Hutchins in the late 1600s. His name was Bergren Hutchins. It appeared that Marigold could legitimately claim the title of Sarah Hutchins's great-great-great-great-great-great-great-great-great-grandniece, or nine-times-great-grandniece.

But there the legacy stopped.

According to Veronica's spreadsheet, the real Marigold Hutchins had died twenty-one years ago. That was the sticking point. Marigold Hutchins was real—she existed, but she was deceased, and the modern-day witch who called herself Marigold Hutchins was an imposter and a liar.

Natalie closed the spreadsheet and logged in to her BLPD database account and began a background check for "Marigold Hutchins" of Burning Lake, New York. She found her listing, but her background information was practically nonexistent. That was odd.

There was an old apartment address in Buffalo from fifteen years ago. Five years later, she moved to Burning Lake. She purchased her current residence seven years ago. Her boutique was listed, but when Natalie dug deeper, she couldn't find any credit history or employment history further back than a decade and a half ago. Nothing from Rochester, New York. No records of any education or special training. It was highly suspicious.

Natalie drew a troubled breath. Then she typed in "Cindy Templeton" of Rochester, New York, age forty-five. A profile popped up. There were numerous former addresses listed, all of them based in Rochester, Syracuse, and Harrisburg, Pennsylvania. She selected "Most Recent," but nothing new came up. The data had dried up fifteen years ago.

She decided to perform a criminal background check for Cindy Templeton. There were several "sealed" juvenile records for driving offenses and shoplifting, but Cindy had apparently been a victim of domestic abuse—that much turned out to be true. Cindy's father had been convicted of assault to Cindy and her mother, along with driving under the influence and drug possession charges.

Natalie did a search for Cindy Templeton's social media profile—but there was nothing there. No Twitter, no Facebook, no LinkedIn, no Instagram, no MySpace. It was as if she'd dropped off the map fifteen years ago.

Natalie sat back. According to what she'd just read, it appeared that Marigold's mother hadn't—as Marigold claimed—changed their last name to Hutchins when Cindy was little. Cindy Templeton was Marigold's real name until about fifteen years ago.

Marigold had been lying about that all along. She'd changed her name to Hutchins when she was thirty years old. It was relatively easy to change your identity as an adult, but you needed a valid excuse. If you were the victim of abuse and wanted to legally change your name to evade your abuser, you could file a petition with the state. Law enforcement agencies provided abuse victims with documented evidence to take to the Social Security Administration to change their SSN. It was all perfectly legal, if you needed to start over from scratch. A mother and child, or the grown daughter of an abusive father—both would be eligible.

Clearly Marigold was lying about her heritage.

She'd lied about her background.

What else was she lying about?

Natalie picked up the yearbook and stared at Cindy's picture. She saw the resemblance clearly now—her eighteen-year-old features were soft and chubby and pliable; her eyes were sweet and scared; her face was buried under too much lip liner and mascara and eye shadow; she had too much wild highlighted hair. In her transformation to Marigold Hutchins, Cindy had lost a lot of weight; she'd dyed her hair from ash blond to black; she'd changed the shape of her eyebrows; she'd exchanged the frivolous bangs for long straight hair parted down the middle; she may have had work done on her face, because her cheekbones were more prominent and her lips were fuller.

But it wasn't just that. Marigold had embraced the lie that she was a descendant of Sarah Hutchins, and this was who she became to the core at age thirty. She adopted her make-believe heritage and her Wiccan roots, and it probably would've killed her to have had someone discover her secret. Veronica picking away at the truth would've stripped her down to the bone. What about Marigold's core made her crave witch status? What did she want out of this way of life that she couldn't access when she was just

Cindy? She said it made her feel empowered. Was she still worried that her abusive father might find her? Was she living in fear?

It wasn't Marigold's fault that her father was abusive, and she probably changed her name for a good reason. She'd made up the ancestry part, but that could be forgiven, couldn't it? Veronica was into forgiveness. The fact that Marigold had lied about being related to Sarah Hutchins, and had used that lie for personal gain, might've ruined her friendship with Veronica and the Pendleton coven, but nothing more than that. At this point, Marigold came across to Natalie as a complicated and sympathetic victim. Not a murderer.

On the other hand, one could argue that she had a lot of problems. She was manipulative and deceitful. She had lied to the community for years. She had committed fraud and conned people out of their money. The real Marigold Hutchins, the twenty-four-year-old who was truly a direct descendant of Sarah Hutchins's family, was dead and buried in her grave. But Cindy Templeton had stolen her identity—legally. With the help of state government and law enforcement. It was quite a magic trick she'd pulled off.

Did that make her a killer?

Holly's mother, Jodi Johnson Stewart, had gone to school with Cindy Templeton, and ten years ago, after Cindy moved from Buffalo to Burning Lake to start over as a direct descendant of Sarah Hutchins, Jodi most likely had called her bluff, but "Marigold" somehow bought her silence. Either through loyalty, threats, or kickbacks. However, Holly knew about Marigold's deception and eventually told Edward, who plotted to blackmail her. But when Holly told Veronica, and she began probing into Marigold's background—it was too much. The straw that broke the camel's back.

Marigold made a good living selling merchandise online and in her boutique, while also working as a Wiccan consultant. She'd used her fake heritage as leverage to become a member of the historic Pendleton coven. That was quite an achievement for an abused girl named Cindy. And Veronica had found out about Marigold's scam. She wasn't related to Sarah Hutchins, after all. She had purchased the costume several years ago through her boutique, Skeletons in the Closet. She could have killed Veronica, because Veronica had discovered her secret and threatened to expose it, but that was only believable if Cindy Templeton was emotionally unstable, as brutal and abusive as her father had been, and had found a willing accomplice.

There was nothing in Marigold's background to indicate any medical condition, bipolar disorder, or psychosis. Natalie was searching for clean lines, but there weren't any. Only more questions. She closed her laptop. She needed to speak to Cindy Templeton as soon as possible.

56

Natalie felt a chill blast of arctic air as she left the house and hurried toward her car. She unlocked the door, hopped in, and turned on the heat. It had stopped snowing, but the sky was looking ominous. Another storm front was moving in.

She took off her gloves and called Luke. When he didn't pick up, she left him a voicemail message. "Luke, we need to talk. Call me as soon as you get this." She hung up and dialed Marigold's number.

The call went straight to voicemail. "Hi, everybody," Marigold's recorded message said. "In case you've forgotten, we're all meeting up at Blackthorn Park today for our own private ritual celebrating Veronica's life. Four o'clock sharp. Don't be late. See you there!"

Natalie checked her watch. It was almost four.

Now her phone buzzed, and she hastily picked up. "Luke?"

"No, it's me, Lenny. Have you heard from him?"

"No, Lenny," she said, turning on the defroster. "Not yet. What's up?"

"The lockbox is missing. Did you or Luke take it, by chance?"

"No, we left it with you. Did you misplace it or something?"

"I don't know what the hell happened. Augie and I have been looking all over for it. Anyway, some good news. The rabbit hairs are a preliminary match to the brown hairs we found in the victim's domicile. I'm sending samples to the state lab for verification, but it's enough to get a search warrant for Justin Fowler's house."

"That's great news, Lenny. The sooner, the better."

"Anyway, if you hear from the lieu, have him call me, will you?"

"Sure thing." She hung up and felt a spike of alarm. She knew they'd left the lockbox in Lenny's possession. And Lenny didn't just lose things.

Blackthorn Park abutted the lake on the south side of town. Sweat beaded on Natalie's face as she swept around the corners, hugging the curve. *Slow down.* At least now they could search Justin's property and pin down the trace evidence, although where that left them, she wasn't sure. Since he was having an affair with Veronica, it stood to reason that his trace would be all over her home. It was called cross contamination. She could feel each bump of broken pavement underneath her discount tires as she headed for the historic park.

By the time she got to the parking lot, it was four ten. She counted at least twelve other vehicles in the lot—unusual for this time of year. She found a cleared space next to a chain-link fence, cut the engine, unbuckled her seat belt, and got out.

As she was locking her car, her phone buzzed.

Natalie picked up. "Luke?"

"No, it's Topaz," the young woman said, sounding scared. "Justin was here, banging on my front door, demanding I let him in. He was shouting at me through the door, asking me what the hell you wanted. I guess he was following you. He saw you go into my house, and he wanted to know what we talked about. He was going to pound the door down, so I let him in. He paced back and forth and wouldn't leave until I told him about Holly and Edward blackmailing Marigold, and about Veronica discovering that Marigold was lying about her heritage. He asked me if Marigold was a suspect, and I said I guess so. Then he took off."

"Are you okay?" Natalie asked.

"Yeah, he didn't touch me. He just stood there shouting like a maniac."

"Okay, listen to me. Lock your doors. If he comes back, call the police."

"I will. I just want this to end." She hung up.

Natalie called Luke again, but he wasn't answering his phone.

Next, she called Brandon and told him to send backup to the park and explained why they needed to find Justin Fowler as soon as possible.

She hung up and walked toward the stone lions at the entrance to Blackthorn Park. Inside the grounds, the mature trees and spindly saplings were covered in icicles like a fairy-tale forest. A low wind hummed through the balsam firs and brittle pines.

The winding footpath was sprinkled with pine needles. Ten yards in, she could hear chanting—a low murmur of female voices. After twenty yards, the voices grew louder. After forty yards, she came to the clearing where a circle of thirteen women surrounded the infamous Witching Tree. A few clouds had been swept away by the wind, and several golden rays of afternoon light dappled the snowy ground. The women were chanting and holding hands. They'd lit candles and incense, and were summoning their energies, chanting and drawing circles in the snow to invoke their deities.

Natalie stood by impassively, while patches of golden light reflected off the snowdrifts. Then the sun disappeared behind the clouds again.

The voices faltered. A few heads turned.

Now Marigold saw her and smiled. Despite her long black hair, she looked like a schoolteacher in her rose-colored wool winter coat with its matching hat and gloves, and her dark red scarf. The women stopped chanting, while Marigold came over to Natalie and said, "Hi, Detective. We're holding a remembrance ceremony for Veronica. We don't have a permit, but they let us in here before."

"I tried calling you."

"We've turned our phones off. Unless you'd like to join us, we'd feel better if you gave us a little space."

"Of course," Natalie said. "I don't mean to intrude, but I'd like you to come down to the station afterwards, if you don't mind. After the ceremony."

"Oh. I see." Marigold desperately held on to her smile. "What is this about?"

"Cindy Templeton."

Her face reddened. She nodded mutely.

Now Tabitha left the group and came over. "Is everything okay?"

"It's fine," Marigold said. "I can handle this."

"What's wrong?" Tabitha asked, looking from Marigold to Natalie. "Can't it wait? We're right in the middle of a sacred ceremony—"

"I've got this," Marigold snapped at Tabitha, who wilted and tugged on her long gray braid like a child clutching a security blanket.

Tabitha walked back to the circle of women.

"I'll come down to the station right after we're done celebrating Veronica's life," Marigold told Natalie. "Okay?"

"I'll be waiting for you by the front gate."

"Why? Don't you think I'll come on my own? I've got nothing to hide."

"I'll be waiting," Natalie repeated.

Marigold stared at her for a moment. Then she turned and rejoined the group.

Once they'd resumed their chanting, Natalie headed back down the trail. But after a few seconds, the chanting stopped.

Natalie turned around.

Marigold had left the group and was running in the opposite direction.

57

Footsteps pounded across the snow and echoed through the woods.

"Marigold? Stop running!" Natalie followed a flash of red darting through the trees as they headed deeper into the woods, where the dense underbrush kept snagging on her coat. She pushed through the brambles, trying not to get stabbed by the thorns.

A few minutes later, Natalie had lost her. She paused on the footpath and looked around. The air was crisp and clear. She searched the woods and heard a virginal crunch of snow. She turned and spotted a figure in a rose-colored coat with a red scarf.

Marigold broke and ran. She tore through a scrim of low-lying tree branches and dashed through the woods, stumbling over drifts and crying out as the branches scratched her face and hands.

"Marigold, stop!" Natalie ran after her, heart thumping, a curdled feeling in her gut. "Stop running! Let's talk about this!"

Marigold seemed panicked, blinded by fear, and only wanted to get away from her. Late-afternoon shadows broke across the trail as the forest gradually thinned out, and the land grew flatter as they closed in on the lake.

Moments later, Natalie burst out of the woods and spotted Marigold running onto the frozen lake with her arms outstretched. Her footing grew unsteady, and she almost slipped but maintained her balance.

Natalie was fearful she might cross a weak spot and fall in, so she stopped where she was and hollered, "Marigold, stop! I won't chase you onto the lake."

The woman slowed to a lumbering trot, then turned around to face Natalie.

They were out of breath, maybe a dozen yards apart. The tip of Abby's Hex Peninsula was less than thirty yards to the west of them, stretching like a lazy arm across the frozen lake.

"Come back, and we'll talk about this," Natalie insisted.

Marigold's long wool winter coat had fallen open, and underneath she wore a pair of black dress pants, a black tailored shirt, and knee-high black leather boots. She'd lost one of her gloves, and her dark red scarf had come undone and was hanging loosely around her neck. Fists clenched, she lowered her chin and said, "My father used to beat me. He killed my dog. He beat my mom. One night, he raped me. He was an asshole. So I changed my identity."

"That's terrible," Natalie said, still gasping for breath. "But I thought you said your mother changed your identities when you were little."

Marigold shook her head. "Yeah, I lied about that. Mom was a coward. She never left my father. He would apologize the next day and buy her flowers, and she'd let him off the hook, and then everything would be hunky-dory again, until the next time he got roaring drunk. We never ran away. We didn't change our names. We were always the Templetons. My mother's face was battered like a boxer's when she died of cancer fifteen years ago. I had just turned thirty. With her dying breath, she insisted that he was a good man, who didn't mean to hurt anyone. So I changed my identity and left Rochester for good. It was legal. My father was still a threat to me. I changed my name to Marigold Hutchins, because I wanted to be a witch. I wanted to empower myself and stop being so scared all the time."

"Why lie about it? Why not just take the name and be honest?"

She rolled her eyes. In the distance, a woodpecker was knocking on a tree. The lake stretched before them, so bright and white with snow, it was disorienting.

"I want to hear your side of the story," Natalie coaxed. "Talk to me."

Marigold shook her head, looking disheveled and defeated. A kind of spiritual surrender had hollowed out her eyes. "I was a good girl, you know. I trusted people. I was so trusting and naïve, people took advantage of me. I got hurt a lot. But eventually, I learned how to survive. I may have broken a few rules, but I didn't kill Veronica. I had nothing to do with that." She smiled derisively. The dying light held a nightmarish resonance. "When she found out about my ancestry and what I'd done, Veronica confronted me with it. I thought it was very hypocritical of her. She's a direct descendant of Thomas Bell, the asshole who condemned the witches to death, and here she is, acting all high and mighty. At least I picked one of the good guys. At least I chose well. I mean, I love witch culture with all my heart. I've absorbed the Craft into my identity—and isn't that what we all do? All of us who choose to embrace Wicca? What's so wrong with that?"

"So Veronica thought there was something wrong with what you did?"

Marigold blinked. The long red scarf billowed and flapped in the wind. "She called me a scam artist. She accused me of cashing in. Hey, I've had a rough life, okay? My father tried to take away my power. And now, the way I figured it, Veronica was trying to take away my power. And I wasn't about to let that happen."

"What were you going to do about it?"

"I don't know. Certainly not kill her."

Somewhere on the lake, the ice shifted with an echoing crack.

Natalie felt a rushing twist in her gut. She dug her heels into the snow and said, "Come off the ice. It isn't safe."

Marigold didn't move. "It took me years to find a place where I wasn't constantly looking over my shoulder. My father gradually wore my mother down. After she passed away, I'll never forget the way he looked at me. I knew . . . I just knew he was going to replace her with me. There was no way I was going to let that happen. So I changed my identity and moved away from Rochester. Buffalo was okay, but I fell in love with this town. Burning Lake has a unique energy. And I think it's cool to blend commercial goals with spiritual ones. I don't see any harm in that. I built up a business with my own two hands. I have friends, people who respect me, a life. Burning Lake has become my real home. I feel safe here. And Veronica was going to destroy all that."

"How?"

"She wanted to hold a meeting, where I was supposed to come out and confess what I'd done. Kind of like the witch trials, you know? 'I confess I'm a witch and I've danced with the devil.' Ironic, huh? Veronica said she and the other members were going to decide what would happen to me. What the next steps would be. She implied they might kick me out of the coven. I begged her not to. I told her how humiliating it would be for me. How long and hard I've worked for all this. But she wouldn't budge, not even a little bit. It felt abusive, to be honest. It reminded me of my father all over again."

"So you felt abused by Veronica?"

"She forgave Justin, but she wouldn't forgive me. I pleaded with her not to do this thing. I asked her to let it go. And I'll give her this much . . . she decided to wait a few days and think it over. You want to know why? Because I reminded her that I know some of her dirty little secrets. And I told her—tit for tat. You tell on me, and I'll tell on you."

"What dirty little secrets did Veronica have?"

"It doesn't matter anymore. Because then she got killed." Marigold stared at Natalie. "And I didn't have anything to do with it. I would never hurt someone, especially in such a gruesome way as that. Why aren't you out there looking for the real killer?"

"We are looking. Do you have any suggestions?"

"How about Justin? Veronica was sleeping with him. He has serious emotional problems. He's extremely paranoid, and—"

A shot rang out.

One side of Marigold's head blew off in a burst of blood. A spatter of crimson blew away in the wind, while she stood dead in her winter coat with her scarf flapping in the breeze. Then her body collapsed in a heap onto the frozen lake.

Natalie screamed and looked around. Someone was standing across the ice at the end of the peninsula next to the bronze monument dedicated to the three witches who'd been executed in 1712. Justin Fowler held a hunting rifle with a scope.

Natalie ducked down and drew her weapon. "Justin!" she shouted. "Put the rifle down! Now!"

He watched her carefully. "She's a liar!" he hollered back.

"Lower your weapon!"

He lowered the rifle. "Topaz told me everything. She said Marigold lied for years about who she was, and that Veronica was about to expose her, so she killed her."

"Stay where you are. Don't come any closer!" Natalie's hands were shaking. She didn't want to shoot him. She refused to kill another human being. She was desperate for him to put down his weapon. "Drop the rifle! Now!" she screamed.

Justin rested the weapon in the snow, then stepped off the peninsula, and slowly crossed the ice toward her with his arms raised. "It's called prison justice." He gazed at Natalie from across the lake. Twenty-five frozen yards. His baseball hat was turned backward on his head. His face was lean and tense. Standing there in front of her was someone who'd survived unimaginable ordeals as an innocent man inside a supermax facility. Because of her sister.

"I'm not going to prison again," he said.

Natalie's hands trembled as she held him in her sights. "Stay where you are!"

"You know this isn't the end of it, don't you?"

"What're you talking about?"

"You're not seeing the bigger picture, Detective." His pain was palpable.

"What bigger picture?"

"You have no idea what you're dealing with here."

She could feel the sweat collecting on her body. Tears filled her eyes. "Stop talking in riddles! Tell me what the fuck you mean!"

"You want a riddle? Here's one. The more there is of this, the less you can see."

She sensed something about to unfold like a shock wave. It came rumbling toward her before she could possibly prevent it from happening. "I don't know. What?"

"Darkness." He pulled a pistol out of his pocket, stuck the barrel into his mouth, and blew his brains out.

58

Four hours later, Natalie listened to the ice shifting and crackling across the frozen lake—an eerie sound. It was nine o'clock on Friday night, and the moon had slipped behind the clouds. The blizzard had not materialized as promised. Snowfall was spotty at best. Portable police lights illuminated the grisly scene. She was staring at a deformed snow angel where Marigold had fallen. It was spattered with blood. The coroner had taken away the bodies, and the area was peppered with orange evidence cards.

Detective Augie Vickers came over, shivering inside his frayed parka, and said, "I'll take over from here, Natalie. Go home and write your report. You look beat to shit."

She smiled weakly. "Any word from Luke yet?"

He shook his head. "But you can rest assured, our guys will be out there all night long looking for him. We'll find him. Okay?"

She nodded. This was what the detectives in the unit had been telling each other since about six o'clock in the evening, when it became clear that something had happened to Luke. He wasn't answering his phone. His voicemail was full. He wasn't at work or at home or any of his usual places. His Ford Ranger was missing.

She could feel her pulse points twitching with fatigue as she gathered up her evidence bags, put everything back in the kits, and headed down the trail toward her vehicle. It was dark in the woods. Her flashlight sputtered for a moment, and she shook the Streamlight until it blinked on again, illuminating the trail ahead.

Ten minutes later, she approached the front entrance of the park and spotted a crowd of onlookers behind the wrought iron fence, many holding up their phones and videotaping everything. Snapping pictures. She recognized some of the reporters who'd hounded her last year, begging for exclusives, and drew her hood up over her head. Fortunately, the chief had just arrived to make a statement, and when they saw him they flocked toward him, leaving the side gate free and clear.

Keeping her head down, Natalie slipped through the gate, then headed for the parking lot, where she could see the red-and-blue flashes of idling police cruisers. She heard sirens in the distance. A news helicopter circled overhead. The roar of the news chopper rattled her nerves. This couldn't keep happening again. It was as surreal as a movie set. The air throbbed with otherness.

Instead of heading home, she drove around town for a while, wondering where Luke could possibly have gone. Nobody had seen him since midafternoon. The lockbox was missing. No one knew where Detective Peter Murphy was, either. It was highly unusual behavior, and it gave her the chills.

She called Brandon again. She called Lenny and Jacob and Mike. She even called Jules Pastor. They all promised to contact her the minute they heard anything.

Finally, she drove past Luke's house. The lights were off, and there was a BLPD cruiser parked out front. Two officers were watching the property and waiting for Luke to return. She'd done all she could. She decided to head home.

On Route 151 heading north, a fire engine raced past, its siren blaring. Panic rang in Natalie's ears. What if something had happened to Luke? She followed the fire truck for a mile or so, before it took the exit toward Bakers Mill Hollow and Meadow Lane. The only person Natalie knew who lived out this way was Peter Murphy.

As soon as she pulled into the neighborhood, she could smell acrid smoke in the air. Highway patrol was rerouting traffic. She parked by the side of the road and got out, showing an officer her shield. She hurried down the sidewalk, past neighbors hugging one another. They stood in their yards, staring at the smoldering ruins of the house at the end of Meadow Lane, where emergency vehicles clogged the driveway. The windows had blown out. The walls were charred. The roof had collapsed. Ashes filled the night, drifting down around everyone and lacing their hair and eyelashes.

At the bottom of the driveway, the state police wouldn't let Natalie get any closer. "Sorry, folks. This area is off-limits."

She showed the officer her shield. "Detective Lockhart, BLPD. What happened?"

"There was an explosion, according to the neighbors," he said.

"An explosion?" The fear was like water rushing into Natalie's lungs—stark and primitive. "Are there any bodies?"

"A couple of firemen had minor injuries, but no bodies have been reported."

"Whose house is this?" she asked.

"Peter Murphy. Stay back, Detective. This area is off-limits."

Assistant Chief Timothy Gossett came loping across the front yard. As soon as he saw Natalie, he waved her inside the perimeter. He raised the yellow tape, and she ducked underneath. They stood in the yard together, while stray ashes floated around their heads. "No bodies have been recovered so far. Murphy's vehicle is missing, so I'm assuming he wasn't inside the house when it caught fire."

"Caught fire?" she repeated. "You mean when it exploded?"

"We don't have all the facts yet."

"Have you seen Luke? Nobody can get hold of him."

"I'm aware of the situation." He brushed a few ashes off the shoulders of his pressed uniform. "It's probably nothing. He'll show up, he always does. Give it time."

"So let me get this straight. Two detectives from your department go missing, and one of these detective's house blows up, and you don't think it's cause for concern? Are you kidding me?"

"No one has gone missing," Gossett said, pushing back, and she despised the arrogant set of his mouth, his cold dismissal of her concerns, and that creepy artificial tan in the dead of winter. He inched the brim of his hat away from his sweaty forehead and said, "Go home, Natalie. We've got this covered. You have your hands full."

"Nobody knows where Luke is," she repeated as if he were deaf. "His voicemail is full. That isn't like him."

"You're done for the day. That's an order."

A window burst from the intense heat, and a thick plume of smoke poured out of the second story, turning the sky inky black. The smell of burning fuel permeated the air. A pulsating fear took hold of her and wouldn't let go.

"Are you sure there are no bodies inside? Are you absolutely certain?"

"That's what they tell me. These brave men know what they're doing. I'm not going to say it again, Detective. Go home," Assistant Chief Gossett repeated with heartless impatience. "That's an *order.*"

With great reluctance, she turned and headed for her car. She passed huddled groups of neighbors and exhausted firemen whose faces were covered in soot. On the sidewalk, amidst the smoldering flakes of ashes, she spotted a photograph and picked it up. The edges were singed from the fire. In the snapshot, Peter Murphy posed in front of the customized van he'd gotten last year, his eyes sparkling with pride beneath those thick Muppet eyebrows. She remembered how giddy he was, giving them a tour of the van and boasting about its many features—privacy windows, a skylight, all-wheel drive. It was dark blue, with a royal-blue interior.

Blue fibers.

Something touched a nerve. She got in her car and called Lenny. "Did you hear about Peter's house?"

"Yeah, just now. They're pulling our guys out of Blackthorn Park to help with the scene over there."

"They didn't find any bodies inside. The assistant chief is here. He told me to go home. He knows Luke's missing, but he doesn't seem very concerned about it."

"Natalie, I don't know what to say . . ."

"I'm holding a picture of Murphy posing with his customized van last year. Remember how proud he was? It's dark blue, with a royal-blue interior—same as the blue fibers you found on the witch costume. Lenny, there's been an ongoing issue about Murphy misplacing crucial evidence. Evidence is missing from one of the boxes we took from Veronica's house, and there were pages torn out of a journal that doesn't match the manifest. There have been problems with the Violinist and Crow Killer cases. Chain of custody seems to point back to Murphy every damn time."

There was a pause. "Are you saying what I think you're saying, Natalie?"

"Last time I spoke to Luke, he said he was going to handle the situation. Maybe it's a stretch, but now he and Murphy are both missing. And then Peter's house fucking explodes. How is that a coincidence?"

Lenny was silent for a long moment. Then he said, "Listen, I didn't mention it before, because I didn't think it was relevant, but Murphy came to the lab this afternoon and asked me about the fingerprint kit. Just a few pointless questions. I didn't put it together until just now, but he's the only other person besides you and Luke who came into the lab today. And then, after he left, at some point, I noticed the lockbox was missing. I thought I'd misplaced it, or that maybe you or Luke took it back for some reason . . ."

"Jesus, Lenny," she whispered.

"And another thing. Yesterday, Augie and I did a thorough sweep of that Dodge pickup and found nothing of significance. But then, during a second sweep, we found trace linking the truck bed to Justin Fowler—and it was right where we'd looked before. And I remember kicking myself, because how the hell did we miss it? Well, Murphy came to see us at the impound lot between those two sweeps. With more stupid questions."

"Do you think he planted the evidence? Why? To throw us off?"

"I don't know. But it's highly suspicious in retrospect."

A deep chord reverberated inside her head. "He's always volunteering to catalog the evidence. He has no family, no responsibilities. I mean, what do we really know about Murphy? He's a blank slate. He's always there, like wallpaper. He just fades into the background."

"Okay, Natalie. Let's take a breath and put a pin in this for now. We don't know anything yet. It's all conjecture. The most important thing is finding Luke and bringing him home safe and sound. There's a statewide APB out for both of them. It's a high-alert situation. We've got everybody working on it. Mike and Jacob are at the scene of the fire. Any information they relay to me, I'll call you the instant I get it."

She could feel thick braids of confusion knitting into her muscles. "So then, are we saying Murphy was involved in Veronica's death? Because he wasn't even on our radar. But the blue fibers in his van could be the source of the fibers on the witch costume. What's his shoe size?"

"I have no idea."

"Could it be that the whole time he was right under our noses, hiding evidence, manipulating us?" she asked with growing concern.

"It's definitely something we need to look into," Lenny said solemnly.

Her phone buzzed. "That's the other line, Lenny. I'll call you back. Hello?" she answered breathlessly, hoping it was Luke.

"Hey, Natalie, it's Brandon."

She felt a stabbing disappointment.

"You need to come back to the park."

"Why? What's wrong?"

"There's something you should see."

59

Moonlight slanted through the conifers and birches, casting eerie shadows across the pine-needled ground. It was midnight. Natalie and Brandon stood in front of Nettie Goodson's Witching Tree, shining their flashlights at the enormous oak.

"Everybody knows you don't touch this tree, or you'll be cursed forever," Brandon said in a hushed tone. "This is the tree nobody touches. Ever."

They were alone in the clearing. Most of the officers and detectives had gone home for the night, or else had been called away to the scene of the fire across town. Natalie's flashlight sputtered for a moment, and the pitchy darkness was unsettling. It blinked on again, illuminating the fresh tree carving on the trunk of the Witching Tree.

"When did this happen?" she asked.

"Sometime tonight."

"How? People have been trekking along this path all night."

Brandon checked his watch. "It's almost midnight. Things settled down here around ten. Whoever did this had a couple of hours." He nodded at the woods. "The state conservation land goes back for miles, all of it virgin forest. They could've entered and left the park the same way, and nobody would've been the wiser." He looked at her. "I must've walked past this tree five or six times tonight, and I didn't see anything earlier. Did you?"

She shook her head.

"I mean, look at that. You can't miss it."

They were on a trail laced with faded brown leaves from last autumn. The path wound around an ornate wrought iron fence that was supposed to protect the tree from vandals, but it was mostly cosmetic. There was a brass plaque on the fence explaining the tree's history.

> Don't stare too long at the Witching Tree.
> Defile it not, or cursed you will be.

Natalie stepped over the fence into the snow and walked right up to the ancient oak. She shone her light across the smooth surface of the bark. A single word had been carved there recently—seven blocky letters. "e-i-l-a-t-a-n."

"At first, I thought it was the name of a demon," Brandon said.

Natalie cringed. The bark of the oak made a pretty good canvas. A few hours ago, someone must've stood in this same spot and carefully carved off the outer layer of bark with a knife. As the tree grew and the bark healed, this carving would become darker and more corrugated around the edges. Eventually it would be swallowed up by the tree, leaving a deformed scar that, as legend had it, only a witch could read.

"It's my name spelled backwards," she said.

"Fuck that shit," Brandon said angrily.

"It's a message. A warning." She didn't dare say hex. In a few places where the knife had cut especially deep, the lines of sap looked like bloody tears.

A flock of birds flew overhead. Little pools of fear flared inside her. The wind stirred her hair. She snapped a few pictures with her iPhone.

"I checked out the area but couldn't find anything. I'll cordon off the scene, and we'll come back tomorrow," Brandon told her, "and gather up whatever evidence we can find. We'll nail whoever did this. Probably some teenage asshole."

She didn't believe that. Fright crept up her spine.

"Natalie? Are you okay?" he asked with concern.

She nodded. "Let's get out of here."

Thirty minutes later, she pulled into the long driveway of Hunter's mansion and got out. It was snowing again. She stood for a moment, relishing the beautiful, breathy chill of falling snow. Snowflakes landed on her eyelashes and enveloped her in a fog of amnesia. How lovely to forget the past—her grief, her many losses. How lovely to forget the entire world.

She tilted her face toward the overcast sky and watched in amazement as big fat flakes mushroomed out of the clouds and landed on her cheeks. She felt gently astonished, like a tired child at a tea party. She opened her mouth and let a few flakes land on her tongue. She could taste her own pain and sadness melting there. She wondered how long it would take for a person to freeze to death. Minutes? Hours? She wondered how long before Hunter's security guards found her lying there? She wondered if, tomorrow morning, they would find her body covered in snow, little blue ice crystals leaking out of her eyes instead of tears.

Sighing with exhaustion, Natalie trudged past the ornamental hedges toward the front door, glanced at the security camera above the fanlight, and got out her keys. Inside it was warm and toasty. She hung up her coat and scarf in the hallway, then took her backpack with her into the living room. Hunter was there. He stood up, and they held on to each other.

She started to hyperventilate. She couldn't breathe. He made her sit down on the sofa. He fetched her a blanket and a cup of herbal tea. He eased off her boots, then sat next to her on the sofa and rubbed her sore feet.

"It's all my fault," she said. "I shouldn't have chased her out onto the lake."

"Nonsense," Hunter said softly. "You aren't responsible. You didn't hold a gun to their heads. You didn't force them to act irrationally. We're all responsible for our own actions. You've got to stop it with the guilt trip."

She eyed him dubiously. "Are you absolving me, Hunter?"

"Yes. I absolve you completely."

She waited a beat, then shrugged. "Sorry. It's not working."

A look of amusement and pity fleetingly crossed his face. Then his eyes raked her slowly—face, lips, neck, breasts. Back to her eyes, lingering there. He let go of the foot he was massaging and leaned forward, his lips hovering beautifully before her, and she could feel his desire in the heat emanating from his body.

"I can't," she whispered.

He drew back. He rested his hands on her shoulders. "All I care about is you."

It occurred to her how cold she was. The house was stuffy hot, but that didn't seem to help. She crossed her arms and shivered. "It's a nightmare," she told him.

"It's a lot to handle for one person."

"No, it isn't. It's fucking out of control." Tears welled in her eyes. "I'm cursed."

He snorted derisively. "Come on. You know better than that. You don't believe in curses. You're not a superstitious person. You've simply had more than your fair share of calamity lately. That's all. A series of random events."

"Random? My life is falling apart."

"Nothing's falling apart. You're with me. I'm going to take care of you."

Heartfelt sobs racked her body.

"That's right," Hunter said. He cradled her in his arms. "Life sucks, and then you die. Some people never make it, Natalie. But guess what? You and I are going to make it." He kissed her softly. Sweetly.

She drew back, shivering. "Justin Fowler warned me right before he shot himself."

"Warned you about what?"

"He said that all of this was much bigger than I realized. That I had no idea what I was dealing with. He told me a riddle. The more of it there is, the less you can see."

He watched her calmly. "The more of what?"

"Darkness."

He looked at her with deep sadness. "You know I'm a hundred percent behind you, Natalie. You're precious to me. Marry me."

"Hunter, no . . ."

"Fuck it, Natalie. Run away with me. A justice of the peace. We'll go any-where you like . . . let's just get away from here."

Her body resonated with self-consciousness. Her face throbbed with ex-citement. She wanted to be loved absolutely. Thrillingly. Eternally. Who didn't want to be loved? But then an overwhelming sadness took hold of her. "Luke's missing."

"This isn't about Luke." His eyes were wide and pleading. "Of course, we'll wait until everything's resolved . . . until Luke returns or whatever happens. I'm sure it's nothing. It's probably just a misunderstanding. But

I want you to be happy. Look at me, Natalie. You're a mess. You're ex-hausted, you're wasting away. If you think I'm going to let that happen, you're crazy. This fucking town isn't your responsibility. I want a future for us. I want to marry you, so that I can make you happy. I swear to God, I'll take you away from here, away from all this pain and suffering. Please . . . marry me."

She watched the vein in his neck tic. She put a finger on it to stop it and could feel the blood pulsing gently through his body.

He caressed her hair and shoulders, then held her close and refused to let go. "Let me take care of you," he pleaded. "It's the one fucking thing I'm good at."

She felt so sorry for him and so moved by this misguided statement that she let him wrap his strong arms around her. His forearms flexed as if to protect her from the world. She smoothed a hand over his tousled ash-brown hair and listened to his troubled breathing.

Her phone rang from the depths of her backpack, jarring them both. He reluctantly released her so that she could dig it out. "Hello?"

"Natalie, we found him," Lenny said urgently. "We found Luke."

She brushed Hunter aside and sat up straight. "What happened? Is he all right?"

"He's in a coma. He's at the hospital."

She felt a suffocating shortness of breath. "I'll be right over," she said and hung up.

"What is it?" Hunter asked, growing pale.

"They found Luke. He's in a coma. I have to go."

"I'll drive you there myself."

"No," she said firmly.

He gave her a solemn nod of acknowledgment. "Be careful. Roads are icy."

Her brain was buzzing. The circuits were frying. Why was Luke in a coma? What the hell had happened to him?

"I'll wait up," Hunter promised.

"No, don't. I might be there for a while. You should get some sleep."

"I'll wait up," he insisted. "Call me if you need anything."

She nodded.

He cupped her face in his hands. "You can trust me, Natalie."

She tried to catch her breath and explain, but it was as if something had been chasing her all her life and had finally caught up with her. She couldn't escape.

He reached for her hand. "I'll be here, waiting for you to come home."

60

L uke was dreaming. Natalie could tell by the way his eyelids moved ever so slightly. It was called REM sleep. What was he dreaming about?

Two hours ago, Lenny had met her at the hospital with the news. Luke's unconscious body had been found two towns over at the bottom of a ravine. A state trooper had spotted his abandoned Ranger on a little-traveled road, and a team of troopers had searched the woods for the missing detective.

Something terrible must've happened. Luke had three broken ribs, a skull fracture, and a two-inch gash on the back of his head, along with multiple abrasions and lacerations. The private hospital room was full of humming, beeping equipment that monitored his blood pressure, his cardiac rhythm, and other vital signs. There was an endotracheal tube taped to his mouth, and Natalie watched the ventilator moving up and down as it kept him alive.

His face was handsome in repose. He wore a thin hospital gown. She allowed herself to look at his arms, his muscles like channels of flesh; the angular cheekbones, the firm jaw, slight crow's-feet around the eyes.

He looked so vulnerable, lying there. His brow was smooth and clear of worry. The weight of the burden was on Natalie now.

She stared at him a little while longer, then settled back against her chair. Across the room from her was the door. She opened her overcoat and unsnapped the strap of her holster. She wanted to access her service weapon on a moment's notice—just in case. She sensed that Luke had stumbled into something he shouldn't have, and now they wanted him dead. Whoever "they" were.

Tell me a riddle.

The more darkness there is, the less of it you can see.

Even in this day and age, the doctors couldn't predict when a coma patient would recover. Luke may wake up tomorrow, or it could take thirty years. At least he was stable, they said. They were monitoring his progress. "Let's wait and see." That was all they could tell her—wait and see.

For a second, she felt herself sinking into despair. Then she bristled. "No." She couldn't afford pessimism right now. "Come back to us, Luke," she whispered, desperate for him to pull through.

Outside, swirling snow pummeled the hospital windows. Inside it was warm. It smelled of medicine and perspiration. She touched the cracked leather holster under her arm and felt reassured by the cold metal handgrip of her gun.

Every morning for almost a year she'd had to accept that Grace was gone. Natalie wasn't going to let the same thing happen with Luke. She could withstand all the great losses in her life, just as long as Luke was there. He had to be there. He was her touchstone. Her rock. A solid presence in her life stretching back forever. He was the clever boy who'd crawled under the fence to introduce himself to her and her twirling, dancing sisters. He was the one thing she could always count on. She couldn't lose him.

Tears sprang to her eyes.

She took a shaky breath and let it out.

She would stay here all week if she had to. All month.

She regarded his handsome face and felt his looming presence in her life.

Luke had fallen down a ravine into a deep, dreamless sleep.

She could not lose him.

She would protect him until he woke up.

ACKNOWLEDGMENTS

Love, respect, and gratitude to my brilliant editor, Alex Sehulster, who keeps me on my toes.

Love to my amazing agent, Jill Marr, and her team at the Sandra Dijkstra Agency.

It's a privilege to be working with the always impressive, inventive team at Minotaur Books—Alex, publisher Andy Martin, associate publisher Kelley Ragland, Joe Brosnan, Sarah Melnyk, Kayla Janas, Paul Hochman, John Morrone, David Rotstein, Steve Wagner, Sabrina Soares Roberts, and Mara Delgado Sánchez. Thank you for helping bring Natalie to life.

Big appreciation and thanks to the Twitter and Instagram writing communities, and to my spectacular readers—thank you for following Natalie so passionately, and for your love of books.

For Doug, my heart and soul.